A SEASON
of Grace

BETTE
NORDBERG

*Judy—
With much thanks
Bette Nordberg*

HARVEST HOUSE PUBLISHERS

EUGENE, OREGON

A SEASON OF GRACE

Copyright © 2004 by Bette Nordberg
Published by Harvest House Publishers
Eugene, Oregon 97402
www.harvesthousepublishers.com

Library of Congress Cataloging-in-Publication Data
Nordberg, Bette.
  A season of grace / Bette Nordberg.
    p. cm.
  ISBN 0-7369-1341-6 (pbk.)
    1. AIDS (Disease)—Patients—Fiction. 2. Brothers and sisters—Fiction. 3. Gay men—Fiction. I. Title.
PS3564.O553S43 2004
813'.6—dc22   2003022503

For Kerrie
You delight in doing everything the Lord wants;
day and night you think about his law.
You are like the trees planted along the riverbank,
Bearing fruit each season and without fail.
Your leaf never withers,
And in all you do, you prosper.

Achknowledgments

I do not know when I first thought of writing *A Season of Grace*. Ten years ago, a friend of mine asked me to read a stage play she'd written about a teenager with AIDS. At the time, her story moved me and I advised her to turn it into a novel. She refused.

I don't remember thinking about it again until three years ago, when somehow, quite miraculously, I knew the assignment had fallen to me. Though this book has absolutely no resemblance to that early play, I'm convinced the two stories are connected somehow.

When I read the writing of Dr. Abraham Verghese, I knew I had to write a novel for the church. For me, writing *A Season of Grace* was an act of divine obedience. Still, I owe many thanks to those who brought the book into publication:

My friend and agent, Chip MacGregor, found a good home for the manuscript.

The enthusiastic team at Harvest House—among them Carolyn, Terry, Nick, and Betty—brought the book to life.

Erin Healy and her attention to detail polished *A Season of Grace* to a high gloss.

Larry, Tim, and Donovan, all suffering with AIDS, opened their lives to my questions.

The folks at Swan House in Portland, Oregon, and the Inter-Faith Care Team in Seattle, willingly shared their wisdom and experiences.

Dr. Dennis Elonka and Dr. Robert L. Thompson, both physicians with Group Health Cooperative, provided additional medical expertise. Dr. Joel Gallant, MD, of Johns Hopkins AIDS Service, regularly answers the questions of hundreds of Internet AIDS patients. Mine too.

My friend, ICU nurse Terry Garner, provided insight into the process of death.

Nurse Pamela Alvey provided access to publications for AIDS patients.

Dr. DeAnna Stoltenberg assisted with pharmaceutical details.

Steve and Wanda Booth answered questions about low blood sugar.

Michael, Shelley, Kerrie, and another friend Shelley openly discussed the issues of homosexuality and the church. All opened their lives to my scrutiny, and added to my understanding.

Food and Friends, Washington, DC, answered many questions about ministry and food preparation for AIDS patients.

Jeannie St. John Taylor assisted in the plotting of *A Season of Grace*, reading early versions of the manuscript and offering wise advice.

Susan Duplissey, as always, provided valuable feedback.

More than any project, this one demanded the support of my prayer team. Without the faithful prayers of Jeannie, Gloria, Petey, Rebecca, Gwyn, Kerrie, Paula, and The Walking Girls, this book would not exist. In the early days, Kerrie's vision for the work held me up.

In *A Season of Grace*, I hoped to put a face on our understanding of AIDS. I wanted my readers to see that every male homosexual is a person first—someone's brother or father, uncle or friend.

For those suffering with AIDS, this book is not intended to provide medical advice. In the two years I've studied this disease, treatment options and protocols have changed dramatically. No one can provide better or more current advice than your personal physician. I advise that you find a doctor you can partner with as you fight the adversary called AIDS.

The rest of us can pray, and we can love. As Franklin Graham said in his 2002 address to the Christian Booksellers Association, "AIDS is the greatest opportunity facing the church today."

CHAPTER
One

I've heard that death is part of life, something that should not surprise or frighten us. We are born. We marry. We have children. We die.

Of course this discussion generally occurs on talk shows between humans currently in the best of health. These sages seem to imply that death is to be anticipated with the same enthusiasm as a summer vacation or breakfast at Denny's. At one point in my life, with death at arm's length, their viewpoint made sense to me. But after what I've been through, frankly I'd rather order a Grand Slam and a glass of orange juice.

I certainly would never have chosen the path my life has taken.

≈ ≈ ≈

On the last Saturday of August, almost fifteen months ago, I left my snoring husband in bed and slipped downstairs to enjoy a few moments of peace before my real day began.

Certain that my teenagers would sleep late, I ate cold cereal alone in the quiet of a dewy summer daybreak. I remember the morning felt cool, but bright, and as I looked out my kitchen window, I felt a certain dread that the seasons had begun to change.

In spite of the deep green leaves on my sweet gum, I'd seen the clues. Nights didn't hold the heat anymore, and days had grown noticeably shorter. Just that week I'd sensed that the afternoon temperatures no longer rose to the usual summertime highs. We'd experienced a few mornings of dense fog, and though it burned off by noon, I could not ignore the implications. No matter how I resisted, summer would make her exit. Fall had her eye on Potter's Hollow, and she was well on her way.

Even though most women love the crisp air and brilliant colors of fall, I don't. I hate the gray skies and early darkness of short winter days. I get tired of being wet and cold all the time. I cope by looking forward to the shortest day of the year so that I can anticipate the coming of spring.

Though it sounds completely crazy, I survive Northwest winters by looking forward to looking forward.

Even though I was raised in the Northwest, I'd move to Hawaii in a heartbeat. I've always felt as though Maui might be my real destiny. As I put my cereal bowl in the dishwasher that morning, I considered begging my husband to consider retiring to a tropical island. No matter how many times he reminds me that perfection grows boring, I argue my position. After all, how hard could it be, living in paradise?

Sighing, I closed the dishwasher and headed for the laundry room.

On that August morning, I faced an enormous pile of laundry left over from our last outing on the Oregon coast. When I crawled out of bed, I'd promised myself that I would wash, fold, and put away every last stray sock, even if it killed me.

Confronting that pile of filthy clothes, I wondered if it might.

I'd invited my mother for Sunday dinner in honor of her birthday, and I knew that if I didn't have my house in order, I'd never hear the end of it. At 82, Mother has no tolerance for a disorganized household. Actually, she's never had much tolerance for anything. Mom never misses a chance to chide me about my household neglect. I wondered what arrows she might launch in my direction if she saw my laundry room.

When I opened the lid of my washing machine, the smell of moldy linen assaulted me and I groaned aloud. I'd forgotten to put this load in the dryer. Holding my breath, I determined not to let this small obstacle set me back. I pulled out the sheets, touching them as little as possible, and dropped them in the dryer. *The heat will kill the smell*, I told myself, and added a second dryer sheet for good measure. With any luck at all, the scent of summer breeze would cover the stink of neglected mildew.

I sorted the dirty clothes into moderately sized mounds of darks and whites, mediums and reds, and stuffed the first load into the washer before escaping to the family room for a quiet moment with my new issue of *Vogue Knitting*. Relishing the shiny pages full of new patterns, I curled up in the corner of the sectional and sipped steaming coffee as I began reading.

In the middle of an article by Meg Swanson, the buzz of the dryer interrupted my concentration. I was reluctant to respond—I'd always wanted to know how to calculate the stitches for a round-yoked sweater.

Holding the magazine open at eye level, I staggered to the laundry room, still reading. I spread the pages across the dryer as I dropped dry sheets into a laundry basket. After emptying the washer I filled it with a load of sandy jeans, all the while considering the yarn in my stash, and wondering which I might use to experiment with the new technique.

Sliding the magazine up over the detergent container, I continued reading as I squeezed the button and filled the measuring cup in my other hand with liquid detergent. Just as I began the section about casting off the under-sleeve stitches, our doorbell rang.

I continued pouring detergent, mentally calculating the stitch formula along with Meg. The sensation of cold liquid seeping through the knee of my pant leg caught my attention. I glanced down. "Shoot," I said, with the enthusiasm of genuine cursing.

All this time, I'd been pouring detergent through a hole in the bottom of the cup—down onto my pants and slippers, over my pile of reds and onto the floor. By this time I'd poured long enough to create a pale pink puddle that oozed under the dryer.

I held my hand under the broken cup, trying to limit the damage, and dropped the whole thing into the washing machine. The doorbell rang again.

"Could someone please get the door?" I asked, raising my voice and exaggerating the words. Though I hadn't heard anyone moving around yet, I expected that our mystery guest had come for one of my teenagers. Certainly I didn't need to answer the door.

I blotted at the puddle, sopping up the liquid with one of my husband's socks. Another wave of pink detergent ran out from under the dryer. Kneeling, I used one of Mallory's hooded sweatshirts to soak up more of the lake. The stuff was everywhere; for every ounce I mopped up, two more emerged from under the dryer. I must have emptied the whole container onto the floor.

By now, liquid detergent soaked through my pants at both knees and had begun to seep through my socks at the ankle. In spite of my best efforts, pink liquid continued running over the floor, back under the dryer, and into the piles of waiting laundry.

I held Mallory's dripping sweatshirt aloft as I lumbered to stand up. My nose began to itch, whether from dryer dust, moldy linens, or dirty laundry, I could not tell. Dropping the sweatshirt in with the jeans, I tried to scratch my nose. Too late. Though I covered my mouth, a sneeze, loud enough to shatter plate glass, rattled my teeth, and I felt the cold sticky detergent now covering my cheeks.

The doorbell rang again.

"The door, for crying out loud!" Hearing no motion anywhere in the house, I continued to mutter as I headed upstairs to the entry hall. With my luck, it would be the paperboy collecting this month's payment, or a neighborhood kid for Travis. I didn't even try to put on a pleasant smile.

With the frustrated energy of an article interrupted, a mess in the laundry room, and having to do everything myself, I threw open the front door without even a glance into the security peephole.

I couldn't have felt more shock if I'd jumped into a pool of ice water.

"Stephen," I said, hearing surprise in my own voice. I sounded like I'd answered the door for Santa Claus. I stood there, one arm holding the door, the other hanging limp beside me, frozen in place. "Stephen," I said again, with the paralysis of a deer caught in the headlights of an oncoming car. I hate myself when I perform like that.

He leaned casually against the brick surrounding our front porch, one foot resting up behind him, both hands in his jean pockets. A lavender gift bag dangled from his wrist. Dropping his foot and turning toward me he said, "Hello, Colleen." He sounded unusually shy, almost reluctant to speak.

"Stephen," I stammered again, finally moving toward him, my arms wide, offering a hug. "I didn't know you were coming." Unwilling to let this awkwardness between us continue, I pulled him into my arms. "What a surprise!" Another brilliant statement by the laundry woman.

I held him close, squeezing his shoulders, smelling the fresh scent of his aftershave. How long since I'd held my brother like this? We lingered in the embrace.

As he squeezed me back, I felt tears sting my eyes. I missed this man, this one who had been so long the center of my world. My brother. My twin. My flesh. "How I've missed you," I confessed, patting his back as I squeezed him again.

"I've missed you too," he said. "Brought you something."

We let go and as I stepped back, Stephen handed me the bag, tissue peeking from the rim. Inside, I found a caramel-colored wooden frame, glossy and smooth. "How beautiful." Turning it over, I discovered a picture of Stephen and me that I'd never seen before.

I recognized the setting, a high-school biology field trip. In the photo, Stephen and I sat together on a log, heads tilted toward one another, deep in conversation. Behind us, the water sparkled in afternoon sunlight. I remembered that we'd had a disagreement that afternoon; a friend had caught us in the act of working out our differences. The picture was beautiful, both for the image itself and the sentiment behind it. "Thank you so much," I said, hugging the photograph. "I love it."

I reached up to brush away a stray tear and felt my sticky fingers. How silly I must look, wet knees, sticky hands. Bubbles where tears should have been. "Oh, no," I said through giggles. "I just spilled laundry soap. I've made a terrible mess."

He looked down at my knees, taking in the dark spots and smiled. "You were always a mess, Colleen. I wouldn't recognize anything else."

"Well then, you won't mind that I've covered the back of your sweatshirt with detergent?" I linked my arm through his and pulled him inside. "Because now you're a mess too."

I led my brother into the kitchen and offered him a clean dish-towel. "I managed to get it all over your shoulders," I said. I turned on the water and began rinsing my own hands and face, drying with another towel.

After I moved away, Stephen rinsed his towel under the faucet and brushed at his shoulders. I watched him, dabbing at the detergent as he leaned against the opposite counter. He wore a half-zip sweat-shirt in sage green with a navy stripe trimming the ribbed collar. The white of a crew neck T-shirt peeked out from underneath the zipper. In spite of warm August temperatures, he'd chosen long, lean blue jeans. On his bare feet he wore slip-on deck shoes—a moccasin style I recognized from outerwear catalogs.

My brother looked good. Really good. And as I eyed him, I couldn't overcome the outright joy I felt in seeing him. I wanted to burst out in giggles. I felt the same longing I have when I see a new-born—that irresistible urge to scoop him up and hold him close, to bury my nose in his neck and smell his skin. The harder I tried to squish my emotions, the more they came alive. I felt tears springing up again. To keep them hidden, I turned away and busied myself brushing crumbs from the counter onto my palm.

Stephen rinsed his hands, dried them, and turned to face me.

"Coffee?" I offered, trying to sound as though he dropped in to visit several times a week.

"Not for me." He smiled. "I've given it up. But I'd take tea, if you have something herbal. Raspberry maybe?"

I raised my eyebrows and laughed out loud. Stephen was the con-summate coffee addict. I'd given him a coffee pot to put in his college dorm room. "I can dig up something herbal. But what on earth made you give up coffee?" I pulled a teakettle out of the cupboard and filled it with water.

"You'd be surprised," he answered. "I'm into clean living these days."

I started the gas stove, waiting for the flame to catch before I put down the kettle. "Clean living?" I turned to look at him, wondering.

"Not that clean." Stephen shrugged, his eyes avoiding mine.

I tried to smile, but this one was forced. "So what have you been up to lately?" I threw the words in the air, trying to keep the conversation flowing. Trying to keep some kind of lid on my emotions.

I wanted to scream, *Why are you here? Why now?* This couldn't be an ordinary visit. Stephen had stayed away far too long to show up now. Almost no phone calls. Very few letters. For more than five years, in spite of my repeated effort, I heard from Stephen only occasionally.

Once after mom had a heart episode, he'd called my husband at work, asking about her test results. On my fortieth birthday, two winters ago, he'd sent me a card with no return address.

I'd cried when I opened it.

Stephen turned forty on the same day, and I had no idea where to send his card. As the silent years passed, I convinced myself I'd learned to live without my other half. But today, I knew—by the twisting pain now shouting in my gut—that I'd never really learned anything.

That part, that hurting part, wanted to retaliate. *How could you just leave me? How could you walk away from everything we've shared and disappear from my life?* Of course I couldn't express it. I sucked it down, swallowed hard, and blinked away the threatening tears.

I listened as he described his last student production. "The advanced class is going to do *Our Town* this fall," he said. "I had to re-block it for the new theatre building on campus. We'll open in late November. So I've just finished that. I'll hold auditions in early October."

"Thornton Wilder," I said, catching this last information like a life ring. The kettle began to whistle and I took it off the heat. "How did your classes go this summer?"

"I took the summer off."

More new information. From our older sister, Carrie, I'd heard that Stephen taught drama at Seattle Community College. Before that, before his big disappearance from my life, Stephen had earned

his master's degree and directed small-scale stage productions in
Seattle. He had a good singing voice and a charisma that flew over the
seats of a theatre, all the way to the back row.

As a kid, Stephen wanted to make it big in theatre. He'd dreamed
of playing Broadway, taking Hollywood by storm.

"Hmm," I tried to sound casual as I poured boiling water over the
tea bag in his cup. "Must have been a good break. What did you do?"
I handed him the cup.

He cradled the mug, warming his fingers around the outside. "I
needed a break. I didn't do anything really. Rested a lot. Read a lot.
It was a good summer."

I pulled a cup off the rack for myself and filled it from the coffee
pot. "We had a good summer too. Some fun with the boat. Some time
on the coast. The kids are growing up so fast." I slid onto a barstool.
"They'll be gone before we know it."

I watched him dunk the tea in and out of the hot water. Stephen
hadn't really told me anything. Still trying to reign in my emotions I
asked him, "So, this is a real surprise Stephen. It's great to see you." I
took a sip of coffee.

A lengthy silence hung in my kitchen as I watched him walk over
to the silverware drawer and remove a spoon. With skill born of practice, he caught the bag and drained the liquid. "Honey?" he asked.

I pointed to a cupboard and Stephen reached inside for the honey
bear, prying it off the shelf paper. He smiled at me across the kitchen
as he held the bear under hot water until the residue dissolved.

"Sorry. Mallory puts honey on her Cheerios. She never cleans up
after herself."

"Right." Squeezing a stream of honey into his cup, he stirred as it
fell. At last satisfied, he put down the spoon and took a sip.

"So," I began, wondering if I might push the limits. "Not that you
aren't welcome—but what gives? Why did you drop by today?"

"Mom's party," he answered. "I heard you were giving her a
birthday party, and I decided that I should come." He took another
sip.

"How did you hear?" I moved to the breakfast counter and pulled
out a chair. He followed my lead, taking the stool next to mine.

"Carrie told me. I called Kevin to ask if I could join you."

"Kevin?" I couldn't hide my surprise. Why would Stephen call my husband instead of me? Why hadn't Kevin told me? I pushed aside another twinge of disappointment.

Stephen nodded. "He said I could come anytime."

"Of course you can," I said, still dumbfounded by this news. I sighed. "You're always welcome, Stephen. You know that."

Looking straight ahead, he nodded, taking my gentle rebuke without comment. Obviously, for reasons I didn't understand, Stephen didn't feel welcome. Something I'd done or said—some silly event stood between us—and I didn't have a clue as to what had happened.

As we sat together that August morning, facing the breakfast bar, it felt to me as though we lived in two separate universes. No matter how much I loved him, Stephen no longer belonged to me, as he had when we were children. He had moved away.

In the silence of my kitchen, I wanted him to know how much his distance hurt me. I wanted to tell him about the times I'd cried, wishing I could share my life with him. I wanted to tell him that losing a brother—a living brother and most especially a twin—felt worse than death. It *had* to feel worse than death.

But I didn't say a word.

Looking out the kitchen window, I drank my coffee. Though I sat close enough to touch him, I could not reach him. Instead, I stole glances—noting the wave in his curly blond hair, the shimmer of his blue eyes, the wide cheeks and ruddy complexion—recognizing at once the similarities between my own face and his more rugged, masculine one.

I noted his lean body and wished that we shared that similarity as well. From birth, I have struggled to keep my weight under control. Stephen had different genes. He ate everything he wanted, buttered, sugared, and glazed. On that summer morning, he seemed even more lean than when I had last seen him, and I stifled a feeling of envy.

I looked for signs of aging, grey hair, a softening of the tummy; Stephen looked remarkably good. His hair remained light blond where my natural color had darkened. Though we shared the same fair skin, light lines surrounded his softer, bluer eyes.

For whatever reason, this stranger had come home. Though I did not understand why he had chosen this moment to return, I decided that I would welcome him. There would be plenty of time for questions and explanations. There would be time for understanding and reconnecting. Lots of time.

That morning, as I sat drinking coffee beside my brother, I hoped that more than the seasons had begun to change in Potter's Hollow.

The first time I heard Stephen's watch alarm go off, I thought it was a mistake.

I'd just put on a fresh pot of coffee and returned to my seat at the breakfast bar when Kevin wandered into the kitchen. Nothing pulls my husband out of bed like the smell of coffee brewing. He'd managed to pull on a T-shirt and jeans, though he clearly hadn't shaved. He staggered in barefooted, with his red-blond hair standing out all over his head.

"Hey," he said, slapping my brother on the back, as if Stephen showed up on our doorstep several times a month. "Glad to see you made it for Mom's party."

Kevin leaned down to deposit my complimentary morning kiss and I felt his sandpaper cheek scrape my own. Kevin hadn't brushed his teeth either. Heading straight for the coffee pot, he filled his favorite twenty-ounce mug and asked, "What's for breakfast?"

Like most men, Kevin Payton likes to keep things simple. When his belly rings, he answers.

Together, the three of us managed to fry bacon and cook hash browns. We'd just begun an omelet of fresh veggies and goat cheese when our banging dishes, slamming cupboards, and rowdy laughter woke the kids. They joined us, surprised and happy to find their uncle in the kitchen.

Mallory, my seventeen-year-old, baked blueberry muffins from berries we'd grown in the garden. And Travis, bless his surly fifteen-year-old heart, managed to set the table in spite of his deep conviction to avoid women's work.

17

It was eleven before we sat down at the dining-room table to the tempting aroma of our cholesterol-laden breakfast. By then, I'd completely forgotten my own early morning cereal and filled my plate to match the rest of my family.

Okay, maybe my struggle with weight isn't completely genetic.

We'd just asked the blessing when Stephen's wristwatch started beeping. Passing dishes of steaming food, we hardly noticed as he fiddled with the buttons of his watch and finally managed to quiet the thing. "It's new," Stephen said, apologizing.

"You should have Travis fix your watch," I said, balancing a forkful of omelet dripping with cheese. "He's a whiz with electronics. Every time I get something new, I give it to Trav." I smiled over at my son. "After he figures it out, he gives me lessons."

"Mom'd still be wondering how to turn on her computer," Travis said. "Can I have another muffin?"

I nodded and Trav leapt toward the platter. I frowned. "We can help if you ask."

"Try to keep your seat on the chair, Trav," Mallory said. "Humans do that when they eat."

Ignoring the kids, I asked Kevin, "What're you planning today?" My husband has the most remarkable ability to escape party preparations. I knew that if he didn't sign his name in blood, he'd be off to the hardware store or down fiddling with the engine on the boat. I think his disappearing acts are the reason I hate having company.

Between mouthfuls, he answered, "Trav and I are going to wax the boat."

"Wax the boat?" I groaned. "Honey, the lawn needs mowing and edging. The apple trees need picking. Mom is coming tomorrow, and I'd like the yard to look presentable."

"Boat needs a coat of wax before winter." My husband shrugged. "Besides, your mom isn't coming to inspect the lawn."

Stephen excused himself and went into the kitchen. I heard water in the sink, and before I could respond to Kevin, my brother reappeared with a tall glass of water. "I can help with the boat," he said, taking his seat again. "That way, Trav can do the lawn."

"Thanks so much, Uncle Steve." Travis slid down in his chair and tossed a paper muffin cup onto his plate. He took the second half of the muffin in a single bite. I made a mental note: At earliest opportunity, work on Travis's table manners.

"Any time, Trav." Stephen smiled at his nephew.

With my family held captive by breakfast, I divided the preparations for Mother's party, making a list on the back of an envelope. Mallory, who would rather cook than clean house, agreed to bake a birthday cake. I planned to change the sheets in the guest bedroom and clean the upstairs bathroom. "I'll put Stephen in the guest bedroom," I said. "And both of you can spend some time today picking up your rooms. I'd like to hear the vacuum cleaner upstairs this afternoon."

The children groaned in unison.

Having covered everything, I excused the kids and made one last attempt to extract a commitment from Kevin. "Please, honey, could you clean the barbeque grill for me this afternoon?" I pulled off my reading glasses and rubbed the bridge of my nose.

"I don't know why we have to do that," Kevin answered. "The smell of smoke flavors the food. It tastes better if you don't clean it. Besides, it only gets greasy again."

"If we follow that reasoning, I shouldn't wash your underwear."

"Point taken," he said. He stood, picking up his breakfast plate. "I think I know when I'm outgunned. How about we retreat to the boat, Stephen?"

And with that, my two favorite men escaped the house.

Saturday night, after dinner, Kevin and the kids started a movie they'd chosen from the video store while Stephen and I cleared the dishes and loaded the dishwasher. As we worked together, I offered what I hoped would sound like a casual invitation. "Stephen, I'm playing piano for the early church service tomorrow. We'd be glad to have you tag along if you'd like." I braced myself for his undoubtedly negative response.

"When does church start?" he asked. The lift of his brows suggested that he might be mildly interested.

"Starts at nine," I answered. "You'd like our pastor. He's really a gentle guy. We have a good service." There. Though I hoped to sound casual, I'd managed to sound like a used car salesman. Why do I do things like that?

"No thanks," he said, carefully folding a kitchen rag and laying it over the top of the faucet. "I'm really tired. I think I'll head upstairs to bed if you don't mind."

"Sure. I've put fresh towels on your bed." I tried to sound upbeat as I accepted yet another rejection. "The bathroom in the hall is all yours."

"Thanks." With a weary smile, he turned to go.

I followed Stephen into the dining room, where I stacked the placemats as I watched him climb the stairs to the second floor. In our split-level house, Stephen had only a half flight to ascend. Still, he leaned heavily on the handrail as he slogged up the treads. Moving like an old man, Stephen looked more than tired; he looked completely exhausted.

Maybe the trip across the mountains had gotten to him. After all, he'd driven more than three hours. Anyone would be tired from a long early-morning drive.

I turned out the dining-room light and joined my family in the middle of *The Emperor's Club.* Though I'd looked forward to the movie, I couldn't focus on the story. I got up and wandered around the house, picking up the Saturday paper, straightening knickknacks, turning out lights. Returning to the television, I picked up my knitting.

A vague feeling of restlessness stirred inside of me, some nameless emotion bubbling just under the surface, thwarting my concentration. I made several mistakes in the color work of a Scandinavian sweater I'd hoped to finish by Christmas. Tearing out the stitches, I rewound the yarn and put the project back in my basket.

Eventually the movie ended, and Mallory turned off the television. While everyone headed for bed, I prowled through the house one last time, at last brewing myself a cup of herbal tea. Perhaps tea would settle my troubled heart. Fatigue gnawed at my muscles, and worry ate at my soul. I drank chamomile in the kitchen darkness.

Later, I crawled under the covers beside my snoring husband. Kevin rolled over and threw a heavy arm around my waist, mumbling affection from somewhere in his dreams. I nestled into his warm, soft frame. As comforting as this place had always been in the past, I couldn't find sleep. Eventually, I squirmed out from under his arm.

Rolling and tossing, my fitfulness woke Kevin. "What's wrong?" he whispered in a sleepy voice.

"I'm sorry," I whispered. "I didn't mean to wake you." I rolled onto my back and stared up at the ceiling. He pulled me close, tucking his nose into my neck. I felt his warm breath on my skin.

"Something bothering you?"

"How often has Stephen called you?"

"Is that what's keeping you awake?"

I resented the laughter I heard in his voice. After all, what did Kevin know about having a twin? He'd grown up in the blustering company of four boys. Athletes, all of them, the Payton boys played every knockdown, killer contact sport that men could enjoy. Kevin had never known the sense of commingled identity that comes with having a twin.

On the other hand, it wasn't Kevin's fault if my brother preferred to contact him. "I guess it is," I admitted. "I don't understand why he would keep in touch with you instead of me. We've always been so close."

Kevin was quiet for so long that I thought maybe he'd fallen sleep. Finally I heard him heave a thick sigh. "He hasn't been calling me, Colleen. He's kept in touch with Carrie."

"My sister?" My voice rose. "Carrie? Why would he call Carrie?" Kevin whispered, "Shush, Colleen. He'll hear you." Kevin slid away, readjusted his pillow, and spoke quietly. "He's afraid. He thinks you don't understand."

"And you do?"

"Not really." The bed creaked as Kevin propped himself up on his elbow and rested a cheek on his knuckles. "I don't understand Stephen at all. But he isn't my problem." Kevin leaned forward, his lips searching in the dark for my cheek. His wet kiss landed below my ear lobe. "I've known Stephen a long time. No one can change him," he whispered. "Not even you. No matter how much you wish for it, you can't change the way things are."

I thought about Kevin as he'd looked when Stephen first introduced us, square and strong. As part of his senior project, in exchange for credit in his electrical engineering program, Kevin had managed the lights for a stage production Stephen directed. Kevin designed the lighting, calculated the electrical load, and designed and built the power packs controlled by the lighting panel. Stephen and Kevin became friends over the course of that winter production.

Stephen introduced me to Kevin at the cast party on opening night.

I loved Kevin from the first moment I saw him. And, after nineteen years together, my feelings haven't changed. Kevin provides the solid, predictable balance to my more artistic and emotional nature.

Of course our differences have also generated more than our share of sparks. What else would you expect of an electrical engineer? So far, we'd survived the struggle.

But on this night, the night that Stephen came to visit, Kevin wanted to balance my emotions once again. And while part of me wanted to believe my husband's assessment, other parts—the concerned sister, the loving twin, the devoted believer—rejected his words. Things had to change. They had to, and I would do whatever it took to make them change. "I don't know, Kevin. I just can't give up on him."

"Stephen never meant to hurt you, Colleen. Don't take it personally."

"But he did," I said, feeling the pain again. "He just disappeared— for so many years. It still hurts." I felt tears roll down my face and into my hair. "It hurts so much to see him again."

This time, I accepted the warm comfort of Kevin's kisses.

≈ ≈ ≈

After Sunday-morning service, we came home, changed clothes, and began the last-minute preparations for Mother's party.

Carrie and her husband, Tim, arrived with Mom around one-thirty. By then, I'd managed to whip myself into a frothy overdrive, worrying about party details. I imagined my house from my mother's perspective, actually traversing the same course she would take from the front door into my kitchen. If I cleaned it perfectly, perhaps I could fend off her critical jibes before she delivered them.

I polished the glass light fixture over the front door and knocked the cobwebs down from the entry-hall ceiling. I went over the powder bathroom, item by item, looking for signs of dust or neglect. I even took a toothbrush to the base of the faucet.

By the time the party began, I'd polished and dusted myself into exhaustion.

"Colleen," my mother said, hugging me in the front hall. "It's so nice of you to have me for dinner. I know you're so busy—I mean you hardly ever have time to come visit. And now, you go to this much trouble. I'm embarrassed."

Zing. Direct hit. I faked a smile. "No trouble at all," I said, glancing at the same time over her shoulder. Kevin, standing directly behind my mother, rolled his eyes. I frowned back at him and put my arm around her shoulders, guiding her into the kitchen. I tipped my lips toward her ear and said, "By the way, happy birthday, Mom. We have a little surprise for you."

"A surprise? For me?" She let me lead her into the kitchen.

"Guess who?" I said as I pushed the swinging door out of the way.

Hearing the hinge, Stephen turned from his work at the sink. In one hand he held a dripping head of Romaine lettuce, in the other, a sharp paring knife. He dropped these on the counter and turned to dry his hands. "Mom," he said, walking toward her. "So good to see you." He gathered her into his arms. "Happy birthday," he said, squeezing hard and patting her back.

"Oh my goodness," she said, standing back. "I had no idea that you'd be here." She glanced at me in surprise.

"He surprised us," I piped up. "Isn't it wonderful?"

"Well, Stephen is always full of surprises," she said.

Tension filled the room as forcefully as if someone had opened the valve of a fire hydrant. "Kevin, time to put on the salmon," I said, picking up the fish basket from the counter beside the sink. "Now that Mom's here. We can eat as soon as you finish." I handed him the basket and the basting brush.

"Don't forget how expensive fresh salmon is," I teased. "No leaving the grill to visit with a neighbor."

"Who me?" He was still smirking as he closed the back door behind him.

"Actually," I said to Stephen, "he has. Last week the guy across the street brought over a new fishing rod and we ate charcoal for dinner." I opened the refrigerator, plucked a plastic tub from the door shelves, and handed it to Stephen. "Would you mind taking this sauce out to him?" I patted my brother on the shoulder. "Keep an eye on him for me, okay?"

"What about the salad?"

"We'll finish it."

Forty minutes later, we sat down to a lovely salmon dinner. Unfortunately, the salmon was the only lovely thing about our afternoon.

As nearly as I remember, the explosion began with a slow fizzle— something like the fuse on a stick of dynamite. And, though my mother has often set off such explosions, I'd hoped to get through this event without one.

"So, Tim," Kevin spoke to my brother-in-law. "Any news about work?"

"Nothing new," Tim answered. "Boeing is still laying off. But at least I don't have to close any more plants for a while."

"Your job is safe, right?" I asked.

"Looks like it, at least for now" he answered. "Since it's my job to help Boeing stay competitive, as long as they struggle with productivity, they'll need me."

"He travels all the time though," Carrie piped up. "I wish they'd send someone else—someone younger. He's getting too old for all this travel. The time zones nearly kill him."

"Now that wouldn't be fair, Carrie," Mother said, as though speaking to a child. "Young men have families. And children shouldn't have their parents traveling all the time."

I heard the condescending tone and actually saw Carrie's shoulders begin a slow creep in the direction of her ears. "Mom, just because we don't have children doesn't mean that we don't deserve time together too."

"I know, Carrie," Mother crooned. "But after all—"

I grabbed the nearest casserole dish and handed it to Mom. "Would you like more rice?" In my eagerness, I nearly threw the dish at her.

"No thank you." She looked pointedly at me. "I have to watch what I eat if I don't want to gain. I'm not getting any younger, you know."

I reached for a glass of water, bracing myself. Mother has harassed me about my weight since junior high. At least I'd managed to distract her from Carrie. "And you look wonderful, Mom," I agreed. "Have you been walking in the heat this summer?"

"Not outside," she nodded. "Silvia Slater and I have become mall walkers. It's air conditioned, you know. We carry identification cards and win prizes for the most miles walked. There's a registered nurse at the mall, and we have our blood pressure taken every Friday. You should walk, you know," she looked toward me.

I felt a brief moment of triumph. She'd forgotten Carrie's childless life. "No mall here," I countered. "But that's great for you and Silvia. We won't worry about you being outside in the weather this winter."

"I'll miss seeing children every morning though," Mother said.

"What children?" Mallory asked. Carrie groaned.

"The kids waiting for the school bus." Mom turned toward my daughter and laid her wrinkled hand over Mallory's. "I suspect they think of us as two old crones. But you know, before long, the children wave to us every morning."

"Well, you haven't missed them yet," Stephen said. "School starts again this week. Maybe you could walk outside for a while until the bad weather hits."

"At least I have Mallory and Travis," my mother lamented. "I mean with three grown children, you'd think I'd have more grandchildren. I'll never understand why Carrie and Timothy quit trying to have children. They'd have made such wonderful parents," she said. "I never understand why some people choose not to have children. Why would anyone be so selfish?" She looked to Mallory for agreement.

Mallory shrugged.

Carrie's eyes glistened, and I felt her frustration. It didn't matter how often we covered this territory, Mother couldn't seem to let the issue of grandchildren go.

"I'm not criticizing you," Mother said sadly in Carrie's direction. "I understand all your health problems. I'm just saying how much I love my grandchildren. With grandchildren like these, I wish I'd had more. That's all. Can't a woman wish?"

"Speaking of wishes," I made a desperate stab for peace, "is everyone ready for birthday cake?" I stood, gathering my own plate and utensils. "Mallory, maybe you could help me with dessert?" I tipped my head toward the kitchen.

My daughter looked up from her plate, still chewing a bite of dinner roll. Her face said it all: *Mom, I'm still eating here.*

"There isn't any hurry, dear," my mother said, her voice soft and wistful. "You don't need to hurry dinner along in order to change the subject." With a deliberate motion, she placed her fork down on her plate. "I've learned to live with disappointment. My only son will never marry." She turned sad eyes on Stephen. "No one will carry on the family name."

I glanced toward my brother just in time to see a flicker of anger cross his face. Stunned, none of us managed to say anything that might deflect the words I sensed heading our way. I willed my wooden mind to think, to avert the disaster, but it refused.

"It's such a shame that the MacLaughlin name will be forever lost." Mother continued, oblivious to the hurt her words spawned.

She looked toward Carrie. "My oldest daughter will never know the joy of children." She wiped the corners of her lips with a linen napkin and then folded it neatly beside her still-full plate. "I can live with these disappointments. When you get to be my age, heartache is part of the package."

"I don't mean to be a source of heartache, Mother," Stephen said, rising from his chair. He nodded toward Kevin and looked directly at Mother's face. "I only came today because it was your birthday. I thought my coming might bring you pleasure." He dropped his napkin on the table. "I hoped that someday we could get beyond these things. But I realize that I can never please you. Never." He stepped away from the table and pushed in his chair. "So, if you'll excuse me, I think I'll be going." Stephen stormed up the stairs to the guest room. Dumbfounded, I put my plate down. Moments later, I heard the front door open and close behind my brother. I dropped into my chair and buried my face in my hands.

CHAPTER
Three

After Stephen's exit, Mother's party took a definite turn for the worse.

Carrie and I—as if by mutual consent—behaved as if all families experienced temper tantrums in the midst of birthday celebrations. Like idiots, we pushed the conversation forward, making vain attempts to distract the family from the bomb that had just exploded.

Timothy and Kevin took a more stoic approach. Neither said anything. In spite of the painful tension, we managed to serve the cake and sing a meager chorus of "Happy Birthday"—though a more heartless rendition has never been performed.

In the kitchen, I caught Carrie crying as she served the cake onto dessert dishes. "I'm so sorry, Carrie," I said, squeezing her shoulders. I felt her stiffen. "Mother can be so insensitive. We all know that."

Diabetes had robbed Carrie of three pregnancies. She and Timothy had stopped trying to have children seven years ago. Because of her brittle diabetes, adoption agencies had turned down her applications. "Mom isn't the only insensitive one in the family." She said, brushing aside a tear.

I set down the serving spatula. "What do you mean?"

"You could have defended me."

My mouth dropped open. "I don't handle Mother's barbs very well." I stood motionless. "I guess I just didn't think."

"You're not so different yourself, you know."

I stared at her.

"You both get a bone in your jaws and just can't let go. With her, it's grandchildren. With you, it's religion."

I shook my head, completely unable to respond. I picked up two pieces of cake and headed for the dining room. We served dessert against a camouflage of chitchat, after which Mother opened and politely exclaimed over each of her gifts. When my bewildered children could stand no more of our phoniness, they asked for and received permission to escape. I heard them head downstairs, taking comfort in the familiar lines of an old Star Wars video. In the meantime, the five of us continued to pretend nothing had happened.

I wished I could join the kids.

By the time she left, Mother had huffed and puffed and justified herself into the second phase of a major pity party. "I'll never understand Stephen," she told us, her eyes glassy with unshed tears. She kissed my cheek lightly and sat down in the back of Timothy's Camry. "We did our best raising you children. What can anyone do with such a tempestuous, emotional child? Stephen takes offense over absolutely everything."

Mother turned in the seat, lifting her feet into the car. With deliberate motions, she tucked her skirt around her knees. "It was a lovely party, Colleen," she said as I closed the door.

As I stepped back to wave, I remembered something a counselor had once told me. "Yours is an elephant-in-the-living-room family," he said. Of course, I didn't understand. "It means that when you have something as big and destructive as an elephant sitting right in front of you, your family would never have the courage to talk about it truthfully."

Just call me Colleen "Elephant in the Living Room" MacLaughlin Payton. I felt guilty about the enormous relief that came over me as Timothy drove away.

～ ～ ～

I spent the next two weeks helping the kids settle into the new school year. Mallory, a senior, had recently transferred to a brand new high school not far from our home. September swamped us in a series of back-to-school meetings and college information nights.

In spite of the busy schedule, I put the finishing touches on my teaching plans for the school year. I teach private piano lessons three days every week from the piano in our living room. My students range in age from five to sixty, and fitting their lives into my three-day teaching schedule would try anyone's tactical ability. That fall, after endless phone calls and arrangements and rearrangements of lesson times, I scheduled everyone.

Then I began my annual hunt for appropriate sheet music.

As exhaustion sets in, I remind myself that I love teaching piano, that I love giving the gift of music to others. And, in the spring, when that encouragement fails, I remind myself that these piano students will send Mallory and Travis to college.

As I worked, I recorded the pieces I hoped to assign for spring recitals. To make certain that no background noise disturbed the recording process, I turned off the telephone and worked during the day while the children were at school, sometimes spending hours at the piano.

In the midst of this busy chaos, I continued chauffeuring Travis to and from the soccer field, where his select soccer team met twice weekly. Of course on my one free afternoon, Travis—who plans to become the next Kenny G—scheduled his saxophone lessons. I'm sure it never occurred to my fifteen-year-old son that I might actually have a life.

In September and October the weather around Potter's Hollow continued dry and clear—long past the time that our winter storms normally begin. People in town began to worry about thirsty landscaping and low rivers. Kevin, the power manager for the bustling city of Potter's Hollow (our population once swelled to seven thousand), found himself sequestered in endless meetings between city officials and power regulators. From these late-evening meetings, Kevin emerged exhausted and short-tempered.

In my typically sympathetic way, I suggested that city officials might have more success holding a citywide rain dance. My advice did not amuse Kevin.

Situated on the eastern edge of the Cascade Mountain range, our town is carved into the rugged hills surrounding the Wenatchee River. Behind the town, the tree-covered peaks rise so high, that to look at the top, you must tilt your head back—far enough to make your neck hurt. In the winter, these hills are covered with snow, and the view is breathtaking. But the view has never been enough to keep Potter's Hollow alive.

In the early twentieth century, Potter's Hollow nearly became a ghost town. When the railroad pulled out and the Troy Brick Company closed the clay mine, the local economy hit bottom. The population dwindled. Businesses went bankrupt.

Fifty years later, in a last desperate effort to save their town, local politicians convinced the townsfolk to transform our tired railroad town into a classic Bavarian alpine village. Reluctantly, business owners agreed. Townspeople covered commercial buildings with plaster façade, added heavy wooden balconies and decorative trim. That together with the obvious overuse of German language on business signs gave Potter's Hollow a whole new look.

And in my humble opinion, ours is the most beautiful city in Washington. Hands down.

In the transformation, more than the face of Potter's Hollow changed. Local entrepreneurs discovered that large amounts of quality kaolin remained in the area where the mine had shut down. Together, they created a cooperative that both removed and refined the clay. Then they recruited ceramic artists to manage the organization and work the clay into beautiful and expensive pieces, destined for the hands of eager tourists.

Today, Potter's Hollow is alive and well because men and women refused to let it die. I had no doubt that our unrelenting determination would guide the town through its water troubles as well.

As the days grew shorter, no amount of teaching or carpooling could drive away the memory of my brother's face. I could not shake the look of rejection I saw in him as he strode from my dining room. I couldn't forget the sound of the front door closing behind him, or of his car as he drove away.

By some wonderful miracle, for one brief moment, Stephen had come into my life again. And then my mother had driven him away. None of my relentless activity could overcome the feelings of anger I felt toward my mother. Part of me wanted to punish her for her selfish attitude and unkind words.

As my frustrations rose, I remembered some of the unkind things I'd said to Stephen myself—not sixteen years before—on the night my brother came to meet Travis in Good Samaritan Hospital.

Stephen arrived late, an hour after Kevin had taken Mallory home. I'd finished feeding my newborn and sent him back to the nursery with a nurse, when a soft knock pulled me out of a light sleep. I sat up in bed, pulling up the covers. Wondering who might visit at that late hour, I called, "Come in."

Stephen entered, carrying an arrangement of blue carnations in a ceramic tennis shoe. "You look tired," he said, kissing my forehead.

"No kidding." I laughed at my brother. "You try giving birth some day. It's like a fifty mile jog with a full pack."

"How would you know? And where is my new nephew?"

"Okay. It might be something like a fifty mile jog," I conceded. "He's down in the nursery. Thanks for the flowers. They'll look great in his room."

"That's better," he said, pulling a chair up beside my bed. "How's Mallory taking the arrival of her new brother?"

"She's so proud. You'd think she did it herself." I straightened a pillow and snuggled down for what I hoped would be a long visit. "She and Kevin just went home for her bath."

"I'd like to see that," he said, a smile spreading across his face. "Macho dad gives three-year-old a bath."

"Oh he's pretty good at it. I give him lots of practice."

"I'll bet you do." Stephen leaned back. "You always tried to get me to do your chores," he said, folding his hands on his lap. He looked at me for a long moment. "I think he's made you very happy."

"Kevin? He's wonderful," I agreed. "Sometimes, when I look at him—even now, after two children—I think about how lucky I am that he chose me."

"You deserve to be happy."

"Thank you," I said, pulling a pillow into my embrace. "I wish you could find someone."

"Please, Colleen. Not that again." Stephen said, emphasizing his words as if he spoke to a recalcitrant two-year-old. "I'm not going to find someone. Of all people, you should know that."

In all our years together, Stephen and I had no secrets—well, almost none. We'd gone to the same schools and shared the same friends. We'd played together, skied together. We'd sung in the same performing choir. We'd even performed duets together. We'd gotten our driver's licenses on the same day.

For years, I believed that we even thought alike.

In all that time, we'd never come this close to talking about our differences. His difference. "I don't know," I said. "I don't understand why you think you are—you know—different." I pulled the pillow closer, hugging it fiercely. "You're a handsome guy. Women like you. You've had a normal life. Why can't you just decide to get married and have a family? I know you'd find someone as wonderful as I have."

"Colleen, it can't happen and you know it," he said. "I am who I am—and nothing you can say will change that. If you can't handle who I am, then I'm sorry. But please, don't feed me these lines about finding some wonderful woman who can make me into the guy you think I ought to be." He crossed his arms and slid down in the chair. "I can't listen to it anymore. Not from you—not from anyone."

"I'm sorry, Stephen," I said. "I'm just afraid for you."

He avoided my eyes, as his lips tightened into a straight line. "Please don't talk about it again."

I hid my disappointment like an old woman tucking a tissue up her sleeve. "Would you like to meet Travis?" I asked, reaching for the long robe draped over the foot of my bed. "I think he looks like a MacLaughlin. Walk me down to the nursery?"

Like a magician, I'd managed a conversational sleight of hand. Once again, I'd agreed to keep the MacLaughlin code of silence. Stephen and I never spoke about his difference again.

I shook my head, trying to brush away the memory.

On the day of her birthday party, Mother hadn't agreed to our cover-up. In her own blundering, inconsiderate way, she'd hurt

Stephen. Unwilling to let go, Mother chose to prod and push and shame my brother. As much as her behavior angered me, I struggled with a nagging question.

Was I all that different?

Maybe Carrie was right. While Mother outwardly resented Stephen, I struggled with an inner resentment, an inner wish that he would just forget whatever it was that made him believe that he was different. I wanted him to change as much as my mother did. I might have had the manners to keep my wishes to myself—but I still had the same wishes.

No matter how I regretted the scene at the party, I couldn't blame Mother too much. I hated whatever it was that had taken Stephen from me. I hated that he had to hide, to run, to miss out on a normal, happy life.

My aching had a spiritual dimension as well. While my brother had moved away from the religious training of his childhood, I had moved toward it.

As children, our parents insisted we attend church. Though we went to Sunday school and services, they made it clear that faith belonged only in the context of the church building. In college, I'd begun attending church again, beginning my faith journey during my senior year. I'd bought it all—the whole thing—hook, line, and sinker. I believed in Jesus. I believed in his sinless life, and his death in my place. My decision amused mother. She thought I'd grow tired of living the zealous life. "Church is a fine thing," she told me. "But you can overdo it, you know. I've seen it happen."

Stephen, on the other hand, greeted my news with disdain. "What a crock, Colleen," he'd said. "I didn't think you were that stupid."

I guess I am—stupid I mean. I didn't grow out of the decision. In fact, over the years, Kevin and I had grown in faith together. My faith launched me into a whole new world. And as I faced that world, my faith became my compass, showing me the way.

During the silent years, the years Stephen had stayed away, we'd heard the sermons and read the articles. We knew the dangers Stephen's lifestyle invited. But we also heard others like him labeled and judged. Though we never actually heard it personally, we knew that some Christian pastors called the AIDS epidemic "God's judgment" on the homosexual lifestyle.

The voices of two cultures pulled me in opposite directions, neither voice fully resonating in my soul. I never accepted homosexuality. But those who condemned it most strongly did not know the pain of losing someone they loved to a lifestyle. And they might never understand how their hateful words and unkind actions helped to build a wall between me and my brother that I could never begin to scale. Stephen associated my faith with their actions.

That fall I spent hours thinking about Stephen. What had driven him so far from me? Did he sense my inner struggle? Did he disappear in order to spare me the pain of choosing between my love for him and my own religious standard?

But after Mother's disastrous birthday party, I missed Stephen more than ever. So much that my chest ached, and breathing sometimes hurt. I cried in the bathtub.

I saw him everywhere. In the clothing ads for the Christmas season. In the face of the men who sang in my church choir. I saw him too, of course, in the picture he had brought me on the day of the party. I'd placed it on the lid of my piano, where I saw it every time I sat down to play.

There were other pictures too. In fact, the pictures of my childhood document Stephen's childhood as well. In every picture of me, Stephen is included. I was twenty years old before I had a picture taken without him. Since then, only my wedding pictures include his face.

In spite of how much I missed my brother, I didn't have the courage to face him. I didn't have the courage to call and apologize for Mother's behavior—or my own for that matter.

Though I could say the words, I could not hide my true feelings. In that way, I was exactly like my mother. Though I loved Stephen, I wanted something else for him. He knew it. He would see through to my heart instantly.

I tried to pray about the situation. But the more I prayed, the more confused I felt. The sister part of me wanted the Stephen of my childhood to return exactly as I remembered him. But that seemed impossible. The Christian part of me wanted Stephen to be completely changed and set free from whatever kept him from me.

But Stephen did not want to be free.

The more my thoughts rolled and tumbled and fought, the more hopelessness began to intrude on my preparations for Thanksgiving. Believing that I'd lost my brother again, I didn't feel very thankful.

Tuesday afternoon, ten days before Thanksgiving, I unloaded the dryer and filled a laundry basket with clothes. I took them to the family room to fold and walked in on Travis and Mallory in a full-fledged screaming match.

"How dare you talk to me like that?" They stood toe to toe, Mallory pointing her index finger at her brother's chest.

"I'll talk anyway I want to talk."

Mallory's voice rose a half step. "I was trying to defend you."

"Okay, time out." I said, dropping the basket on the couch.

"I don't need your defense," Travis said, ignoring me. "I don't need my big sister butting in on my problems."

"Wait a minute," I said, stepping between them, my hands on their shoulders like a boxing referee. "Time for a break."

"Mother, we aren't children." Mallory crossed her arms. With a toss of her head, she managed to throw her long blond hair over one shoulder.

"Funny, you both sound like children," I said. "Now take a seat," I ordered. "Now."

"Mom," Travis said in a whining tone I recognized from his early days. Though the boy grows, some techniques stay the same.

"What is this about?"

"I was trying to defend my brother," Mallory said, flopping onto the arm of the couch.

"Against what?"

"Against nothing." Travis fell into a lounge chair across the room, slamming the seat back with one hand. The chair jerked flat, nearly turning over backwards. I turned to Mallory and repeated my question. "Against what?"

"Some of the guys were making fun of him at lunch," Mallory said.

"It doesn't matter." Travis said.

"Apparently, it mattered to your sister." I sat down on the couch with Mallory. "So?"

"The winter youth retreat is the same weekend as solo contest," she said. "The guys want Trav to go with them, but he won't. They said only sissies play classical junk."

"Sissies?" I asked. I glanced at Trav, who put his arms behind his head and stared at the ceiling. I barely managed to stifle a smile. "What did you say?"

"What *didn't* she say," Travis spat, crossing his ankles and shaking his head.

"I told them that anyone could be a cud-chewing, brainless couch potato who watched professional football for the rest of his life. But people with talent make something of themselves."

"You said that?"

"I did." She pulled her hair into a ponytail and tossed it behind her head. "But I wasn't that nice about it."

My imagination whirled with images of Mallory verbally thrashing her brother's persecutors. It had taken a lot of courage for Mallory to stand up to them in front of everyone in the cafeteria. Part of me felt more than a little proud. *You go girl.*

And then it occurred to me. I hadn't defended my brother against my mother's hateful words. The thought caught me unaware, and I sank back into the memory of the birthday party. If only I'd have said something. Could I have stopped my mother?

"Mom," Mallory's voice broke into my thoughts. "I only defended him. That was right, wasn't it?"

"I don't need her in my business," Travis growled.

I reached out to touch the arm of the lounge chair. "You know, Travis, you should be grateful that you have a sister who loves you so much."

"Great, she can humiliate me because she loves me."

"You can both go clean your rooms," I answered. "Discussion over." Whenever I run out of expertise, I use this parental backup technique. I can end any argument by sending children off to clean their rooms. If nothing else, it gives me time to regroup.

I thought about Stephen as I folded clothes. I worried as I mixed meatloaf. By the time I made dressing for the broccoli salad, I'd decided to call Stephen and invite him for Thanksgiving. I called Carrie for his home phone number.

With the phone number in one hand, I began a relentless harassment of Stephen's telephone. I never got past voice messaging. Stephen never returned my calls, and I began to wonder if he was avoiding me. The silence only made me more determined to reach him.

I called the operator at Seattle Community College and asked for the drama department. I wanted to speak with a human. "That office is in the English department," the operator explained. "I'll transfer you."

"Seattle Community, Dr. Lyndon's office," a cheerful voice answered.

"Yes, I'm trying to get in touch with Stephen MacLaughlin," I said.

"I can give you his voice—"

"No, not the voice mail," I practically shouted. I couldn't handle being clicked into never-never land again. I took a deep breath, calming myself. "I'm his sister, his twin actually, Colleen MacLaughlin Payton. I'm having trouble reaching him at his extension, and I'm wondering if he's changed his number or if something is wrong. I'm not sure why I'm not catching him."

"Let me transfer you to the department chairman's office," she said, maintaining her cheerful composure. "Dr. Dennison is at his desk this morning. Perhaps he can help."

I'd heard an entire chorus of Burl Ives singing "Frosty the Snowman" before a gravelly male voice picked up the line. "Dr. Dennison."

"Dr. Dennison, this is Colleen MacLaughlin Payton. I'm Stephen MacLaughlin's sister."

"His sister? I didn't know he had a sister."

I pushed aside a stab of hurt. "His twin sister, actually. I haven't been able to reach him lately and I'm trying to find out if anything is wrong." Why hadn't Stephen mentioned me?

"Perhaps he hasn't felt well enough to check his messages."

"Not well enough?"

"He called in sick last week. Stephen hasn't been on campus for about five days now."

"He's sick?" I felt a queer mixture of relief and apprehension roll around in my stomach.

"Yes, though we're expecting him back any day. I'm sure it's nothing to worry about. You know how those fall colds can put you down." He cleared his voice. "I don't think you should worry. You'll find him at home, tucked in bed, probably enjoying an old movie."

"Of course. I'm sure you're right." I managed to excuse myself and hang up without giving any hint of the rock that had landed in the bottom of my gut.

Something was wrong. Nothing would keep Stephen from campus with the approach of his play's opening. I don't know how, but I felt completely certain; Stephen didn't have a cold. He hadn't succumbed to the flu. My brother, my twin, battled something much worse.

CHAPTER
Four

"Mom, do you know where my tux jacket is?" Travis's voice interrupted my cartwheeling, worried thoughts. I glanced up as he came through the kitchen door and began prowling through the pantry for food.

"Sure I do. I sent it to the cleaners to get ice cream off the lapel."

Travis pulled out a box of Ritz crackers and tore open a tube, taking half the stack. "Will it be done in time?"

Those words always catch my attention. I stopped drumming. "In time for what?"

Travis popped three crackers into his mouth and headed to the refrigerator for what I knew would be a super-sized glass of milk. "For tour. We leave Thursday morning."

The four-day band tour to Canada. How could I forget? "Oh, sure. Right." I said as calmly as I could. "I'll pick up the jacket Wednesday before lessons. Do you know where the pants are?"

"Yep," Travis nodded as he filled a huge glass with milk, holding the gallon over the glass until the last drop fell from the container. Tossing the jug on the counter, he added, "Thanks, Mom."

"In the trash please."

Travis groaned. "Don't forget, okay?" He backed out the swinging door.

"No crackers downstairs," I reminded him just before he disappeared.

My fingers started drumming again. Ignoring the milk on the counter and the crumbs on the floor, I let a fresh idea gather steam, rolling it around in my mind like a hard candy on the tongue, savoring the taste.

Because of band tour, Mallory and Travis would be gone from Thursday morning through Sunday afternoon. Kevin had a series of out-of-town meetings on Thursday and Friday. Maybe I could drive to Seattle and visit my brother. I could make amends in person, invite him for Thanksgiving, and, best of all, find out about his illness. To me, it seemed like a perfect plan.

≈ ≈ ≈

I told Kevin as we prepared for bed Sunday night.

"What on earth can you do over there?" Kevin asked. Looking in the mirror, he glanced at me, water dripping from his chin. "Make chicken soup?"

"Don't be cute."

"I'm not being cute. I'm being practical." Kevin dried his face on a hand towel. "Stephen's a big boy. He doesn't need you."

"How do you know what he needs?" I said, putting paste on my toothbrush. "We haven't talked to him since the party."

"Exactly, Colleen." He put his towel on the rack. "He knows our number."

"He's not going to come to us, Kevin. He tried that. We let Mother eat him alive. For all he knows, we hate him like she does."

"Of course we don't hate him."

"How would he know that? We didn't say anything."

"Why don't you just call him?"

"I can't get him to answer the phone."

"Has it occurred to you that he doesn't *want* to talk to you?"

"No," I said honestly. "Listen, Kevin, you don't know anything about having a twin brother. No matter how bad things are between us, we don't give up on one another. We spent our childhood believing that it was us against the world."

"This time, the world could win." Kevin said, picking his glasses off the counter and pointing them at me. "And you might be making things worse. I think you should leave well enough alone."

With that, Kevin went to bed.

I decided not to mention the trip again. I dreaded having to listen to Kevin tell me how useless it would be to visit Stephen. Kevin hadn't forbidden my going—he simply believed I was wasting my time.

Oh well, it was mine to waste. My only real problem was that I didn't know exactly where Stephen lived. With three days to spare, I called my sister. Though I got her home answering machine, I never reached her. She didn't return my messages. I finally called her at the office.

Sometimes my sister's post-graduate education makes me feel a little insecure. Truthfully, I'm happy that she's is a successful attorney. But next to my sister's career, my music lessons seem a little insignificant. "I'm looking for Carrie," I told her assistant.

"I'll see if I can reach her. Please hold." Classical music came over the line.

"Carrie Bergstrom."

"Carrie, hi. It's Colleen."

"You never call in the middle of the day."

"I've tried you at home, and I'm running out of time."

"Out of time, for what?"

"The kids are headed on a band tour this week, and Kevin has a business trip. I thought I'd go over to Seattle and visit Stephen."

My sister didn't answer.

"Carrie?"

"You're going to visit Stephen?" She clucked her tongue. "That's rich."

"Rich?"

"I was there. I heard him take off. Weren't you listening? He doesn't want to hear from you again."

"He was upset with Mother. We all were."

"If that's the way you want to see it."

"Carrie, I didn't call to argue about Stephen. I just need his latest address. The last thing I mailed came back with no forwarding."

She paused again, and I wondered what could be so difficult about my question. "I don't know," she hedged. "I don't think you should try to interfere."

"Carrie, for crying out loud. Interfere with what? He's my twin."

"I know you're twins. Sheez, you tell me that every time you see me. I'm so aware of that fact."

"So why not give me his address?"

"Because I don't know if I should."

"Oh come on."

"Just because you're his twin doesn't give you the right to barge in on him."

I could hardly contain my frustration. "Carrie, listen to me. I'm trying to make sure he's all right. I called the school and they said he's been out sick. I'm a little worried. That's all. If I find that he's okay, I promise I'll turn around and come home. I'll leave him alone if that's what he wants."

"Alright," she finally said. "Give me a minute."

She came back on the line and read the address to me.

"Thanks. I'll try not to mess him up too much when I go see him." Without a word, she hung up.

∼ ∼ ∼

By the time I reached the freeway Thursday morning, my conscience had begun to prickle. I soothed it by tuning the radio to a Christian music station. An hour later, my stomach signaled for attention, and I stopped for a soft-serve cone at a drive-through window. I've heard that soft ice cream is lower in fat and calories than its more solid counterpart—a rumor I've never chosen to investigate. Sometimes, ignorance is bliss.

I licked the top off my cone as I headed back to the interstate. I had no idea how to find the address Carrie gave me. My plan included getting close enough to stop at a convenience store and ask for directions. Okay, so I never said I was brilliant. At least I had a plan.

As the miles slid by, I watched the pastures east of the Cascades rise to higher elevations. Thin stands of long-needle pine trees replaced the dry, rolling grassland as the highway began to climb into the foothills. Puffy white clouds dotted the sky. Before I reached the summit, I spotted a thick cover of black clouds hugging the highway. I've lived in Washington long enough to know what those colors meant.

Before me ominous dark streaks began to spot the sky between rugged mountain faces. I recognized the streaks as rain, falling hard on the west side of the pass, and I glanced at the temperature indicator above my dome light, wondering if I would encounter snow.

Douglas fir and western hemlock began to replace the pine trees, and just as I reached the first summit exit, I turned on my windshield wipers. What began as heavy rain soon gave way to mixed rain and snow, driven by heavy wind. Feeling deep concern for Stephen, I began to pray for my brother. "Help him to see you, Lord," I prayed, clutching at the steering wheel as I fought the wind buffeting my car. "Show me how to help him, Father."

The road grew slick and traffic slowed to a crawl. I tucked myself in behind an eighteen-wheeler just as my radio went into terminal static. My fingers ached from clenching the steering wheel; I stretched them, easing the discomfort as I leaned forward to turn off the radio. My cell phone rang.

I picked it up out of the console. "Hello."

"Colleen." Kevin's voice came through clearly. "I thought I'd call and see what you decided."

"Decided?" I glanced in the rearview, trying to sound vague.

"About going to see Stephen."

"Well, I'm headed over the pass now."

"You got his address?" He'd asked a direct question; I couldn't very well lie.

"I got it from Carrie." No need to mention our bizarre conversation.

"Well don't come crying to me if things don't work out the way you hoped." My normally patient husband sounded more than a little perturbed. "Not everything works out like it does in a fairy tale."

"Worked for me," I said. "I married the prince."

Dead air. "No one gets to live happily ever after," he said.

"Thanks for your support."

"I'm just trying to warn you."

"I get the warning. Now, if you don't mind, I'm on the highway."

I switched off the call and reached forward to drop the phone back into the console. At the same moment, the truck in front of me swerved and braked. I looked up in time to see my hood bear down on his rear bumper. Hitting my own brakes hard, I pulled into the center lane without checking traffic. I heard a horn blast behind me and looked into my rearview mirror as a pickup truck swerved to avoid hitting me, honking again as he sped by. Though I remained in control of my car, the pickup began a breathtaking slide that seemed to go on forever.

"Jesus," I prayed, slamming on my brakes and holding my breath as I watched the truck travel sideways down the road.

Eventually, the driver regained control. I ignored his angry gestures as he pulled away. My heart pounded and I felt my face grow warm with shame. A single moment of inattention and I'd nearly caused a terrible accident. How many cars might have been involved?

I breathed thanks for the Lord's protection and thought again about my journey. Should I have come? Would my actions—this pursuit of my brother—cause a wreck of an entirely different kind?

Already my sister questioned my motives, while my husband questioned my judgment. What more would this quest ask of me? Where would it take me?

Did I have the constitution for the mission I had already begun?

~ ~ ~

By mid afternoon, I found myself on Capitol Hill. To the urgent beat of windshield wipers, I began my search near Seattle University, at the south end of a major arterial. Between the condensation on my windows, and the blur of heavy rain, I had difficulty reading the street signs. Focusing on the progression of numbers, I passed block after block, cautiously navigating busy afternoon traffic and thick crowds of pedestrians as I drove north.

Unfortunately these streets were identified not by numbers, but by the last names of deceased presidents. Wanting to concentrate, I turned off the radio again, listening instead to the steady rhythm of rain and wipers.

At a stoplight, I pulled the yellow slip of paper from my purse and stuck it on the leather seat beside me. Drumming my fingers on the steering wheel, I waited as an old woman crossed in front of me pushing a wheeled walker. The light changed, but the woman, hunched forward, shuffled across the street. As she approached the middle, she stopped, took a deep breath, and seemed to rest before continuing across.

I felt a moment of pity for her, her damp hair covered in a wet black kerchief, her twisted bare hands holding on to the cold metal. She rested without looking up, whether to keep her face from the blowing rain or because of some infirmity I could not tell.

In the time she took to cross the street, I spied a convenience store toward the end of the next block and signaled my intention to turn. I found a parking space, turned off the car, and wished that I'd had the foresight to bring an umbrella.

Inside, I poured myself a cup of steaming coffee, added three cartons of creamer, and brought it to the counter. A teenaged clerk, sporting a gold ring perfectly spaced halfway between the tip of her chin and her lower lip, took my money without comment. Her hair, dyed in red stripes of every hue, was cut in a perfect line at ear level.

"I wonder if I could ask you for directions?" I handed her my yellow note. "I'm from out of town." She nodded, her blue eyes taking in the numbers on the paper.

"Up this street," she pointed, "like about four more blocks. Turn right at the second light and head...like...that direction"—she turned her back to me and gestured with her right hand, meaning east, I assumed—"another ten blocks. You'll come to this street." She pointed back to my yellow notepaper. "And then turn right. I can't tell you how many blocks, but you'll be real close."

I thanked her, accepted change for my coffee, and went outside to face the weather. The wind blew off the hood of my jacket, leaving my hair exposed as the rain soaked my face. Inside the car, I turned the heat on high and directed warm air over my steaming windows.

The chin-studded clerk had given accurate directions. Before long, I crept past closely spaced old homes posed along a narrow street lined by leafless trees. Some of the houses showed a great deal of pride, with well-tended gardens and short chain-link fences.

Others had not fared as well. Among the uncared for, the state of disrepair varied greatly. One, in faded sea-green, leaned crazily toward its neighbor. The entire first floor had been boarded up and grass grew knee-high in the yard. Discarded household items covered the porch.

Ten minutes after leaving the convenience store, I parked across from the house I believed to be Stephen's. The numbers hung in a mismatched diagonal, the seven upside down on the center nail. I turned off the car and sat looking anxiously at the house.

I never expected to find Stephen in a house like this. He'd always been meticulous, even fastidious about his living space. This was not Stephen's kind of house.

His last home had been a proud two-story with a large yard, where Stephen had tied blooming perennials to garden stakes with perfectly matching ribbons. Now, according to the address in my hand, Stephen lived in this old home on a narrow lot jammed in among its equally elderly neighbors. This house had no driveway, no garage, only a few cement steps leading up to the narrow sidewalk that made its way to a red porch. I wondered why my brother had allowed so much gardening to go untended. Glistening brown leaves still covered the yellow lawn, and weeds had begun to invade the flowerbeds.

The shake siding reminded me of cake frosting, thick with heavy layers of gray paint. The trim around the single-pane windows flaked scales of mildewed white, and the edges of the glass showed layers of paint as well. These windows had long since been painted shut. Lined curtains completely covered the front window, and no lights were visible from the street. The house looked empty to me—not like the home of someone home sick from work. Cobwebs skirted the naked bulb over the front door, and the empty wooden frame of an old screen door leaned against the house. I noticed a single newspaper, soaked with rain, hanging off the top step of the porch.

The whole effect confused me, and I began to wonder if I'd written down the wrong address. Sighing, I slipped on my raincoat and threw my purse over one shoulder.

CHAPTER
Five

With a deep breath, I ran through the rain, gingerly sidestepping puddles as I crossed the street to the house. I lifted the latch on the cyclone gate and pushed hard. It moved only a few inches before stopping against the uneven surface of the walk. I tried again, this time lifting as I pushed open the gate. Reluctantly, the gate opened and I slid past, making my way up the cracked walk to the concrete porch.

I pushed the doorbell, leaning forward and tipping my ear as I did, noticing that I could not hear the tone inside. I pushed again and stood back, brushing rain from my jacket as I waited. No one came to the door. I threw back my hood and pounded on the front door. No answer.

At the front window, I cupped my hands against the glass, trying to peek through the dark space between the curtains. I saw only a single sliver of furniture and a bit of dark carpet beyond.

I'd come too far to leave without knowing for certain that Stephen lived here. I stood with my hands on my hips as I thought. It was in this position that I first spied it, a tiny black mailbox hung low and to the right of the front door. Stuffed to overflowing, the box appeared to hold more than a single day's mail. Magazines folded lengthwise enclosed junk mail and numerous envelopes. If each folded collection represented a day's delivery, Stephen hadn't retrieved his mail in at least three days.

As I pulled the collection out, envelopes tumbled down over my wet jacket and onto the porch. I bent to retrieve them, examining each one as I brushed the water off and put them back on the stack of mail.

Bingo. I'd found him. Stephen MacLaughlin.

With the fallen mail in hand, I straightened, then unfolded the magazines, anxious to put the loose envelopes back with the rest. Suddenly the title of a single magazine took my breath away.

HIV Plus.

I had to sit down.

I have no idea how long I sat on Stephen's front porch, with my legs exposed to the rain. I did not feel my jeans soak through with water. I was not aware of the chill as it crept from the cement into my bones, at least not until I felt myself begin to shiver. I might have stayed there forever, were it not for the shivering that gradually increased until my teeth chattered like dice in a Bunko game. I remember spending the entire time trying to explain away the presence of the magazine in Stephen's mailbox.

Surely Stephen had not been infected with the virus that caused AIDS. He hadn't told me anything. How could anyone face a disease this serious without telling the ones you love most in the world? It couldn't be true.

As I put his mail back in the box, another thought came to me, and I clung to it with a desperate, irrational hope. Perhaps Stephen had subscribed for some other reason. Maybe someone he cared about had HIV. Perhaps Stephen had a roommate.

I tried the idea on for comfort. It didn't fit, but I chose to buy it anyway.

I dried my face with my hands and wiped my nose with the sleeve of my jacket, thinking how my mother might chide this lack of feminine discretion. My eyes filled with tears. Mother. If Stephen really were ill, how would Mother take the news?

I wondered what to do. Stephen hadn't asked me to come. And frankly, at that moment, I wasn't sure I could face him. My body felt as heavy as if I wore a suit of armor. My soul was bruised. Maybe I should just go home. With a heavy heart, I clumped back down the porch steps.

Just as I reached the front walkway, I noticed a series of small paving stones leading around to the back of the house. On a whim, I followed them around through the side yard, past another gate and into the back.

This yard received no more care than the front. Neither did I recognize any signs of my brother. Just as I considered giving up, I noticed a light spilling from what must have been the kitchen window. I went up four concrete steps to the back door and peered inside. Through sheer curtains covering a half window, I found myself with a perfect view.

Dirty plates and half-filled glasses covered the white tile counter. Newspapers stood open on the small round table at the side of the room. On top of these stood several prescription bottles and two half-empty bottles of Gatorade.

I tried the door. Locked. I banged again with all my strength but could not rouse anyone inside. Looking down, I noticed an opening that filled most of the lower half of the wooden door. Over the opening swung a sheet of heavy plastic. Whoever installed that opening owned a very big doggie.

I prodded the flap with my foot and found no resistance.

I got down on my hands and knees and started through. By carefully twisting my head and shoulders, I managed to get the upper half of my body through with ease.

"Stephen," I called, "I'm coming in."

As I moved forward, I realized that my lower half did not fit quite so perfectly. I crawled backward without success. I stopped, panting, and tried to think. I imagined the neighbors spotting my wiggling behind as I struggled to get inside. How on earth would I explain this to the police?

Then a more frightening thought struck me. In a movie I'd seen somewhere, a character had entered a house using the same technique, only to be confronted by a vicious guard dog. I stopped moving momentarily, wondering what it might feel like to have my face attacked with only my hands to defend myself. The thought spurred me forward.

I dropped onto my tummy and rolled onto my left side. I had crawled part way into a small alcove just off the kitchen. Above my head, a line of hooks held outdoor coats. I pulled on one as I wriggled forward. The coat fell off the hook and landed on my head. Tossing

it away, I grabbed the edge of the nearest doorframe and pulled hard.
Dragging myself along the wood floor, I managed to squeeze into the
house. I took a moment to collect myself before I stood up.

"Stephen?" I called again. "Stephen, are you here?"

I heard a sound, something like the squeak of a chair, coming from
the front of the house. "Stephen? It's me, Colleen," I said, starting
down a long hall toward the front door. "Stephen?" I called again,
passing the doorway to a small formal dining room. I glanced inside.
The upper half of the room had been covered in wallpaper with an
oriental print.

Though small, the house exuded craftsman quality, with bare
wood floors and half-paneled walls lining the hallway. I heard the
squeaking sound again, the sound of someone moving inside a chair—
if that was the sound I'd identified—and a soft moaning.

I peaked into a doorway on my left and found a small half-bathroom
tucked under what had to be a stairway. Empty.

At the end of the hallway, I came to a small alcove behind the front
door, where a wooden stairway led up to what was probably the
bedroom area. To my right, through a plaster archway, I spied the living
room.

It too had wooden floors, with a large oriental rug in front of a
smallish leather couch. A dark coffee table covered with napkins and
dishes sat before the couch. I stepped into the room and gave myself
a moment for my eyes to adjust to the darkness. Though I saw lamps,
they had not been turned on.

At first, I didn't see him. When I did, the difference in my brother
startled me. Stephen lay fully reclined in a leather chair in the corner
of the room. Beside him, a small table held tissues and an empty water
bottle. "Stephen," I said, rushing toward him. "I was worried about
you. Are you okay?"

He didn't seem at all surprised to see me. Instead, he gave me the
smallest of smiles. "I was hoping someone would come," he whispered.
"I can't seem to get out of this chair."

I found myself breathing through my mouth as I crouched in front
of my brother. I couldn't identify all of the smells that made my
stomach rebel. But the room reeked, and I knew without asking that

Stephen's illness afflicted him with both nausea and diarrhea. I longed to open the front door and let in some fresh air.

"How does it work?" I asked, moving around to the side of the recliner.

"The lever," he answered, his voice weak and breathless. "It's stuck."

I followed his gestures and found a long handle below Stephen's right hand. "It should go forward?" I pushed at the lever, but the chair did not move. "Can you help me by sliding yourself forward?" I asked.

He tried. Clearly, Stephen had very little strength. His eyes appeared to have shrunk down into the sockets. And though he seemed clearheaded—he knew who I was—he wasn't himself. He moved as if in slow motion, sluggish and half aware.

From the front of the chair, I slipped my arms around his shoulders and pulled him forward. Nothing moved. I let go and grabbed him lower, toward his hips.

"Okay, on three," I said, and began counting. On three, we both threw ourselves into the effort and, reluctantly, the chair folded up. Stephen's T-shirt was wet where he'd been stuck against the vinyl. His skin felt warm to me, and I wondered if he had a fever.

"I need to go to the bathroom," Stephen said, embarrassment in his sheepish expression. "I've been stuck here a while."

"Can you get up?"

"I can do it myself," he said, his voice a small bark. His lips seemed sticky somehow, as if coated in egg whites. He glanced up at me and leaned forward, straining to stand.

I let him try several times before suggesting help. "Alright," he agreed reluctantly.

I pulled him out of the chair, holding both his shoulders until he stopped swaying. Pulling him up hadn't taken as much effort as I expected. Stephen had lost weight.

His stood for a moment, eyes closed.

"Can you walk? Do you need help?" Already my back ached from the bending and lifting. I'd never have made it as a nurse.

"I can do it," he said, the stubborn tone returning. With that, he began to shuffle across the room, his stocking feet never quite leaving the wooden floor. As he reached the corner of the entryway he reached out, bracing himself as he swayed. "Your timing is impeccable," he said, his voice barely a whisper.

I smiled back at him. "Always has been."

I stood next to the chair, listening as he shuffled down the hall to the bathroom. I heard the door shut, and the sound of the toilet seat dropping onto the ceramic bowl. He would need time to clean up, I thought, and then I realized that he had no clean clothes with him.

I followed him down the hall, knocking gently on the door. "Stephen, would you like me to get you something clean to put on?"

"I can manage," he said.

"Are you crazy? You can't get out of your own chair. Let me help. Are your things upstairs?"

He was silent for a minute. "In the front bedroom."

"Will you be alright for a minute?"

"I'm not dead, Colleen."

I smiled at the door, glad to hear his old independence reassert itself.

Upstairs, I passed the open door of the back bedroom, peeking in as I went by. Stephen had made this bedroom into an office, though I doubted he had been inside for a while. The shades over the single window were pulled shut, and dust covered the surface around his computer keyboard.

I scanned the rest of the room and found my gaze arrested by the trunk sitting in front of a simple sofa. Stephen was in the middle of a project. I stepped inside to take a look.

Spread across the dark leather top were pictures of my childhood—and Stephen's of course. In one, my parents stood behind us and our brand new tricycles. In another, toddler Stephen sat in his father's arms, grinning at his older sister.

Stephen had organized the pictures, as nearly as I could tell, chronologically. I picked up a photograph and gazed at tow-headed toddlers holding hands in front of a small outdoor table. Two candles topped the birthday cake behind them.

At the moment the shutter opened, my attention was focused not toward the camera, but on something off to my right, my index finger pointing at the distraction. Stephen, on the other hand, looked directly at the lens, and I saw something old and familiar in his expression. Stephen always made me feel as though he could see clear through me.

I shook my head, smiling as I replaced the picture. In the center of the trunk, I recognized the leather cover of an album nearly a foot square. I opened the cover, leafing lightly through the black pages. Stephen was in the process of creating a scrapbook, the pictures inside carefully mounted and labeled. His was a labor of precision.

So like him. I turned out the light and moved on.

Passing the upstairs bathroom, I went into the front bedroom and switched on the lights. Lovely yellow walls surrounded a cherry sleigh bed. Ornate wall lamps balanced the spaces on either side of the front window. The dresser stood on my right, and a small square closet in the corner beyond. I peeked into the closet. Stephen's clothes hung in neat rows on double racks. All his shoes stood at attention, toes pointing to the wall, along a wooden rack at the end of the closet.

This closet represented the Stephen that I remembered, and I sighed thinking about the mess downstairs. It must kill him to live like that. I chose a pair of jeans, neatly folded over a hanger, and moved to the dresser, where I found clean boxers, a T-shirt and a sweater. How long had it been since Stephen had showered? It occurred to me to stop in the bathroom and bring down a towel and washcloth.

Downstairs, I knocked again at the bathroom door. "I brought some clean clothes, Stephen. Maybe you'd rather take a shower?"

"No," he said, exhaustion in his voice. The door opened about five inches and he put out his hand for the clothes. I placed them in his fingers and watched as he pulled his hand back through the opening.

Stephen clearly didn't need my help dressing. Rather than wait in the hall, I decided to tackle the mess in his kitchen. At least I could help there.

Dirty dishes filled the dishwasher, and I crammed the few remaining spaces with glasses from the counters. I found detergent and started the dishwasher. I filled the sink with hot soapy water and began hand washing the remaining dishes. Working quickly, I had most of the counters cleaned and wiped and the dishes drying on a nearby towel when I began to wonder about Stephen. I dried my hands and started down the hall.

"Stephen," I called. "Are you okay in there? Can I get you anything?"

He didn't answer. I knocked gently. "Stephen, do you need anything?"

Still no answer. Even as I began to worry, I chided myself for being so easily thrown into a tizzy. I paced the hallway, then listened for a moment, my ear against the wooden door. I couldn't hear anything. Had he fallen asleep? Or worse?

I banged on the door. "Stephen, I'm worried. Are you okay?" Still, no response. I rattled the doorknob. He had locked it. Part of me felt angry for his foolishness. What did he think I would do, walk in on him? "For heaven's sake," I muttered to myself, heading back to the kitchen. No locked door had ever stopped me.

In a drawer under the telephone, I found a small screwdriver. If my skills held, I could unlock a bathroom door faster than any mother on earth. I stuck the screwdriver into the tiny hole of the doorknob, turning the tool while at the same time wiggling the handle of the door. The lock clicked open.

Too bad there isn't a gold medal for entering a locked bathroom.

I pushed at the door, but it didn't open. It took a moment to realize that the door had stopped against the unconscious body of my twin brother.

CHAPTER
Six

As soon as I finished calling 9-1-1, I slammed the phone on the cradle and ran down the hall to the bathroom. "Stephen," I shouted, banging on the door. "Stephen, wake up!" My knuckles hurt from the impact, and I realized that no one knows, unless you've experienced it, the heart-pounding terror of waiting for an ambulance.

I felt so helpless waiting there in the hall, the blood crashing against my eardrums and my heart pounding against my chest. I began to cry.

Anxious to flag down the ambulance. I hurried to the front door and tossed it open, letting it crash against the wall in the entry. As I stepped outside, hoping to hear the sound of approaching sirens, my thoughts buzzed like bees in a confused swarm.

For some reason it occurred to me to call Stephen's doctor and let him know what had happened. As soon as I had the thought, I realized that I didn't have any information about Stephen's health care.

The hospital would need that information—his insurance, his physical history, his doctor's name. Still listening for the sound of the ambulance, I realized that I couldn't fill out an admission form, because I didn't even know my brother's social-security number. With mounting concern, I watched the road in front of the house while chewing on the side of my thumb.

I glanced at my watch. Hoping for enough time, I ran back inside and up the stairs to look for my brother's wallet. Perhaps he had an insurance card. If I could find Stephen's wallet, at least I'd have some of his emergency information.

In my desperate hurry, my foot missed the top stair and I stumbled, banging my shin against the wooden lip. "Shoot," I said, brushing away tears that had nothing at all to do with the spreading bruise on my leg.

I looked in Stephen's bedroom. Every evening, with the regularity of the setting sun, our father had unloaded his pockets onto the top of his bedroom dresser. Perhaps Stephen had picked up the same habit. I turned on the light and scanned the bare top of Stephen's chest of drawers. Disappointed, I sighed.

His nightstand held only a lamp and a paperback book lying face down beside folded reading glasses. Here too was new information; I didn't know Stephen needed glasses. I hurried to the closet door and opened it, scanning inside for a jacket.

Perhaps Stephen habitually left his wallet and keys in his coat pockets. I pulled out anything that might carry the information I sought—sport jackets, raincoat, suit coat, feeling each of the pockets for the bulk of a wallet. Nothing. I checked the bathroom and the office. Still nothing.

I ran back down the stairs, this time clutching the banister for security, limping a bit from the ache in my shin. I made another attempt to rouse Stephen. Leaning hard against the door, I tried to shove his unconscious body out of the way—with no success. I called out to him, realizing as I did, how silly I sounded. "Stephen, hang on," I said to the paneled door. "Help is on the way. We'll have you out of there in a jiffy." I sounded like a commercial for vitamin optimism.

Jogging to the kitchen, I searched the two long counters for his belongings. I hadn't noticed anything while I did dishes. Still, I looked the room over carefully, feeling along the windowsill and on the lowest shelves of the upper cupboards.

From the street outside, I heard the faint sound of an approaching siren, and I let out a sob of relief. Just as I turned back toward the hall, I caught sight of the medicine bottles on the kitchen table. Of course! The labels would list the prescribing doctor. Someone in the emergency room could trace Stephen's information from these bottles. I grabbed two as I started for the front door.

Ignoring the pounding rain, I hurried off the porch and through the gate into the street, waving down the ambulance. I'd never felt so relieved in my life.

"You called for us?" A man emerged from the passenger side door, pulling up the hood of his coat with one hand, holding a small blue case in the other.

"He's inside." I pointed at the house and turned to lead the way, holding the stubborn gate open for the angel who had just arrived. "My brother is sick in the bathroom, and I can't open the door. I think he's unconscious."

"Let's have a look, then," he said, leading the way to the front porch. At the front door, he turned and waited for me. Only then did I notice his startlingly green eyes hidden behind a dark fan of long lashes. I took comfort in his composed smile.

"He's just right here. The door on the right." I gestured down the hall toward the bathroom. Green Eyes led the way into the house, and as I turned to follow, I noticed that the ambulance driver had left the van, lights flashing, in the middle of the street. Just behind them, a fire truck, engines roaring, emergency lights flashing, pulled up and parked.

Inside, as I approached the bathroom door, I called again, "Stephen, they're here. We have help." Even I could hear the tearful relief in my voice.

The medic knocked loudly, asking me as he did, "His name is Stephen?"

I nodded.

"How old?"

"Forty-two."

"Any medical trouble?"

"He's been sick. Maybe dehydrated." I felt something inside resist volunteering the information I'd gained from Stephen's mailbox hours earlier. What if I was wrong? How would misinformation affect this crucial effort to care for my brother? "He went into the bathroom just after I got here, and when I went back to check on him, he wouldn't respond."

I heard the high pitch of my own voice and realized how frightened I must sound. I brushed away another tear, trying to compose myself. "I think he may have fainted."

"Stephen, can you talk to me?" Though Green Eyes raised his voice, his tone sounded calm, reassuring. "We're here to get you out. Can you move away from the door?"

"He hasn't said anything since I came downstairs with his clothes."

The medic nodded and pushed hard against the door, leaning his whole body into the wood. Reluctantly, the door moved inward two inches. "You may be right," he nodded. "It feels like he's fallen against the door."

I watched as he examined the doorframe, feeling along the wood. "It hinges on the inside. We can't take it off from here." He paused with his hands on his hips, looking at me.

A voice from behind me spoke and I jumped. "Any other way in?"

I'd forgotten about the ambulance driver. When I turned to look at him, I found him staring intently at the doorway. "Another door?"

Of course I would have told them about another door. I barely managed to contain my frustration. "Nothing." I shook my head.

"A window?" His eyebrows rose.

I hadn't considered this option. "I don't know. I just drove over to check on him." I sighed. "I've never really…" I shrugged. "He just moved here."

"Let's look." With confident steps, the driver strode to the front door, his partner following close behind. They bounded down the porch stairs and, ignoring the rain, jogged around the house. By now, Stephen's front yard was decorated with a collection of firemen adorned in matching yellow rain gear, boots, and helmets. One fell into line behind us.

The three of them congregated under a narrow leaded-glass window above the side yard. "Just what we need," the driver said, a note of triumph in his voice. "It lies further inside than the stairway. It has to lead to the bathroom. We're in."

Green Eyes held down the button on a radio holstered beneath his jacket and tipped his mouth toward the speaker. "Base. Unit 519."

"Unit 519, what do you have?"

"We have a forty-two-year-old male, perhaps unconscious. Looks like he's lying against the only door to a bathroom. We're going to try going in via the window." He paused, nodding at the fireman who had joined us. "Will contact you with vitals when we get inside."

"Be right back," the fireman turned and ran back toward the group waiting in the front yard. Moments later, two firemen managed to pry the window frame loose. Fortunately, someone had managed to frame the antique glasswork in a single unit that came out easily.

I held my breath as two firemen scrambled through the opening.

I watched as they slid Stephen's stretcher into the back of an ambulance. They had already started fluids through a line into his arm, but Stephen had not regained consciousness. I spoke with the driver as the medics worked inside the closed cab.

"Can I go with you?"

"Sorry, ma'am," he responded. "We can't allow you to ride with us. We don't have any way to buckle you up."

"Where are you taking him?"

"Swedish," he answered, as if I'd know exactly where that was.

"Where?"

"You can follow us in your own car," he said, as he stepped to the driver's door and got inside. "Or you can call a cab." He slammed the door shut and the ambulance pulled away. By the time they turned the corner, the piercing siren completely covered the sound of the big diesel still running behind me.

I looked back at the fire truck and realized the firemen had piled back inside. They too were ready to leave. I stepped back toward the sidewalk, watching helplessly as the truck drove away. Standing alone in the street, I felt more lonely than I had at any point in my life.

By the time I gathered my car keys, the emergency crews had evaporated. For a moment, I wanted to put my hands around the driver's throat. What did he think I was, a private detective? I'd have to figure out how to find this hospital by myself.

At least I remembered the name. In Stephen's kitchen, I found a telephone book and looked up the number for the hospital the ambulance driver had mentioned. I called and asked for directions.

By the time I locked Stephen's house and returned to my own car, the rain had stopped and the clouds had dropped so low that the streets seemed to be wrapped in a heavy white shawl. Though technically still daylight, the dismal weather cast a depressing gloom over the streets. Already cars had their headlights on.

It was the beginning of the rush hour, and traffic had proliferated to the point that Capitol Hill streets were nearly impassable.

I counted nine lights between Stephen's house and the hospital. I hit eight of them on red. On five of those, I waited through two cycles while cars blocked the intersection in front of me. It would have been a trying trip under ideal circumstances.

Emotions, raw and painful, tumbled around inside of me. I prayed as I drove—a bumbling, scattered prayer—something like confetti blowing through a box fan. Still, no more earnest prayer has ever left my lips than the one I uttered on the way to the hospital. God would just have to sort out the confetti.

I found the hospital, a group of buildings covering several city blocks, but soon realized that I'd never find a place to park. The paid parking lots were full. I circled the campus once and then extended my search in wider and wider circles. Time crawled as I searched for a place to leave my car.

Eventually I gave up and parked in a stall labeled "ER Doctors Only." What can I say? I'm a fallen woman.

Inside, I found the emergency department and spoke to a pudgy blonde with hair the color of overripe Bartlett pears. "My brother was just brought in by ambulance," I said.

"His name?"

"Stephen MacLaughlin."

I waited while she shuffled through papers on her desk. If each of those papers represented a patient, it looked as though an entire city had been admitted in this emergency room. She took one from the stack and paused. "Oh yes, here we are."

"Can I see him?"

"He's with the doctor now."

"But can I see him?"

"Actually, I'd like to have you help me with some paperwork if you could." She turned her chair to the computer and began typing. "I have a previous admission for Mr. MacLaughlin," she said, tipping her head backward as she looked at the screen. She seemed to have trouble getting the print focused in the right section of her bifocals. I took a deep breath, willing myself to be patient. "Could you confirm his address?"

I did.

"And his home phone?"

I gave her the number.

"His place of employment?"

"You have all of that information—" I began.

"Still, I must confirm everything," she interrupted, as calmly as though she were selling perfume. I felt the muscles of my jaw begin to ache. Eventually satisfied, she fetched papers from the printer behind her and handed them to me. "I'm going to have you sign these admission slips, since your brother is unavailable." She gave me a fountain pen and a plastic smile.

"He isn't unavailable," I growled. "He is unconscious."

"Of course." She pasted false concern on her face. "Anyway, if you'll sign them, we can get the records for this visit underway." She pointed to the lines requiring a signature. "Just write the words 'his sister' there beside your name."

I signed without reading the sheets. "Now may I see my brother?"

"Certainly. If you'll just wait over there," she pointed. "A nurse will speak to you shortly."

I took a chair beside an enormous aquarium in the lobby. Little did I know that this wire-framed, vinyl-coated chair would be the first in an endless parade of waiting rooms. I picked up *Newsweek* and leafed through the pages. Though I saw the headlines and looked at the pictures, my mind could not concentrate enough to read.

After scanning several magazines in this way, I changed chairs, looking for a position where I could keep a better eye on the door leading into what had to be the treatment area. Though medical staff, all clothed in brightly colored scrubs, regularly went in and out of the door, no one even glanced in my direction.

I couldn't begin to guess what had happened to Stephen. As I waited, my mind conjured up all kinds of horrible scenarios playing themselves out beyond the doorway. I decided I'd never watch another rerun of ER. Desperate to distract myself, I went out through the automatic doorway and used my cell phone to call my sister.

As I listened to her telephone ring, I chewed on my thumb. On the fifth ring, her voice mail picked up. I left a voice message asking her to call as soon as possible.

Inside the hospital, I stopped at the nurse's desk, where a gray-haired nurse wrote notes on an aluminum chart. "I'm Stephen MacLaughlin's sister," I said.

She glanced up, holding one finger in the air as she continued writing. I waited obediently. Finished, she put down her pen. "And what can I do for you?"

"I want to know what is happening with my brother. Stephen MacLaughlin."

"Actually, I'm working with another case. Would you like me to check?"

"Please."

"And you said you are his sister? Your name please?"

"Colleen MacLaughlin Payton." She nodded and disappeared beyond the doorway. As soon as the door closed behind her, I leaned over the counter, shamelessly trying to read every piece of paper on the nurse's desk. Perhaps something here held some clue as to Stephen's condition.

"May I help you?" Another nurse, younger, with brown hair twisted into a knot above her collar, stepped from behind me into the cubicle, moving into position to block the papers I'd been trying to read.

"No, thank you. I've been helped."

"You'd be more comfortable in the waiting area." She pointed to the aquarium.

"I've been there." I smiled, probably the same plastic smile I'd gotten from the admissions clerk. "I'll wait here, thanks."

The older nurse reappeared at the doorway. "I'll take care of this, Courtney," she said, nodding. With another glance at me, Courtney pulled a rolling chair out from behind the desk and sat down, her back to us.

"Ms. MacLaughlin," the nurse began.

I took a deep breath. "It's Payton. Mrs. Payton."

"Yes, Mrs. Payton," she came around the outside of the counter. "I'm sorry to have to tell you this, but I can't give you any information about your brother."

I was stunned. "What?"

"It's a new law. We aren't allowed to give out information to anyone without the patient's permission."

"But he's my brother," I stammered. "I brought him in. If I hadn't, he might be dead."

Her eyes shone with sympathy. "I didn't write the law, and believe me, it just makes my work harder. But it's just the way things are these days."

"What am I supposed to do?"

"I'm not sure, actually. You might try talking with one of our social workers." She patted my shoulder. "Now, if you'll excuse me, we have a full house back there."

I stood there, shocked into silence, watching the door swing closed behind her.

CHAPTER
Seven

I fought a fresh onslaught of tears as I slumped against the nurse's desk. What could be so hard about giving me a report—some indication of how Stephen was doing?

For a moment—a short moment, I admit—I considered storming the back door to the emergency department.

Then, I remembered what the nurse had told me. She'd suggested something; my mind struggled to bring back her words. I strode over to the admissions desk and slammed my palm onto the bell. The Bartlett pear clerk turned from the copy machine to face me, her eyebrows raised. "May I help you?"

"I want to see a social worker."

"Do you have someone particular in mind?"

"Whoever covers the emergency room," I answered, still angry. "I need to talk to someone immediately."

She nodded and picked up a telephone, mumbling quietly into the handset. I took a deep breath, hoping my courage wouldn't fail me. My heart fluttered with the thought of confronting anyone about anything. My breathing was so shallow, so frequent, that I felt as though I might faint. The clerk had barely replaced the telephone before it rang.

I watched as she tipped her head down, whispering slightly as she explained my request to the caller. Hanging up, she spoke formally, "If you'll take a seat in the waiting area, Ms. Gilbrethson should be down in a moment."

"I'll wait right here, thank you." I said, standing my ground for the first time that day.

I spotted the social worker as she came down the hall toward the lobby, her broad silhouette boosted by enormous shoulder pads, a pair of reading glasses bouncing against her ample bosom as her heels clicked a tight staccato rhythm on the cold linoleum floor. She approached the clerk's desk, still scanning the lobby as she moved. So intense was her search that she nearly ran into me before she saw me.

She glanced at the clerk, nodding. "I'm Ingrid Gilbrethson," she said, offering her hand. "I facilitate hospital admissions through the emergency department."

"Colleen Payton," I said, disarmed by her direct, businesslike approach. She was perhaps sixty, with dark hair cut at chin length. Her pasty white skin reminded me of egg whites beaten into meringue. She wore a bold stripe of berry lipstick on thin straight lips. Other than this dash of color, Ingrid Gilbrethson wore not a single stitch of makeup.

"Shall we find a place to speak privately?" She directed me to a door beside the admissions counter, where she punched in numbers on a security pad. When the buzzer rang, she pulled open the door and held it for me.

"We keep an office just for these occasions," she said, tip-tapping her way down the bare floor. In a uniformly gray room the size of a bedroom closet, she offered me my choice of two wire chairs. I sat down, putting my purse on the floor beside me.

"Tell me what I can do to help," she began. As she settled into the chair, she focused her attention on my face. Ingrid Gilbrethson did not carry a notepad or a purse, but somehow, I had no doubt that she kept detailed notes tucked away in her mind—a mind that I felt quite certain already knew what I was about to tell her.

"I don't know where to begin," I said, hesitating. I'd never called anyone's bluff before, and I really didn't know how to make my case. "I'm from out of town, and I came to visit my twin brother here in Seattle today. After I arrived, he fainted in the bathroom. I called the ambulance, and they transported him here."

She nodded, her brown eyes intense. "Has he been admitted?"

"He's still in the emergency department, I think."

"And what seems to be the problem?"

"I can't get anyone to tell me what's happening to him," I said, concentrating on every word. "I spoke to a nurse, and she told me she isn't allowed to give medical information to a family member without the patient's permission." With these words my voice broke. I took a deep breath and plunged on. "Stephen was unconscious when they put him in the ambulance. Right now, he can't give anyone permission for anything."

Ingrid caught her chin in her thumb, her index finger gently caressing her upper lip as she considered my story. "Is your brother married?"

"No."

"Does he have other family members?"

"Just my sister and me. Our mother is in her eighties and lives out of town."

"Does your brother have a local physician?"

"I honestly don't know. Until I arrived, I didn't know he was this sick."

"Have you heard of HIPAA?"

The image of a baby hippopotamus came to mind and I shook the picture away. "What? What does HIPAA have to do with my brother?"

"HIPAA is an acronym for a new law all of us are still getting used to." She smiled. "It was designed to help patients maintain health coverage when they change jobs. But a big part of it has to do with patient privacy." She smiled at me, her features expressing genuine concern. "Believe me, the nurses back there are some of the most compassionate people I know. But with this new law, we all have to do things very differently. We're required to safeguard all the information about the patients we treat." She stood. "Sometimes, we get a little carried away with it all. But I'll go talk to the charge nurse and see what I can find out."

"I don't know how to thank you," I said, offering her my hand as I stood. In spite of my determination to keep my emotions out of the conversation, my eyes filled with tears.

"You don't have to thank me," she said. "I know what it feels like to worry about family." She stepped into the hallway. "I'm going back right now. Would you rather wait for me here, or in the waiting area?"

This time, I chose the chair by the aquarium.

~ ~ ~

Another thirty minutes passed before Ingrid returned and took the chair beside me. "I've talked to the nurses caring for your brother," she said, reaching out to touch the back of my hand. "And I've been in to see Stephen. He's doing much better now than when you last saw him, so you can relax about that." She smiled. "The doctor here has called your brother's primary care physician, and they are consulting on his condition. Stephen's doctor will drop by the hospital this evening."

"But I still don't know what's going on."

Ingrid referred to a small notepad in her left hand. "Well, right now, it looks as though your brother is severely dehydrated. They're giving him fluid through an intravenous line. He's regained consciousness, and he isn't in any pain." She watched my face carefully, and I felt her trying to gauge my reaction. "However, the emergency doctor has decided to admit him to the third floor. That way they can respond to any other problems as soon as his test results come in."

"What problems?"

"Something has led to his present condition. The doctor has ordered blood tests, and he's taken a chest x-ray. We can't be absolutely certain what's going on until the tests results are back."

"When will that be?"

"A few hours at least."

More waiting. More wondering. I couldn't help the resentment I felt toward the staff who had deliberately kept me out of the loop. "I don't understand why they will talk to you but not me." I sighed. "And when the test results come back, will I have to page you again?"

"I've convinced the staff to consider you Stephen's next of kin. Because Stephen was unconscious when admitted, they need you to make any decisions that he isn't able to make for himself. It's complicated, but it seemed the best way to handle it for now."

She stood again, offering me her business card. "The emergency staff will keep you informed of your brother's condition. If you need to speak to me, you can reach me here at the hospital. In an emergency, you can page me at that number." She pointed to the card. "The one on the bottom." She patted the pager on her waist. "I'm available at any time."

"Thank you so much. You don't know what this means."

"They're moving Stephen upstairs now. You should be able to see him in the next fifteen minutes or so." She smiled and offered her hand. "Don't forget to call if you need me." She turned to leave. I watched Ingrid hurry down the hall, listening to her shoes tap on the floor until she disappeared around a corner.

~ ~ ~

It was a full hour before I saw Stephen in his third-floor room.

In the meantime, I called Kevin from the pay phone in the third-floor sunroom. I knew when his voice mail picked up on the first ring that Kevin was still in a meeting. He'd turned off his cell phone.

I left a lengthy message about Stephen's condition and emphasized how grateful I was to have visited when I did. I've never liked having disagreements with Kevin; I guess I hoped that this report of Stephen's illness would smooth over Kevin's resentment. "I don't know what would have happened if I hadn't dropped by," I said. "Call me and I'll tell you the lastest news." Since cell phones were not permitted in the hospital, I left the phone number for the front desk.

I neglected to tell him about the doggie door.

I caught my sister on her way to the office from the courthouse. "Stephen is in the hospital," I began.

"Where?"

"Swedish."

"What happened?"

"He fainted," I said and took a deep breath. "He didn't wake up for a long time. I called an ambulance. He's so sick, Carrie. They are taking blood and doing tests. No one here will tell me anything."

"I know," she said, so quietly that I barely heard the words.

"You know?"

"I have for a while."

Her words stunned me. For a moment I couldn't respond. Why would Stephen tell Carrie this kind of information without telling me? "You know?" I repeated, and this time, even I recognized the hurt in my voice.

"We can talk about it when I get there," she said. "I'll be over by six."

I hung up. Surprise and hurt fought for priority in my swirling emotions. I'd always felt as if Stephen were exclusively my brother. He was attached to me. Whenever something happened to either of us, we always told the other first. Then, and only then, did we ever consider sharing information with anyone outside our bond.

It never occurred to me—not ever—that he would confess anything to Carrie that I didn't already know. In all my life, I'd only kept one secret from Stephen. Of course, I'd never told Carrie or Kevin either, for that matter.

My sister's admission left me so completely stunned that I didn't hear anyone enter the sunroom. "Ms. Payton." I jumped. A technician who had come to take samples of Stephen's blood stood just inside the door. "I'm all finished with your brother. You can go in to see him now." She left without seeing my tears.

Outside Stephen's room, signs declared isolation precautions in bright red letters. I read the sign, noting with disappointment that visitors were expected to check in with nurses before entering the room.

Another obstacle.

After two inquiries, I finally found someone who could help me. "The precautions are for body fluids only," she said, reading from a chart. She must have recognized my confusion. "Visitors don't have to follow any real precautions. Just wash your hands before and after you leave the room."

With no further understanding, I approached Stephen's room, knocking gently on the open door before I went in. A soft green curtain partially obscured the bed inside his small private room. I stepped around the curtain and spoke softly. "Stephen, it's me, Colleen."

He lay against the pillows, eyes closed, looking completely spent. "Hey," he said, opening his eyes with great effort. I leaned over him, kissing his forehead.

His skin, normally a warm peachy color, looked bleached, and his lovely eyes were rimmed in a red line of fever. "Thanks, Colleen."

I knew he referred to the ambulance crew and the harrowing escape from his own bathroom. I decided to act as if I routinely rescued people from near-death. "Not a problem," I said. "You look much better than the last time I saw you."

He smiled—the tiniest, weakest smile turning up the corners of his pale lips.

"Have you seen your doctor yet?"

He shook his head. "Not yet."

"I hear he'll be coming by."

Again he nodded. I took his hand in mine. "Stephen, you're sick, and I don't understand what is happening. Can you tell me?"

He looked away, deliberately avoiding my gaze.

"You're my brother," I said. "We've always been closer than any two humans on the planet. Why can't you just tell me the truth?"

"You wouldn't understand."

"What? What wouldn't I understand?"

My brother pulled his hand from mine and closed his eyes. "Colleen," he said, his voice a feather drifting along on a silent breeze. "It's too late now."

"It's never too late, Stephen."

"I tried. I went to the house."

Though I'm not sure how, I knew that he referred to mother's party. "I know you tried." I reached over the bed rail, taking his hand once again. "And I didn't help you then. I'm so sorry, Stephen. Please forgive me."

He shook his head. "It's too late," he said. "Too late for all that now."

"No, Stephen. You're wrong. I can help you," I said, wondering about my words even as I said them. Could anyone help Stephen now? Would I ever be able to breach the insurmountable wall that separated me from my brother? I held his hand to my cheek, and repeated the words. "Never too late, Stephen."

He closed his eyes, fatigue softening the lines of pain into blessed sleep. I placed his hand on his chest, caressing it as I let go, letting my fingers drift along his forearm as I took a chair beside the bed.

Then, with all the intensity I could muster, I prayed for my brother's life.

~ ~ ~

A nurse came in to change and adjust the medicines flowing into Stephen's arm. She fussed over the plastic bags hanging from the pole, and then focused on Stephen's arm, poking at the place where the tube disappeared into his skin. "Oh no," she said, more to herself than to me. "I'm going to have to restart this IV." She probed the skin of his hand and fingers. "It's infiltrated. If you'll give me just a minute," she said, "I'll try not to keep him for long."

"Infiltrated?"

"Means that the catheter is dripping into the interstitial space rather than into the vein. Not a big deal. I'll just restart the IV on the other side." She leaned against his bed, watching the fluid drip from the smaller bag into the tube. "Shouldn't take but a minute."

"I've been here a long time, anyway. He could probably use some rest." I stood up, stretching as I did, working out the creaking objections of my muscles. Though I didn't intend to leave the hospital, I wanted time to gather my thoughts, to put my emotions in order. I stepped out into the hall and stopped the first employee I saw. "Could you tell me where the newborn nursery is?" I asked.

"It's on the fifth floor," she said. "As you get off the elevator, turn left."

"Thank you." Moments later, I stood in front of a broad glass window, gazing at tiny bundles of new life, each wrapped in tight swaddles of blue and pink. Some slept peacefully. Others, their faces twisted with frustration, cried with vehemence.

I identified with these little guys.

Caught up in events I cannot change, I have often struggled, as ineffectually as these newborns, to free myself from the confines of situations I would not choose. I would never have chosen this life for Stephen. I would never have wanted this disease for him.

"Howl," I said out loud. "Scream for all you're worth." The scene before me blurred as tears gathered once again. "Don't ever quit fighting," I whispered.

CHAPTER
Eight

When I returned to Stephen's room, I found Carrie sitting beside his bed. We hugged, a long embrace full of grief and comfort. "I'm so glad you came," I told her.

"I didn't want to disturb him," she whispered. "I haven't been here long." She pointed at Stephen, her voice low. "He's been asleep the whole time."

"Have you had dinner?" As always, I assumed food would take the edge off of a difficult day.

"Not yet." She glanced at her watch. "I should, anyway. My sugar is getting a little low."

"Want to go down to the cafeteria? We can talk there."

Carrie did not miss the urgency in my voice. She nodded, tossing her purse over one shoulder. I led the way to the elevator.

In the dining room, we chose a table by the window, each making a great show of moving our plates from cafeteria trays onto the table, arranging our food just so. We sat down and gazed out the window, though condensation obscured the view outside.

I saw Carrie scan the food sitting on the plate before her, calculating the carbohydrates contained in her choices. She removed the insulin pump from her skirt pocket, fiddled with the buttons, adjusting the dose for the meal she was about to eat. Then, she picked up her fork.

I bowed my head, asking silently for a blessing that covered more than food. Too late, I realized that my prayer had embarrassed my sister; she put down her fork and bowed her head, following my lead.

Putting my napkin in my lap, I came right to the question. "Carrie, what's going on with Stephen?"

She took a long deep breath, and without taking a bite, put down her fork again. She glanced away, taking in the room. "I've known for a long time," she began. "Stephen has AIDS."

I blinked and stared. In spite of all I'd been through, the barefaced fact still hit me with a brutality I did not expect. My eyes filled with tears. "AIDS?" I repeated. "You're certain?"

AIDS equaled death to me. Without thinking, the faces of African children orphaned by this massive plague flashed before my eyes. I banished them, trying instead to focus on my sister's words. "His partner died almost six years ago," she said. "They were both positive for years before that," Carrie spoke without emotion, reciting the facts as she would in a meeting between competing attorneys. "Glen's death hit Stephen really hard. He went into a depression I thought he'd never recover from."

"Depression?" So far, my only part in this conversation had been that of a sick echo. I shook my head, trying to take in this new information. "And Stephen told you?" Betrayed on two fronts—by the news itself and by my brother's secrecy—I could barely comprehend the revelation.

"I'm his sister too. He has every right to tell me anything he wants to." Her voice took on a hard edge, and I resented the severity of her tone. She shot an angry glance in my direction. "Don't take it so hard, Colleen."

"I didn't mean it that way."

"You did. You think that Stephen is your personal property. You think that just because he's your twin, no one else can love him like you do. Well, he's my brother too and I love him every bit as much as you ever could."

It didn't take a psychologist to hear the resentment in Carrie's words. Was this her low blood sugar talking, or genuine emotion? How long had this bitterness clouded my sister's feelings toward me? What had I done to make her feel like a second-class sister? "I'm sorry, Carrie. Please don't take it like that. It's just that we…I mean, Stephen has always told me everything." I tried to stem the stammering by taking a drink from my water glass. "I can't believe he'd keep something this huge from me."

My apology didn't begin to soothe my sister. She dug in again. "He didn't tell you because he knew what you would say. He knows how much you hate his orientation. He couldn't face your hate and Glen's death all at the same time."

"Hate? I don't hate Stephen."

She sputtered. "Yeah, right. Love the sinner and hate the sin? Is that your philosophy?" She hugged herself, turning away from me. "You're the worst homophobe ever."

Carrie's overflowing anger surprised me. "How can you say that? What have I ever done that would make you believe that?"

"You're always throwing the Bible around. You leave it around your house. You mention it in conversation. Sheez, Colleen. Anyone could see how you feel about homosexuals."

Her words hit deep and I felt my stomach turn to lead. "Carrie, I've never said a single word to you about homosexuality. What makes you think you know anything about what I think or how I feel?"

She took a long drink of her bottled juice. "I don't have to be a mind reader. I can tell. You agree with every other Bible thumper out there."

My voice was laced with sarcasm. "Oh, really?"

"Okay, so let's have it, Colleen." She picked up her knife and cut a bite-sized piece of turkey from the slice on her plate. "How do you feel about homosexuality?"

I resented being put on the spot at the same moment she dropped the AIDS bomb onto my dinner plate. "Do you think this is fair? Hitting me with all of this and then asking for an extemporaneous dissertation on homosexuality?"

"If you weren't so prejudiced, it wouldn't be a problem, would it?"

"Carrie, please. Can't we just talk about Stephen? Can't we leave philosophy out of it?"

She rolled her eyes and shrugged. "I don't think so. What you believe comes out in how you act. I see it every day in my cases. Harassment, discrimination, sometimes criminal assault."

"You don't have any idea what I believe! Come on, Carrie. Don't lump me in with your clients. I've never been guilty of any of that stuff. This isn't a case we're talking about. It's our brother."

She shrugged. "You don't have to openly harass. Your beliefs are discriminating enough. Stephen knows that. I know that. And, when Glen died, Stephen lost hope for his own battle with the disease."

"If Stephen hates me so much—"

"Not hate," she corrected me. "Let's just say he mistrusts you."

"Okay, mistrusts me. Why did he come to the house for Mother's party?"

"I think that he was just starting to come out of the depression. In his mind, he was trying to reach out to you. He's had some trouble with his medications, and I think he believes that he doesn't have much time left." She scraped gravy off the potatoes on her plate and glanced up at my face. "What? You don't believe me?"

"Not much time?"

"I don't know for certain, and neither does Stephen." Carrie continued eating as if death were part of every dinner conversation. "With this disease, the facts seem to change from day to day."

The charged air turned my stomach to wood and I pushed my plate away, vaguely aware of a growing nausea rolling around in the pit of my stomach. *How much am I supposed to take, Lord?* "You know, Carrie, I think I'm just going to head back to Stephen's house for the night," I said. As I stood, I grabbed my coat up from the back of my chair.

"So you're going to run?" She said, her eyes cold. "Take off without facing the truth?"

"You really don't get it, do you?" Other diners looked our way. I lowered my voice, speaking with a quiet intensity. "You've just told me that my twin brother is dying. And to top that off, you're telling me that he doesn't trust me. That he thinks I hate him. And best of all, Carrie, you accuse me of prejudice without any evidence whatsoever."

She bristled. "I don't need evidence."

"How reasonable is that? You tell me. You're the lawyer." I put on my coat, my anger bubbling over. "So far, the only evidence you've given me tonight is what real attorneys call hearsay."

"I only call it as I see it."

"Then you see it wrong." I said. "Enjoy your dinner, Carrie."

I left my sister in the cafeteria and drove to Stephen's house without going up to say good night to my brother. I needed time to think about what she'd said. As I drove, I realized that parts of her story—at least the pieces concerning Stephen's illness—fit together with what I knew of my brother's disappearance.

I tried to remember the last time I'd had regular communication with Stephen. The only clear memory I had involved Mallory's twelfth birthday party. Stephen had attended, and he'd spent the three weeks before calling twice a week to make certain he'd bought the perfect gift. After the party though, he disappeared. I called, but he didn't return the calls. I sent cards, with no response. At first, I thought he was caught up in his work, too busy to keep in touch. Later, I wondered if he was mad at me.

It seemed as if he'd dropped off the face of the earth. Now I realized that emotionally, he had.

I continued to my brother's house through fog heavy enough to leave droplets on the windshield, my thoughts as thick and hopeless as the air around me. After driving around Stephen's block twice, I found a parking place and squeezed the Honda into it.

As I turned the key in Stephen's front door, I heard the sound of fierce barking inside. The owner of the doggie door I'd climbed through had come home at last. I wondered if the dog held grudges.

The bark coming through Stephen's front door was deep and menacing, and I considered going to a hotel. Instead, I gathered my courage and began talking even before I opened the door. "Good doggie," I cooed in a voice I normally reserve for newborns. I held the door partially closed as a golden nose pushed through the space toward me, still barking.

I pushed the door open, wishing I'd had the foresight to bring home a hunk of the meatloaf I'd just thrown in the trash. Still talking, I offered the golden giant my hand and forearm, hoping that this hairy protector of the castle could smell my relationship to Stephen. Shouldn't twins smell alike?

I pushed the dog backward into the entry, stepping inside as I closed the front door. I reached out to caress the long blond fur on a head that easily cleared my waist. Apparently I passed the smell test. Immediately, the golden monster rose up on her hind legs and washed my face with kisses.

In spite of the day, I laughed at the greeting. "Ooh, it's cold in here," I told the dog, pushing her down and shivering at the cold blast of air that blew through the old house. I turned on the entry lights and checked the thermostat on the living-room wall. The temperature had dropped to sixty degrees. Only then did I remember the missing window in Stephen's bathroom.

Sure enough, the door to the bathroom was still open, and a cold wind blew into the hallway through the gap where the window had been. I turned on the bathroom light to discover a puddle of water in the linoleum and a connected trickle running onto the wood floor, probably from the afternoon monsoon.

I dropped a towel on the floor and dragged it around with my foot. Something needed to be done about the missing window. I stared at the problem for a long time before a temporary solution occurred to me.

I found heavy pushpins in the upstairs office. Then, stretching a plastic garbage bag and two layers of heavy bath towels over the opening, I managed to hold them in place with the pins. It wasn't much, but it would block the wind and keep the rain from ruining the wood floor. I would find someone to repair the window in the morning.

The phone rang, and I wrapped myself in the comfort of Kevin's voice. "I'm so glad you called," I said, curling up in the corner of the living room couch.

After I told him everything, Kevin expressed sympathy for the remarkable detour my trip had taken. "I'm sorry about Stephen," he said. "I didn't have any idea he was HIV positive."

"I didn't either. But I can't even begin to get my mind around that problem," I answered. "Carrie blindsided me with all this stuff she's carrying around. She's angry with me about everything." I told him what my sister had said.

"It doesn't make any sense to me," he replied. "You've always been there for her—when she lost the babies. You've always been the one to support her, even when your mom was so unkind."

"I guess I wasn't kind enough. She thinks I'm anti-homosexual."

He paused. "We are, aren't we?"

"Not the way she means it."

"What do you think she means?"

I sighed, exhaustion clouding my thoughts. "I'm not sure what anyone means today."

"Maybe you two could talk about it again later—when you've both had some time to calm down. A good night's sleep will do you good."

"I'm not sure I want to."

"Sleep?"

"No. Talk about it."

"She's your sister."

"I know," I admitted. "Today, I wish she weren't."

We visited for a few moments before Kevin said, "Well, I have an early-morning breakfast meeting. I'd better get to bed."

"Thanks for calling."

"I love you, dimples," he said, and hung up.

Even Kevin's love name didn't lift the heaviness I felt. In a way, Carrie was right. I've read my Bible, and the restrictions about homosexuality on those pages couldn't be clearer. I don't doubt those words.

At the same time, I could not doubt my love for Stephen. What bothered me now, what gnawed at me like a splinter festering in my index finger, was a much stickier question: How could I express my love without compromising my values? And would my love ever be enough for Carrie and Stephen, if I could not combine it with absolute acceptance?

I've never considered myself a theologian. I don't dwell on thoughts more lofty than today's menu or separating darks from whites on laundry day. But that evening, I sensed God moving me from my comfort zone into regions I'd never explored before. Frankly, I didn't want to go.

I placed the telephone on its cradle and sat for a long time in the dark, the dog curled up on the rug near my feet. Eventually, I stretched out, face down on Stephen's couch. I could have spent the next hour interceding for Stephen, or for my sister, or asking for wisdom. That would be the mature and godly approach. But I have never claimed to be either mature or godly.

Instead, I cried, begging God to let me out of the whole mess. And then, with a grieving heart, I fell asleep.

In the morning, I ate cold cereal while calling glass companies for someone to reinstall the window in Stephen's bathroom.

I called the hospital to ask about my brother and got a new version of the same runaround I'd experienced the day before. I thanked the nurse and asked to be transferred to Stephen's hospital room. He answered on the fifth ring.

"Stephen, it's Colleen. How are you feeling this morning?"

"Better," he answered. "Much better. The doctor says I may be able to go home this afternoon."

"Great. I'm glad for you." The dog, hearing Stephen's voice, came to sit beside my chair, her head on my lap, whining. "Your dog misses you."

He laughed, a hearty, happy laugh. "Tell her I miss her."

"I fed her last night. And we've been out for a little walk already this morning. I hope that's okay."

"Good. I didn't think to ask anyone to take care of her."

"You were a little out of it yesterday."

"So I hear."

"I'll be by the hospital as soon as the guys come to fix your bathroom window."

"My window? What happened to the window?"

I told him the story of the firemen and the crowbar. "They were really lucky, I think. They took it out without breaking anything. It just has to be reinstalled. Maybe you should think about having it made into an entry—like a doggie door."

"Then you could come in through the bathroom or the back porch." He laughed at me.

"Look, Stephen, if you want to keep me out of your life, you're going to have to get a smaller doggie door."

"And a meaner dog," he said, and laughed again.

The sound of his laughter made my heart sing. "By the way, she and I haven't been formally introduced," I said. "What's her name?"

"Colleen," he answered, his voice suddenly sober. "I named her after you."

CHAPTER
Nine

It was nearly noon before I arrived at the hospital. Stephen's floor seemed quiet, the patients having completed their preparations for another day of healing. That morning, as I walked toward Stephen's room, I glanced into the other rooms of the third-floor hallway. Most of his fellow patients slept.

"Hey, Stephen," I said, peeking around the curtain in his private room. "Good morning." He lay propped up on pillows, a thick hardbound book open on his lap. Blond hair circled his pale face in broad waves, and his skin was freshly shaven.

He smiled, ignored my greeting, and said, "Did you think to bring me clothes?"

"You didn't ask for clothes."

"I know." He shook his head. "I can't go home in this stuff. I don't know what I was thinking." He plucked at the blue gown draped over his shoulders. "Why didn't you think of it for me?"

"It would entertain the neighbors to see you come home in a backless gown." I laughed. "But you can relax." I said. Grinning, I held up a grocery bag I'd filled with underwear, jeans, and a sweatshirt I'd plucked from his bedroom.

"You're a lifesaver. A mind reader." Stephen smiled. "Just like the old days."

"No mind reader. I'm just a mom. After a while, these things come naturally."

He closed his book, leaned back against the pillows, and pointed to a chair beside the bed. "I hear that you and Carrie had a heart-to-heart last night."

"I wouldn't call it that." I took off my coat and sat down. "In fact, I think it was more like a verbal sword fight. She drew blood—lots of it." I had a hard time picturing Carrie telling him all that she'd told me; but then, Carrie had done and said a lot of surprising things over the last twenty-four hours.

"I tried to get the details out of her, but she wouldn't budge."

"Good thing," I muttered. "So what does your doctor say?"

"Carrie told me that you know."

I sat down, feeling the weight of the issue. "I guess I'm now officially in the loop." I looked directly into his eyes. "Stephen, why didn't you tell me?"

"I don't know. It was so much to deal with, so much grief. It just swallowed me whole. The meds. The illnesses. The doctor visits and hospital stays." He sighed heavily. "Everyone I cared about was caught in this living hell. I spent a year teaching and taking care of Glen at the same time, and in the end, I had to find a home for him. I just couldn't bring you into the torment I was living."

"I'm so sorry you had to go through all of this." His explanation didn't resemble the one Carrie had offered. I couldn't rectify the two versions. Whether out of instinct or desperation, I chose Stephen's. "I could've gone through it with you."

"At the time, it took all the energy we had to just keep living. You couldn't have made it any easier." Stephen reached over to his bedside table and poured himself a glass of water. "My doctor's trying some new meds. If I can keep my food down, and stay hydrated, he says I can—"

"Stephen?" I heard a gentle knock and looked up as a male face peeked around the curtain. Olive skin surrounded dark, intense eyes. A tall man with a full beard smiled as he entered the room.

"Rodney!" Stephen's greeting held genuine welcome. "Come in." My brother pulled himself up in the bed, straightened his bed covers, and reached out to shake the hand of his visitor. "This is my sister, Colleen," he said, pointing to me.

"So, he named the dog after you?" Rodney asked, shaking my hand.

I smiled. "I'm trying to take it as a sign of affection."

"That's a good attitude." He put one hand on Stephen's foot, "So, how are you feeling?"

"Better," Stephen said. "I guess I got a little dehydrated."

"I suppose so," Rodney winked at me. "Generally, you don't have to call an ambulance to break you out of your own bathroom." He spoke to Stephen. "The guys said they'd be by to visit tonight."

A creepy feeling had begun to make itself known in my gut. Though I saw nothing inherently unusual in the mannerism or behavior of this visitor, I began to suspect that he was one of Stephen's gay friends. "Stephen should be discharged this afternoon," I volunteered. "So, Rodney, do you work with Stephen at the college?"

Rodney buried his hands in the pockets of his dress slacks. "Actually, no. I'm an accountant. Stephen and I have been friends for years."

I nodded and smiled. The creepy feeling grew.

"I talked to Sean last night." Rodney directed this information to my brother.

"What is going on with the house?"

"They expect to close on it today and move in this coming weekend."

"No real renovation to do?"

"Nothing more than cosmetics. A little paint. New carpet."

Stephen made an effort to include me. "Some friends bought a condo in West Seattle."

"Well, actually, it's new to them—but in a really old building," Rodney added.

"I haven't seen it. Does it face the water?" Stephen asked.

"Northeast. They have a lovely view of the Space Needle."

"I'm sorry I won't be able to help them move." Stephen sighed and leaned back against the pillows, his energy running out like a car out of gas.

"Of course not," Rodney said. "You should be resting. Besides, they'll have plenty of help. You don't have to worry about it." He patted Stephen's foot and straightened up, "I need to be going. I'm on my lunch break, and I've got to get back to the office." He reached out to shake my hand again. "So nice to meet you, Colleen. Take care, Stephen. I'll call you tomorrow."

"Thanks, Rodney," Stephen said. And in a moment, his guest was gone.

≈ ≈ ≈

By three in the afternoon, after signing several pages of discharge instructions, I had Stephen safely belted in the passenger seat of the Honda. "Take this next left," he told me, pointing. Obediently, I turned the corner.

"Stephen," I began, guiding the car down the middle of the narrow street, "Can I ask a question?"

"Shoot."

"I'm wondering about last summer. Did you take off work because of AIDS?"

He hesitated. "Yes," he said, and looked away.

"Were you sick?"

"Colleen, you don't know anything about this disease. You can't possibly understand. With AIDS, you have ups and downs. Last summer was a down."

"How about now? Is this a down?"

He put his elbow up on the passenger door, massaging his forehead with his fingers. "I guess it is. But I'll swing out of it. Once I get back to school, we'll put on the play and I can take more time to rest."

"When will you go back to work?"

"Monday."

"Is that wise?"

"What choice do I have? Quit work? What then? AIDS is a disease I have to live with. There isn't any alternative. Living means working."

"You're right. I don't really understand what you're facing. I just hate to see you push yourself so hard." I stole a glance at my brother, trying to gauge his response to my concern. Finally exasperated, I admitted, "I'm worried."

"Now there's a surprise." He sighed. " Look, I started the quarter and I can finish it. We'll put on the play. Then, during winter break, I can reconsider how much time I can spend working—if I need to."

I made the last turn into the alley behind his house. "Stephen, I'll help you, anyway I can. Don't forget to let me help? Please?"

He patted my hand as it rested on the steering wheel. "You worry too much, Colleen."

Moments later, I pulled the car into the space beside the little one-car garage in the alley. As we stepped through the back gate, Colleen-the-dog received us with happy barks and a furiously wagging tail.

I unlocked the back door and turned on the lights as Stephen shuffled down the hall toward his favorite living-room chair. "I think I'll take a little nap," he said, sitting down in the recliner.

"Before you do, can I show you what I bought for you today?"

He seemed amused. "A gift?"

"Sort of. I bought it at the pharmacy when I picked up your new meds." I opened the bag I'd carried into the house and removed a pill holder exactly the size of copier paper. "Let me show you," I said, opening several of the tiny containers. "It's a one-week pill minder. You can use all of these little openings to remind you of all the pills you take during the week. See?"

I showed him the container, each plastic door clearly labeled with the day of the week and the time of the day. I removed the column of slots labeled "Wednesday." "Each day's slots will come out in one piece. You can take a whole day's worth of pills with you to work."

"You think of everything." He used the lever to drop the chair into the reclining position, closing his eyes as his head hit the back of the chair.

"You're making fun. I just thought with so many pills, you could use some help staying organized."

"Stop worrying. Besides, you're the one who needs help staying organized."

"Okay. If I get sick, you can loan the pill organizer to me."

"Great. Can I take that nap now?"

I shrugged. "Sure." I sat on the coffee table, watching his chest rise and fall. Only moments later, I recognized the soft purr of a snore. The clock in his entry hall struck five, and I got up to make dinner.

～ ～ ～

Before I drove home the next day, I'd made several meals and put them in the freezer over Stephen's refrigerator. I made an elaborate chart showing the drug dosage and schedule for each of the drugs on Stephen's kitchen table. Though it took several tries to get every-thing exactly right, I left my brother with a clear and easy-to-read diagram.

By the time we added the discharge medications, Stephen had thirty-four tablets to take every single day. Some had to be taken with food, others had to be timed carefully—so many hours before or after a meal. Not only did his medications require careful planning, but by my calculations, his meal schedule could not vary by more than an hour in either direction without interfering in some way with his medication schedule.

Secretly, I made a list of Stephen's medications and tucked them into my purse. With Stephen feeling so protective about his illness, I knew I'd have to find some other way to learn what I could about his condition. I planned to take that little sheet of paper home and find out as much as I could about these drugs and the disease that bat-tered Stephen.

I would never allow him to keep me in the dark again.

I ran several loads of laundry, changed the sheets on his bed, and vacuumed and dusted downstairs. For my last chore, I did one final round of dishes; Stephen came into the kitchen just as I hung up the dishtowel.

"Aren't you about finished?" he asked, pulling out a chair and sitting down to the table. He picked up the latest version of the chart I'd left for him. "What's this? I have a master's degree. I can read drug labels."

I ignored his complaint. "I'm just finishing up."

"You have a long drive home. I don't want you heading over the pass in the dark."

"When did you become my father?" As soon as the words came out I regretted them. A shadow passed over Stephen's features. I tried to soften my tone. "Look, I've been driving since I was sixteen. I think I'll make it."

"Can I bring down your bags?"

"Already by the door." I smiled at him. "I really am leaving you know. I'm not going to haunt you forever."

"Thank goodness."

"I feel so appreciated."

Stephen smiled and shook his head.

It isn't easy having someone invade your space—no matter how much you need the help. It must be even harder for those with streaks of independence. And Stephen's streak of independence was more pronounced than the stripe on a skunk.

With a hug and a promise to come see the play, I left Stephen on his back porch. I started the car and pulled out into the alley, giving him a final wave from my car window.

I arrived home shortly after eight, anxious to spend time at the piano, preparing music for Sunday. So far, the offertory sounded like the undifferentiated tones of a rock tumbler. If I didn't put in some time on the piano bench, the whole congregation would suffer the consequence.

When the automatic garage door opened, I found Kevin in the garage, tinkering with our snow blower. I'd barely turned off the ignition when he came around the car and opened the door. "Hey, dimples." He leaned down to kiss me.

"Hey yourself." I wrapped my arms around his waist and leaned against his chest.

"Tired?"

"Very."

"What can I take in for you?"

"Just an overnight bag. Any messages?" I handed him my car keys.

He opened the trunk and pulled out my duffel. "Jackie called to remind you about practice."

I leaned in to retrieve my purse from the passenger seat. "Practice?"

"Isn't it on your schedule?"

What had I forgotten this time? Kids? A women's trio? Jackie, one of my closest friends, directed our youth choir, sang special music for church, and even arranged music for other performers. Whenever Jackie volunteered to lead music, I ended up at the piano. We came together, Jackie and I, like garlic and onions, salt and pepper, bass line and melody.

"Oh, right. I promised to play for her solo at the Christmas lunch."

"How's Stephen?" Kevin closed the trunk and threw the strap of my duffel over one shoulder. Coming around the car, he returned the keys.

"I can't tell. He never even told me what put him in the hospital. I mean, I thought AIDS wasn't a problem anymore. You know, you just take drugs and—" I opened the door into the house.

Kevin stepped in behind me, finishing my sentence. "The whole thing is under control, like diabetes or hormone replacement."

"I don't know about hormone replacement." In my experience, hormones have always been wildly out of control.

"It's his body. Let him deal with it."

I put my bag down on the kitchen counter and reached for a glass from the cupboard. "We're talking death here. AIDS isn't a common cold. I need to figure out what is happening to him."

"He's not your responsibility."

"I know that." Once again, I considered telling Kevin about the meaning of my relationship with Stephen. How can you tell anyone what it means to survive childhood with a twin? How can anyone understand being so closely tied to a sibling that you scratch whenever your twin itches? Believe me, I've tried to paint this picture for Kevin.

How can I explain what I don't understand?

On those rare times that I've tried to pour out my past, my husband has responded in grunts or shrugs. On that particular Saturday, it didn't make sense to try and explain it all again. I was too stressed and too worn out.

Instead, I opened the refrigerator, poured myself a glass of water, and walked over to my purse. "I brought home a list of his medicines. I thought I might be able to find out something from the Internet."

"Colleen, if he isn't telling you everything, maybe it's because he doesn't want you to know." Kevin took the list from my hand and gave it a cursory glance.

"I won't interfere. I just want to understand."

"And then what? You have a family to take care of. Kids. Students."

"And you of course."

"And me."

"I can still care about Stephen."

"Sure. You can pray. You can phone. But Colleen, all the understanding in the world can't save him from this battle."

CHAPTER
Ten

Jackie tossed her lyric sheet onto my piano and sat down on the bench beside me. "What's going on with you today?" she asked, with more than a touch of irritation.

"I'm sorry. Really. I'll get it." I reached up and turned my music over, looking again at the first four bars of her solo. "It's just that I'm not good at improvising jazz. You do remember that I teach the classics, right?"

"I know exactly what you teach. You can do this. It's a great song. You just have to settle into a pattern." She ruffled the crest of her spiked brown hair. "Do you realize that you've rewritten the intro three times in the last four tries?"

Jackie had chosen to perform a jazz rendition of "No One Ever Cared for Me Like Jesus." Her sultry alto caressed the melody in a way that gave me goose bumps. The song would be wonderful, if only I could pull the accompaniment together. Jazz demands a kind of swing on the half beats that I've never done well—even on my best days. "I know," I said. "I try so hard to get the feel of the music that I lose track of the chords."

"Oh please, no whining. You're not concentrating."

"Of course I am. It isn't like you actually gave me music." I pointed at the handwritten chords and lyrics on the piano. "This dumb cheat sheet is all I have to go on. Give me some time." I began the introduction again.

"I have a better idea. Let's take five and break open that coffee cake I smelled when I came in."

"Not until we've finished." This had to be the first time I chose work before snacks.

"Forget it," she said, waving me off. "You need to shake that mental block. I'll pour coffee." Slapping both hands on her lap, she stood up.

I felt reasonably sure that coffee wouldn't cure my lackluster performance. Still, I followed her into my kitchen, where she had already begun filling two mugs with fresh coffee. "Slice that cake before I eat it whole. You know better than to bake when I'm coming over."

"I didn't bake," I countered, dropping onto a stool. "I opened a box of biscuit mix and added water." I didn't mention that I'd planned to serve it for dinner.

"That's baking in my book." She pushed the cake pan toward me. "Hurry, please. I missed breakfast."

Oh well, I had time to bake another. "Hand me a knife," I said, pointing at the oak block on the counter.

"This one?"

I nodded, accepting the utensil she offered. "How big?"

Jackie opened a cupboard and brought out two small plates. "Big enough to spoil my lunch," she answered, sliding the plates across the counter. "Oh forget it. Make them big enough to *be* lunch."

"Not a problem." Like Stephen, Jackie can eat anything she wants and still stay as slim as she was when she graduated from high school. I've seen the pictures that prove it. And though I'm jealous, I still feed her.

I pulled the knife through the crisp brown-sugar crust. "You must have the metabolism of a hydroelectric dam," I said, envy dripping through every word. "Every year, I have to work harder just to keep from gaining weight."

"I watch my weight," Jackie said, putting two forks on the counter. "No matter what I do, I don't gain an ounce."

"Cry me a river." I pulled a napkin from the holder and threw it at her.

I met Jackie the first week after Kevin and I arrived in Potter's Hollow. Since then, she has been my closet friend. Her tall sinuous body and short spiky hairstyle make her look ten years younger than her real age. Convention does not hinder my friend. She says what she means and means what she says. In spite of her no-nonsense personality, her dark brown eyes betray the compassionate heart beating at the center of her soul. My life would be bland without her.

Jackie made a face and sat down beside me at the counter. "So how was your visit with your brother?" She stabbed a piece of coffee cake.

I groaned. "Don't ask, please."

"It's my job to ask," she said. "You're the one who called and begged me to pray. So what happened?"

"You want the long or the short of it?"

"I want all the gritty details."

I told her the whole story, or at least most of it, though I glossed over the episode with the doggie door. I even managed to give her a quick rundown of dinner with my sister, complete with Carrie's hateful accusations.

"Everyone should have a loving sister like Carrie."

"I must be a complete dunce. I didn't know she felt that way." I crossed the kitchen and opened the refrigerator. "It isn't like I've tried to force anything on Carrie or Stephen. I've tried to be considerate."

I poured milk into my coffee cup and offered some to Jackie. "The whole trip was one huge shock. My brother is in desperate health. My sister hates me. What am I supposed to do with all of that?"

Jackie nodded, stirring her coffee with a spoon. "I don't think hate is the right word. Maybe resentment." She shook her head. "You might even consider jealousy. You and Stephen have always been so close that Carrie must feel like a third wheel on a bicycle. But what really frosts my cookies is that Stephen never told you any of this."

I nodded. "I don't understand that at all. It's only been two days. I haven't even begun to accept the fact that Stephen has AIDS." We ate without speaking. "Anyway, the doctor started him on new medication, and Stephen bounced back from whatever it was that made him pass out in the bathroom. He looked sick, but not dying. Still, I don't even know what happened."

"So this explains why you're so distracted this morning."

"The whole thing keeps rolling through my mind over and over again. I just wish I could do something. But I can't."

"Of course not. No one can cure AIDS."

"It isn't like it's a death sentence. At least not in the same way it used to be." I took another bite of cake. "I've been on the Internet nearly every spare minute since I got home. I've found dozens of Web sites and printed everything I thought might help. I've even ordered a couple of books."

"And what did you learn?"

"More than I ever wanted to know."

"So, tell me."

I glanced at my friend, wondering if she really wanted to hear all I'd discovered. Jackie leaned forward, her eyes intense, focused. "I learned that some of the treatments are so effective that the virus seems to be completely eliminated from the bloodstream."

"They're cured?"

"Not at all. The virus stays there; it's just hiding. If patients stop the medications for any reason, even just missing a dose, the virus can take over again." I pointed my fork at her. "Only it's worse. Because the virus changes so quickly—"

"You mean it mutates."

"Right. Anyway, if you stop meds, your virus turns into one they can't stop."

"So patients have to keep taking the meds, right?"

"Yeah, but the cost is shocking. Some treatment regimens cost more than the mortgage on an expensive house. The average cost is twice our house payment."

"Don't AIDS patients have insurance?"

"Not all of them. Only the ones who can still work. But if they get sick, really sick, and have to quit, they lose medical coverage."

Jackie used the fork to catch the crumbs on her plate. "I had no idea."

"I didn't either. And that's not everything. I wrote down the names of the medicines that Stephen is taking. Then I looked them up."

"And?"

"And, the list of complications looks about as dangerous as the bubonic plague."

"No kidding?"

"Okay. I'm exaggerating. But they're bad. Real bad. Diabetes, high blood pressure, nausea, diarrhea." I ticked the list off on my fingers. "And there's high cholesterol, heart disease, anemia. The list of side effects goes on and on."

"Still, it has to be better than the old days, when the disease killed you."

"I guess. But now the drugs can kill you." I sipped some coffee, wishing that I had more information. "Stephen's in trouble."

"Stephen has been in trouble for a long time, Colleen. Maybe not medical trouble, but trouble just the same."

"I know," I agreed. "I don't know what to do. I've tried to talk to him about his homosexuality. But I can't get anywhere with him. He shuts me down as soon as he thinks I'm headed there."

"You can't force him. Maybe this is your opportunity to love him."

I buried my face in my hands. "I don't know what that means. And what if I'm too late?"

"We don't get to control other people."

"We don't get to control anything." I dabbed at the corners of my eyes with my fingertips. "While I was there, Stephen had visitors and I realized how much of his life is centered around other people just like him."

"You mean the homosexual community? How did you know?"

I stared at Jackie. Her eyes held no guile. "You can tell."

"The gay guy who came to visit. That's what you're referring to, right?"

In spite of myself, I shuddered. "Okay. Yes. I want Stephen to move toward faith. How can that happen when those are the only kind of people he hangs out with?"

"Don't be silly. He works at a university. He has heterosexuals all around him."

"It's a community college," I corrected her. "And I saw it myself. Homosexuals are influencing him, drawing him away from the Lord."

"Wait a minute," Jackie said, a cryptic smile toying at the corner of her mouth, "From what you've told me, no one is drawing Stephen away from the Lord. He was never close, right?"

"Okay. They're blocking him from seeing the truth."

Her smile broke out like sunshine. "Colleen, my dear sweet friend. I've never seen Jesus blocked by anyone. Not by the Pharisees. Not by the Romans. Not even by a sealed tomb." She picked up her fork and plate and set them in the sink. Then turning, she asked, "So, are you ready to try that intro again?"

Two weeks later, after a big Sunday lunch, I found Kevin in the family room, watching a fly-fishing show on television and pulling line off of a fishing rod. I sat down on the couch beside him, picked up my needles, and settled into the reassuring rhythm of knitting.

"I'm thinking about Stephen's play," I began.

He nodded without looking up, intent on the task before him. "What about it?"

"It's this Thursday."

He glanced at me, his eyebrows drawn together. "Okay?" He said it like a question.

"I'm thinking that I want to drive over and see it."

"You're going to drive across the state to see a community college play?" He shook his head, as if I'd lost my mind.

"I could drive over in the morning and come back the next day."

"Colleen, you don't need my permission."

"I know. I'm not asking permission." I paused, took a deep breath and continued, "I was thinking maybe you'd like to join me."

"Why don't you ask a friend? Maybe Jackie could go with you."

"I already asked her. She's busy."

"I'm not much for plays." My caveman husband, the original hunter-gatherer, pulled the last of the line off his reel, leaving a translucent bird's nest on the couch beside him. He reached for a new package of line and tore open the plastic with his teeth.

"I know," I agreed. "But I think we need to make an effort, you know. To try harder to connect with Stephen. I don't want to let him get so far away from me again. We should support his work, don't you think?"

"He's your brother. Besides, I work on Thursday and Friday."

"You could take two days off. Heaven knows you take time when the fish are running."

"I count that as vacation."

"Can't you come with me?"

He threaded the reel with the new line, concentrating entirely on the task.

"Couldn't you think about it?"

"Colleen, I'm not going to drive two hundred miles to see a play," he said, his voice gentle but firm. "You can go. I'll hold down the fort here."

So, on Thursday, I drove across the state to view the community college production of Thornton Wilder's *Our Town*. I arrived in Seattle early enough to spend the morning at a downtown music store browsing through sheet music I didn't need. From there, I drove to the University District, visiting a store chock-full of hand-spun yarn and weaving supplies.

I spent hours reveling in the textures and colors of natural fibers—touching, caressing, smelling, and squeezing. I sat at a small table, savoring the latest knitting books, examining every single photograph for style and design. Eventually I chose delicious wool in a dark teal and bought enough for a man's sweater.

It occurred to me that Stephen would look wonderful in teal.

Later, I ate Thai at a restaurant not far from the community college and waited in line at the ticket window of the performing arts center.

Inside, I made my way to the balcony, stepping over a set of obviously proud parents, both holding camera cases and multiple copies of the production credits. They had draped the empty chairs between the aisle seat and my own with various handbags and coats, all in anticipation of a crowd yet to arrive.

I smiled at the woman as I passed, and dropped into my seat with relief. At least I didn't have to climb over the rest of them.

I'd last read *Our Town* for a literature class I'd taken during a particularly troublesome semester in college. I remembered the play as overtly boring. Somehow though, I'd managed to bluff my way through the required paper for class. At the time, I couldn't see what all the fuss was about, couldn't understand why Wilder won such acclaim for a story in which nothing really happened.

While I waited for the curtain, I perused the credits. At ten minutes past seven, the house lights blinked and patrons hurried to their seats. As the lights dimmed, the curtains rose to a Spartan but intriguing set, depicting the small town of Grover's Corner, New Hampshire.

Stephen's class had designed a monotone grouping of silhouettes, beautifully backlit by an ingenious design crew. In the first act, the lights glowing behind the shapes changed from pale raspberry to warm yellow, portraying the path of the sun as it evolved from dawn to dazzling sunlight. The effect was striking.

The narrator reminded me somehow of the Ghost of Christmas Past—as morose as a funeral director—though I could not tell if his was a case of stage fright or passion. The audience twittered at his portrayal, and I bit my tongue to keep from giggling with them.

Gradually, the characters of Grover's Corner launched into their small-town conversation. I recognized the everyday picture of small-town life that Wilder projected in the play; I lived it every day in Potter's Hollow. The students hadn't been on stage long before I remembered why I thought the play was so boring. I fought drooping eyelids through the entire first act.

By the second act, when ordinary conversation gave way to stories of love and marriage, I fell into the rhythm of the story and the people of Grover's Corner. With the rest of the audience, I enjoyed the charming portrayal of Emily Webb's marriage to George Gibbs.

I listened carefully as Emily delivered her lines from the graveyard and grieved as she tried to recapture the joys of life. I cried as Emily showed us that life is wasted on the living. Just as Wilder intended, I recognized the importance of life's little moments.

At the same time, I saw more than the rest of the audience, something frightening. While they reflected on the performance, I wondered about the message behind the play. Why had Stephen chosen this particular drama for his theatre group?

Was Stephen interested in little moments because he believed he had so few left to enjoy? Was the message of the play really the message of the teacher?

As the audience clapped, I brushed away tears. After the curtain dropped, I sat for a long time, wondering about the play and its message. How should a Christian feel about the little moments of her life?

Do I sometimes sacrifice the moments for the mission? Does my busyness please my Savior? For a moment, I wished that Wilder had given me answers instead of questions.

As members of the audience filed down the balcony steps to the exit, I thought about how guilty I feel when I sit in the sun and enjoy its warmth. How I squirm when I'm asked to wait in a doctor's office. I thought about the lists hanging at that very moment from the front of my refrigerator.

I didn't know why Stephen had chosen the play. I couldn't guess his feelings about his battle with AIDS. I couldn't say for sure what fears motivated him to keep his disease a secret. But even as I stood to put on my coat, I realized that if I wanted to help Stephen, I could not remain silent.

No matter how much I hated the idea, eventually I would have to ask.

CHAPTER
Eleven

From the back of the theater, I caught a glimpse of Stephen leaning against the stage as he accepted the congratulations of his audience. Even in the semi-dark, I noticed that he'd lost more weight; the angles of his face stood out over deep shadows cast by the overhead lighting.

He looked tired, relieved perhaps, and his smile seemed more obligatory than genuine. I felt a little sorry for him as I made my way down the center aisle toward the horde of gushing parents and proud actors. I've had to put on that same smile at more than one piano recital.

Ducking into a seat near the front, I people watched as I waited for the throng to die down. Amid the flash of cameras and the exchanging of bouquets, I recognized the young woman who played Emily. Already in street clothes, she beamed with pleasure as she accepted yellow roses from a young admirer. Beside her stood an older man, his arm draped around her shoulders. In his expression, I saw the obvious glow of fatherly pride. Side by side, they seemed to bask in the triumph of her first major stage role.

Before I could stop them, tears came to my eyes. Though I knew better, a wave of envy swept over me as I watched Emily and her father. Staring at them, I wondered if she knew the treasure she had in his love. For the briefest moment, I allowed myself to imagine how my life might have been different had I basked in the reflected adoration of a proud father.

An older woman hovering over Emily glanced toward me and I looked away, aware that my observation had drawn her attention. It didn't matter anyway. My father was gone.

Moments later, Emily's father draped a coat over her shoulders and led her up the aisle toward the lobby. As they passed my seat, I tried to hear his words of praise but could not make them out over the noise of parents and performers.

"I'm glad you came," Stephen said, pushing down the seat as he dropped into the chair beside me.

"The show was wonderful. The kids did a great job."

"Oh, there were a few glitches."

"Not that anyone noticed."

"You all alone tonight?"

"Kevin was busy." Even as I said it, I wondered why I felt obligated to make excuses for him. "I did some shopping in the city this morning. It would have driven him mad."

"Congratulations, Stephen," A heavyset man with startlingly black hair reached over a row to shake Stephen's hand. "It went splendidly."

Stephen stood to accept the handshake. "Thank you, Dr. Lyndon. The kids did the work."

"Still, you should be proud."

"I am, sir."

As his colleague moved away, I stood to join Stephen. "Are you going to a cast party?"

"Only for a moment. I have to put in an appearance." Acknowledging another parent, Stephen waved and nodded at someone behind me. "Why don't you come along? They'll have snacks. There isn't much to eat at my house."

"I didn't expect you to cook for me. You've been busy."

He nodded. "Every spare minute. So, do you want to ride along in my car?"

I agreed and picked up my coat. Together, we made our way up the aisle. "Thanks for letting me spend the night at your house. I'm getting too old to make the trip over and back in the same day." I buttoned my coat. "I'd hate to go to a motel this late at night."

He smiled down at me as he slipped his hands into his coat pockets. "No problem," he said. "I can't very well deny shelter to the woman who saved my life."

Just before midnight, Stephen unlocked the back door of the house. Flipping on the lights, he stumbled across the linoleum and collapsed into a chair at his kitchen table. Obviously exhausted, he leaned his chin onto one hand and asked, "Would you like some herbal tea?"

"Look at you," I said, and giggled. "You look like you've just gotten back from a war zone." I took off my coat and hung it on the hook by the back door. "Tea sounds good, but you don't have to make it, silly. I'll start the water. You want some?"

Stephen's watch alarm began beeping. He switched it off with one hand. "Guess not." He pointed to the watch. "I need meds before bedtime," he said. "Have to take them with food."

I opened the fridge and scanned the meager contents. "Milk okay?" He shook his head. "How about crackers and cheese?"

In the time it took me to make food suggestions, Stephen had opened a medicine bottle and removed a pill as big as the end of my pinkie. "Just crackers and juice. I can't eat dairy with this one."

I poured orange juice from a pitcher and gave him the glass. "Isn't that for a horse?"

"I wish," he said, placing the tablet as far back on his tongue as he could manage. He lifted the juice glass.

I opened a cupboard, pulled down a box of Wheat Thins and gave it to him. Satisfied that he had what he needed, I filled his electric kettle and plugged it into the wall outlet.

"Stephen, this drama thing has really taken it out of you. You look so worn out. You're losing weight. Your face is beginning to look like a skeleton." I took the chair across the table from him.

"Thanks so much." He tossed a cracker into his mouth. "Considering the situation here, that might not be so far off."

I made a face. "Please don't make jokes about that. You know what I mean. Aren't you supposed to keep your weight up?"

"How do you know that?"

"You aren't the only one in the family who can read, you know." I dipped into the box and pulled out a handful of crackers for myself. Fingering one I said, "I've been looking into the whole AIDS thing. You know, research, reading."

He nodded, clearly impressed. "So what have you learned?"

"Not enough to show off." I ate the cracker. "I learned that everything I ever thought I knew about this disease is completely out of date."

Stephen smiled. "You and everybody else in the world. At one time, AIDS was a death sentence. Most people didn't live eighteen months after the diagnosis. Now, teenagers think that doctors have it cured."

"You're kidding. Not cured."

"Almost. Kids think they can come down with AIDS and just start taking a pill. Like it's a sinus infection or something."

"I've read enough to know that isn't true." I ate another cracker, listening to the clock over his sink tick away the midnight hour. "But I have so many questions. So many things I don't understand."

Stephen ignored me. "The kids are the ones who are getting it now. The normal, heterosexual kids who think they're invincible."

I shuddered, thinking of Mallory and Travis. I made a mental note to review the facts with them as soon as I returned to Potter's Hollow.

"No one is invincible," Stephen said, turning the medicine bottle around and around between his fingers. "No one."

"I've been thinking, Stephen," I said, expressing a thought that had only begun to form itself in my imagination. "Why don't you come home with me? Take a week to rest. You get Thanksgiving off anyway. You'd only have to miss a couple of days of work.

"We could baby you. You could sleep as much as you want. I'll cook for you and you could get some strength back. Maybe you could even put on a few pounds—especially if you don't have any everyday worries to handle."

Stephen didn't answer right away. "Colleen, you can't save me from this."

I felt my breath catch in my throat. Those were Kevin's exact words. "I'm not trying to save you," I said. It was as close to a lie as anything I'd said in the last twenty-four hours. "I'm trying to invite you for Thanksgiving dinner. It won't be a big crowd. Mom will be at Carrie's house. Kevin's folks are in Florida. Just us." I shrugged.

"Colleen, get real. You've been trying to save me for the last twenty years." Stephen laughed. "Besides, I think it might be hazardous to my health to eat turkey at your house."

"I can cook when I put my mind to it."

"Anyway, I have two more weeks in the quarter. I still have midterms to grade. Final tests to prepare. Then after finals, I'll have to turn in my grades. I can't take a break right now." He leaned his forehead onto the long slender fingers of his left hand.

In Stephen's gesture, I saw longing mixed with a kind of emotional fatigue that I couldn't begin to understand. The need to have Stephen come home with me became even more urgent. "Alright, then. Come when you've finished the quarter. Spend your whole Christmas break with us. I promise not to harass you. You can rest, or read, or just veg out. Whatever you need. Just come." I reached over and covered his hand with my own. "Please come," I whispered.

Two days later, late on Saturday afternoon, I sat at the grand piano in our little church.

"Alright, let me have your attention." Jackie clapped her hands in a vain effort to control the teens gathering along the bottom two steps of the platform. Jackie had spent her day off at school grading papers and come straight to rehearsal. Though she had to be both famished and tired, Jackie displayed the patience of a saint.

Smiling, she clapped again, and this time, I saw her tension in the fine lines between her eyebrows. These kids took every ounce of patience she could muster. I relished my position at the Yamaha grand, on the side of the platform.

I kept my mouth shut while Jackie struggled through the first hour of youth choir. "Come on. Take your new positions," she said, using her command-teacher voice.

As the children settled into place, their conversation gradually died off.

"Much better," Jackie said. "I was afraid I'd have to call Doug."

"Kitts only responds to malicious property destruction," a blonde quipped from the back row. "Right, Andy?" Andy Dorman's face turned bright red as the group burst into laughter.

"It pays to have a policeman in the congregation. Besides, the way you guys sing, you're destroying my music," Jackie answered. "I'd be thrilled to press charges." She turned back a page on her music and looked toward me. Lifting her arms to direct, she said, "Let's take it again from letter A. Pick up the music two measures back, please." She raised both her arms, gave a subtle lift of both shoulders and dove into the section.

Taking signals from her shoulders, I tapped two beats with my left toe and began the lead-in to the requested section. Ten measures later, the boys in the back row lost the harmony notes, and the song drifted into an undistinguishable mush of musical oatmeal. I dropped the accompaniment and began plucking out the men's part.

"Cut." Jackie said, dropping her hands to her sides. "Okay, men, let's try that alone at letter A. Try to read the music, please. When the notes go up, so should your voice." Jackie always sugarcoated her sarcasm with a heavy dose of genuine amusement. The kids loved her.

She looked at me. "Colleen, could you play both the men and the women's notes?" To the choir she said, "Men, I want you to sing along, but as you do, listen. See how the parts fit together. By knowing the harmony, you will be better able to find your own part." She waved the desired tempo, and the boys came in on cue, trying valiantly to improve.

After several repeats, Jackie gave up. "Alright, that's it for tonight. But"—she stopped mid-sentence, holding up her index finger—"I want all of you guys to listen at least twice every day to the tape. Sing along. Pick it out on the piano. Do whatever you have to do to be ready for next week. We'll start off right at letter A."

She closed her music and smiled at the kids. "And I have donuts for you. Stop by the kitchen on your way to the parking lot." With a roar, the teens headed for the kitchen. They reminded me of a flock of starlings exploding from a tree at precisely the same moment.

I closed the grand and locked the cover, dropping the key into my purse. "Quite a rehearsal, maestro." I said.

"I have a horrible headache. Do you have anything?"

"I do. For occasions such as these." I pulled out a tiny pill bottle and dropped two tablets into her outstretched hands. "Truthfully, though, they're coming along. It's going to be fine."

"If I survive until the performance." We walked together from the sanctuary into the hallway, where Jackie bent over the water fountain.

"You will."

"Don't be so sure of yourself." She tipped her head back to swallow the pills. "By the way, how is your brother?"

"I don't know. I went to see his play."

"And?"

"It was great. Have you seen *Our Town?*"

"I think I've read it, but I don't remember much. It's pretty depressing, isn't it?"

"I came home and got a copy at the book store," I said as we walked slowly through the hallway toward the front doors.

"Once through wasn't enough?"

"Something in it struck me, and when I got home, I couldn't remember the lines. I wanted to read it, to see what I'd heard."

"What did you find?"

"It was near the end of the play. One of main characters says this: 'That's what it was to be alive. To move about in a cloud of ignorance; to go up and down trampling on the feelings of those…of those about you. To spend and waste time as though you had a million years. To be always at the mercy of one self-centered passion, or another. Now you know—that's the happy existence you wanted to go back to. Ignorance and blindness.'"

"I was right. It was depressing."

"I can't figure out why Stephen chose that particular play for the kids to do this fall. What was he trying to say?"

"How am I supposed to know?"

"Silly, I didn't mean that you're supposed to tell me."

"Why don't you ask him?"

Why are these things so obvious to everyone else? Fortunately for me, at just that moment, the kids burst through the foyer, heading for waiting parents in the parking lot. Distracted by the tumult, Jackie said good-bye to the kids, admonishing them again to practice.

When the front doors slammed behind the last teen, I said, "I invited Stephen to spend his Christmas break with us."

Jackie's eyebrows rose and her mouth dropped open. "The whole vacation? Kevin doesn't mind?"

"I haven't told him yet. It was spontaneous, you know. We were sitting at his kitchen table and I just invited him to spend some time with us. Besides, he might not come."

"And then again, he might. Colleen, why on earth did you do that?"

Her shock surprised me. "Why wouldn't I? He needs a break. He's exhausted. He's been sick. I thought it would be good for him."

"And good for you?"

"What do you mean?"

"Well, you can keep a really close eye on him if he's at your place. None of his gay friends can get at him on this side of the mountains. And, if you're really lucky, you can try to pry information out of him."

How could my best friend make such accusations? "What information?"

"You can try to find out the truth about how this disease is affecting him."

"Did it ever occur to you that I love my brother? Could it be that I just want to spend time with him? To catch up on the years we've missed?"

Jackie smiled, a mysterious knowing smile. "I know you love him."

"Of course I do."

"And I know that you are willing to do anything at all to save him."

"That isn't true. I'm just trying to love him." Standing at the church's front doors, I turned on my friend. "Isn't that what we're supposed to do?" Why did she make me feel so defensive?

"It isn't your job to save your brother." Jackie pulled her church key from her purse, opened the door to the alarm box, and punched in the electronic security code.

"I know that. What makes you think I have ulterior motives?"

She leaned against the door, backing through the opening. As we stepped into the cold winter air, I hugged my music to my chest, holding my coat tight against the chill.

"I didn't say you had ulterior motives," she said. "I'm not the enemy here." In silence we walked toward our cars, parked side by side under the streaming light of a single street lamp.

Still a little overwhelmed by her response, I stood nearby as she unlocked her car, wondering what she meant. What had I done to deserve these accusations?

As she opened the door and slid into the driver's seat, she said, "I'm sorry. I'm tired. I've probably said more than I should have." She closed the door and rolled down the window.

I blinked against tears, feeling falsely accused and a little betrayed by my friend. Reaching out to the car, I put my hand over the edge of the window. "Really, Jackie. I'm not trying to accomplish anything."

"Okay," she said, starting the car. "I'll accept that. It isn't my business anyway, and I won't mention it again. Let's just forget I said anything." With that, she put the car in reverse. Her car stopped suddenly, and I saw the brake lights reflected on the pavement behind the car as the driver's window came down. "One more thing," she said as she tipped her head out the window. "If what you say is true—and I'm willing to go along with it just for the sake of argument—I guess I'm just wondering why you haven't told Kevin about it yet." She smiled at me, shrugged, and leaned back inside.

With that, Jackie pulled out of the parking space and turned toward home.

I couldn't shake Jackie's warning. It stayed with me through the Sunday morning service and through our weekly trip to the grocery store. I felt it tremble in my conscience while I made beef sandwiches for lunch.

It would not leave, even as I sat at the kitchen counter, looking through cookbooks and planning our Thanksgiving meal. In a *Southern Cooking* book, I found a recipe for hot fruit compote and began writing it out on a three-by-five card.

"Ah, planning the big meal," Kevin said as he came in the kitchen. "Have you seen my little snub-nosed pliers?" One after another, he opened the top drawers, stirring up the contents in search of his beloved tool. "Yellow handle. 'Bout this big." He held his two index fingers apart to indicate the size. "I thought I saw them in one of these drawers."

"Have you asked Travis? I don't borrow your tools."

"He used it on his bike last week. Said he left it in the kitchen." Kevin dug through three more drawers in the time I transferred the compote ingredients onto a grocery list. "Have you decided what we're having on Thursday?"

"Not entirely."

"Well, if I had my way, I'd say don't make it so fancy this year. We aren't having company. Let's just have the basics. You know, turkey, gravy, potatoes, that yam casserole you make. And pie. Don't forget the pie." He opened the drawer with my kitchen towels. "Ah hah! Look at this. Covered in—ugh, what is this? And why are my pliers in here?" He turned on the faucet, rinsing something sticky from the yellow plastic.

"It's a sweet-potato casserole," I corrected him.

"Right. What do you think about inviting someone from church?"

"I'm thinking about having Jackie and her family."

"That would be fun."

"I asked Stephen."

Kevin, drying his beloved pliers on a clean dishtowel, stopped dead in his tracks. "You did? Is he coming?"

"Relax. He can't come." Leaning on the counter, I turned the pages in the cookbook. "So, I asked him to spend his Christmas break with us."

Still clutching the towel in one hand, Kevin bent forward, resting his palms on the counter before him. I saw confusion in his eyes. "You asked him to do what?"

"He's tired, Kevin. He needs a break."

"How long? Two weeks? Three weeks? With us?" He shook his head. "What were you thinking, Colleen? We promised the Thompsons that we'd spend the week between Christmas and New Year skiing with them." He picked up the towel and draped it over the rack. "Stephen won't want to do that with us. Besides, I took that week off. I thought we'd spend it together as a family."

"Stephen is family," I protested. Suddenly my plan to offer refuge didn't seem like such a great idea. "Anyway, I don't think he'll come."

"But what if he does? Three weeks is a long time for a houseguest. Even when it's someone you love."

"What is that supposed to mean?"

"Don't read so much into it."

I couldn't help taking offense for my brother. "Why not? I thought you liked Stephen." Even as I said it, I knew I shouldn't have. But the reaction, my protective, mother-bear reaction came naturally, a response built from years of practiced repetition and reinforcement.

"Don't be silly, Colleen. Of course I do."

"So why can't we offer a place for Stephen to rest? I can take care of him. I can cook and wash his clothes. He needs someone to give him a real break."

"Okay. But why does it have to be us? And why during our vacation?"

"Because he needs us now, not when it's convenient."

"What about the kids? Shouldn't you have asked the kids? It's their vacation too. Maybe they don't want to give up a ski trip for three weeks of hanging around the house, baby-sitting your brother."

"Now who's overreacting? Stephen doesn't need us to baby-sit. He just needs food and rest and love. That's not so hard, is it?" I slid off my bar stool and came around the counter. Wrapping my arms around Kevin's waist, I said, "We can still go skiing. Stephen can house sit while we're gone."

"I just wish you would have asked me first. I don't want the kids to feel like their vacation isn't important."

"How can they learn to care for other people unless we model it? After all, someday they'll be taking care of us."

"Sooner than I used to think." Kevin rubbed the thinning hair at the crown of his head.

"I'm sorry I didn't tell you sooner. But it will be fine. Really, everything will be just fine." And even as I said it, I wondered if anything would ever be fine again.

Snow fell in Potter's Hollow on the day before Thanksgiving. On my last trip for groceries, I drove by the wrecking yard out on the highway. The rusted graveyard had already taken on the purified persona of a winter fairyland; soft white snow blurred the distinction between cars, covering the sharp edges of decaying metal with a false beauty, a frozen mystique thrilling the likes of highway beautification enthusiasts. By Thursday afternoon, a six-inch mantle clothed Potter's Hollow, the first snow of the season.

To me, this snow miracle, this blanketing of everything harsh and ugly, proved to be the only redeeming quality of the winter season. Darkness and snow would persist in Potter's Hollow for most of the next five months. Nothing I could do would change the course of the seasons; at least the brilliant reflection of sunlight on snow made our short days more bearable.

We shared a quiet Thanksgiving afternoon with Jackie's family, followed by a movie they'd rented for the occasion. Later in the evening, after our company left and the snow continued to fall, I nursed hot chocolate while Kevin and Mallory and Travis waxed and tuned our skis.

The long skis and close quarters created a scene worthy of vaudevillian comedy. I wondered if they would finish without knocking someone over. Still, working together brought out the best of them, and I embedded the memory in my mind. Someday, when they left home, I would have that memory to pull up whenever connections between us grew tenuous.

On Friday, we cut down a Christmas tree, which we decorated on Saturday. By the end of the weekend, Christmas had begun a fullfledged onslaught on the Payton household.

Tuesday morning, after the last of my early students left the house, I grabbed a quick breakfast of bran flakes and coffee and returned to the living room, where I pulled out the tape of Jackie's solo. I'd recorded her singing a cappella, with the intention of working out the intricacies of the accompaniment without her.

I turned the recording on and sat down at the piano, the lead sheet before me, my hands resting on the keys. I heard the cue for the tempo and began the introduction we'd devised together, pausing at the exact moment Jackie's taped voice began to sing, "I would love to tell you what I think of Jesus."

I made it through the first two lines of the verse, filling the pauses between the lines with jazz chording that embellished the style Jackie had chosen to sing. At the end of the third line, I heard a mistake in the harmony we'd planned. I stopped playing to pick up a pencil, making a note of the necessary changes. Putting new chords above the words, I put the pencil in my teeth as my fingers tried to catch the music on the tape. And then Jackie began to sing the chorus:

No one ever cared for me like Jesus.
There's no other friend so kind as He;
No one else could take the sin and darkness from me,
O how much He cared for me.[1]

As I listened to her voice, low and rich, I stopped playing, caught by the way in which the lyrics resonated with the reality of my life. For me, they were absolutely true. Nothing in my life, in my childhood, or in my teen years had prepared me for the overwhelming love I'd found in my relationship with Jesus. And as I sat at the piano bench, a parade of memories trooped across my mind's eye. Bits and pieces of my past, mistakes I wished I could forget, came calling like scenes from a daytime soap opera.

Because I'd submerged these pieces in the forgiving blood of Jesus, I knew that they had no power over me. But no matter how many times I recalled them, I continued to feel regret. How I wished I'd had the power to choose a different path.

As the memories marched past, I thought again about how little I deserved the love I'd found in Jesus. I guess all Christians feel that way, but sometimes the knowledge leaves me weak with gratitude. Instead of playing, I leaned against the keyboard and wept.

When the music ended, I turned off the recorder and began playing again, though not the chords of Jackie's solo. Not music represented by notes written on a page. Instead, I began playing the worship choruses I'd learned from years of playing with the worship team at church.

One song after another, I let my fingers praise my Savior with notes and melodies my voice could not express. I thought through the words rather than singing them—I no longer have a public singing voice—but in my soul, the song lyrics rose on the wind of exuberance.

As I played, I lifted up the needs of my family, alternating my prayers with choruses of praise played by my own imperfect human hands. I don't know how long I played like that, praising and praying. Over the course of it all, I felt the presence of the Lord in a profound, nearly tangible way, as real though invisible as the scent of a woman's perfume.

I marveled at the holiness of the moment. Certainly, my own skills hadn't brought the wonder to the music. In fact, if I was to guess, I would think that the holiness of the One I worshipped made my meager keyboard skills holy without changing or improving a single

note. It is a marvelous thing to let my hands worship without the dis-
heartening interference of my own inadequate voice.

And then the doorbell rang.

Once again, Stephen stood on my front porch, this time holding
a small duffel bag in one hand. A suitcase leaned against his other leg.
He wore a heavy wool coat in dark green watch plaid and a brown
beret set low over his forehead. Already, snow had begun to gather on
the top of his hat, leaving his head looking a bit like a frosted acorn.

"I'm so happy you decided to come," I said, this time expressing
welcome rather than shock. "Come in. Come in."

"I heard you playing," he said, with a shyness I recognized from the
old days. "It was beautiful. I didn't mean to interrupt you."

"You aren't interrupting. I was just, umm…" I searched for words.
"Fooling around." I gestured to the bag. "Can I take that for you?"

He shook his head, picked up the bag, and stepped across the
threshold. "I wish I could fool around like that." He dropped the bags,
stamped the snow off his feet, and unbuttoned his coat. "Where shall
I put these?"

"I'll put them in the closet."

"Where am I staying?" he asked, taking off his coat.

"Upstairs. I've cleaned the guest bedroom." We climbed the stairs
and turned the corner toward the back of the house. "You used to
play the piano better than I did, Stephen. Why did you quit?" I
turned in time to catch a glimpse of anger cross his face. "What happened?"

"You didn't know?"

"I thought you were tired of it. I guess I never really asked."

"Dad was tired of it. He thought it wasn't maaaahnly enough."
Stephen stretched the word for emphasis.

"He made you quit?"

Stephen shrugged. "No. I quit because I wanted to please him. I
turned out for football." He dropped the smaller bag on the antique
double bed. "Broke my collarbone in the first game."

"That, I remember."

"When I got here, I stood outside listening for a while before I
rang the bell. What were you playing?"

For the slightest moment, I considered avoiding a truthful answer. Who would understand the wild worship of a second-rate pianist? Instead, I shrugged. "I was supposed to be practicing for a solo my friend is singing for our Christmas Eve service."

"But you weren't?"

"Not really. I just sort of let myself go." I glanced away, took a deep breath, and came out with it. "It was church music."

"Not any church music I remember."

"True," I laughed. "Today's music doesn't resemble anything you and I sang in that old church in Spokane."

"Or in D.C. or Virginia, or California or Nevada or Texas."

"Or in Germany," I agreed. Between the two of us, we'd managed to list most of the places we'd lived as children. I shook my head at the parade of homes. "Dad certainly got around, didn't he?"

"Which wouldn't have been nearly so bad if he'd just left us behind."

"You'd rather he left us alone—without him?"

"The whole family would have been better off, don't you think?"

"I don't think Mom would have liked that arrangement much."

"It would have made everything easier."

I changed the subject. "How about something hot to drink? Hot chocolate?"

"Sounds good."

Moments later, I'd guided Stephen and his hot chocolate into a club chair in our living room. I switched on the Christmas tree lights and sat down in the matching chair. I pulled a magazine toward me and put my sugar-free chocolate on the table between us.

"Nice tree," he said, pointing to the noble fir standing in the curve of the grand piano.

I smiled. "The kids chose it."

"In a lot?"

"No, we always go to a tree farm about six miles up Highway 2. We've done it since the kids were big enough to wade through the muck with us."

"Ah," he said, nodding. "A tradition."

"Not much of one. It takes about an hour. We go out, choose a tree, cut it down, and drag it back to the car."

"Still, it's something you do together."

"Right. Most years we get caught in a freezing downpour that always starts at exactly the same moment Kevin pulls into the parking lot. It's a very important part of the tradition."

He laughed. "Well, at least you have something."

I took a drink of chocolate. "You have something. You have us."

He looked away. "It's not the same."

"Not the same. But good."

He looked at me, and I recognized a startling sadness. A sadness that made me want to reach out and wipe it away, like a wet cloth washes the ink off of a whiteboard. I wanted to ask about it, but chose not to. "I have professional family," he said.

"Speaking of school, how was the end of the quarter?"

"Not bad. I have papers to grade."

"Have you recovered from the play?"

"I'm getting better. It threw me for a loop." He leaned back, resting his head against the back of the chair as he slid his hips forward, nearly reclining in the overstuffed chair. "I don't have the energy I used to. Someday I'm going to have to quit working, I think."

"But you love teaching."

"I do. But it takes so much energy. I need to conserve that now. I need all of my resources if I'm going to beat this thing."

"What would you do?"

"Some writing maybe. Some freelance. I've always wanted to publish. Anything that will pay the mortgage."

"Tell me," I said, "whatever happened to the man you used to live with in that big old house on the hill. He was your partner, wasn't he?" Though I knew the answer, I asked anyway, wanting to lay open the subject that had kept us apart.

It was the first time I'd openly mentioned Stephen's lifestyle, and the newness of the admission set off a little quiver in my stomach. Afraid that the quiver would move to my hand where Stephen could see it, I put my mug down on the table again and rested my hands on the arm of the chair, my fingers spread in an effort to appear relaxed.

He nodded. "Glen died six and a half years ago."

"I'm so sorry."

"AIDS," Stephen continued. "He'd been positive for years. We'd done all the medicines, followed all the advice. Still, we couldn't hold it back forever. And, in the end, we didn't want to. We wanted to get it over with. To spare him the pain. It was a terrible death."

"Is that why you moved? To get away from the loss?"

"I moved because we'd refinanced the house to pay for his medicines. I couldn't afford to stay there alone, and I couldn't face having someone else live with me. I had to sell the house to minimize the damage. I can barely afford the house I have now."

I picked up the mug again, blowing on the hot liquid. Six and a half years. The numbers stuck in my mind, seeming significant, and yet I couldn't quite say why. I took a sip, watching Stephen gaze out the window onto the yard behind our house. The trees, dressed in white cloaks, looked like the inside of a child's snow globe, with big flakes drifting, falling, and settling on the landscape beyond our comfortable chairs.

Not a breeze stirred the trees in the distance.

It hit me then. Stephen had disappeared from my life at almost exactly the same time his partner had died. Had grief caused his disappearance in my life? Of course, it had to be. What else would keep him from me? What else but anguish would account for his intermittent efforts at communication?

But why had he chosen to tell Carrie instead of me? Was there some truth to her accusations? Had my zeal driven my brother away? Or did the truth of my faith drive him from me? I shook these questions from my mind. It didn't matter now. At last we had begun to talk to one another again.

"That was when you stopped talking to me."

He nodded, still staring out the window.

"It was grief."

He turned his head, looking into my eyes, as if by staring he could force my understanding. "Grief, yes. But more than grief. It was the beginning of fear."

CHAPTER
Thirteen

I fixed a light lunch of soup and toast. To my surprise, when we'd finished, Stephen asked for dessert. I gave him a bowl of ice cream and fudge sauce, which he polished off while I cleared the dishes. When he'd finished, I suggested a short walk down by the river. "We wouldn't have to go far," I explained, hanging a towel on the rack beside the stove. "There's a trail along the river, and the light off the water is breathtaking in the afternoon."

"I'd like that," he said. "Seattle rain keeps me inside most of the winter."

After putting on coats, we added hats and gloves from a box I keep in the front hall closet. "Just like when we were kids," I said, opening the front door.

"Not quite," Stephen said and then chuckled. "You always lost your stuff and ended up borrowing mine." He stepped back from the door and said, "Hey, do you have a water bottle I could carry? I'm really thirsty."

"Sure." I headed for the kitchen. "The kids have dozens of them in a drawer. The problem is finding the right lid for the right bottle." After rummaging through the cupboards, we managed to locate and fill a Nalgene bottle. Moments later, we headed outside.

The early-morning snow flurries had ended, leaving a beautiful though thickly overcast sky. We trudged through squishy wet snow to the end of the street where a path, used by children on their way to and from school, cut through a field of bare cottonwoods. Neither of us could resist the lure of untouched snow. Veering off the path, we kicked our way into the perfect whiteness. The snow, lying on top of tall grass, came in over the top of our boots, sending doses of cold surprise onto our feet.

We tossed snowballs at one another and laughed.

Well, to be completely truthful, Stephen laughed at my abominable attempts to aim a snowball. In all the years since our last snowball fight, my skill hadn't improved. Over and over, I missed my brother by wide margins. Each failed attempt left him doubled over with laughter and gasping for air. I tried not to take it personally.

In the end, I gave up. After all, I didn't want him to hurt himself laughing.

We came out on Robin's Road and cut across the fifth fairway of the community golf course. Crisp cold air bit into my lungs, and I wanted to hug the pillars of late afternoon sunshine streaming through heavy clouds. I couldn't hold back my gratitude for the opportunity to spend this time with Stephen.

By the time we crossed the edge of the golf course to the path along the river, Stephen's breathing began to sound labored. Deliberately, I stopped walking to gaze at the river, giving him time to rest.

Even as he stood beside me, the heavy breathing continued. He gulped water from the Nalgene bottle, drinking nearly half the contents.

"Let's sit down," I said. "The air burns my lungs."

He nodded and we walked another fifty feet to an old wooden bench along the river, moving slowly, my hands deep in my pockets. I brushed snow from the bench and waited for him to sit down. Hugging himself, he relaxed into the bench, gazing at the river flowing below the bank. "It is beautiful," he said.

"I wish I could paint it. I've tried photographs, but it doesn't quite come out on film." I gestured widely with my arms. "I love the way the late afternoon sun turns the air apricot. Even on a cloudy day the white of the clouds and snow changes color. It's the best part of winter here." Sighing, I leaned back on the bench.

"Better than rain," he agreed.

Below us, the dark Icicle River sang a fairy song, light and staccato, as it tripped over the river bed on its way south and east. So far, no footprints marred the thick, perfectly shaped top hats of snow covering islands of grass in the river. "Do you remember floating the river that first summer we lived here?" I asked.

"Sure. Mallory was only a little tyke. She insisted on floating with me on my inner tube."

"She only had eyes for you."

He laughed. "I didn't think you'd let her go with me."

"I wouldn't have. But Kevin said her life jacket would keep her floating face up all the way to Wenatchee."

"That would comfort me." He seemed to have recovered from the difficult hike to the river. His shoulders relaxed and his breathing eased. He opened the bottle and drank again.

"It didn't. I only let her go after I realized that the whole river was only six inches deep between here and the takeout. Still, I stood in the middle of the river waiting until the minute I saw you both come around the bend."

"You waited on the bank." He looked at me, certain I'd lost my memory.

"You only thought I was on the bank."

"You little sneak. You didn't trust me."

"Don't be offended. As a mother, it's my duty to worry." We sat in silence for a moment, each of us reveling in memories. I remembered those late-summer float trips, resting bottom-down in a gigantic black inner tube, letting the river take us wherever it wanted. Sometimes we'd get caught on branches or dragged into little eddies at the side of the river. Then we'd paddle with our hands or shove against the obstruction and push ourselves back into the current.

And sometimes, while others waited, caught at the side of the creek, we would be swept away, far downstream, being carried faster and farther than we felt comfortable. "It was the not knowing that made it exciting," I said.

"Excuse me?"

"We never knew how it would go. Every trip was different."

"Do you still do it?"

"The kids do," I said. "Especially late in the summer. They get a big group together and take two trucks. They leave one truck down at the sandy beach, and the other shuttles them up to the bridge. They go in there. I can't handle the cold any more."

"How long?"

"How long is the float?" I asked. Stephen nodded, and I shrugged. "I don't know. Two miles maybe. You should come back this summer and try it again. You wouldn't have to carry Mallory."

This time, Stephen laughed. "I don't think she'd let me."

"It would be a good vacation for you, staying here for a week during the summer."

For a long moment, Stephen didn't answer and I wondered if he hadn't heard me. "Maybe we should start back," I said, scooting forward on the bench. "Piano lessons start right after school."

Stephen caught my arm. "Not yet. I need to tell you what is happening with me."

I shook my head, as if by refusing his request, I could deny the truth of what I already knew. I tried again to contain the fear by avoiding the truth. "You don't have to tell me anything. I trust you, Stephen."

"I don't know if I'll be here next summer, Colleen." He looked up, staring at the bare branches of trees hanging over us. "I mean I don't know if I'll be alive next summer. I want to, but my meds aren't working like they should. My blood tests are bad. I've held it off for so long, tried so many things—from the very beginning but..." his voice trailed off and I reached for him, touching his mittened hand with mine.

"You can change medications," I protested. "I've read a lot about it. There are so many. And new ones coming out all the time."

"Not for me. I've stopped responding to the meds. We did genetic tests on the virus and there isn't anything that will stop it. The meds made me sick, sicker than most other patients. That was part of what was going on when you came to visit."

I nodded, acknowledging the incident.

"We changed meds shortly after I got home from the hospital. I'm on my last combination."

"So, what are you saying?" Though I determined to remain calm
and supportive, my voice sounded harsh and frightened. "This is it?
This is the end?"

This time, Stephen comforted me, holding my hand in both of
his. "I'm not saying that at all. I'm saying that things aren't certain
any more. With the new meds, we expect my blood levels to return
to reasonable numbers, but we aren't even sure about that. Who
knows how long I'll stay well?"

"You don't know?" I echoed, unable to let the idea sink in. All my
wondrous joy in the beauty of winter vanished; I slumped against my
brother's shoulder. Tears began trickling down my face and I brushed
them away with my mitten. "I don't want to lose you," I said, my
voice low and thick. "You stayed away for so long, and I barely survived. I've only just found you again. I can't lose you now."

He didn't answer. Instead, he put his arm around me, patting my
shoulder with his hand. We sat there, the two of us, each grieving in
our own way until I felt the first shiver rattle through Stephen's bony
frame. "We need to go back," I said. "You're getting cold. We've been
out too long, and you're tired." I stood up, offering my hands to pull
him up off the bench. "You can nap while I teach piano."

"That sounds difficult."

"I have earplugs," I said. "Most of my students sound better
through earplugs, anyway."

He stood and we started back toward the house, arms wrapped
around one another as we walked. I couldn't shake the image of an
inner tube hopelessly caught in the strong current of a determined
river. In my mind, I saw the tube swept around the bend and out of
sight.

By loving Stephen, I had gotten into the inner tube. Now, the
course of events would carry me toward a destiny I could only
imagine. That afternoon, with Stephen leaning against me as we
trudged along through the snow, I didn't think about where things
would end up. I didn't worry about my part in the drama that lay
before me.

I only thought about the warm and loving man my brother had
become, and about how empty the world would be without him.

~ ~ ~

One evening, three days later, as we finished cleaning up the kitchen, Mallory came through the swinging door with the salt and pepper from the table. "Why don't we make sugar cookies tonight?"

"Cookies?" Normally, I try to avoid Christmas goodies. I end up making them, cleaning up, and worst of all, I eat more than my fair share. "None of us really needs cookies."

"We can't have Christmas without cookies," she moaned.

I made one last effort to think of a valid excuse. Then, wiping my hands on a towel, I gave in. "Alright. If you promise to help," I said. "I hate getting the whole baking thing started and having you go off to bed."

"You hate cleaning it up," Travis said, closing the dishwasher and turning it on.

"True," I agreed. "I hate cleaning anything up—especially your room."

"Baking sounds fun," Stephen volunteered from his position at the sink.

"Alright," I said. "We'll make cookies. How many batches?"

"Four should be enough." Mallory said, heading to the freezer for butter.

Four. Inwardly, I groaned. Four batches of dough to cool and shape and decorate. We'd be baking until midnight. "Okay, we'll do four. But you have to stay with it to the end," I warned.

"Not a problem," Travis said. "You can write an excuse and we'll sleep in."

"Not a chance, Trav," I said, popping him on the top of his head. "Why don't you sift flour for me? I'll measure powdered sugar."

"First we need some Christmas music." Stephen disappeared into the living room.

As the sound of Mannheim Steamroller came pulsing through the speakers, Stephen came back into the kitchen.

"Sift?" Travis, obviously bewildered, didn't seem to know where to start.

"I'll show you," Stephen said. I pulled the sifter from a lower cabinet and handed it to my brother. He scooped flour from the drawer while I pulled out a length of wax paper. Moments later, both of the guys were covered in white flour.

And so was the kitchen floor.

I creamed butter and sugar while Mallory measured the flour and scolded Travis. "It's all over the floor. I'm not cleaning that up. It's your job."

"Stephen will do it," Travis offered.

Eventually, though the kitchen looked like an alien landscape, we developed quite a reliable production team. Stephen rolled and shaped the dough. I monitored the cookie sheets going in and coming out of the oven. The kids decorated the shapes as soon as they were cool enough to take icing. I lost count of the finished cookies the three of them ate.

About ten o'clock, Kevin came in from a council meeting and snatched a frosted reindeer from the waxed paper. "Ah, I thought I could smell something when I came in the house," he said. With one arm, he hugged me, gave a quick kiss and devoured half the animal in a single bite. "Very good. About time we had some Christmas goodies around here." He reached for another.

"Dad, don't eat them all tonight." Mallory gave him a good-natured slap on the back of his hand. "We have thirteen days until Christmas," she scolded. "Pace yourself. Okay?"

"You can make more," he said, finishing off another reindeer.

I took a tray of cookies from the oven and turned to take off my oven mitt. I paused to lean against the stove, enjoying the scene. At that moment, I watched Kevin take in our teamwork. Even as it happened, I knew what he was thinking. I saw it in his eyes the moment Kevin saw Stephen pressing a cookie cutter onto the dough.

Kevin put his second, unfinished cookie on the counter beside him. "Colleen," he said, his voice low and calm. "I have some stuff out in the car. Could you help me bring it inside?"

"Sure. Let me grab a coat." I put another cookie sheet into the oven. No use letting Kevin's anxiety interrupt our production line. I set the timer. "Mallory, would you watch that for me? I'll just be a minute."

I headed for the mudroom and grabbed my down parka. As I stepped out into the night, Kevin closed the back door behind me. Our driveway leads directly to a detached garage, which I've always hated. In the winter, we have to shovel a path from the door to the garage and then use the snowplow attached to our tractor to clean off the driveway.

So far, we hadn't had enough snow to start shoveling. From the top step of the back porch, I saw the garage door closed, the lights off. The driveway glistened in pale moonlight, shrouded by a thin layer of packed snow. By morning, I knew, the driveway would transform itself into an ice rink.

I stepped down off the porch and onto the snow-covered grass, waiting patiently for Kevin to get to the point. I zipped my coat and put my hands in my pockets. In the moonlight, I saw tiny clouds of steam coming from his mouth.

"Colleen, what is going on in there?" Kevin said as he stepped off the porch.

I knew what he meant, but I refused to participate. "We're making Christmas cookies."

He put his hands on his hips and looked around the yard, trying to avoid saying what he meant. "Should he be doing that?"

"Travis?" I asked with as much innocence as I could muster. "I think all kids should learn to cook. Tonight, he learned to sift flour." At that moment, I had the same feeling a cat must have as it toys with a doomed mouse.

"You know what I mean," Kevin said, his voice terse. "Stephen. Should Stephen be making cookies?"

"Why not?"

"Colleen, don't be foolish. He has a disease. He shouldn't be making food for other people. What about our kids?"

"Kevin, you're an engineer. You have people who work for you. Don't they train you about these things in city government?"

"Obviously not."

"The virus that causes AIDS isn't transmitted by casual contact."

"That's what they say. But do you really know?"

I shook my head. "Please, Kevin. The disease has been around for more than twenty years now. Use that brain of yours. Don't you think that doctors would know if people got it by touching, or cooking, or coughing?"

"How do you know it's safe?"

"I don't know anything but what I've read. I'm not a researcher. I have to depend on the information I get from other people. I can tell you that I looked up the precautions on the Internet when I first found out about Stephen. It's safe, Kevin. Really safe."

He paced back and forth, obviously unsettled. "How do you know where the information came from? I mean, don't the people who have this disease have a big stake in keeping everyone else calm? Don't they want to avoid being kept in isolation?"

"I can't answer that," I said honestly, a little saddened by this side of my husband.

"I'm only trying to protect my family," he said, turning again to face me. "I'm not trying to be mean. I don't want—"

The back door opened suddenly, a metallic slam resounding through the night air as the wood crashed against the dryer in the mudroom. "Mom!" I recognized Mallory's voice, frightened and urgent. "Come quick. It's Stephen."

I took the steps two at a time, landing on the porch as she stepped back inside. "He's in the bathroom. Upstairs. Calling for you."

"It's alright, honey," I said, pausing to grasp her shoulder as I passed. "I'll go see what he needs."

I had already cleared the kitchen by the time I heard the back door close behind Kevin. I sprinted up the stairs to the bathroom door. This time, it wasn't locked.

Inside, I found Stephen, draped over the toilet, convulsed by furious contractions, his stomach heaving. Clearly, he had nothing left to empty. I touched his shoulder. "I'm here, Stephen," I said. "What can I do?"

Another wave of nausea threw him forward, his hands gripping the edge of the toilet. He could not speak, and as the wave passed I saw him shake his head. He leaned back, his face white, expression blank as he gasped for air.

I went to the linen closet beside the door and pulled out two wash-cloths. "I'm sorry. This should help." I rinsed the cloths in cold tap water. "You can suck on one of these to rinse your mouth." I squeezed out the excess water and handed him one. "Wipe your face first."

He accepted the cold washrags, putting one in each hand and holding them to his face. With a trembling voice, he spoke. "I think I need to go to the hospital."

CHAPTER
Fourteen

On the way to Wenatchee, the snow began to fall again in earnest. Though Kevin's Cherokee took these difficult road conditions in stride, I could not help but wonder if all of nature had conspired against Stephen's life.

"We should be there in about fifteen minutes," I said, turning in my seat to look back at my brother.

Stephen lay across the back seat, face down, head draped over the edge so that he could aim for a glass mixing bowl I'd placed there. "It's not worth an accident," he said, his voice low and pained.

I looked at Kevin who, with a glance into the rearview mirror, pulled into the left lane to pass a struggling VW bug. "We're making good time," Kevin said. "No hurry."

In the quiet that followed, I heard Stephen crawl across the leather seat and heave into the bowl. My stomach tightened in sympathy and I caught Kevin's eyes across the console just before the car surged forward.

We arrived at a quiet emergency room shortly after ten-thirty. This time, with Stephen mostly coherent, the check-in and exam happened without delay. The emergency-room nurse put Stephen on a gurney in a secluded exam room, a tiny plastic bowl beside his head. The nausea and vomiting continued, in spite of the fact that his stomach held nothing at all.

Kevin and I sat with him as the doctor, who introduced himself as Dr. James Stein, checked him over, poking and prodding, listening and tapping. Moments later, a nurse checked Stephen's blood with a

130

glucose monitor—one similar to the model I'd seen Carrie use. She shook her head as she wrote down the results.

Dr. Stein, a young man with curly dark hair and a full beard, had a small bald spot beginning to expose the crown of his head. His swarthy skin and black eyes gave him the look of an outdoorsman, the kind of man who might be more comfortable stream fishing with Kevin than running an emergency room. Even his hands, thick and rough, implied that he lived another life, one far away from latex gloves and disinfectants.

As soon as the doctor read the nurse's notes, he ordered a shot for Stephen. The nurse, a slim grey-haired woman, injected medicine directly into the plastic tubing that now dripped fluid into Stephen's left arm. Within moments, his nausea relented and Stephen dozed off. Occasionally, the sound of his own snoring woke him and he opened his eyes, blinked at the lights, and slid away again.

In the meantime, the doctor shot questions at Kevin and me with the relentless pace of a machine gun. We tried to answer accurately, but knew too little to be of much help.

"Do you have a record of his latest CD-4 count?"

"I don't even know what that is," I said.

"Viral load?"

"Stephen only came to spend a couple of weeks with us. He's been working very hard and he came to rest and recover."

"How about previous illnesses?"

"He was in the hospital about three weeks ago. We had to call an ambulance."

"Where?"

I gave him the name of the hospital, explaining as much as I knew about Stephen's previous admission and illness. "They sent him home twenty-four hours later," I said.

"I'll have them fax the records," he said. "Do you know the dosage on his diabetes medicine?"

This question caught me completely off guard, and I blinked, staring at the doctor. "Diabetes?" I looked at Kevin.

"Yes, he told the nurse that he was taking Glucophage. Do you know the dosage?"

"We really don't know anything," I explained again. "We just learned about his, umm, his condition."

"He's staying with us for Christmas," Kevin repeated.

The doctor slid his pen into his jacket pocket. "I can't make any judgments about his general condition without more information," he said. "For that we'll have to wait on some lab work. But I can tell you this. His blood sugar has skyrocketed. Five-seventy-five by my measurements."

"Shouldn't have eaten that cookie," Kevin joked.

The doctor frowned at Kevin before continuing. "We've started an IV. He's badly dehydrated. I've given him an antiemetic. Next, we'll begin insulin therapy, along with an insulin-resistance medicine, and see if we can get that blood sugar headed in the right direction."

"Our sister has diabetes," I said, regaining my focus. "She got it as a teenager."

"That might explain why your brother's blood sugar isn't responding to his present medications." Dr. Stein continued with a lengthy explanation about protease inhibitors and multiple therapies. He added something about insulin resistance as a result of AIDS medications, but he lost me early into the lecture.

I knew Stephen would want a full explanation when he finally returned to his old self, and I tried desperately to remember the details for him. When it comes to medi-speak, however, I'm lost. Most of the doctor's words floated right over my head. I sometimes wonder if medicos use the language to discourage patients from asking questions. When the doctor wound down, I asked, "Will you keep him here?"

"Overnight, at least." The doctor swung his chair around and began typing at a keyboard beside Stephen's gurney. "It depends on how he responds. We have to stabilize his blood sugar before we can discharge him. With diabetes in the family, this may or may not be related to his antiviral medications. That could make his blood sugar harder to manage.

"Stephen should be feeling better shortly." The doctor finished typing, closed the program and stood to leave, sliding his stethoscope into his jacket pocket. "When he's more alert, I'll get a list of his medicines from him."

Kevin offered his hand. "Thank you, Dr. Stein," he said.

"I'm going to have the nurse start that insulin now," he said, nodding at me as he reached for the curtain separating us from the rest of the emergency area. "I'll leave him right here for an hour or so, and watch to see how his blood sugar reacts. Then I'll write orders and send him upstairs." He disappeared behind the curtain, pulling it closed as he left.

∽ ∽ ∽

Two hours later, Kevin and I started up the highway toward Potter's Hollow. The wind had died down and the snow fell more lightly. In the twin telescopes of the headlights, tiny specks of snow fell quickly, telling me that the temperature had dropped and the worst of the precipitation had passed.

Kevin put the windshield wipers on intermittent, and I counted the beats between swipes, listening for an imaginary melody marked by their rhythm. After about five miles, I broke the silence. "Would you switch cars with me tomorrow? The Jeep would be easier to drive to the hospital."

"You're going to visit him?"

"Of course. Why wouldn't I?"

"It's snowing."

"Oh come on, Kevin. We live in the North Pole. It snows all winter here. I drive everywhere."

"You have piano students tomorrow. He doesn't need you to visit. He's a big boy."

"Where does it say that big boys don't need hospital visits? Besides, he's my brother."

"You can stop reminding me of that. I think I've got that down."

"What's behind all this sudden animosity? I don't understand you. First, you don't want him to come to our house for the holidays, then you don't want him cooking, and now you don't want me to drive to the hospital."

"You can't seem to let go of him, Colleen. He's made choices. Bad choices. The choices have consequences. If you keep trying to rescue

him from the consequences, how can you expect him to want to
change? And that's the goal isn't it? Having him change?"

I felt my hackles rise. "What makes you so holy? Haven't you ever
made any bad choices?"

"Of course. I'm not saying that."

"And for every one of your bad choices, you've suffered through
the consequences?"

"Yes, pretty much." Kevin dimmed his headlights as an oncoming
car came around a curve in the highway. "Actually, yes, I have. It's
been good for me. I've learned from the consequences of my mistakes."

Against my bidding, memories came flooding into my vision. Doctors. A hospital. Canned music. Bright lights. A tiny cry piercing the
night. I pushed the images of my secret away, refusing to surrender to
the power of those emotions. "I don't think so, Kevin. We've all made
mistakes. Every one of us. And fortunately, most of us don't have to
take a death sentence for them."

"But your brother hasn't made just one mistake. He's made a series
of bad choices. He's chosen a lifestyle. If you rescue him, how can he
learn?"

"We aren't talking about a puppy here, Kevin. He's a person. My
brother. Nothing I do will ever keep him from suffering the consequence of his actions, his choices. This thing, this disease, is going to
kill him. Don't you think that's consequence enough? I'm talking
about compassion. Love. Don't you get the difference?"

"But what about our family? Are you willing to risk our kids?"

"What risk? What are you talking about?"

"The virus. He was cooking food at our house, Colleen." I glanced
at Kevin and saw him squeeze the steering wheel, stretch his fingers,
and squeeze again. "Food. Mucus. Virus. It makes me nervous."

"You're afraid we'll be exposed to the virus?"

For some minutes, Kevin didn't answer. "And what about his
influence on the kids? He's gay, Colleen. Aren't you afraid of having
him influence Travis?"

"Three-girls-a-week Travis?" I laughed. "We'd be lucky if it would
slow him down.

"That's not funny." Kevin's voice was serious. "Really. We don't want our kids to adopt the attitude that gay is okay." Kevin sent me a scolding look. "It's the gay agenda. Get the kids to see homosexuality as an acceptable choice in life."

"I don't know anything about agendas, Kevin. I don't even care about agendas. You keep talking about consequences. I can't see anything healthier for our kids than observing firsthand the results of the gay lifestyle. AIDS. Wasting. Diabetes. Medicines. Hospitals. Fatigue. There it is, for all to see, and it isn't pretty. It doesn't make me believe the propaganda. I don't think it will convince Travis to consider the lifestyle." I reached out to take Kevin's hand. "I trust our kids. I think they're smart enough to see that."

Kevin was silent for a long while, and I went back to keeping the beat of the windshield wipers. This time, I let my mind play with parallel rhythms, tapping my fingers on the leather upholstery. I began thinking about our kids and the great adults they seemed to be growing into.

Silently, I thanked the Lord for the work he'd begun in them. And I wondered...

My secret poked its nose into my thoughts again. It took me to the little safe that sat on the highest shelf in my side of our walk-in closet. I've never worried about the safe, never even hidden it, though I've always kept it locked. In all these years, I've never opened the safe, never relived the secrets hidden there.

But on that night, to the rhythm of the windshield wipers, in the company of my husband's bewildered silence, I allowed myself to go through the contents. To think about the photo of the baby they'd named Jonathan. My last letter from the people he would call "Mom" and "Dad." And for the millionth time in more than twenty years, I allowed myself to wonder.

What would Kevin say tonight if he knew the whole truth? What consequence would he believe that I should pay?

∼ ∼ ∼

The next morning, Friday, I finished my piano lessons, did some laundry, and cleaned up the mess from the cookies. I couldn't shake the sadness I felt over Kevin's rejection of my brother. I hadn't seen this side of Kevin before, and though I thought I understood his position, I grieved over the obvious pride I heard in his voice.

It was as if Kevin saw his own sins as less horrible than Stephen's.

For lunch, I drank a tall glass of milk and ate two large frosted cookies. After all, depression is best treated with large doses of refined white sugar. The phone rang before I could finish the second cookie.

Stephen's voice came over the line, "Colleen, I'm glad I caught you," he said. "I'm wondering if you're coming to visit today?"

"I was just about to get in the car."

"Great," he said, with obvious relief. "Could you go up in the guest bedroom and find that little duffel bag I brought to the house? I'd love to have it here."

"Where did you leave it?"

"I think it's beside the rocking chair in the corner."

"You got it. I should be there in about forty minutes."

He thanked me, and I was about to hang up when he interrupted me. "Oh yeah, and Colleen, could you bring a few of those cookies?"

"Are you supposed to be eating sugar?"

"I don't care; I'm starved. Sneak 'em in if you have to. Please?"

"I'll think about it; no promises though."

I finished my afternoon snack and wrapped a single frosted Christmas tree in saran wrap. I found the duffel bag exactly as Stephen described, dropped the cookie inside, and drove to the hospital to visit Stephen. I found him lying in a private room on the third floor.

Still tethered to an intravenous line, my brother had nothing to entertain himself but the television. Just as I stepped in the room, I heard him change the channel with the remote. "Hey," he said. "You made good time. Roads must be clear."

He lay on a deep stack of pillows, his bed partially elevated, his face freshly shaven, his curly hair tousled around his head. Normally, Stephen never let his hair curl in public. He hadn't had time or energy to stretch the curls out with a brush and hair dryer.

"The plows take good care of the highway," I said, leaning down to kiss him before dropping my coat over the back of the chair. "Did I just catch you listening to Christian television?"

He switched off the television. "A Billy Graham crusade," he admitted. "I had to change the channel. It was too much."

I ignored the comment. "Here's your duffel bag," I said, plopping it down on the bed beside him. I caught his hand as he reached for the bag and squeezed it. "How are you feeling today?"

"Much better. No nausea. I guess I should have known I was in trouble. Especially now that I think about it. I've been thirsty and hungry ever since the play. Water went through me like I was made of sand." He shook his head. "Stupid, huh?"

"We rarely see things in our own lives very clearly." I put my knitting bag on the floor next to the chair and sat down.

A knock on the door drew our attention. A short man with salt-and-pepper hair and blue wire-rimmed glasses paused on the threshold. He wore a long white coat over a blue shirt and dark tie. His perfectly trimmed silver moustache gave the impression of a man consumed with meticulous order. "I'm Dr. Erickson," he said, smiling broadly. "Dr. Stein in the ER asked me to come see you."

"Come in," Stephen said.

I stood up, sliding my chair toward the doctor. "Please. Sit down."

"No thank you," he said, smiling at me. "I just wanted to come in and talk about your case for a few moments."

"Do you want me to leave, Stephen?" I touched the rails of the bed, looking into his eyes.

"No," Stephen said. "Dr. Erickson, this is my twin sister, Colleen."

"A twin, eh?" The doctor shook my hand. "Not often that I get to meet a twin," he said. "You live here in Wenatchee?"

"In Potter's Hollow."

"Ah. And you, Stephen, where do you live?"

"I'm over from Seattle."

"So you don't mind discussing your medical condition in front of your sister?"

"Not at all," Stephen said. "We're past that, I think."

I sat down, folded my hands on my lap, and waited politely for the discussion to begin. Dr. Erickson held open the cover of the hospital chart. "I'm an internist," he began. "I specialize in the treatment of diabetes and other endocrine disorders."

Stephen nodded.

"I see that you've been managing your diabetes with drugs that reduce insulin resistance."

"My doctor thought that the protease inhibitors caused the blood-sugar problems."

"Not an unreasonable conclusion. Are you still taking the PI's?"

"Yes. We're trying to manage without quitting them. It should be on the chart. I told the nurse all about my drugs this morning."

"Oh yes, let's see." The doctor flipped several pages in the chart and came to the nurse's handwritten notes. "Hmm," he said, fingering his mustache as he read. "Yes. The diabetes educator, I see her notes. It's all right here. Well, we know for sure that the condition hasn't reversed itself with your other medication." He flipped a page in the chart. "And to be honest, we still don't have your sugars down where I'd like to see them. You know, of course, that we've been adding insulin to manage the higher numbers."

He looked up at Stephen and continued, "At some point, I'd like to do some specific tests to challenge your pancreas. I'd like to get a better picture of where you are in the disease. When was the last time you saw your infectious-disease specialist?"

Stephen glanced at me. "Not since the last time I was in the hospital."

The doctor's eyebrows shot up. "No follow-up?"

"It didn't seem necessary, " Stephen said, shrugging.

"Try me."

"Well, my insurance coverage covers only 70 percent of my bills up to twenty-one thousand in a single calendar year." Stephen said. He seemed embarrassed and frustrated, the wrinkles on his forehead underscoring the emotion in his voice. He spread his hands. "I can't even afford the other 30 percent. I figured I could see the doctor at my next regular appointment and save the co-payment."

"Reasonable," Dr. Erickson nodded. "But not wise." He looked back at the chart, again flipping through the pages of notes. It seemed impossible to me that a hospital could generate so much paper in less than twenty-four hours. He closed the chart and put it down on the bedside table. "I have an idea," he said. "I don't think you'll like it, but I'll give it a shot anyway."

"Go ahead," Stephen said.

"I think you should take the time to visit another infectious-disease specialist. We have one who's new in town. She's from Tennessee, trained at Johns Hopkins, came here because she wanted to get away from the huge populations of AIDS in the city."

"She'd be thrilled to see me."

"I don't think you'll be much of a surprise. There are far more folks struggling with this out here than you know." The doctor looked at me. "Even in little towns like Potter's Hollow," he said. "This disease is no secret any more. We're seeing it everywhere."

The doctor leaned down, resting his elbows on the end of the bed. "I know that with AIDS, there are as many treatment plans as there are doctors to prescribe them. There are lots of variations, new opinions, new combinations. You may have more options than you thought."

Dr. Erickson straightened up and pulled a prescription pad from his pocket. "I'd do it if I were you," he said. "I know it's hard to start over again. The history, the tests. It's all very exhausting."

"Very expensive," Stephen interrupted.

"But if it changes the course of the disease, it's worth it." Doctor Erickson printed on the pad. "You'll find her over on Benson across from the post office."

With that, the doctor washed his hands and began what looked to be a routine check of Stephen's heart and lungs. He wrote more notes in the chart and shook hands again with Stephen. "I enjoyed meeting you, Colleen," he said. Washing his hands again, he left the room.

"So, what did you think?" I asked Stephen. "He seemed nice. Maybe we should go see another doctor."

"Don't kid yourself," Stephen said, bitterness in his voice. He picked up the remote control and turned the television on. "I'm not going to go see anyone else. I'm not going to spend a month's wages just to find out that they've done everything they can do."

The next morning, Saturday, marked the first weekend in December. It was the day of our church's annual Christmas luncheon, where I'd accompany Jackie on the jazz solo we'd been working on.

I planned to arrive early so that she could run through a verse or two in the fellowship hall before the women began arriving. Our rehearsal would give the sound team a chance to set up microphones and check monitors before the actual performance.

In spite of my full schedule, I got up early and snuck over to visit Stephen in the hospital. He looked much better to my unprofessional eyes, and he told me his blood sugars seemed to be responding to the new treatment regimen. I noticed that his intravenous line had been removed, though a small plug remained attached to the skin. I asked about it.

"They left it in, in case I don't do as well as we hoped. I'm supposed to be drinking like a man hiking though Death Valley."

"I can only stay a few minutes this morning," I said from my usual bedside chair.

"Then let's make the most of it." Stephen sat up and swung his feet over the side of the bed. "I'd like to go for a walk." He slipped socks onto his feet and stood up, grabbing a striped robe from the end of his bed. Though his hair had seen better days, Stephen looked strong and energetic. I rejoiced in the improvement.

"Are you sure you should?" I jumped out of my chair and grabbed my purse, hurrying to catch up with him.

"They're my nurses, not my parents," he said disappearing into the hallway. "How about coffee?"

"I don't know if I have time," I said, checking my watch.

"Make time." Stephen punched the button on the elevator door with an intensity that surprised me.

I saluted. "Yes sir, anything you say, sir."

As the elevator doors opened on the basement floor, I smelled the delicious scents of bacon and freshly brewed coffee. We crossed the hall and stepped into the serving area of the hospital cafeteria. "Would you like breakfast?" Stephen asked. "I'm hungry again."

I tried to ignore the warning marked by his constant hunger. Stephen's blood sugar was not mine to worry about. "No thanks, just coffee."

We moved through the line behind two women wearing tropical-print scrubs. The women moved slowly, filling their trays with breakfast foods, until I could hardly resist the siren aromas of sweet rolls and sausages. Instead, I filled a twelve-ounce cup with coffee. Stephen put a glazed old fashioned on a paper plate and chose raspberry tea.

At the cash register, I realized with amusement that though Stephen had invited me to the cafeteria, I was the only one with any cash available. "Smooth move, brother," I chided him. "Invite me for breakfast knowing that I'd have to pay."

"What do you expect? I'm a dying man."

It was too soon to laugh at such maudlin humor. Though I smiled on the outside, pain squeezed my heart. "Always the mooch," I told him. "Just like that first year in college."

"You wanted to do my laundry."

"Right. I could hardly hold myself back." We chose a table by the window and I sat down across from him. Stephen added two packages of sugar and a carton of cream to his tea. Stirring gently, he looked outside for a moment and then focused again on his tea.

"So, have you thought any more about seeing another doctor?"

He shook his head. "I won't do it over here. It doesn't make sense."

"Because you live too far away?"

"That, and I'd get better care in Seattle where there are more of us."

I nodded, disappointed. In my mind, I'd already blown Dr. Erickson's recommendation completely out of proportion. I saw the opinion of another doctor as the perfect opportunity, another chance to save Stephen's life. "Will you see someone new when you go back?"

He tipped his head, stirring the tea again, a gesture I was coming to recognize as Stephen's way of staying uncommitted. "I really wanted to talk about something else, Colleen. Something important."

"Okay," I said, bracing myself. Though I did not know what he was about to say, my stomach did a little flip-flop and I began to worry.

"Yesterday, after you left, a man came to visit me," Stephen said. "He introduced himself as Dwayne Charboneau, the pastor at your church."

It seemed quite incredible to me that Dwayne had come to visit Stephen. As far as I knew, Dwayne didn't even know that my brother was in Potter's Hollow, let alone that he had been admitted to the hospital. "How did he know you were here?"

"I was going to ask you the same question," Stephen said.

"I didn't call him."

"He wouldn't tell me who sent him."

"You asked?" I couldn't believe that the visit had gone that badly. "Dwayne is a nice guy. Why are you so upset?"

"Because he shouldn't have come, Colleen." With his cup between his two hands, Stephen turned the base in tiny circles. "He said a lot. Way too much, actually. He'd hardly been in my room two minutes before he launched into the dangers of the sin of homosexuality.

"Pastor Dwayne waxed eloquent about all the places in the Bible where it is expressly forbidden." Stephen shook his head as if he still couldn't believe the pastor's behavior. "I mean the guy doesn't even know me, and he's hitting me with all this stuff. He never even stopped to ask if what he'd heard about me was true. He just launched into me, like he hoped to have me cut into little pieces before dinner."

"Are you sure? Maybe you just misunderstood him?"

Stephen's eyes filled with tears, and I knew the encounter had humiliated him. Along with brokenness, I saw anger, a deep rage tightening the muscles of his jaw, narrowing his eyes.

"I'm so sorry," I said. "I've never seen Dwayne do anything like that. Our family loves him. Even the kids." The kind of behavior Stephen described sounded so unlike the pastor we loved.

"I don't care about what a nice guy he is to your family," Stephen said. "You are the only reason I didn't give him a piece of my mind. I mean, the nerve of the guy." Stephen shook his head. "I asked you down here for one reason," Stephen said, poking the Formica table with his fingers. "I want you to be absolutely certain he never ever comes near me again. Because if he does, I won't even try to restrain myself."

Though I promised Stephen that I would take care of the problem, I had no idea how to do it. In the silence that followed, my mind whirled with questions. In the first place, I didn't know who had told Dwayne about my brother. I considered Kevin and then dismissed the idea. Stephen was the kind of brother-in-law Kevin would like to keep secret.

Who would think it their duty to pass that information along to our pastor? And beyond that, how could I call my pastor and tell him to leave my brother alone? How could I tell him that his visit may have effectively set any evangelistic effort back into the Dark Ages?

And then again, did I dare trust Stephen's evaluation of the visit? Maybe my brother had overreacted.

As I drove back to the church at Potter's Hollow, these thoughts gnawed at me, leaving the coffee lying in my stomach like a pond of industrial pollution.

I arrived at church a full hour before the luncheon began, dressed in my best black wool pantsuit, my performance face on, music in hand, ready to play. In the fellowship hall, ladies bustled around placing centerpieces, setting tables, and arranging name cards.

The smell of chocolate drew me to the kitchen, where I found a whole team of my friends baking caramel fudge brownies for dessert. I managed to lick a spoon before getting kicked out of the kitchen.

To my surprise, the grand piano had not been moved into the fellowship hall. Instead, I had only the electronic keyboard from the sanctuary. I'm not fond of electronic keyboards; the touch is very different from a regular piano, and the vast array of electronic voices—even though they are adjustable—provide too many variables for my taste.

I put on the earphones, adjusting the sound, playing through segments again and again in different combinations of voices, at different volumes, before saving my final choices in the instrument's memory bank. Satisfied, I took off the earphones and played until Jeff, our sound guy, was happy with the volume levels.

While the women put the final touches on the tables, I accompanied Jackie though a single verse and chorus of her song, and when we finished we both escaped to the church foyer, happy to greet and visit with old friends.

When we re-entered the fellowship hall, I could hardly believe the transformation. With the lights turned low, candles glowed from holly centerpieces. Red napkins accented angelic white tablecloths. Tiny clear lights, swathed in ivy and white tulle, wrapped every post in the room. The room looked enchanting.

Nearly 150 ladies enjoyed a luncheon of salads and breads, followed by hot brownies resting under scoops of homemade ice cream. While the women chatted, I tried hard to keep my mind in the room. Over and over, I found myself thinking about Stephen and the hurt he'd revealed at the hospital.

After lunch, the women sang Christmas carols, which I accompanied on the electronic keyboard. Then it was time for Jackie's solo.

When she finished, the applause was spontaneous and generous; I deemed our work a complete success. She gestured to me, and I made a small bow before returning to my seat.

And then something happened that made my stressful morning much, much worse.

The women's committee had scheduled another solo after Jackie's, a Christmas piece to introduce the speaker. The hostess introduced the solo, and the singer stepped up to the podium. I happened to glance at the keyboard, where another woman took my place. As I watched, she did the most amazing thing.

She switched off the power to the keyboard. While everyone waited for the music to begin, this woman removed a sanitary cloth from a small foil container and proceeded to wipe down the keys. With deliberate precision, she wiped every key—both black and white—from high C to low A. She didn't miss a single one.

At last satisfied, she turned on the power and began the introduction to the solo.

I could hardly believe my eyes. In all the years I've played the piano, I've never seen anything like it. Even in my home, where all winter long, child after child sits down to play at my grand piano, I've never done anything like it.

I take that back.

Once, during a particularly bad flu season, I had a fourth grader sneeze through an entire lesson. Though I offered her tissue, she'd repeatedly wiped her nose with her fingers whenever she came to a rest in the music. Then, undisturbed, she would place her slimy little fingers on the keys and continue playing as if nothing had happened.

I wiped the piano with alcohol after she left the house.

But this woman's behavior seemed to me the most ignorant, most foolish display of selfishness I'd ever encountered. I could hardly control my anger.

While the soloist sang of a virgin birth and a Savior's love, I fumed. By the time the speaker came to the podium, I had worked myself into a froth. I never heard her speech. Instead, I used the time to write a speech of my own. One I would never deliver.

As soon as the speaker finished, I fished through my purse for my car keys, anxious to leave before I said something I would deeply regret. Instead of my keys, I picked up my cell phone and turned on the power. It started beeping.

Voice messages.

Generally, though I've never confessed this to my children, I don't listen to voice messages. For the most part the message is out of date by the time I hear it. But for some reason, on this particular Saturday, I walked through double doors into the quiet of the office wing and dialed the number for my voice mail.

I listened through four messages before I heard the one that made my heart skip a beat. Kevin's voice, low and somber, asked me to call home immediately. My hand shook slightly as I pushed auto dial, and I tried to imagine simple explanations for the message. But even as I dialed, I knew this was no ordinary call.

"Kevin? It's me. We just finished."

"Oh good. I hoped you'd call soon."

"What is it? What do you need?"

"Colleen, the hospital called."

"Okay." As I waited for the rest of the message, the power of those words sucked the air from my lungs.

"It's Stephen, Colleen. The hospital wants us to get over there right away. They wouldn't give me any information over the phone."

Since I had the Jeep at church, Kevin agreed to drive my car over to meet me. I put my phone away and leaned against the wall, needing something to hold me up. I ran my fingers through my hair. *What now?* I wondered. *What more could possibly go wrong?*

I'd just seen Stephen that morning. He'd looked fine. Angry, but fine. He'd given me no indication that anything was wrong. I took a deep breath and walked to the water cooler outside the receptionist's office, where I filled a paper cup. After all, until I knew exactly what had happened, there was no use worrying about it, not yet.

In spite of my own wise counsel and the cool winter weather, I felt the silk blouse under my suit jacket grow damp with perspiration.

I tossed the paper cup and backed through the double doors, buttoning my wool dress coat as I entered the hallway outside the fellowship hall. Though most of the women had already left, Jackie stood in the doorway, engaged in deep conversation with one of the women on the planning committee. She saw me, and without appearing to lose a word of the conversation, signaled that I wait for her.

I didn't feel up to it.

I walked to the outer doors and leaned against the side window, staying warm while I kept an eye on the parking lot. I heard her steps on the floor behind me.

"Thanks for playing, Colleen," Jackie said. "It turned out well, no matter how much you groaned about making it work."

I glanced at her and nodded. "Thanks."

She looked over my shoulder to the parking lot, and back again to my face. "Something wrong?"

I shrugged. "Long day."

She leaned up against the window so that her body blocked my view of the lot. "Not yet. It's not even two in the afternoon. What's going on?"

"I can't even begin to tell you," I said. "Stephen is mad at me about a visit from the pastor."

"Pastor Charboneau?"

I nodded, turning to lean on the wall by the window. "I don't even know how he knows about Stephen. And did you see Elaine Gregory wipe the keys of the Roland after I played? Did you see that?"

Jackie put her finger to her lips while glancing over her shoulder. "Shh. I don't know if she's left yet."

"I don't care if she's still here."

"Trust me. You do," Jackie said. "She just doesn't know. She's ignorant, not unkind."

"I don't even care." I turned back to the window. "I have to watch for Kevin."

"Kevin? Something wrong with your car?"

"I drove his car today." I saw my Honda turn into the parking lot, my beloved Kevin at the wheel, bundled in his favorite fleece-lined denim jacket. "No," I said, slinging my purse higher on my shoulder and bending to pick up my music briefcase. "Kevin is meeting me here and we're taking his car to the hospital. I think something has happened to Stephen."

Something passed over Jackie's face, and I expected her to express sorrow over Stephen's latest distress. "I told him," Jackie said,

reaching out to catch my shoulder as she spoke. "I told Pastor Charboneau. I asked him to visit Stephen. I didn't know he'd be unkind."

I stared at her, unable to respond. Why would she feel the need to
interfere? What gave her the right to make such a request on my
behalf? I stepped around Jackie. "We can talk later," I said. "I have to
go now."

~ ~ ~

At the hospital, we went immediately to the nurses' station on
Stephen's floor. A plump woman with perfectly curled blond hair
approached the counter. The name on her tag read LaDelle Lewis.
"May I help you?"

I glanced at Kevin. "We had a call from the hospital," I explained.
"Someone requested that we come right over."

"And you are?"

I took a deep breath and started again. "I'm Colleen Payton. My
brother is Stephen MacLaughlin. Someone here called my home and
asked me to come the hospital."

"You didn't get a name?"

Kevin spoke up. "I took the call. They just said that we needed to
come here immediately."

LaDelle turned to her computer and typed in my brother's name.
"M-C-L-A," she spelled as she typed the letters.

I corrected her spelling.

"Oh yes, he's moved to the second floor." She pointed to the elevator behind us. "Down one floor. The nurses' station will be to the
right at the end of the hall."

"Why was he moved?" I asked. "Has something happened?" I felt
panic rising in my chest, and deliberately lowered my voice to ask
again. "Has something happened to my brother?"

"I'm sorry, Ms. Payton. I'm not a nurse. I wouldn't be able to tell
you anything. You'll get all the information you need from the nurses
on the second floor."

"Why was he moved?"

"You'll have to speak with the nurse in charge of his care."

"What about his doctor? Why can't I speak with his doctor?"

"I'm sorry, Ms. Payton. I'm sure the nurses downstairs…"

"Thank you, Ms. Lewis." I felt Kevin's hand pressing gently on the small of my back, turning me away from the counter and back toward the elevator. "Come on, Colleen. Let's not waste any more of the lady's time."

When the elevator doors closed, I pounced on him. "Why did you do that, Kevin?"

"You weren't going to get anything from her. We might as well go where we can get the information we need."

"I can't believe this. They call us to the hospital, but they don't tell us where to go or who to speak to."

"Colleen, try to relax," Kevin said, putting his arm around me and holding me close. "I answered the phone in the garage. If I'd been thinking, I would have gotten more details, a name, a unit—something—it's my fault. We'll know more in a minute."

"It isn't your fault," I said, leaning into him, wrapping both arms around his waist. A lone tear made its way down my cheek and I wiped my face on Kevin's flannel shirt.

When the elevator doors opened, we hurried to the end of the hall, where we found the nurses' station hidden behind two automatic doors. Apparently, the clerk on duty controlled the doors from behind a partial glass window.

But I didn't have to speak to the woman behind the glass. I knew everything I needed to know about my brother, simply from the words printed on those two doors. In fact, those words told me more than I ever wanted to know.

As I reached for his hand, Kevin read them out loud. "Cardiac Care Unit."

Sixteen

We announced ourselves to the clerk, who promptly admitted us through the electronic doors. Inside, patient rooms spread from the nurses' station like spokes on a hub, sliding patio-style doors providing entry into each room. From her chair at the desk, a nurse could supervise the welfare of several patients at the same time.

I found the array of patients and families and professionals distracting. My attention was focused not on the clerk behind the desk, but on the faces beyond the glass, in search of my brother. Kevin, always the single-minded one, waited patiently while the clerk telephoned someone about Stephen.

I heard the doors of the elevator open and turned in time to see a woman dressed in solid scrubs and a white jacket step toward the security doors. She swiped her ID card through the slot and the doors swung open.

"Hello, I'm Candice Loper," she said, extending one hand to Kevin as she stepped toward us. "I called you this morning about Stephen."

Kevin took the hand. "I'm Kevin Payton. And this is my wife, Colleen." He pointed at me. "Stephen is Colleen's brother." Candice, a woman of medium height, heavy build, and dark complexion smiled. With dark eyes under heavy lids and a thick nose, this woman would not have won a beauty pageant. Still, something about her made me trust her immediately.

"My twin actually," I said, shaking her hand.

"Of course. I see the resemblance." She directed us down the hall. "Why don't we step into my office, and I'll fill you in on what's happening."

We followed her around the corner to a small office adjoining the nurses' station. The sign outside listed Candice Loper as the cardiac care charge nurse. "Have a seat," she said, gesturing to two wire chairs opposite her desk.

In the tiny office, one wall displayed her college degrees. On another wall, a poster sporting a nurse in an intensive-care setting had a caption that read, "Nursing: The science of medicine dominated by the art of caring."

Obediently, Kevin and I sat down. As I did, Kevin reached out to take my hand. Neither of us removed our coats.

She glanced down at our hands. "First, I should tell you both to relax. Though the situation is serious, I don't want you to worry excessively."

"What's this all about?" Kevin asked.

"Dr. Erickson, the internist in charge of your brother's care, gave me permission to call you. He's asked another physician, Dr. Ken Otta, to come in and evaluate your brother. It seems that your brother had some kind of cardiac episode here in the hospital this morning."

"What kind of cardiac episode?" I asked. Kevin's hand gave mine a gentle warning squeeze. Careful, Colleen, the squeeze said. Stay calm.

"I wasn't with him at the time," she answered, "so I'll have to rely on the nurse's notes. Apparently, Stephen has been up walking quite a bit today. At some point, he took a shower." Candice lifted a piece of paper from the desk and read it before continuing. "Apparently, your brother's nurse responded to the bathroom call button. She found your brother dizzy and lightheaded. He needed assistance getting back to bed.

"The nurse recorded his vital signs, checked his blood sugar, and called his physician. Dr. Erickson ordered some blood tests and asked Dr. Otta to see Stephen immediately."

"So what was it? What happened?"

"We can't say for certain." Candice folded her hands across the papers on her desk, perfectly manicured nails accenting strong, relaxed hands. "His blood work indicates that he may have had a slight heart attack."

"May have?" Kevin asked.

"Dr. Otta ordered Stephen to be transferred up to the CCU. He's ordered more tests. In the meantime, he wants to keep a close eye on your brother."

"I don't understand," I said, still confused.

"We don't know exactly what happened. But Stephen asked me to call you," Candice Loper continued. "He was worried when he moved into the unit—not that worry is unusual here—but he wanted you to know exactly what had happened."

"What's next?" Kevin asked.

"When we have his test results, the doctor may schedule a procedure for tomorrow morning. In the meantime, Stephen has a heart monitor and is under restricted activity. We're monitoring his blood sugar, his heart rhythms, his blood work, and vital signs. If anything changes, he'll be close to the help he needs.

"You can call me or the nurse on duty twenty-four hours a day to check on him. Of course, you can phone him or visit any time you'd like. Please keep your visits short. We don't want to tire him."

Smiling, she stood up. "Now, I'm guessing that you'd like to visit your brother?"

Stephen was lying on his side, resting against a mound of pillows, his eyes closed, his face slack. "He's sleeping," Kevin whispered. "Maybe we shouldn't wake him. We could go downstairs for lunch."

Resting my hands on his bed rails, I scanned the equipment behind his bed. Tiny high-pitched bleeps accompanied lines darting across green monitors. A line dripped fluid into his arm. Twin tubes entered Stephen's nostrils—oxygen, I guessed from the sign prohibiting smoking. Underneath his gown, I made out the clear delineation of devices connecting him to the heart monitor.

I felt worry climb onto my shoulders, squeezing my throat from behind, like a deadly mugger in an urban alley. I tried to shake it off.

"We can come back later," Kevin suggested.

"You go on down to the cafeteria. I'd like to sit with him."

"You sure? I don't have to go."

I nodded. "I'm fine." I spotted a chair on the other side of the bed and pointed to it. "I've eaten. I'll just wait with him."

Kevin squeezed my shoulders and gave me a kiss. "Be back in a few minutes then."

I nodded, watching my husband as he crossed to the automatic doors by the nurses' station. I stepped around the bed. Stephen stirred and opened his eyes. I counted the long seconds it took for him to recognize me.

"Hey," he said.

"Hey yourself."

He stretched slightly. "This isn't turning out to be such a great day."

"Tell me about it."

He smiled. "I'm sorry. I never meant to drag you into this."

"Stephen, we got dragged into one another's lives at the very beginning. I don't know why it happened, but I kinda like it that way. Don't you try to change anything now." I tousled his hair and then turned to pull the chair close to the bed. "How're you feeling?"

"Tired. I've had an ultrasound and an EKG. I've been carted all over the hospital by kids Mallory's age. I've been pushed into walls, caught in elevator doors, and I nearly froze to death waiting in the hall for someone to take me back upstairs. Can you believe this? A tropical-weight hospital gown under a single sheet."

"Hard to get good help these days."

"No kidding." Stephen rolled over on his back and brought both hands to his face, rubbing his eyes. "I hate sleeping in the middle of the day. Makes me so groggy."

"You need the rest."

"Rest isn't going to make any difference here."

"Sure it is. Your body has taken a beating in the last three days. Give yourself a break."

"I can't afford it."

"Of course you can. It's your winter vacation. You don't have students. No obligations. You can take all the break you need."

"You don't get it, do you? I can't afford to be here. I'm up to my ears in debt." He pulled himself into a sitting position. "It won't make any difference if I get over this episode or not, because there will always be another, and another and another."

I glanced at the monitor behind him, as if I expected the machine to reflect his grouchy frustration. "You're just tired."

"I'm worn out," he said, closing his eyes again. "And I don't mean today."

Who wouldn't be discouraged fighting such an invincible beast? I tried to think of some way to lighten the mood. "Stephen, did I tell you that I had a ladies' luncheon this morning?"

Without opening his eyes, he shook his head, and I launched into an animated and largely exaggerated accounting of the women's meeting. I didn't tell Stephen about the piano incident, and I chose to leave out Jackie's confession about Pastor Charboneau. "It was beautiful," I said. "But there wasn't enough food. I guess they had more ladies than they expected. I've never been able to manage on those rabbit lunches that women are supposed to enjoy."

"Hungry, huh?"

"You know better than that. I'm always hungry."

"How did your friend's solo turn out?"

"It was beautiful. I thought about you while she was singing. I wished you could have heard it. You would have enjoyed it."

"Maybe," he admitted. An alarm began beeping at the head of the bed, and I stood up to see what might have happened.

"What's going on in here?" A small-framed, muscular man in pale green scrubs entered Stephen's room, scanning the dials above the bed. His gaze settled on the IV pole. "Ah. You're drip is out." He flipped a switch and the alarm went off. "I'll be right back."

When the nurse left, Stephen asked, "Did Candice Loper call you?"

"We met with her as soon as we got to the hospital."

"What did she say?"

I gave Stephen a condensed version of the report. "Do you like your cardiologist?"

"He's okay. Just another specialist in a long line of specialists."

"Come on, Stephen. These guys are here to help you."

"You don't understand, Colleen. Some things aren't fixable."

"What do you mean? You don't know what happened this morning. Maybe it was the diabetes, or fatigue, or dehydration."

"Not true." He sighed. "They have the results of a blood test that implies muscle damage. I've known it was coming for a long time."

"What?"

"The medicines. They change your blood lipids."

"Lipids?"

"Cholesterol. I have scary cholesterol levels. Like someone living on eggs and cheese and steaks four times a day." He ran his hand through his hair. "I knew this would happen eventually." I tried to take it all in, all the things Stephen faced. Diabetes, heart disease, AIDS, side effects. By the time the nurse returned with another bag of fluids, I'd lost track of the list.

His voice sounded heavy, discouraged, and I wished that I had some magic wand to wave over my brother's disposition. If I could, I would have given him a full dose of fight. I took Stephen's hand, squeezing it gently. "You know, I'm here for you. Whatever you need, you can count on me."

"I knew you'd say that. I didn't want you to have to do this. It's too hard. No one should have to love someone going through this. Don't you see that? Can't you see? It's why I tried to stay away for so long."

And in a rare moment of truth, I answered from my heart. "And it didn't work, did it? So don't ever try that again."

The edges of his lips softened in an almost smile.

"The nurse told us not to tire you. So I have to take off. But I'm wondering if you need anything? Is there something I can bring you? A book? Some clothes? Slippers?"

He shook his head, opening his eyes again. "You've done more than you should already." He paused, and then continued. "Well, there is one thing."

"What?"

"Would you bring me the duffel bag from the closet there?"

Until then, I hadn't noticed the locker-sized storage space behind my chair. I shoved the chair out of the way and opened the locker. His robe hung on a single hook inside, the red duffel bag on the floor. I placed it on the bed.

He unzipped the bag and brought out what appeared to be a writing tablet covered in black paper. While I wondered what he was up to, he flipped the paper over and ran a finger around the edge, separating the cover from the tablet. Then Stephen handed the paper to me. "I did this for you yesterday. I meant to give it to you when I saw you next, but I got a little carried away this morning. Guess I forgot."

I looked down at the paper, surprised to discover a perfect image of the Icicle River as seen from the bench where Stephen and I rested on our afternoon walk. Somehow, Stephen had managed to use watercolor to convey the warm apricot of winter sun, and the glow of sunlight on snow. At the same time, the sketch perfectly captured the dark and swiftly moving river and the untouched mantle of fresh snow on the trees nearby.

I'd never seen anything so lovely. "How on earth did you do this?"

"After you left yesterday."

"Not when, Stephen. How? I didn't know you could paint."

"You don't know very much about me."

I reached over the bed rail to hug my brother. "It's beautiful. I can't thank you enough."

"I think maybe you already have."

CHAPTER
Seventeen

Early Sunday morning I called the hospital to check on Stephen. The nurse told me the doctor had already come by. "They've scheduled a coronary angioplasty for three o'clock this afternoon," she said.

"Do you have the results of yesterday's tests?"

"They haven't been dictated yet. But the procedure is a sure indication that they found some blockage in the heart."

I wished I understood more about his condition. Unanswered questions had swirled through my dreams during the dark hours of the night. They shook me awake at the first sign of dawn. How much blockage had the doctors found? Did they know the extent of the damage? I sighed; she'd given me all the information she had.

"When will he go to surgery?"

"I suspect he'll go downstairs around one-thirty."

"Will they discharge him today?"

"That I do know," she said. "The doctor left orders to transfer him back to his room in CCU. He's going to spend at least one more night with us."

"Why not send him home?"

"His blood sugar continues to have wide swings. And of course, infection is a serious concern because of both his diabetes and his HIV status. We'll keep a close eye on him overnight."

"Of course," I agreed. "Could you transfer me to the telephone at Stephen's bedside?"

After a series of clicks, Stephen picked up the phone. "Good morning, kiddo," I said with as much cheer as I could muster.

He laughed. "Kiddo? I'm forty-two."

"Yeah, but you'll always be younger than me."

"By what, four minutes?"

"Six. Ask Mom."

"No thanks. I'll take your word for it."

"I just wanted you to know that I'll be there for your procedure today."

"Don't, Colleen. It's not that big of a deal. You have family to take care of."

"It's okay. I won't spend the day. But I'll be there before they take you down to the surgery area. And I'll stay until they tuck you back into your own bed."

"I guess I can't stop you."

Though he sang a very independent song, I sensed a lost and discouraged little boy under all that bravado. "No," I agreed. "You can't. I'll be there with bells on."

"I can't wait to see that."

"Take care, Stephen," I said. And then, without even thinking about it, I added, "Do you know how much I love you?"

I think my words surprised him. "Of course I do," he answered. "You don't have to say it." He cleared his throat. "I love you too, sis."

In all this time, I'd been so wrapped up in my own problems that I hadn't discussed Stephen's health with Travis and Mallory. Certainly they suspected something; they'd seen too much to ignore. But they hadn't brought it up. Frankly, until Stephen's confession at the river, I didn't have enough information myself to answer the questions my children were sure to ask.

Kevin and I had been careful not to talk about Stephen in front of the kids. We'd explained our trip to the hospital with Stephen's recent diabetes diagnosis. We hoped this made sense to them. After all, their Aunt Carrie has diabetes.

But that Sunday morning, with Stephen in the hospital, I felt the time had come to lay out the whole situation. I didn't mean to hide things from our kids, and I didn't want them to resent my silence. Reluctantly, Kevin agreed with me.

I went upstairs and told the kids—Mallory through the bathroom door, and Travis in his bedroom—that we were having a sit-down breakfast before church.

Travis looked at me as though I'd announced that we were having ice-cream sundaes. "You made breakfast?" he asked me, astonishment ringing through his voice.

The kids joined Kevin and me in the dining room, asking questions even before they took their seats. "What's all this about?" Travis said. "We never eat breakfast before church."

"And we never get waffles." Mallory took a long drink of orange juice. "I don't know what's up, but I like it."

I passed the serving dish to Travis. "I decided we needed to eat together this morning, so that we could talk about something important."

He stabbed four waffle quarters and dropped them onto his plate, passing the tray to Kevin without comment.

"What's up?" Mallory said.

"We need to talk about Stephen," I began, passing the gravy bowl to Travis. I wondered if the scent of hot blueberry compote would forever remind me of the morning I told the children about Stephen. "I haven't said anything to you guys so far, because I really didn't know much. But your Uncle Stephen is sick."

"You mean diabetes?" Travis spoke with a mouth full of waffles and blueberries.

I glanced at Kevin who nodded almost imperceptibly. "No. There's more than diabetes. Stephen has the virus that causes AIDS."

Both children stopped moving, turning their heads toward me, eyes wide. "I was right. I told you," Mallory said to Travis.

Ignoring her, I continued. "He's been HIV positive for many years. Lately, though, the disease has progressed. He's been sick, and that's the reason behind this last trip to the hospital."

Travis paled. "Uncle Stephen has AIDS?"

I nodded.

"Is he going to die?" Mallory picked up her napkin and brought it to her face, catching the first tears as they spilled over her cheeks.

Reading the distress on my face, Kevin answered for me. "We don't really know what will happen. We do know that the diabetes was probably caused by the medicine he's taking for the HIV virus. It's sort of a side effect, not the disease itself."

Travis seemed caught in disbelief. His head followed our conversation back and forth like the gallery at a tennis match.

"How long will he live?" Mallory's voice trembled, though I saw how hard she tried to maintain control.

"We don't know that either," I answered. "It isn't like it used to be. They have medications. Lots of them. They can help a person live for many years without ever having any symptoms of the disease."

Travis suddenly came alive. "He's staying here? With us? And he has the virus?"

"It isn't contagious that way, if that's what you are worried about."

I could see doubt written all over my son's features, "I don't care if it's contagious." He looked at me. "Stephen's gay, and you're letting him stay with us?" I didn't have to wonder what Travis thought about homosexuality. Disgust rang out in the tone of his voice.

I nodded.

"You knew that? And you let him stay here? What about me?"

"I think I've known for a long time," I admitted. "But you're perfectly safe around him, Travis, if that's what you mean."

My brother does not fit the stereotype of the gay male. He is not effeminate. He does not dress like a Nordstrom's model. Though he is thoughtful and well read, his wrists are not floppy and he does not speak with a lisp. Still, I guess I thought that Travis knew about him. I was wrong.

Neither did I anticipate Travis's antagonism. I heard blame in his voice, saw it in his facial expression. "I don't understand why you would bring him here! He's gay!"

Though I wanted to defend my brother, I tried to remain calm. "I brought him because he is my brother. No matter who he is, or what he's done, I love him." In spite of my effort, tears pooled in my eyes. "You don't stop loving someone just because they make bad choices."

"Mom, he's gay!" Travis put down his fork and shook his head. "How disgusting."

"Oh Travis, get off it. You liked him just fine before you knew he was gay." Mallory's voice rose, and her anger suddenly found a target. "You don't have to be such a homophobe."

I'd hoped that expression would not arise in our family discussion. But nothing had gone as I had hoped. I put my head in my hands and prayed for help. "Mallory, I appreciate what you're trying to say. But I don't think Travis is a homophobe. He's just a little surprised. Maybe a little afraid."

"Like I'm not surprised?" Mallory put her napkin on the table. "Here is this relative that I'm getting to know again. And I love him. And he's here with us. Even if I guessed he had AIDS, I didn't think he was actually dying. How am I supposed to deal with that?"

Kevin, bless his heart, intervened. "I think we should take a break here. What's happening to Stephen is a surprise to all of us. Maybe once we've all had a chance to think about it, we can come back with questions and ideas. Right now, we need to calm down and finish breakfast, or we'll all be late for church." Kevin reached out and gave Travis's shoulder a sympathetic squeeze. We ate the rest of our Sunday breakfast in miserable silence.

As is our custom, Kevin and I took the kids to church, arriving in time for Sunday school. While we attended our usual adult class, Travis joined the high schoolers. Mallory had drawn nursery duty for the month, and she spent the hour before church rocking and changing babies. Nothing makes Mallory happier.

Unlike Mallory, I had trouble being happy that morning. Something had begun to break inside of me, though I couldn't begin to identify it. I'd always prayed for Stephen. But since he came to visit, my quiet time had taken on a new fervor. I tried to read the Bible, but all I could think about was my brother. I tried to pray, but all I could do was plead for my brother's soul. On that morning, I experienced a tenderness and empathy that bordered on hormonal madness.

When I first learned about Stephen's homosexuality, I wished that
he would change. It was a wish based on love, rooted in misunder-
standing. I wanted him to be like me—happy in the mainstream sub-
urban life.

Later I began to see that his lifestyle held him in bondage, locked
in a prison he would not leave. No matter how much he protested,
Stephen was not happy. His orientation, as he called it, left him
empty, wanting something he could never have. I think Stephen first
taught me about the power of sin.

I wanted to give him the key to his own prison. I ached with
unbearable longing for the health of his soul. It was as if I lived in a
parallel universe, watching him from this fourth dimension, wanting
to help him see the whole truth. That something bigger exists. That
eternity is real. That sin brings death.

As the classroom lesson progressed, my mind wandered back to a
time that Stephen had come to visit Kevin and me before we'd moved
to Potter's Hollow. I was pregnant with Mallory at the time and desperate to see my brother saved.

One morning before he got up, I made fresh muffins and boiled
eggs, put Christian music on the stereo, and waited for him to appear.
We ate together, and after we finished, I hit him with what I hoped
would be an irresistible presentation of the gospel. I followed my
evangelistic training to the letter. I even drew a diagram to illustrate
the points.

Unfortunately, Stephen didn't follow the script they'd given me
in evangelism class. He listened quietly, and when I finished he said,
"Don't you think I know what you're doing here Colleen? I hear the
music. I see the setup." His expression was tight, his voice angry. "It's
nothing more than proselytizing. Trying to get me to buy into your
stuff."

He got up from the table, throwing his napkin onto his plate.
"Don't ever do it again. Do you hear me, Colleen? I don't want you
notching your gun with my name. It won't work. I'm not buying."
And with that, my brother stormed from the room.

I felt my face burn with the memory. From that morning on, Stephen completely shut out any mention of spiritual things. Part of me blamed myself. If only I'd done it differently.

In a way, I'd chosen to let go of my desperate concern for Stephen's soul. As he faced this deadly disease, I'd put all my energy into saving his life.

As long as Stephen stayed alive, perhaps someone else could break through the shell encasing his soul.

These were the kinds of aches churning in me on that long and painful Sunday morning. I found myself left with a desperate restlessness that kept me from being fully present in the here and now.

I cried during the opening prayer of class. I cried during the teaching lesson. While everyone else moved their chairs into discussion groups, I slipped out to find more tissue. When I returned, red-eyed and puffy, Kevin leaned over and asked, "What part of your cycle are you in?" I nearly kicked him.

After slogging my way to the choir room, I cried through the choir warm-up. The more I cried, the more tender my heart became, until I began to worry that I wouldn't make it through the worship service without breaking down at the keyboard. My last thoughts before putting my hands on the piano were, *Lord help me; I'm in deep trouble here.*

After the song service, I sat with Kevin, ignoring his curious glances in my direction. Though I tried to concentrate on Dwayne's sermon, a cycle of thoughts presented itself over and over in my mind. Stephen's face, with its expression of humiliation and anger, kept coming back to me. The more I tried to push it away, the more vividly it returned. And behind that would follow the image of the woman wiping the keys of the electronic piano. And behind that, Jackie's face as she confessed calling the pastor about Stephen.

About this time, in the progression of my thinking, the tears would start again, and I would pull another tissue from my purse. Though I was crying on the outside, on the inside I felt anger. Anger at the insensitivity and presumption of the people I considered my family. Anger over lost opportunity with Stephen. Anger over Travis's inconsiderate response. Anger over the humiliation of having someone clean my fingerprints off the keyboard. Anger that the key-boardist believed that I somehow carried the AIDS virus.

And at the bottom of it all, I felt angry because I was completely unable to do anything about the circumstances in which I'd been caught up. Maybe I was angry with God. As surely as the inner tube had been caught in the river, he had dragged me away from all things comfortable, familiar, and secure.

On the fifth time around this emotional merry-go-round, some-thing different happened. Something quite miraculous. Something so holy and so mysterious that it feels sacrilegious to explain.

As I came around again to tears, I realized in an instant that I was in the process of a God-ordained experience—a birth of sorts. Though I don't know how, I knew with absolute certainty that God had chosen this event, or more accurately, this series of events to push me through a kind of spiritual constriction.

And in that same instant, I knew that if I would surrender to the process, I would emerge in a place of new freedom, new effectiveness. If only I would surrender.

In my mind's eye, I saw a picture of myself like an infant in the birth canal, holding both arms out, pushing as hard as possible to keep from moving forward. The Holy Spirit showed me that to move for-ward I had to let go. I had to let go of my evaluations—about Dwayne and Jackie and Travis and the piano lady—and trust that God would set them straight. I had to let go of Stephen. I couldn't force him to accept my faith. I had to let go and trust Jesus' care for my brother. It was Jesus' job to set the record straight. Jesus' job to bring Stephen into faith.

My job was to obey.

In the quiet moment after the sermon, while Dwayne gave his altar call, I let go of the walls. I decided to let God give birth to the new thing he intended to accomplish in me. Whatever that entailed.

≈ ≈ ≈

On the way home, Kevin asked, "What was all that about this morning?"

I didn't answer.

"I mean, why all the tears?"

"It's hard to explain."

"Try me."

I glanced into the back seat, where the kids huddled together over a CD a friend had given Mallory. Neither seemed interested in our conversation. "I don't know what to tell you." I shrugged. "I just felt overwhelmed this morning. I've been angry with Dwayne for the way he talked with Stephen."

"You don't know what he really said."

"You're right. I don't."

"We know Dwayne well enough to know that he would only tell the truth. Everyone needs to know the truth." Kevin put on his blinker, slowing for the turn onto Main. "I think Stephen over-reacted."

I didn't want to argue the point with Kevin. After all, I'd only just let go of it myself. Why bring it all up again? "You didn't see his face after it happened," I said. "Kevin, when you want to talk to someone about the gospel, where do you start?"

"I don't know. I try to figure out where the gospel fits into the person's needs."

"You don't start by listing the person's sins and demanding that they repent?"

"I don't think I've ever done it that way."

"Me either." He braked for a stoplight. From the car window, I watched John Mueller shovel fresh snow from the sidewalk in front of the video store. "When I learned the four spiritual laws, they told us to begin with, 'God loves you and has a wonderful plan for your life.' As nearly as I can tell, Dwayne didn't use that technique with Stephen."

"You don't know what his technique was."

"I only know what Stephen told me. And I know how it affected him." The light changed, and we drove slowly through the downtown section of Potter's Hollow. Kevin waited patiently while the car in front of us released a group of teens in front of the grocery store.

"However he did it, I just wonder why," I continued. "I'm not angry anymore. But I wish it hadn't happened. I think it gave Stephen one more brick to put on the wall he hides behind." We crossed Icicle River and took a right onto Robin's Road.

"How would you do it differently?"

"I don't know. No matter what I say, he shuts me down."

"So you don't get much further than Dwayne did."

"I guess not." I leaned back against the seat, closing my eyes, trying to recapture the peace I'd felt during the altar call. If only I could resist picking up all that anger again.

"Mom, can we go skiing this afternoon?" Travis asked from the back seat.

"At the golf course? Is there enough snow?"

"A bunch of kids from church are going to meet there in an hour. Afterward, we're going to Brian Dalley's for a movie."

"You going, Mallory?" Kevin asked, glancing into the rearview mirror. Kevin didn't want to go out after dark and pick up Travis.

"No. I'm going over to Nicole's house to work on our duet for the contest."

"I guess it's okay," I said to Travis.

"Why don't we get out our skis and head up the river?" Kevin said, reaching for my hand. "I saw some people out yesterday afternoon."

"I can't."

"Why not?"

"I promised Stephen that I'd be at the hospital for his angioplasty today." I turned to look at Kevin. "Why don't you come with me? I could use the company."

"I'd rather stay home," he said, his expression carefully blank.

CHAPTER
Eighteen

When I arrived in the CCU, I found Stephen watching a play on BBC television. I leaned over the bed to kiss his cheek. "How're you doing this afternoon?"

He shrugged, pointing the remote at the television, muting the sound. "I've been up since about five this morning. Of course I can't eat anything, and I'm starving to death. I just wish we could get it over with."

"Have you seen the doctor?"

"Are you kidding? Only nurses and vampires."

"Vampires?" I sat down in my usual chair.

"Blood suckers."

"That's a good one."

He nodded, grimacing. "It's a wonder I have any blood left."

"You're really Mr. Cheerful today. What's bothering you?"

"Have you even thought about how much this little visit to the hospital will cost?" He rolled to face me. "I have. It was bad enough being admitted through the emergency room for the diabetes, but the coronary care unit? And to top that off, now surgery."

"We'll figure something out."

"What do you mean we? There's no we here. I can't even begin to imagine the cost. And whatever it is, I don't have it, Colleen. I'm going to have to sell the house."

"You don't have any savings? Investments or something?"

"It's all gone. I live from paycheck to paycheck—just like the undisciplined riff-raff that Dad used to look down on. Now, with this..." He shook his head and looked away. "I can't think of anything to do but sell the house. I don't have any other options."

"Stephen, it can't be good to go into this procedure worrying about money. Let's agree to tackle the problem after they send you home. We'll figure something out."

"You can't squeeze blood from a turnip," he said. "And in this case, I'm the turnip."

"Ah, I hear they squeezed bunches of blood from you this morning. Maybe it just takes special equipment."

Though it wasn't a real belly laugh, a small chuckle escaped from Stephen. I hadn't relieved his fear though; the smile never quite reached his eyes.

Moments later, someone from transportation came with a wheelchair to take Stephen downstairs. I watched as they lowered his bed, dropped the bed rail, and parked the chair near Stephen's mattress. Stephen raised the head of his bed and, looking like a little old man, took tiny steps to the wheelchair, where he collapsed.

"Wait," I said to the attendant. "Could you give us a minute?"

The young man behind his chair shrugged and stepped back. "Only a second though. I have to have him downstairs right away."

I went around the bed and bent in front of the wheelchair. "Stephen, can I pray for you?"

He shrugged, turning his head away. "If it will make you feel better."

I took his hands in my own. "Father, I don't have to tell you about how much I love my brother. And I know that nothing pleases you more than love. You are love. And I'm asking that you protect Stephen. Keep him safe during the procedure. Give his doctors wisdom bigger than their training.

"And give my brother peace. I ask that as he goes through this, you draw close to him. Let him sense your nearness and your love for him. Give the procedure success. I ask this all because of the work Jesus did in our behalf. Keep my brother, Lord. I trust you with him. Amen."

I looked up to see Stephen's eyes glassy, his face tight with emotion. And then the young man rolled him away.

~ ~ ~

I brought Stephen home early Monday afternoon. Doctors had managed to place a stent—an expandable tunnel, as I understand it—in a blocked heart vessel and prop it open. The procedure had gone well, and according to the nursing staff, Stephen was recovering nicely.

Still, Stephen seemed to have aged several decades in the four days he'd been in the hospital. He moved slowly and had almost no appetite. He rarely spoke. When we got home, I walked him, with one arm around his waist, up the sidewalk, into the house, and directly up the half-flight of stairs to the guest bedroom, where he collapsed in the bed. Pulling up the covers, he rolled onto his side and closed his eyes.

I wondered if Stephen suffered as much from his disease as he did from depression.

Since I'd already finished teaching for the month of December and my own teenagers had another week of school before Christmas break, I spent the next week focused entirely on helping my brother. Even without the distraction of students and children, it took all my energy.

Once again I sorted through his medications and set up a schedule. During his stay in the hospital, he'd managed to add five medications to his already crowded list—one to lower cholesterol, two for the diabetes, one to prevent infection, and a daily aspirin to prevent clot formation where the stent had been placed. Combining these with his other medications required the skill and wits of an air-traffic controller.

During that week, I wondered if Stephen's depression had other manifestations. It seemed that my brother had no interest in managing his blood sugar. He would not use his monitor regularly, and when he did, he refused to record the sugar reading in the small notebook they'd given him at the hospital.

This neglect, combined with almost no appetite and regular doses of insulin, made for a nearly catastrophic battle of wills between us.

On Thursday afternoon Stephen backed me into the wall. "I brought you lunch," I said from the door of his room. "Hot soup and fresh bread."

He was lying on the bed, eyes closed, face unshaven. "I'm not hungry." He rolled away from the door to face the window.

"You need to eat. We can't manage the blood sugar if your food intake isn't regular. Besides that, you're messing with all the antivirals. You've got to eat."

"I'm not hungry. And it isn't your job to manage my blood sugar."

"I know. But it seems pretty clear that you aren't doing it."

He didn't answer. I set the tray on the dresser and walked around the bed, placing myself between my brother the window. "You know, I've about had it with this self-pitying attitude, Stephen."

He looked up at me, and I saw anger flash through his normally calm blue eyes. Still, he made no response.

"You can't spend the rest of your life in bed. You've got to get up and get moving. It's the only way you can get better."

"What do you know about the rest of my life?"

"I don't know anything," I said. "But neither do you. You can't just decide to quit. You have a lot of time ahead of you. And you don't want to waste it here, between these sheets."

"What difference does it make where I waste it?"

His words reminded me of the play I'd seen at his school. "What about *Our Town*, Stephen? It was your play. You chose it. What about that?"

He looked at me, surprised. "What are you talking about?"

"I'm talking about the play at the college. Remember the line at the end? I don't remember who says it, but someone says we spend time and waste time as if we had a million years. Is that what you want to do? Waste the time you have? Throw it away as if you had forever?"

"I don't have forever."

"And neither do I. So let's use the time we have. You might have more than you think."

He frowned at me. "You might have a lot less than you think."

"Is that a threat?"

"I haven't decided yet."

"So, are you going to have lunch?"

"No."

"No?" I took a deep breath, deliberately swallowing the words I wanted to say.

"No. I'm going to the bathroom first. And then I'm going downstairs and eat at the table with you." He threw the covers back. "If you aren't going to leave me alone. I might as well give up. It's my only hope for some peace and quiet this afternoon."

I couldn't help the smile that spread across my face, and I stepped back to let him pass.

"Wipe that smile off your face," Stephen said, patting my cheek as he moved by. "You didn't win the war. You just won lunch." I heard the bathroom door close behind him.

"I'll carry the tray downstairs," I said. "Hurry. You don't want the soup to get cold."

Even from the hallway, I heard my brother groan.

After one week, my concern for Stephen had grown. His general weakness lingered in spite of his renewed efforts to exercise and eat regularly. He moved slowly, and on that next Monday morning, Stephen spent hours sitting in a living-room chair, staring out the window.

I asked if he would like me to bring him something to read. "I couldn't concentrate on a book," he answered. "Thanks, though."

With schools recessed for Christmas vacation, Travis and Mallory slept in late. Travis headed off to hang out with friends. Mallory invited Stephen to go with her to a movie. He smiled and refused. She went with a girlfriend.

A couple of hours after lunch, Stephen went up to take an afternoon nap. I set up the ironing board in the family room and turned on the television. While Stephen slept, I planned to catch up on my ironing and enjoy an old movie on A&E.

About three o'clock, the doorbell rang. I looked through the peep-hole to find an older man wearing a dark blue down coat, standing on the front porch. Grey hair peeked out from under a black fedora. I opened the door. "Yes?"

"Hello," he said, removing his hat. With low, straight eyebrows, a tight mouth, and eyes the same stony grey as his hair, this visitor looked as though he worked for the FBI, or perhaps the Mafia. "My name is David Dennison. I work at the community college with Stephen MacLaughlin. I understand he's staying with you for the winter break?"

"Yes, he's my brother."

"I hope I haven't come at a bad time. I just wanted to drop in and say hello."

I barely managed to stifle a grin. Dropped in? From 300 miles away? I invited Dr. Dennison inside and showed him to a seat in the living room. "I'll run up and let him know you're here."

I found Stephen standing at the side of his bed, swaying slightly as he slid a flannel robe over his bony shoulders. "There's someone here to see you. Dr. Dennison."

He nodded. "I heard. I'm coming."

"Would you like me to bring him upstairs?"

"I don't want him to see me in bed." Stephen sounded angry.

"Alright. I'll tell him you're coming down," I said, shrugging. As I pulled the door closed, I wished that this visitor had the good sense to call before arriving on my front porch.

I offered the man a hot drink and paused to switch on the Christmas tree lights as I headed for the kitchen. I passed Stephen as he shuffled forward, offering his hand to the visitor.

Dr. Dennison did not take Stephen's hand.

In the kitchen, I put a teakettle on the stove, poured cider mix into two coffee mugs, and waited for the water to boil. I knew this had to be more than a simple visit. Though my brother had many friends at the college, none had called or visited during his last stay at the hospital.

Dr. Dennison was my brother's first visitor.

I suppose I should have been glad for the company. Instead, in this dearth of personal contact, his arrival aroused my curiosity, even my suspicion. I wanted to join the men in the living room and hear firsthand the reason for this peculiar visit.

As are all watched pots, my kettle seemed reluctant to boil. Eventually, I poured steaming water into the mugs, arranged some sugar cookies on a plate, and served it from a hand-carved wooden tray. Keeping one eye on the liquid in the cups, I balanced the tray carefully and took it to the living room. As I came around the corner I heard Dr. Dennison say, "You know how much we value your contribution to the college."

Stephen did not respond. Instead, he waited as I served the cider and placed the cookies on the table between them. "Thanks, Colleen," Stephen said. I gave a little curtsey—my own pathetic attempt to humor him.

Stephen shook his head.

"Well, I guess I'll leave you two alone," I said into the silence. "I'll be in the kitchen if you need anything,"

In the kitchen, my curiosity took me by the throat. I tried to sit at the counter and make a grocery list for Christmas dinner. I tried to clean under the burners on my stove. But I felt drawn to the conversation in the living room.

Unable to stop myself, I crept through the swinging door between the kitchen and dining room. Then, holding the door with one hand, I leaned against the wall and slid onto the floor. I resisted the door as the automatic hinge slowly pulled it closed. From this position on the floor, Stephen could not see me, but I heard every word coming from the living room.

"I know," Stephen said. "I've used all my sick leave."

"And family leave," Dr. Dennison added.

"I thought I'd be stronger when I came back this fall."

"We all hoped so. How much time do you think you'll need this time?"

"The doctor says four weeks."

"And how long since surgery?"

"Only a week."

"And what about you? What do you think? Will you be up to full speed in four weeks?"

"From now?" A pause grew as Stephen considered his answer. "Maybe four weeks is pushing it."

"That's why I came," the visitor said. "You know how much the college values you. You've been teacher of the year twice since you've been with us. Your students write the best papers of anyone on campus. And I don't want to do anything to discourage you from continuing your career." Another pause, and I leaned toward the living room, unwilling to miss a single detail.

"If you want to continue teaching, we'll do everything we can to help. We can hire substitutes. We can get you a teacher's assistant. We can limit your class size or give the drama productions to someone else. We can do whatever you need."

"Thank you for the offer," Stephen said. "But I don't want you to do all that."

"It's the least we can do," he said. Then the professor's voice took on a serious tone. "But I have something I want you to think about. Really think about. After what you told me on the phone last week, I have to wonder what teaching is doing to you. Is it robbing you of the strength you need to fight this disease? Because none of us want you to risk your health in order to keep this job."

"Are you asking me to resign?"

"Never," he answered. "I meant what I said. You can keep the job for as long as you want it." His voice became urgent. "But you don't have to do it. You can quit. You have some money in the retirement fund. You have the house. You don't have to keep pushing yourself."

"I know," Stephen said.

"It's okay to think of yourself first. I just want to give you permission to do what's best for you. Whatever that is. Don't let your obligation to us keep you working longer than you should."

"I do think of myself. I take good care of myself."

"Alright then, you keep that up. And you let me know what we can do for you." I heard a chair groan, and I guessed that Dr. Dennison had stood up. "Well then," he said, "you look like you could use some rest right now. I think I'll be going. Don't forget what I said, Stephen."

Afraid that Stephen's guest might see me as he walked past the dining room, I crawled back through the swinging door to the kitchen, pausing to slow the door as it shut behind me.

My brother's illness had brought me to new levels of depravity.

I stood up and brushed off my corduroy pants. Then I began pulling things out of the refrigerator. If Stephen came into the kitchen I wanted to look busy. I kept it up until I heard the front door shut behind Dr. Dennison.

Then I threw my rag in the sink, put all the food back inside, and slammed the door. In that moment, I discovered what all busybodies understand: Sometimes it's better when you don't know everything.

I sat down on the bar stool and let myself have a good cry.

CHAPTER
Nineteen

Later, after I managed to compose myself, I rinsed my face with cold water and headed upstairs, tiptoeing on the treads so I wouldn't wake Stephen. I peeked into his room to find him lying on his side, his head on his hand, staring out the window. "Hey," I said, knocking. "You checked your blood sugar lately?"

He glanced over his shoulder at me and frowned. "Leave me alone, Colleen."

"I will if you really want me to. I just thought maybe you could use a friend."

"Now, why would I need a friend?"

I sat down in a corner chair. "He didn't stay long. Was he your boss?"

He nodded. "He didn't need to stay long." Stephen's focus never moved from the wintry scene outside the bedroom window.

"He traveled a long way to see you."

"I'm sure I should be honored. I just don't feel that way right this minute."

Trying to sound curious, as though I didn't know what the two men had discussed, I asked, "So what did he have to say?"

"He wanted to know when I'd feel up to teaching again."

"What did you tell him?"

Stephen glanced at me, a look of irritation passing over his features. "You writing a book?"

"No. I'm just curious. I know it's not my business. But I do care, Stephen. I do."

Stephen rolled onto his back and closed his eyes, bringing both hands up over his face. With drawn-out exaggeration, Stephen spoke. "Dr. Dennison is concerned about my welfare. He's worried that I'm using too much energy. He wants me to think of myself first."

"That doesn't sound so bad. I'd give you the same advice."

"You don't understand, Colleen. What he really wants is for me to resign."

"Did he say that?"

"It's what he meant."

"Why would he want you to resign? He said you're the best—" I slapped a hand over my mouth.

"Listening in, were you?"

"Just a little bit. I…" I took a deep breath and blew it out slowly. "Okay, I confess. I listened in. I was curious. And to be truthful, I was worried."

Stephen swore. "Can't you mind your own business for just one minute, Colleen? Just because I'm your twin doesn't mean that you own me. It's my life. It's screwed up. It's a nightmare. But it's mine." His voice rose to a frightening level.

"I'm sorry," I said, feeling tears threaten. "I didn't mean to hurt you. I just wanted…oh never mind. It doesn't matter what I want."

Once again Stephen's gaze retreated to the scene outside his window, and I sat on the chair in silence. I heard Mallory come into the driveway with the Honda. A few minutes later the door to the kitchen opened and she yelled, "Mom, I'm home!"

As the door to the dining room opened, I heard Travis tramp into the kitchen behind his sister. The back door slammed and he shouted into the emptiness, "Mom, what's for dinner?"

"I suppose I should go tend the troops." I stood up. "Forgive me? I know you're right. It is your life. I shouldn't have eavesdropped." I touched Stephen's hair as I turned to the door.

"Don't be sorry," he said quietly. I looked back to see that Stephen hadn't turned away from the window. "He's right, you know."

"Who is? Who's right?"

"Dr. Dennison. He's right. It's time for me to quit."

~ ~ ~

Stephen's depression deepened with every passing day. My worry grew, swelling like raisins in hot water. Somehow, with the approach of Christmas, I felt extra pressure to fix things. After all, no one has permission to be sad over Christmas.

On Wednesday morning, four days before Christmas Eve, I decided to call my sister. "Carrie, it's me, Colleen."

"Hi," she said, offering no welcome, no questions about Stephen's health or my welfare, no merry holiday greeting. Maybe this wasn't such a great idea.

Pushing aside my doubt, I came right to the point. "I've been thinking about Christmas. You do know that Stephen is staying with us over the winter break, right?"

"I've heard. Mom told me he's had surgery. It would've been nice if you'd called me. I'd like to hear the bad news directly, you know."

"Carrie, the whole thing was a surprise. I didn't think you'd mind hearing from Mom. I asked her to call you right away. I was only trying to save some time." In truth, I'd hoped to avoid a conversation exactly like this.

My sister made no effort to let me off the hook. "So, calling me would waste too much of your precious time?"

"Carrie, will you cut it out? I'm trying to communicate here. I'm sorry I don't do everything exactly the way you'd like it. I'll be sure and call you personally next time." I took a deep breath, letting it out slowly. After such a grand beginning, I had trouble coming up with the desire to issue an invitation. Why would I want my oh-so-loving sister to come for a visit?

"Anyway, I've been thinking. Stephen's a little depressed lately, and I was wondering if you and Tim would consider coming to our house on Christmas day."

She stuttered in frustration. "Christmas is only four days away. How can you drop an invitation like that with no notice?"

"I know. It's inconvenient. I should have called earlier. But I've been so busy taking care of Stephen. For a while I thought that a quiet day would be better for him. But now, I'm worried. I think you should come."

"You think so, huh? What about Mom?"

"I'm going to call her too."

Carrie took a deep breath. "We had plans, Colleen. Tim and I were going to spend Christmas Eve with his parents. Then we have reservations at Whistler. We need this time away together." Her voice took on a desperate, defensive edge. "If only you'd called sooner."

I decided that now might not be a good time to observe that since Carrie and Tim lived alone, they didn't really have anything to get away *from*. "I know. I should have," I said, again apologizing. "Mom told me you had plans. I just thought maybe you could spend Christmas day with us and then go skiing."

She hesitated. "I don't know. I'll have to talk to Tim."

"Please do," I said. "And get back to me?"

As soon as I hung up the phone, I remembered. We had plans too. And so far, neither Kevin nor I had mentioned our ski trip with the Thompsons. At that moment, I couldn't see how I could leave Stephen alone while we went off to ski. But what would I tell Kevin?

Another straw for this camel's ever-weakening back.

Later that morning, I called Jackie. "Hey, I have a favor to ask."

"I'm listening."

"I've been so busy with Stephen that I haven't finished getting ready for Christmas. I'm thinking about having company and I need to hit the grocery store, and spend a couple of hours at the mall to finish up my shopping. Do you think you could stop by tomorrow morning and stay with Stephen for me so I can get out of the house?"

In the lengthy pause that followed, I heard water running and cupboards doors banging closed. I'd caught Jackie washing dishes. "Hmm," she said. "I'd like to help, really I would Colleen. But I've promised to spend tomorrow morning at the Leavitts's house. I'm supposed to watch the kids so Sandy can get some rest."

"She had the baby?"

"A little girl. Seven pounds, six ounces. Twenty inches long. They named her Chloe."

"When?"

"Monday morning, just after midnight."

"I've been so out of it. I didn't even know. Is everyone alright?" It hurt that Jackie hadn't thought to let me know about the baby's arrival. I tried not to feel left out.

"Both mom and baby are doing great. But Gary is out of town for a couple of days. We're all pitching in. With three kids at home, she needs all the help she can get."

"I understand." I pushed aside my own disappointment. "Well, then how about Friday?"

"I have the program Friday night."

"Oh shoot."

"You didn't forget!"

"No, of course not. I just wasn't thinking about it."

"Well, I hope you find someone to help. What about the kids?"

"I don't know. Stephen has been depressed, and he isn't monitoring his blood sugar."

"I can't do that. I don't have the foggiest notion about blood sugar."

"I know. But you'd know what to do in an emergency. I hate to leave the kids with that much responsibility. What if he had a seizure?"

"I'm sure the kids can manage a couple of hours at home with Stephen. It's the least they can do. He's their uncle after all."

As I hung up, I tried to shake off a nagging feeling of disappointment. In a way, Jackie was right. Stephen was my responsibility. I'd invited him to stay with us. Jackie had no real obligation to help me out. And it was true that I could curtail my children's highly important social schedule in order to get some help with Stephen. It wouldn't hurt Travis or Mallory to stay home for a couple of hours. Maybe I could make certain Stephen checked his sugar before I left.

With any luck at all, Stephen could manage to stay alive until I got home.

~ ~ ~

After lunch, I asked the kids for help. "Are you kidding? Alone with him?" Travis shook his head. "No way."

"Travis, would you lower your voice!" I couldn't believe his behavior. "And I've had just about enough of this attitude of yours lately. I don't care what you think about Stephen. I want you to be kind to him."

"You mean you approve of him?"

"That isn't the point," I answered. "The point here is kindness. He needs us now."

"I'm not staying alone with him." He crossed his arms and leaned against the counter.

"Don't worry, Mom," Mallory said, dropping her silverware into the dishwasher. "I'll stay with Uncle Stephen. I don't mind at all."

When I left them, Mallory and Stephen were hunched over a chessboard they'd set up on the ottoman in the living room.

Even though I carried a cell phone, I hurried through the grocery store, dropping items into my cart with no more thought than someone winning a shopping spree from a radio station. Hopefully, in that mound of groceries, I'd have something to fix for company.

The mall was a nightmare, made slightly more hyperactive by the recent heavy snowfall. Even though we Eastern Washingtonians pride ourselves on our ability to handle the snow, we often stay home until the highways are plowed and the parking lots are cleared.

Hoping that Carrie and Tim might join us, I chose gifts for them and had them wrapped while I went off in search of a gift certificate at the electronic game store for Travis. I bought my mom a robe and Mallory a pair of birthstone earrings to match the sweater I hadn't finished.

I couldn't think of anything Kevin would want at the mall. He's not exactly a GQ kind of guy. So instead of worrying about it, I stopped at a sporting-goods store and picked up a gift certificate.

With the back of the car packed with goodies, I pulled into the bakery parking lot. Inside, I was greeted by warm, humid air laced with the sweet smell of cinnamon. I tried to ignore the fresh donuts and went straight to the case filled with cakes and pies.

"What can I get for you, Colleen?" Marie Swanson smiled from behind the display case.

"I need a couple of things for dessert this weekend, Marie. Got any ideas?"

"How many people?" Marie has run the bakery in Potter's Hollow for more than twenty-five years. If you need to know anything about sweets, Marie is the person to ask. Having sampled everything, I'd guess that she weighs nearly three hundred pounds.

"Five, seven, eight," I counted out loud. "Eight, I think."

"Eight?" She pointed into the case. "Well, this apple pie would keep nicely if you froze it. And this turtle cheesecake is very good. Gets better with age."

I nodded, overwhelmed by the sight of so many choices.

"I recommend the turtle."

I turned to face the familiar voice and recognized our pastor, Dwayne Charboneau, waiting in line behind me. He wore a heavy parka and jeans. "Dwayne," I said, "Good to see you." I gave him a sideways hug.

"Having company?" he asked.

"Not sure yet. I asked my sister and my mom to come for Christmas."

"Will they be here for the program on Friday?"

"I don't think so. I can hardly get them to come for a family dinner."

"Speaking of family, how's your brother doing?"

Marie broke in. "If you tell me what you want, Colleen, I can box it while you chat."

I felt myself blush. "I'm sorry, Marie. I'll take the apple and the turtle. And could you seal them so I can put it all in the freezer?"

She nodded and turned to grab a box from the counter behind her.

"That's a good question," I said to Dwayne. "I think Stephen is really depressed."

"Understandable."

"Yeah. But I'm worried about him. He isn't recovering from the latest physical blow. I don't know how to help him pull out of it."

"He needs Jesus. I tried to tell him that when I went to visit him at the hospital."

"I know. You're right." I glanced around at the crowded bakery. "Stephen quit listening to me about those things a long time ago."

"So would you like me to stop by the house? I could present the gospel."

"No," I said, entirely too quickly. I definitely didn't want Dwayne visiting my brother again. I made an effort to cover my blunder. "It's the holiday season and I know you're too busy to stop by the house. Maybe you could pray for us?"

My pastor nodded, his face sympathetic. "I already have been."

"Your total comes to thirty-two sixteen," Marie said. I turned to face her, digging in my purse for the exact change.

"Thanks so much," I said, taking the boxes from the counter. "You've saved me again."

"That's what we're here for," Marie winked. "Not everyone can bake like I can."

I drove home slowly, pondering the situation with Dwayne and Stephen. My pastor was absolutely right. Stephen needed Jesus. I couldn't argue with that. Though I didn't expect that salvation would heal Stephen's body, I knew it would heal his soul.

But the question was how? And who? Who would he listen to?

It really didn't matter what Dwayne had said when he'd spoken to Stephen. It probably hadn't gone exactly as Stephen had painted it. But in truth, whatever had been said, Stephen had closed his ears to Dwayne Charboneau. Probably nothing our pastor said would ever get through my brother's thick and very stubborn skull.

No one knew that better than I.

As I crossed the river, heading toward our house, I shook my head, worry churning in my stomach, fear making acid rise in my mouth. Who could ever get through to Stephen?

CHAPTER

Twenty

At home, I pulled into the detached garage, used the electronic control to shut the door behind me, stashed my Christmas purchases inside the tool cabinet, and put the newly purchased desserts into the freezer chest. Then I reopened the garage door. In moments, I'd backed the car up to the kitchen, honking twice to announce my arrival.

By the time I opened the trunk, Mallory appeared in the doorway, putting on her letter jacket. "You were sure gone a long time."

"Lots to do. Everything okay here?"

"Uh-huh."

"Stephen doing okay?"

"No problem."

"Any phone calls?"

"Grandma called." Mallory loaded her hands with the handles of plastic grocery bags. "She said to tell you that she'd be arriving on the day before Christmas Eve, the 7:15 bus."

Great. I'd have to have someone else pick her up. By seven, I'd be playing piano for the Christmas program. "I'll call her when we get this stuff inside," I said. Maybe I could convince her to change plans.

Mallory glanced over her shoulder as she stepped into the mudroom. "Did you remember to buy gel?"

I knew there was a reason to make a list. "Oh no. Sorry, honey." I lugged four gallons of milk, two handles in each hand, up the steps into the kitchen and over to the refrigerator. "You can pick some up this afternoon. I'll let you take the car."

Stephen came in from the living room. "Did you finish all your errands?"

"Well, not everything exactly. But enough." I placed a bag of canned goods on the counter nearest him. "Put those away in the pantry, will you?"

I watched Stephen carry the bag to the pantry closet and open the sliding door. No ninety-year-old would move that slowly. "How're you feeling today?" I asked.

"About the same," he answered.

I reached up behind him, placing a box of dry cereal on the shelf. I couldn't help but notice the fruity, almost fermented scent coming from his body. I've lived around diabetics long enough to recognize the smell. I first smelled it when Carrie came down with diabetes. I'd recognized the same scent in Stephen on the night we took him to the hospital.

It only happens when blood sugar levels rise dangerously out of control. I wanted to strangle my brother. Instead I asked, as casually as I could, "How's your blood sugar today?"

He turned from the cupboard, a can of soup in one hand, and lied, "My sugar is right on. Couldn't be more perfect."

"Hmm." I said, trying to stifle my anger. I noticed that his cheeks seemed a little too pink, and I looked for other signs of fever. With difficulty I resisted the urge to place my palm on Stephen's forehead. After all, I'm not his mother.

Though I still hadn't heard from Carrie, on Friday morning I began earnest preparations for Christmas day, thawing, cooking, and freezing. I hurried through my chores, hoping to find time to run through my piano pieces for the Christmas program. Late that morning, I put Jackie's tape on the recorder and played through her accompaniment. Stephen came downstairs in the middle of the second run through. "That's beautiful. Who's singing?"

I stopped playing and leaned over to shut off the recorder. "Jackie Moore," I said. "She teaches at the middle school. That was the solo she sang for the women's lunch."

"She teaches music?"

"Nope, math."

"That's a surprise." He wandered over to his favorite chair and turned it toward the window. The snow had begun to fall again and wild birds fluttered around the bird feeder, eager for breakfast. "Don't let me stop you. I just came down to listen. I haven't heard you play in a long time."

"Thanks a lot," I made a face at my brother. "Now you'll make me nervous."

"I don't think so. You play for people all the time."

"It isn't the same," I said. "People you love can make you more nervous than strangers." I leaned over and rewound the tape. "But it will be good for me to play for you. Might ease my nerves for tonight." I switched the machine to "play" and waited for the lead-in tempo.

After so much practice, I'd finally managed to imitate the sound and phrasing of a lounge pianist, and I have to admit that I enjoyed the new style—though I'd never make it in a tavern. For a brief moment, I visualized a huge brandy snifter sitting on my grand piano, filled with dollar bills. By the time I finished Jackie's song, I could almost smell the cigarette smoke and hear the tinkle of glass.

I ended with a downspin of jazz chords and let the last note fade into the morning.

"Bravo," Stephen said. "That was really good. I wish I'd learned to play like that."

"You mean jazz?"

"No. I mean by ear. I learned from a teacher who didn't believe in that stuff. He thought that the only real music was music written on a staff sheet."

"I know. I had the same teacher, remember?"

"So, where did you learn?"

"In Seattle, while Kevin finished his fifth year in engineering."

"Who taught you?"

"A lady in the church we attended."

"Is it hard?"

"To play by ear?" I considered the question for a minute. "Actually, Stephen, it's a miracle."

"Oh please don't."

"I'm not kidding. You start with the most basic information. Nothing more than a melody and some understanding—stuff no one bothered to explain while we were taking lessons. At first your fingers have no idea what they're doing. The chords don't come easily and you feel like a fool trying it. Everything sounds bad.

"But then something amazing happens. I don't even know how, but suddenly, your fingers can sing—just like your voice. They find notes without looking for them. They know what chords will go with the melody without ever making a conscious decision about them. And then eventually, you get this freedom. You can play almost anything you want. Any way you want. You have no walls. It's a miracle. Honest. There isn't any other way to describe it." I laughed at myself. "I sound like a street preacher. Sorry."

"You sound like a teacher," Stephen said, correcting me. "Can you teach it?"

"I don't know. I've never tried."

"Maybe you should," he said. "I'd like to learn."

His words surprised me. "You? It isn't easy. It takes time."

"So? Just this week, you told me that I have all the time in the world."

"You're right—I did. But you're going home soon. We don't have time to learn that much, and you don't even own a piano."

"So maybe we only get started. We can do more later," he said. In spite of my brother's illness and age, his voice had the eager sound of a child wishing for his first bicycle.

I considered his request, half afraid to try. What if I couldn't teach it? What if Stephen didn't have the patience to practice? Still, I hadn't heard this much energy in his voice in the three weeks he'd been with us. "Alright. Let's make a deal," I said, turning toward him on the bench. "I'll teach you piano if you'll teach me to paint."

"You? You can't draw a stick man."

"I know," I shrugged. "So, your job is just a little more challenging."

This time Stephen thought for a moment. "You're on," he said. He stood up and plopped himself down beside me on the bench. "So, what do we do first?"

At four o'clock, I put on my coat and headed out to pick up Mom at the bus stop. Fortunately, I'd been able to convince her to come on an earlier bus. "But the Garrisons have already planned to give me a ride to the bus depot," my mother complained. "I don't want to have to call them and change the schedule."

"Mom, the Garrisons can take you earlier. They're retired. I'm playing the piano Friday night and the kids are doing drama. Kevin is managing the sound system. It would help us if you would come on the earlier bus."

"Well, I don't want to be an inconvenience," she intoned.

"That settles it then," I said, before she could change her mind. "I'll be here waiting for you."

George Endicott, our resident snowplow driver, had recently cleared the roads in Potter's Hollow, easing my drive into town. Christmas lights twinkled from every building, and tourists strolled the sidewalks, arms laden with packages, moving in and out of the various upscale shops.

Some paused in front of breathtaking window displays, featuring moving trains, elaborate Christmas decorations, and hand-painted murals. As always, traffic downtown slowed to a crawl as local drivers accommodated the lazy pace of pedestrians. We've long since learned to cope with the unexpected dash of a tourist into traffic.

I turned into the Tyrolean Inn, parked in the side lot, and got out to wait for my mom in the hotel lobby. Just as I reached the front doors, the Greyhound pulled in behind me and I waited as the big bus came to a stop and opened its pressurized door. The driver climbed out and opened the baggage compartment while my mother descended the huge curved stairway, carrying a small satchel. As I watched her, I was struck by how small and frail she looked coming down those steep stairs.

She clung to the rail as she dangled one foot out into the air below the bus. I saw her look down at the pavement, apparently worried about the presence of ice. "It's just wet, Mom," I said, hurrying forward to offer my hand.

"Thank you. I'd hate to fall now that I've come so far." Leaning heavily on me, she took the long step to the ground.

"Which bag is yours?"

"The blue one." She pointed to a small bag. "The handle pulls out, so you can roll it."

"I've got it," I said, grabbing the handle. "Why don't we go inside? I thought maybe you'd like to have a cup of hot coffee before you head to the house."

Her eyebrows rose as she considered this very unusual offer. "Well, I suppose I could use a little something," she agreed. "I hope they have a bathroom here. I wouldn't use that filthy thing on the coach."

Inside, I settled Mom onto the couch in front of the lobby's two-story fireplace. In the Tyrolean, the owner himself maintains the fire, using logs in a wood box large enough for a grown man to walk around in. Between the warmth of the fire and the luxurious surroundings, you can reach a level of relaxation at the Tyrolean that seems slightly immoral for a public place.

Together we managed to keep up a long run of chitchat, talking about nothing more important than the weather and Mother's bridge club. When the silence rolled around again, she asked directly, "So what is it that you want to tell me before we go home?"

"You don't mess around, do you?"

"I'm old, not stupid. Something is bothering you."

"You could always tell, couldn't you?"

"Still can. I know from the way you answer the phone how things are going."

"I wonder if I'll be that good when Mallory grows up?"

"You have a lot of time yet. So, what is it? What's going on?"

"It's about Stephen." I paused and took a deep breath. "He's been sick, and I don't know how much anyone has told you."

"I've wondered. No one gives me the courtesy of a straight answer anymore. You kids don't think I notice anything."

"I know better than that." I patted my mother's soft hand. "You notice everything."

She nodded. "So, what's wrong with Stephen?"

No matter how much I dreaded it, I couldn't avoid it any longer. "Stephen has the virus that causes AIDS."

Her face remained expressionless. Only the slightest tightening of her lips told me that she'd heard my words.

"Do you know anything about HIV?" I asked.

"Certainly. I read the paper; I watch the television." I'd insulted her.

"Stephen has had the virus for years." I toyed with my paper cup, not wanting to tell her, and yet knowing that she had to be prepared for the changes in her son. "Lately, he's developed diabetes and complications with his heart. He's had trouble eating."

With each additional problem, her shoulders sank visibly. "He's dying, isn't he?"

"Mom, I don't know that." I gave her shoulders a squeeze. "I don't think anyone knows where we are in the course of the disease. I just wanted to tell you. To warn you."

"To warn me about what?"

"Stephen doesn't look very good, Mom. He's skinny. He's weak. He moves like an old man. I just don't want you to be too surprised when you see him."

"You mean you don't want me to overreact when I see him."

I smiled. "I guess it's something like that."

"Because he doesn't look like Stephen any more, does he?"

"No, not like the old Stephen," I agreed.

At home, Mallory and Travis came out to greet their grandmother with enthusiastic hugs. "Merry Christmas," Travis said, wrapping her in his long adolescent arms. "I love you, Grams," he said. "Let me help you in the snow," he said, offering his arm.

I couldn't overcome a suspicious smile. It was, after all, the Christmas season. And certainly Travis knew that somewhere in my mother's bags was a gift for her only grandson.

If my mother felt used, she did not let on.

I carried Mother's bags into the house and dashed upstairs to change clothes. I'd promised Jackie that I'd help her test the microphones and monitors on the stage before the teenagers began their warm-up at six-thirty. I needed to hurry.

When I came downstairs, everything appeared to be under control. Mallory had baked a frozen lasagna and convinced Travis to set the table. I spotted a green salad on the table in the breakfast nook and guessed that Stephen had been pulled into service.

I found my mother reading the morning paper in the living room. "Mom, are you sure you wouldn't like to come to the Christmas service? You could ride with the kids."

"Is Stephen coming?"

"He said he isn't feeling well enough."

She folded the paper and thought for a moment. "I'm awfully tired, dear. I think I'll just stay home and rest." I forced myself to smile. "Well, then. We'll be home before nine-thirty. Mallory has dinner ready. Help yourself to anything you need."

"I'm sure I'll be just fine." She picked up the paper.

I streaked through the kitchen on my way to the mudroom. As Mallory was taking the lasagna out of the oven, she said, "Oh, Mom, I forgot. Aunt Carrie called. She said to tell you that she won't be able to come on Sunday. I told her I'd tell you." Mallory dropped the tin pan onto the stovetop. "Whew, that's hot."

I made a face. Leave it to Carrie. I wondered if she hoped staying away would hurt me.

"That's okay, isn't it?" Mallory said, reading my expression. "Should I have said something else?"

"Sure, Mal. It's fine. I'm just disappointed, that's all. See you at church."

At six-forty-five, Jackie and I finished our preparations for the Christmas service and handed the auditorium over to the drama team for a final run-through.

I headed to the foyer to fill my water bottle. Just outside the entry to the classroom wing, I spotted Gary Leavitt holding his newborn, bundled into an enormous handmade quilt. Michael, Gary's three-year-old, clung to his father's leg.

"Gary, welcome home!" I said, walking toward him. I bent down to address Michael. "Hey, I hear you're a big brother this week. Do you think I could see your new sister?"

Leaving his thumb in his mouth, Michael Leavitt nodded, his face a mask of serious responsibility. "Don't touch her, though."

"I promise," I said and stood up in time to see Gary roll his eyes.

Gary turned his body so that the bundle in his arms faced me, and lifted the blanket covering the sleeping newborn. Chloe squirmed at the intrusion of artificial light and then settled back to sleep, her baby hands fisted beside her perfect pink face. "She's beautiful," I said, resisting the urge to take the baby. "I'd forgotten how tiny newborns are. Where's Sandy?"

Gary nodded toward the hallway. "She snuck off to the ladies' room." At that moment, the diaper bag he'd slung over his shoulder slid down to his elbow, jarring him. "Here, would you mind holding her for me while I take Michael to class? I'm afraid we won't get a seat in the sanctuary if I don't hurry. Sandy should be out in a minute."

"Mind? Are you nuts?" I held my arms wide to receive the bundle. "I'd love to hold her." I'd no more than tucked Chloe into my arms before I began to sway in motherly rhythm. With one hand, I tossed back the cover on Chloe's face and let myself be mesmerized by her beauty.

I don't know how long I stood like that, completely entranced, when a sound caught my attention. I glanced up to see Sandy Leavitt hurry across the foyer, her face an expression of horror. "Colleen," she said, reaching out to snatch the baby from my arms. "Let me take her. You shouldn't—I mean, I don't expect you to hold her."

For an instant, the slightest fraction of a second, I resisted Sandy as she took Chloe. Then, as understanding dawned, I let go, watching as she covered the baby's face and hugged it protectively against her chest. Sandy did not smile; she made no effort to feign a polite cover for her distress. "I'd better get inside," she said, her face contorted with fear, her voice trembling as she backed away. "I need to save a seat for Gary."

Completely stunned, I stood frozen to the spot, disbelief and anger whirling inside me. I heard the organ begin the prelude, and still I remained unmoving. And as I stood there, an anger too large to contain welled up inside of me. How dare she take that baby! What made her think that I shouldn't have it?

Just as I came close to venting that anger, I recognized the source. Déjà vu clung to the moment. As my mind moved back in time, I realized that like this experience with Sandy, the other had been unfair. Unreasonable. Irreversible.

And I felt other things too. Things I had not felt in many years. Rejection. Disdain. Contamination. All familiar and painful emotions, ones that I had hoped never to feel again. And as the words for the feelings broke on my consciousness, my emotions dissolved into tears.

What was happening to me?

"Colleen, I've been looking for you everywhere," Jackie put one arm around my shoulder, guiding me toward the sanctuary. "You'd better get up to the piano. They've started—" Jackie stopped speaking suddenly. "What happened to you?"

She suddenly changed direction and began guiding me down the hall toward the rear stage entrance. I dabbed at my eyes, catching the first stray tears before they rolled over my cheeks. "Nothing," I said. "Nothing happened. I always act a little crazy around newborns."

Traditionally, our Christmas service is a family affair. All the children perform, whether they are three or twenty. Proud grandparents and happy relatives fill our sanctuary, laughing and applauding in the relaxed atmosphere of unpretentious fun.

I played Christmas carols as the congregation sang, and then listened as the elementary-aged students gave a rousing rendition of "Go Tell It on the Mountain" with the wild enthusiasm of the very young. One curly-headed kindergartener stood on the top row shouting the lyrics, his mouth wide open, waving at the end of every line. His voice had all the melody of a chain saw; the audience could hardly contain itself.

When our turn came, I played for the teen choir as they sang "O Holy Night" and an unusually rambunctious arrangement of "The Drummer Boy." The high-school drama team performed a short sketch about the meaning of Christmas. Both Mallory and Travis surprised me with their skill, and I have to admit, I felt chest-busting pride as the audience showed its appreciation.

Just before the sermon, Jackie sang the solo that we'd worked on for more than a month. Though the song is old, the jazzed version seemed to draw the audience in, and I sensed them warm up and lean toward Jackie as she sang. I think I heard sniffles.

And Jackie, who has never shunned the spotlight, milked their enthusiasm for all it was worth. The audience's applause was spontaneous and enthusiastic.

After I'd finished all my musical responsibilities, I sat down next to Kevin. In the quiet moments before the sermon began, the event I'd experienced before church came back to haunt me. I couldn't keep my mind from wandering back to the look of horror on Sandy's face when she'd discovered me holding her new baby. And with every remembrance, I felt again the struggle between us—the tiny, almost imperceptible tug-of-war I felt when I refused to relinquish the baby. I shuddered, trying to push the memory away.

Kevin noticed. "You okay?" he whispered. Dwayne Charboneau had taken the platform to give his sermon; I tipped my chin toward our pastor. Kevin shrugged.

Dwayne's sermon seemed an unlikely choice for a Christmas service. He'd selected his text from the book of Luke, reading aloud the story of the demon-possessed man delivered by Jesus. While Dwayne elaborated on the history and context of the story, I continued to struggle with memories, trying desperately to erase the images that had been conjured up by the tug-of-war in the foyer. Over and over, I tried to return to the sermon.

"Each of us must be like this demon-possessed man," Dwayne said as he brought his sermon to a close. "We must be willing to tell our own story to those around us. We must tell our neighbors. Tell our friends. Tell our families. And don't just tell the end of the story," at this moment he paused. "Tell the whole story of the wonderful things Jesus has done for you."

His words riveted my attention. Certainly Dwayne did not mean the whole story. Isn't every believer entitled to her secrets? After all, when our past is forgiven, isn't it forgotten as well? What possible benefit could result from digging up the past?

As I thought about his words, I felt the certain understanding that Stephen needed to know about my past. Though I could not explain how I knew, I felt certain that this sermon was for me alone. As I recognized the application, every cell in my body rebelled. Stephen was the last one who needed to know about my past.

Before I knew it, Dwayne asked me to return to the piano. Mesmerized by his closing words, I hadn't thought of an appropriate closing hymn. I made no clever association between the lyrics of a chorus and the sermon for the evening. I fought a moment of panic.

I sat down at the keyboard, desperate for something to play. Distracted and frantic, I began a more traditional version of Jackie's hymn. I focused on the chords, watching my fingers as they found their home among the keys.

Dwayne closed the service. "Remember, the demon-possessed man just wanted to travel with Jesus. But Jesus told him no. He sent the man back to his hometown." Dwayne paused for effect. "Back to the people who knew him best. Back where his brothers and sisters lived. Back to everyone who knew the whole story of his life.

"Jesus didn't give the man a fresh start with new people and new surroundings. No. Instead he gave the man these simple instructions: 'Tell them how much God has done for you.' "

At that moment, Dwayne turned his attention to me. "So for that reason, I'd like to close tonight's service with the same carol the kids sang earlier tonight. Let's all sing, "Go Tell It on the Mountain."

His instruction caught me off guard, and as the stage light came up over the piano, I felt myself freeze for an instant, and I committed the cardinal sin of keyboardists. My fingers stopped moving. I felt the sweat bead up on the tips of my fingers and wished there was some inconspicuous way to wipe my fingertips on my skirt.

Dwayne sensed my hesitation. Turning to the congregation he said, "Let's stand and sing hymn number 241."

His instruction gave me time to open the keyboard hymnal and find the music. I began the introduction and relaxed as Dwayne led out the first line of the hymn. While the congregation sang, I wrestled with our pastor's words. Should I tell Stephen the whole truth?

At home, Travis and Mallory brought out ice cream and root beer to celebrate their drama success. "You want some?" they asked as I passed through the kitchen.

"Just a small one. I'll be right back."

Apparently Mother had already gone to bed. I found Stephen stretched out on the family-room couch, sound asleep under a wool afghan, while Animal Planet played on the television. I shook his arm and was surprised by the warmth broiling through his shirt. "Stephen, wouldn't you be more comfortable in bed?"

He stirred and opened his eyes. "Hmm? You home already?" He sat up, dropping his long legs over the side of the couch. His sock had a hole in the toe. He threw back the afghan. "Seems like you just left."

"Just got home."

Stephen rubbed his eyes and yawned. "Man, I'm tired. What time is it?"

"Twenty to ten." Taking a seat across from him, I turned on a lamp. A red line circled the rim of Stephen's eyes, and the crimson color in his cheeks persisted. "Would you like a snack before bed? The kids are making floats."

"No. Thanks though." Snatching his shoes from the floor, he stood up and stretched, putting one hand to his forehead. He ran his fingers through his hair. "I would like something for a headache though. I'm working on a tiger here."

"Sure," I said, standing. "You go on upstairs and I'll bring it to you." I followed him up to the main floor, fighting with the urge to ask about his blood sugar.

Not my disease, I chanted to myself as I opened the medicine bottle and put two tablets out on the counter. *Not my disease*, I thought as I poured Stephen an ice-cold glass of water from the container in the fridge. *Not my disease*, I said again as I climbed the stairs to his room.

Later, Kevin came into the bathroom while I brushed my teeth. "Colleen, I'm wondering if you want to take your mom to the bus on the way out of town, or if you'd rather drive her over and come back. The kids and I can pack the car while you drive into town."

The time had come to face my decision. I rinsed my toothbrush and placed it in the ceramic holder. "Actually, I needed to talk to you about that."

He frowned. "We're supposed to leave on Monday."

"I know."

"So we need to plan the morning."

"I don't think I should go." I dried my face with a towel. "I don't think I can leave Stephen alone."

Kevin threw both hands in the air, exasperated beyond words. "Why not? He's a grown man. He's been taking care of himself for years without you."

"I know. But you saw what happened the night he got sick. He needed us, Kevin. And what if his heart acted up again? Who would be around to help him?"

"Colleen, I can't believe this. Are you saying that you've decided to stay home while we go on vacation without you?"

"It's only this once, Kevin." In an effort to keep my hands from shaking, I hung up the towel. "We have four weeks of vacation a year. I've never done anything like this before. We can't take Stephen with us. If something happens, he would need his own doctors, his own records. I don't know if he'd even be treated in Canada."

"So, how long have you known you weren't coming?"

"I don't know. I've been worrying about it for the past few days."

"When were you going to tell me? When it was time to get in the car?"

"Kevin, don't blow this out of proportion."

"Out of proportion?" He put both hands on his hips, and his cheeks grew ruddy. I noticed the tiny furrow between his brows that only shows when Kevin is in pain or under great stress. "It's our vacation we're talking about here. I can't believe you're throwing it away." His voice rose, and I put my index finger over my lips.

"I'm not throwing away anything," I said, as quietly and deliberately as I could. "It's only one week. You and the kids can still go. You'll probably have more fun than you would if I came along anyway. I can't ski as well as you guys; I only hold you back." I moved toward Kevin, slipping my arms around his waist and laying my head on his chest. "I promise to make it up to you."

Kevin didn't put his arms around me. Instead, with his palms on my shoulders, I heard a long sigh as he let out his breath. "Colleen, you can't make up a vacation. These are our kids, and they're growing up too fast as it is. We're supposed to be making memories here. I don't see how you can choose your brother over the kids." He patted my shoulder and pulled himself loose, stepping back as he spoke.

What Kevin really meant was, *How can you choose your brother over me?*

He took a deep breath and then spoke. "I can't make you change your mind. But I don't have to pretend that I understand it."

As the light in the bedroom went off, I smoothed moisturizer onto my face. I slipped between the covers, pulling the down comforter up around my neck against the cold of the open window. I rolled onto my side and put one arm around Kevin.

Without a word, he slid out of my embrace.

We celebrated Christmas with as much of our usual Scottish festivity as we could muster, considering our unusual circumstances.

Early the morning of Christmas Eve, I used the bread machine and a mix for fresh oat bread. Mother made the crust for a chicken potpie, our American adaptation of the traditional mincemeat. While I cooked the chicken breast and put together the sauce, Mallory and Travis cleaned vegetables, then steamed them in the microwave.

By four-thirty, we slid the pie in the oven, an enormous two-and-a-half-quart monstrosity, and collapsed on kitchen stools with hot chocolate and cookies. As the smells of chicken and spices filled the kitchen, Mom pulled out a large pot and poured in apple cider. When it came to a boil, she added a muslin bag filled with traditional mulling spices.

The door to the dining room opened and Stephen came in. "Mmm, I smell wassail," he said, opening the lid to take a deep whiff.

"After a fashion," Mother answered. "Colleen won't let me add any whiskey."

"Not with the kids," I said, nodding my head at the two of them.

"We don't mind," Travis piped up. "Feel free to lead us astray."

"Oh no. I wouldn't want to pollute Colleen's children," Stephen agreed, dropping the lid in place with a grin. "I couldn't live with myself." He reached over and wrapped one arm around Travis's head, giving his hair a five-knuckle rub.

I saw Travis stiffen and pull away. My son had grown more distant from Stephen since the morning we told him about the AIDS. Surely Stephen felt Travis's rejection, but I didn't quite know what to do about the situation without drawing attention to it.

After an early dinner, we gathered around the Christmas tree. During my childhood, my father had always insisted on the Scottish preference for opening gifts on Christmas day. But as I blended my traditions with Kevin's, we moved the exchange to Christmas Eve. And, because we had created our own family, we added some traditions of our own, ones reflecting our mutual faith.

As soon as the children could read, we began reading the Christmas story straight from the Bible. Though it didn't always go smoothly, we've perfected the procedure over the years. Actually, Mallory, being a natural leader, straightened us all out when she became our official story director.

"Alright, everyone," Mallory said, taking her place before the fire. "It's time for our annual reading of the Christmas story. As most of you know"—she looked at her grandmother and winked—"we pass out various versions of the Bible, and then we draw Bible passages from this basket." She held it up in one hand. "You have to look up your passage and read it out loud. That is," she paused and looked directly at Travis, "if you can read."

Travis lifted both hands palm up. His expression said, *See how she abuses me?*

Mallory continued. "What you get is what you read."

Mallory gestured to Travis. "You may pass out the Bibles now."

Though Mother had joined us for other holidays, this would be Stephen's first Christmas with us. I glanced at him, anxious about how he would take the Payton festivity. I saw his expression change slightly as he watched Travis lift a stack of Bibles and begin moving around the room.

We hadn't been raised with Bibles. I couldn't help a little shiver as it shimmied up my spine. Mother's face was carefully composed as she accepted her Teen Study Bible.

Travis gave Stephen a well-worn New American Standard. In spite of his smile, Stephen's shoulders and face looked tense. He teased Mallory, "I take it we aren't talking about the story that begins, "Twas the night before Christmas, and all through the house…'"

"Nice try," I said. "I thought you were the literary genius in our family."

"Well, even geniuses have their limits."

Lightly clapping her hands, Mallory spoke again, "Alright everyone, we have the Christmas story divided into sections, which are numbered chronologically. We each take a section until all the papers are gone. Then, we look up the passages and read them out loud, in order of course." No matter what Mallory chose for a profession, I knew it would include telling others what to do.

Instructions finished, Mallory walked around the little circle, offering the basket first to her grandmother and then to each of us in turn. When all the pieces had been passed out, she spoke, "Alright, who has section number one?"

"I do," Kevin said. He opened the leather-bound New Living Translation and began reading, "It all begins with a Jewish priest, Zechariah, who lived while Herod was king of Judea…"

As Kevin read, I leaned back in my chair, letting my mind drift over the words, thinking again about the miracle of Christmas. Though I had worried all day about this part of our celebration—worried about how Stephen might respond to this tradition—at that moment, I chose to let go of my concerns.

When Kevin finished reading his selection, Travis followed, and then Stephen and myself. As we continued, one after another, our individual voices knit together the story of God's intervention in the course of men. Though the individual readings were unique, each from a different translation, together they told a story more improbable than any Disney could imagine.

The voices told the story of God's unquenchable love for his children, lost to sin.

When we finished, Kevin stood and announced the burning of the yule log. He sent Travis out to the mudroom to bring in the birch log he'd selected early in the summer. Travis, now carefully trained in the peculiar customs of the Scottish Christmas, returned with the log and handed it to his father.

In a more traditional Scottish family, the head of the clan would pronounce a blessing on the group, asking God to increase their number and to protect them from loss. Instead, Kevin stood in front of our fireplace, the log cradled in his forearms, while he began another Payton adaptation. With somber voice, Kevin prayed for each member of our family, gently lifting individual needs to the father, pronouncing a blessing over each before moving on to the next.

When he came to Stephen, Kevin began, "Father, we lift our brother, Stephen, to you. You know how he struggles with his body. You know the illness he faces. Father, we ask that you would touch his body. Give him health for the coming year. And we ask that you would rain down a blessing on Stephen's inner man. Help him to grow closer to you. Surprise him with your care for him. Let him feel your nearness and your comfort. We ask in Jesus's name."

I admit that I hadn't closed my eyes as Kevin prayed. Instead, I'd focused on the floor in front of my feet. And, in the moment that Kevin moved on to Mallory's blessing, a movement caught my eye. With my head down, I glanced at Stephen just as he wiped his eyes.

≈ ≈ ≈

On the day after Christmas, I got up early and cooked breakfast for my family. Even though it was my decision, I ached to send them away. The kids, keenly aware of the tension between Kevin and me, demonstrated a single-minded determination to change my decision.

"Mom," Travis said, "you can still come. I can load your skis into the Jeep, and you could throw a bag in the back. We'd wait for you."

"Not this time, Trav," I said. "You'll have lots of fun skiing without me. You won't have to wait for me at the lift."

"But what about Dad?" Mallory asked. "He'll miss you."

"Dad will be just fine," I said, patting her shoulder. "You'd better hurry, though. Your bags aren't downstairs yet. And, no matter what Travis says, your dad doesn't like to wait."

I stood in the entry hall, a coffee cup in one hand, while Mallory ran upstairs for the last of her things. Already, Kevin and Travis had begun taking things out to the car.

"You guys have enough junk here?" Kevin asked, starting his second trip to the car.

"Dad," Mallory dropped her pillow onto the floor. "You can't get it all in one bag. We need one bag for ski clothes, and another for regular clothes."

Kevin grimaced as he backed out the door, both arms full.

"Take this out to the car." I handed Travis a cooler full of food.

"Mom, we're gonna eat pizza," he lifted two bags and started for the door.

"Not all week you're not." Travis must have heard the warning in my voice; he dropped the bags and returned for the cooler. "Thank you," I said. "You'll appreciate this later."

"Right." He didn't sound convinced.

The winter sun rose just as the car pulled out of the driveway. The sky was clear, and the air very still. I pulled the front of my robe closed against the cold, retying the belt as I watched the little Jeep round the corner onto the street.

"So, they're off," my mother said, standing beside me in the dawning light. "I hope they have a good time." She crossed her arms. "I still think you should have gone."

"They'll be fine this one time," I said, pulling the storm door closed. "Stephen's staying for another week at least. I don't think he should be alone yet."

Mother looked directly at me. "Ah, well. I guess you know what you're doing." I saw doubt in her eyes.

Mother ate breakfast while I cleaned up the mess in the kitchen. "Oh shoot. Kevin didn't put the lunch meat in the cooler," I said, standing in front of the open refrigerator. I shut the door and turned to Mom. "Do you need any help with your things?"

"No," she said. "I'm all packed. I just have to bathe and dress." She brought her dishes to the sink. "What a wonderful Christmas, Colleen. I just wish Daddy could have been here. He would have loved it."

I murmured agreement and bent down to close the dishwasher. While mother bathed, I dressed and picked up our bedroom, hanging up the clothes Kevin had worn on Christmas Day. I wondered about Stephen, sleeping through the morning noises. Part of me wanted to wake him so that he could say good-bye. But another part, the protective part, wanted to let him rest.

I needn't have worried. When I came into the hall, my winter parka draped over my arm, I found Stephen's door open and Mother inside talking quietly. I slipped by the door to carry her things out to the car and start the engine.

As I waited, letting the car warm up, I wondered what Mom would say to Stephen. She had such a unique ability to humiliate him. I watched as she came down the sidewalk and got in the car. "So you got to say good-bye?"

"You don't have to worry about what I said," my mother huffed. "Even I can see the boy is sick. I wouldn't hit him while he's down."

I pulled the car out of the driveway.

"Daddy so loved the Scottish Christmas traditions," Mother said from the passenger seat of my car. "He loved the yule log. Remember how we left it decorated by the fireplace?"

I smiled over at her while I turned on the blinker. "Which house were we in?"

"We did it everywhere we lived." She sounded defensive.

"Oh. Sure." I pulled into traffic. "I guess I hadn't thought of it."

"Your daddy loved the tartans and the carols, and the tree."

And the booze, I thought wearily.

"He loved having the family together and being with you kids."

Funny, I didn't think he ever came home. I bit my lower lip and forced myself to remain quiet. Mother has the most remarkable ability to remake the memory of my father. Sometimes, while she praises him, I wonder if we are thinking of the same man. I took a deep breath and tried to focus on the speedometer. I slowed the car down to exactly twenty-four miles an hour and concentrated on keeping the needle steady.

Mother continued. "Do you remember his last Christmas with us?" She looked over at me, as her eyes began to fill with tears. "He was so happy that year. It was as if he knew."

In spite of my effort to disconnect from my mother's reminiscing, I shook my head. I could not think of a single moment when my father had ever been happy. Neutral perhaps. But never really happy. I bit the inside of my cheek; after all, it was Christmas. No use picking a fight with Mother now.

"He'd love to see the grandkids now, all grown up and so mature. He was so proud of you—of all of you really."

"Too bad he never said it." The words came out before I had a chance to stop myself. Mother's face registered shock and her features hardened.

She puffed her chest. "It wasn't the thing to do in those days," she said. "Fathers didn't gush over their children the way they do today."

Ah, heck. Christmas was over. I might as well face it. "Mom, I never heard him say, 'I love you.' Not one single time."

"Of course you did." She crossed her arms across her chest.

"Not once." I slowed to a stop, yielding to a pedestrian.

"You just don't remember."

"Mom, don't you think I'd remember those words? He was never home. The Air Force had him off on some mission most of our lives. If it weren't for pictures, I wouldn't know what he looked like."

"How can you say these things about your father? He isn't here to defend himself."

I felt anger push against my chest. "How can you try to change him into someone he wasn't? He was what he was. I've dealt with that. But what is the point of canonizing him now? It's over. He's gone."

"He was a good father. He did the best he could." Her voice trembled as the first tear trickled down her cheek.

"Mom," I began, trying to keep the anger from my voice. "I know you loved Dad. And that's great. Maybe he was a great husband. But he wasn't such a great dad. I don't think he knew how. He was gone too much to figure it out."

"How can you be so ungrateful? He sacrificed to give you a good home. Good medical care. A good education. You had new clothes. He made sure that you had everything you needed."

Without another word, I pulled into the parking lot of the hotel and turned off the engine. Turning in my seat, I took a deep breath and said, "Mom, I'm grateful for what Dad gave us. He wasn't all bad. No one is. I'm not saying that.

"But he wasn't all good either. I can't speak for Carrie or Stephen. But I can speak for me. The one thing I needed he didn't give me. He never gave me love. I never felt it, not once. Maybe he didn't know how. Maybe he didn't believe in it. Maybe he thought it would turn me into a sissy or something. But he didn't give me what I needed most in life."

Tears spilled freely down my mother's cheeks, and her lips formed a straight hard line across her small face. The light went out of her eyes as the crow's feet hardened around them. Though I hadn't meant to start a war, I knew Mother would not forget this conversation. Not for a long, long time.

"Well for all of your resentment, you didn't turn out so bad. He couldn't have done such a terrible job," she said, getting out of the car.

Mother didn't speak as I got her bags out of the trunk, or as we waited in the lobby for the nine-thirty Greyhound. When the bus pulled up to the entrance of the hotel, we went outside and waited in silence while the driver put her bags on board.

When it was time to go, I gave her an awkward hug, much like hugging a stack of firewood. "Thank you, dear," she said, her voice formal and cold. Then, she pulled herself up the steps and disappeared inside.

No wonder I became an elephant-in-the-living-room person. Telling the truth isn't all it's cracked up to be.

≈ ≈ ≈

When I got home, I found Stephen in the kitchen, rinsing his cereal dish. "Well, I got Mom off," I said, pouring myself another cup of coffee. "But she was none too happy when she left." I went to the fridge and added milk to the strong dark liquid.

Stephen didn't answer and I turned to look at him as he put his dish in the dishwasher. His cheeks glowed pink, and the sagging shadows under his eyes had darkened. I smelled the funny, fermented fruit smell again, and I bit back the urge to ask about his blood sugar. "You don't look well," I said. "You feel okay?"

"Why is it that everyone feels the need to comment on my looks all the time?"

"We care, that's why. So no whining." As I put away the milk, I grabbed a pitcher of orange juice. "Would you like some juice?" I poured two glasses, handing him the larger.

"Yeah, thanks," he said, accepting the glass. Leaning against the counter, he drank deeply. Immediately, he started coughing—a hard, racking cough that sounded as though it shook his very bones. "Are you okay?" I patted his shoulder.

"Yeah. Fine," he said. "Went down the wrong pipe." His coughing continued, little spasms that began with an irritation and increased to earth-shaking strength.

Trying to hide my alarm, I carried my own glass to the sink and slid a box of tissues across to him. This sounded much more serious than juice gone down the wrong pipe. I made a display of wiping the counters. "I think you have a fever," I said, folding the rag and draping it over the faucet.

"Look, you're no nurse." He rested against the counter, spent and listless, as if this bout of coughing had wrung the life from his body.

"I don't claim to be a nurse. But I do own a thermometer."

"Anyway, I've been thinking," Stephen said, ignoring me. "I'm thinking that I'd like to head home today. I need to get back to Seattle."

I choked back my resentment. If Stephen were planning to go home all along, why didn't he tell me? Why had I sacrificed my vacation so that I could stay home with him? "Oh really? I thought you planned to stay through the New Year."

He folded his arms across his chest. "I'm thinking that I should get home. I'd like to get in to see my doctor."

CHAPTER
Twenty-Three

Stephen sat down at the kitchen table. Even this small change in posture triggered another bout of coughing. Part of me felt sorry for him. But the other side, the less compassionate side of me spoke, "I told you so," I said, pointing. "I knew you weren't feeling well."

Stephen frowned. "It must give you great pleasure to say that."

"I relish it, my good man. Have you called your doctor?"

"Not yet," he said.

Stephen visibly wilted. Looking at him, I wondered how he could expect to drive himself home in his condition. "Why don't you call first? You might get an earlier appointment than if you wait until you get home."

"That's probably a good idea."

I handed him the cordless. "Do you have the number?"

"In my wallet."

I sat in the chair next to him, drinking coffee as he pulled a card from his wallet and called his medical clinic. I listened to his end of the conversation. "Alright, I understand," he said into the telephone. "Yes, Tuesday. That would be fine." He clicked off and handed me the phone.

Sitting close, I could not miss the bead of perspiration outlining Stephen's upper lip. He had a fever. I asked, "Next Tuesday, or tomorrow?"

He nodded. "My doctor is taking the week off. I can see one of his partners tomorrow, but I'd rather see my own doctor." He shrugged.

"So next week it is. I'll be fine." He punctuated his faith in the future with anther series of racking coughs.

"Sounds fine to me," I agreed.

Stephen frowned at my sarcasm. "I'm going upstairs to pack." He got out of his chair and stood up, coughing again as his body stretched into a standing position.

Clearly, my brother was very sick. Some bug had chosen to camp in his lungs. But just as clearly, Stephen didn't want me to interfere in his plans. Now, with this new collection of symptoms, the fruity smells I'd caught emanating from his body made more sense. Whatever caused his fever and cough had clearly thrown off his blood sugar.

I knew from Carrie that even a cold had the power to send her blood sugar into the stratosphere. Our mother made more than one trip to the emergency room because of this potentially fatal combination of illness and diabetes.

"I have another idea," I said, trying to sound casual as I studied the flowers on the outside of my coffee mug. "Since you can't get an appointment with your own doctor, why don't you stay here and see if you can see that new doctor in Wenatchee. You might get in sooner, and you wouldn't have to drive home sick."

"I just told you that I want to see my own doctor."

"I know. And I understand, really I do." I noticed the sheen of perspiration on Stephen's face reflected by overhead lighting. "I'd feel the same way."

"No you don't. With this disease, there're as many treatments as doctors." Stephen coughed again, doubling over with the effort. "You just have to pick one and stick with it. You make yourself crazy going from doctor to doctor and from treatment plan to treatment plan. I can't do it any more. I won't."

"You've already seen more than one doctor?"

"Not me," Stephen said with a rare bitterness.

I made a guess. "You aren't Glen, Stephen," I said. "One new doctor isn't going to mess everything up. In fact, she might help." Though I didn't want to tell my brother what to do, the words came out anyway. "Besides, you can't drive in this condition."

Stephen coughed again, swaying this time, as he collapsed into another chair. "Alright," he said, stubbornness oozing through his words, "here's my deal: If you can get an appointment for me today, I'll go." He wiped his face with his palms. "But if you can't, I'm going home."

Slowly, he stood. "I'm going upstairs to pack."

I called the infectious-disease specialist Dr. Erickson mentioned when Stephen was in the hospital. These calls to Dr. Kurian went unanswered, and I worried that she might have taken the week between Christmas and the New Year off.

In desperation, I called the internist I'd met in Stephen's hospital room. His nurse listened to my predicament, promised to check with the doctor, and call me back. The moments ticked by as I heard the shower upstairs stop running. Eventually, I heard Stephen start the hair dryer.

I was running out of time.

The phone rang. "Dr. Erickson has your message," the nurse reported. "He's called Dr. Kurian himself. You should be hearing from her office before long."

I hung up and glanced at the clock. Stephen had been upstairs nearly twenty minutes. If the office didn't call soon, I'd have to let him go. I went into the living room and picked up my knitting, hoping to lose myself in the pattern of stitches. I heard Stephen's cough echo off the high bare walls as he came downstairs.

"Well," he said, sitting in the chair across from mine. "Did you get an appointment?"

"We should get a call any time now."

He shook his head. "Colleen. Just give up. I'm going home. I'll be fine." Stephen's arms and hands hung over the arms of the chair.

I sat forward on the couch. "If you insist on going, at least let me drive you."

"Right. And then what do you do?" He leaned his head back. "You'd end up stranded in Seattle." He chuckled, and the chuckle disintegrated into a full-blown convulsion of coughing. I waited for the coughing to end. "No, thanks. I'll drive myself home."

Sometimes Stephen is so stubborn I'd like to box his ears. "That makes so much sense. And how are you going to stay on the road if you have another fit like that?"

"I'll be fine." He closed his eyes and crossed his arms. There was no use fighting with him any more. If he wanted to die on the highway, I'd have to let him. I didn't say anything for a time, and he seemed to have drifted off.

I put my knitting aside and stood up, trying to cross the room quietly. I hoped that Stephen's sleep would buy a few more minutes.

His eyes opened as I passed his chair. Stephen stood up. "I'm coming," he said. "You don't need to carry my bags."

"Oh be quiet," I said, making no effort to cover my exasperation. "I'll carry your stuff if I want to." I opened the front door and stepped out onto the porch. "You might as well get going. If you wait any longer, you'll be dead before you leave."

He put on his jacket and followed me out to the car. We hugged and he climbed inside.

"Do you have everything?" I asked, leaning toward the open car window.

"I think so," he said. He started the car and put it in reverse. "Oh wait," he said, shifting into park. "I have a bottle of medicine in your refrigerator. I forgot it."

"I'll run back in."

I found the medicine in the refrigerator door, and as I turned to leave, the telephone rang. I picked up the cordless. "Hello," I said, panting.

Moments later, I ran back outside, waving a note at my brother. "Turn off the car," I said, grinning with triumph. "You lose. Dr. Kurian just called, and you have an appointment at two."

≈ ≈ ≈

Three hours later, Stephen and I stepped into the smallest waiting room I'd ever seen. Six oak chairs defined the perimeter of a tiny square, two on each of three sides. On the fourth, the receptionist sat behind a tall counter. In the only clear space, a second door led to the back of the office, an area I assumed contained the exam rooms.

I chose the chair closest to the second door as my brother checked in with the receptionist and began filling out the mountain of required paperwork. Though it didn't seem possible, Stephen seemed to grow weaker with each passing moment.

His hand trembled as he handed the clipboard back to the receptionist.

My worry grew as he collapsed into the oak chair beside mine. I brought my knitting out and began working. "Would you like a magazine?" I asked, gesturing to the table beside me.

"No thanks." He leaned his head against the wall behind his chair.

The coughing began again, and I held my breath, willing the sound to cease. "Some water?" He opened his eyes and frowned at me. I got the message. "Okay, right."

I began to count stitches, trying to remember where in the pattern I had quit knitting. A man entered the office from outside, bald and stooped, his downturned face emaciated. He moved toward the counter, where he signed in. When he'd finished, he stepped over my knitting bag and took a seat in the chair farthest from Stephen.

The door opened again, and an older woman entered. Though she appeared to be in her mid-sixties, perhaps seventy, she wore her light brown hair quite long, down past her shoulders. Heavily streaked with gray, her wavy hair had been caught at the neck with an elegant turquoise clasp. With a long fleece skirt and a corduroy artist's jacket, she seemed the antithesis of any grandmother I'd ever known. Hand knit stockings peeked out above her Doc Martens. Travis would have dubbed this granny "hip."

Moving with spry grace, she smiled and greeted the receptionist by name. "Had to park down the street," she said, gesturing with one arm. "When is Dr. Kurian going to get more designated parking?"

"We have to share with the whole building," the woman answered. "I don't know if we'll ever get more spaces."

"This rain has made muck out of the snow," the newcomer said. "Everyone will be soaked by the time they get in here today." She stepped in front of me, heading for the chair between Stephen and the man who had preceded her.

I tried to pull my knitting bag out of the way; but somehow, in the tiny space, the woman caught her shoe in my yarn, trailing it with her as she passed. Before I could stop her, my knitting jumped from my fingers. "Excuse me," I said, embarrassed. "You've got my yarn there." I pointed to her shoe, a Mary Jane style that would have left Mallory miserable with envy.

"No, no. It's my fault," she said, sitting down. "I should have been more careful." She leaned down to unwind her foot.

"It's small, isn't it?" I said, accepting the yarn. "I mean the office."

The second door opened, and a nurse with hair the color of orange soda announced a patient's name. The emaciated man stood and the older woman reached up to catch his arm. "Be sure to ask about the shot," she said. "I can wait if you need one."

He nodded and followed the nurse into the recesses of the office. When the door closed again, the grandmother reached down into her leather purse and pulled out a small leather-bound book, which she opened and placed on her lap. Though I could not see the cover, I guessed from the gold edges that this woman had brought a Bible to the office.

She caught me watching and smiled. Realizing that I'd made her uncomfortable, I returned to my knitting. Once again, she bent to dig in her bag. This time, she removed a plastic sheet, which she spread across the pages of the open book. I realized, as I stole glances in her direction, that she used the sheet to magnify the words on the page.

When the nurse returned, she called Stephen's name, and I watched him stand as another episode of coughing caught him off guard. "Would you like me to go in with you?" I asked. Though he could not move for the convulsions racking his chest, he shook his head. I stood, prepared to catch him, as I waited for the cough to subside.

"No," he said. "I'm fine."

Yeah, right. I frowned.

The door had no more than closed behind the nurse when the older woman spoke. "They can be so stubborn, can't they?"

"Men?"

She considered for a moment. "Yes. Them too. Actually, I was thinking of these patients." My eyebrows rose with an unspoken question. Did this woman have contact with more than one patient? "Was that your son?" I asked.

She smiled. "Jake? Oh no. I just drive him to his doctor's appointments. He's a friend." She closed her book, leaving the magnifier inside. "How about you?"

"Stephen is my brother. My twin actually."

She nodded, understanding in her eyes. "Hard, isn't it?"

Without permission, tears filled my eyes. I nodded.

She stood up and took the chair beside me, wrapping one arm around my shoulders and giving me a swift, firm hug. "I know what you're going through," she said.

I blinked back the tears, forcing myself to stay under control. She put her hands in her lap and turned in the seat. "Tell me about it," she said.

I looked into her dark brown eyes and saw the compassion I'd missed so much while Stephen had been with me. For a moment, an instant really, I considered telling her everything. But I let the moment pass. "Oh, there's too much really. You don't want to hear it all," I said. I pointed to her book. "Is that a Bible you're reading?"

"This?" She lifted the book. "Sure. I carry it when I take the doctor's run. It helps me to pass the time waiting."

"Doctor's run?"

She squirmed a little, and her lips pressed together. I felt her wonder if she should explain it to me. "I'm a volunteer. I drive HIV patients to their doctor's appointments, or to the grocery store or to therapy. Whatever they need."

"I didn't know there was anyone who did that," I said, surprised. "Do you work with a group?"

"In the big cities there are lots of organizations that do those things."

"But around here?"

"An organization, you mean?"

"Is it a hospital, or a hospice? What is it?"

"Actually, I work for a little group I started myself."

"Really?"

"Fifteen years ago now, over at my church." She snapped the cover of her Bible closed and bent down to stuff it back into her purse. "By the way, I'm Glorietta Hubbard," she said, offering her hand. "Folks call me Gloria." She smiled again, and the skin around her eyes folded into well-worn creases. Though Gloria showed her age, something about her complexion and the glow in her eyes looked very young. I found myself irrationally drawn to her.

"I'm Colleen Payton," I said, shaking her hand. "Where do you go to church?"

"Valley Bible."

"Where is that?"

"It's a tiny church over on Meeker, out on the east side of town. No more than about a hundred folks there."

We talked for a time about our churches, and she asked about my family. "My husband used to work for the county," she said smiling. "Road Maintenance. I'll bet he knows your Kevin."

"Could be. It's a small county. What does your husband do now?"

"He's retired. We both are. I worked for the county library. Now he grows tomatoes and apples, and he wants to turn into one of those snowbird types that head to Arizona every winter." She tossed her hand toward me. "I could never be happy in Arizona."

"Winter's pretty hard here. It might be nice to have a little sunshine and warm temperatures."

"I'd get tired of it," she said, dismissing my idea. "Besides, what would my boys do without me?"

"How many boys do you take care of?"

"Well, now, do you mean me personally? Or the group?"

I shrugged. "The group, I guess."

"Well, at any given time, we have about fifteen we keep track of. We cook dinners for those who aren't doing well. Others, we just visit every once and a while, to give 'em a little company. And then the ones like Jake here"—she pointed to the door again—"he needs a ride quite often. Doesn't drive any more." Her words were soaked in compassion. "I have help, of course. I couldn't do it all myself. Still, I'd hate to leave it to someone else."

"You don't think they'd get the job done?"

"No," she shook her head and reached out to pat my hand. "That isn't it at all."

"If you don't mind my asking," I said. "Why do you do it?"

"To tell you the truth," she said, leaning toward me as though to reveal a dark secret. "I don't want to miss a single moment of it. I want to be here. These boys need someone. And when I'm here, there's no joy like it."

"You still haven't told me why? Why did you start a ministry like this?"

She smiled a broad, bittersweet smile. She tipped her head to one side as she admitted the truth. "My son," she said, nodding. "I lost my son to AIDS in 1987."

CHAPTER
Twenty-Four

My new friend leaned over and dug through her purse. Opening her wallet, Gloria brought out a small plastic folio of pictures. "There he is," she said, offering me the collection. "I took that picture a couple of years before he got sick."

I held the picture gently, realizing that this mother had just given me entry into her most private pain. In the picture, a tall, slim, dark-haired man stood on a riverbank, his hands on his hips, smiling at the camera. "He's handsome," I said. "A beautiful smile."

"Always was," she said, reaching to take the picture. "It was harder then, you know. They hardly knew what caused AIDS, let alone how to treat it. We couldn't do anything but stand by and watch him die."

I leaned toward her, "How did he get it?"

She laughed at me. "You don't have to whisper, Colleen. He was gay. I never knew where he got the actual infection. But he told us he was gay right after he graduated from college. It broke our hearts, of course. And we didn't handle it very well."

"What happened?"

"I tried to talk him out it." She laughed at herself and the memory as she placed the picture back in her wallet. "He blew up and stopped talking to us. We didn't hear from him for almost ten years."

"Was it hard for you?" As soon as I said it, I realized how foolish the question appeared. "I mean, having him pull away?"

Gloria reached back and tugged at her hair. "I can't tell you how hard it was. I believed my son was headed for hell, and I was so afraid for him."

"What did you do?"

At that moment, the door to the inner office opened, and the orange-haired nurse reappeared. "Colleen MacLaughlin?" she asked, looking straight at me. I began to gather my things and turned back to Gloria, waiting for her answer.

"I let go," she said. "It wasn't my job to save my son. Ten years after that, he got sick."

I stuffed my knitting into my bag, wishing that we could continue the conversation. Then, an idea struck and I picked up my purse. Digging inside, I pulled out my checkbook. "Ms. MacLaughlin," the nurse said again, with growing irritation.

"My name is Payton," I answered, with obvious frustration. "MacLaughlin is my brother's name." I turned to Gloria. "Here," I said, handing her a deposit slip from our checking account. Kevin would have a fit if he knew I'd done it. But I didn't care.

Gloria had survived the same struggles that I faced. She was like me. A person of deep faith watching someone she loved die. I didn't want to lose touch with her. I needed her wisdom. "Could we talk again?" I asked.

She held the deposit slip in the air, waving it as her face broke into a smile. "I'll call."

~ ~ ~

The nurse led me to an office in the back corner of the complex. Unlike many of the offices I'd visited on this adventure with Stephen, this one contained no desk, but rather a floral loveseat and two swivel rockers set around a glass-topped coffee table. A small bookcase stood in the corner, with several photographs on the top shelf.

"Have a seat," the nurse said, pointing. "The doctor will be right in."

I chose a place on the loveseat as the nurse closed the door. Across from me, two windows, covered in mini-blinds, let in slivers of afternoon sunshine. Dust danced in the sunlight over a hand-hooked wool carpet. I took a deep breath, trying to calm the flutter of my heart. I had no idea why the doctor had invited me into this room. I tried to push away visions of bad news, grasping at a fleeting memory of scripture. Why is it that the words never come when I need them? *You give peace, Lord*, I prayed. *I could use some right now.*

The door opened, and Stephen entered. His shoulders sagged, and he looked too tired to walk. I heard him pant as he crossed the room to one of the rockers and collapsed. "What is this about?" he asked me.

"I have no idea," I said. "What did the doctor say?"

" 'Get dressed and meet me in my office.' " He shrugged. "I don't know any more than you at this point." He started coughing again, clutching at his stomach. I imagined how sore his muscles must be by now. "She—"

His doctor entered the room. "Good afternoon," she said, stepping toward me with her hand outstretched. "I am Dr. Kurian. Martha Kurian. Thank you for joining us." Her English accent was pleasant, clear, and clipped.

I introduced myself and we shook hands. I glanced at Stephen as the doctor took a seat in the remaining chair, wondering what he thought of his new physician.

She was very small, barely over five feet, with tiny hands and feet. She wore black pants and a well-fitted pale blue blouse under a three-quarter-length lab jacket. Her skin was the color of a tigereye stone, rich and dark, and reminded me of a pendant Kevin had once given me for an anniversary gift.

She had plaited her thick hair into a braid that extended almost to her waist. Around her face, tufts of black curls escaped, softening the margins between her skin and hair. Her startlingly black eyes seemed warm and direct.

The features of her face were as delicate as her stature, softly arched brows and a broad though attractive nose. "Thank you for joining us, Colleen," she began, smiling at me. "I wanted you here because I've found that my patients do better when they have someone with them when they talk to their doctor."

She looked at Stephen. "I understand that Stephen is reluctant to burden you with information about his health. But I asked if we could try to talk through this together, and see how it goes. So far"—she glanced down at her chart—"he has agreed.

"Now, normally, I begin with a detailed history on every patient I see. And of course, I have much of that information from Stephen. It would be nice to have some of the lab results from your doctor in Seattle."

"We could have those faxed to you," I said.

Stephen shot me a warning glance.

"We may come to that. But as I was saying, the more urgent issue is to discern the source of the cough and fever that Stephen is experiencing. I've cultured some of Stephen's sputum, and I've sent a slide to the lab for analysis. I should have some of those results today, and the rest of the test results in a couple of days." She pulled a large preprinted tablet from under the manila file on her lap. "In the meantime, I'd like to send him for a chest x-ray and a blood draw. I can have the radiologist's report almost immediately. We can proceed from there."

"What do you think it is?" Stephen asked.

"I'm quite sure that you have an early case of PCP. However, the cough is unusual in this diagnosis. Since the pneumocystic carinii fungus cannot be cultured, we'll know more conclusively if the cultures come back negative."

The abbreviation "PCP" seemed to mean something to Stephen. He frowned and began picking at a piece of lint over the knee of his pants.

I must have looked completely bewildered, because she stopped writing and spoke to me. "PCP is a pneumonia caused by a fungus—one that lives in the lungs of most adults without causing illness. Generally, because it can't be cultured, we diagnose it by eliminating the other possible causes of disease. We hope to find the organism itself in the sputum, which confirms the diagnosis. The x-ray will let us know how extensive the infection is."

Dr. Kurian began writing, her tiny perfect print filling up the empty places on the top of the tablet. She pulled the sheet from the pad. "Here," she said, handing the page to Stephen. "I've already called the hospital. They're expecting you. Then, once I've talked to the radiologist, I'll call you at the hospital. If things go well, we'll start treatment by midafternoon."

"What kind of treatment?" Stephen asked.

"Depends on the severity of the infection. It could require hospitalization."

"Not the hospital. Not again." Stephen's shoulders slumped and he slid down in his chair.

"We can do the hospital if we need to," I interrupted. "Whatever it takes to get better."

"We can't do the hospital," he shot back. "I can't afford it. I need to go home."

"Clearly, you shouldn't be driving in this condition," Dr. Kurian said. "I suspect that you aren't getting enough oxygen in your blood. Hopefully, we won't admit you. But it's a possibility."

"I can't afford it."

She looked pointedly at Stephen. "I don't practice medicine by bank account. We take care of your body first. We ask questions later."

A smile snuck onto my face as I scooted forward on the couch and bent down to reach for my purse. I expected the doctor to dismiss us, but Dr. Kurian hadn't finished. She leaned back in her chair. "Now, there is one more urgent issue that we need to discuss. And that is the implication of this infection."

Though I had no idea what she meant, I felt the rhythm of my heart accelerate. Now what? I sat back into the couch.

She continued. "By this I mean that we assume that PCP does not occur in anyone with a CD4 count over two hundred cells per milliliter of blood. To me, the most important question we should be asking is this: If your antiviral medications are working, why did you get this infection?

"I think PCP tells us that your HIV is not under control." She paused, folding her dainty hands in her lap. "Perhaps your virus has mutated, or the medications may not be working. We should certainly check your CD4 and your viral load—even though your present illness will skew the test results."

She slid her pen into the chest pocket of her lab coat. "I've ordered those tests, along with an arterial blood gas. That will tell us exactly how well your lungs are working under the pressure of an infection. Unfortunately, I'll have to wait about four days for the CD4."

"I'm sorry," I said, feeling overwhelmed. "I haven't known about Stephen's illness for long. I don't understand all of these abbreviations. Could you explain this again in English?"

She smiled. "Sure. I forget how confusing our terminology can be; I assume that everyone speaks AIDS." She took a deep breath and looked at the ceiling, considering her presentation. "The viral load test simply counts the number of viruses present in Stephen's blood." She smiled. "But the CD4 is more complex. When the HIV attacks the body, it focuses on one white blood cell in particular—the T lymphocyte. The destruction of these cells, called the CD4 cells, marks the various stages of the progression of AIDS. As more cells die, the number of total cells drop, and the body grows vulnerable to infection. Not your average cold and flu, mind you, but these rare funguses and viral diseases—like PCP and certain tumors and unusual infections.

"When the level of CD4 in the blood is high, we know the body has strong immunity to infections. Unfortunately, in the years we've been working with HIV, we've discovered that we can accurately predict which illnesses correspond with which CD4 numbers. That is how I associate PCP with a CD4 count under two hundred cells per milliliter."

She opened the file and directed her next question to my brother. "Stephen, do you remember the numbers on your last viral load?"

"No. But they were up."

Dr. Kurian frowned. "Would you consider letting me contact your doctor in Seattle for the test results? I'll need your written permission."

Stephen coughed, covering his mouth and leaning down over his knees. When he recovered, he sat up. As he spoke, his voice sounded like a man who had smoked from childhood. "I don't see the point.

I'm going back to Seattle as soon as I can. Viral loads don't make any difference. I have to treat the PCP and get on with life."

"Not exactly," Dr. Kurian said. "If you do have PCP, you'll have to take prophylactic therapy for the rest of your life, no matter what the results of your viral load."

Her words slapped Stephen, and he shrunk visibly with the news. "We use Bactrim," she said. "It's inexpensive and simple to take, even for many years."

"Well. That's doable," I said. Ever the Pollyanna.

"Alright," she said, looking at each of us in turn. "One other thing. It is crucial to monitor your blood sugar. As you know, an infection can throw off your normal insulin demand. You must keep a close eye on that. Test regularly, and document the results. Keep a journal.

"In the meantime, we'll treat this infection and let your regular doctor consider the changes in your viral load. When I get the test results, I'll fax them to Seattle. We'll know more about what we're up against when we talk again this afternoon."

Stephen and I trudged back to the car, crossed town to the hospital, and headed for the outpatient admission desk. Three hours later, we'd been to the x-ray department, dropped by the lab for a blood draw, and returned to the waiting area. We watched CNN while waiting for the radiologist to check Stephen's pictures and report to Dr. Kurian.

Eventually, the receptionist paged Stephen to the telephone. I waited, knitting tight irregular stitches as I kept one eye on my brother. I've always believed that I could read his mind, that by the posture of his shoulders, or his facial expression, I would know what news the doctor had for us.

He crossed the lobby, hands in his pocket, eyes down. "She wants us to come back to the office," he said.

"Now?" I folded my knitting.

"Right now." Stephen slumped against the wall as he waited for me to gather my things.

"Did she say anything?"

"Not really. I guess we'll know more when we get there."

~ ~ ~

As we crossed town to Dr. Kurian's office, a thought occurred to me. "You know, Stephen, it can't be all that bad. She had us at the hospital. If she thought that you were in really bad shape, she'd have admitted you by telephone."

My brother didn't respond, and I wondered if he'd fallen asleep. With his head turned toward the window, his body looked fully relaxed. I drove in silence, praying for the doctor who now directed his care. I'd only known about Stephen's illness since mid-November. So far, I'd watched him endure two hospitalizations and a heart procedure. Less than three weeks after having an angioplasty, Stephen faced yet another serious assault on his health.

It was after five when the nurse showed us back to the office. We waited for almost thirty minutes before Dr. Kurian came in. She shut the door quietly and took her usual seat. "I'm sorry to keep you. I've had an emergency over at the hospital." She folded her hands over the manila file in her lap. "Well, I have some good news and some bad news," she said, looking first at Stephen and then at me.

"I'll take the good news," Stephen said. "I could use some."

"From the preliminary tests, you have a mild to moderate case of pneumocystis carinii pneumonia."

"That's the good news?" Stephen coughed. "That's good news I'd rather do without."

"It's treatable. That's always good news," Dr. Kurian said. "Especially with HIV. The x-rays look quite definitive, and the preliminary sputum results are negative for other bacterial culprits. We'll do a culture to make certain nothing bacterial grows, but that should take a few days. If it's all right with you, I'd like to start treatment now. I feel quite confident of the diagnosis."

"Sure," Stephen said, his face a carefully composed mask.

"We use Bactrim for PCP, and you can take that at home. I've already written the prescription." She handed Stephen the paper. "Fortunately, you don't need hospitalization."

"You mentioned bad news?" I didn't know how much more bad news I could take.

"Well, the bad news is that we have a clear case of PCP. As I said before, this diagnosis indicates that Stephen's antiviral therapy might be failing. If I were you"—she looked at my brother—"I'd want to get right on it. I'd want to do something about it before the virus does any more serious damage." She paused. "Before another disease gets a foothold."

"I'm on my last possible drug combination right now," Stephen said, his voice breaking. "There isn't anything to do. My virus is resistant to everything else. Over the last fifteen years, I've taken every new thing they've put on the market. There's nothing to change. Nothing to add. They've done everything they can."

"I couldn't agree without knowing for certain which medicines you've tried," she answered. "There are many different approaches to managing the disease."

Gently, I placed my hand on Stephen's knee, hoping he would hear the silent testimony of my solidarity.

"What you're really saying then…" A long hacking cough interrupted him. Catching his breath, he tried again, "I've reached the beginning of the end. That's the bad news, isn't it?"

I knew that Stephen was begging Dr. Kurian to argue the point. *Tell me I'm going to live*, Stephen seemed to be saying, his eyes pleading with the doctor. *Please tell me I'm wrong.*

But she did not argue. Instead, she stood up, tucking her manila folder under one elbow. "We don't know that for certain. Not with you. Not with anyone. Some people, even at this stage, find the right drug combination and their viral loads become completely undetectable."

I thanked Dr. Kurian for seeing us. And as she left the room, I heard the words she did not say echoing in the silence:

Some patients never find the right combination.

CHAPTER
Twenty-Five

I turned on my windshield wipers as we pulled out of the basement lot and turned toward home. With sunset only minutes away, gray skies hovered over nearby buildings, darkening even as we watched. Snow, plowed and piled along the edges of sidewalks and parking lots, blended with the rain and slid into the streets, where it formed a thick dark slop flung up by passing cars.

Late-afternoon traffic filled the streets, clogging the intersections and slowing our progress. As we waited through our third red light at the same left turn, I asked Stephen, "So, did you like Dr. Kurian?"

He shrugged.

"She seemed to know what she was talking about."

"Hmm."

The light turned green and we inched forward. "Would you like to stop for dinner?"

"No thanks."

"You should eat something."

"I really want to go to bed."

"I know you must be tired. It's been a long day." I reached out to touch his arm as I turned left and inched my way across the lanes of traffic. "I have to stop at a pharmacy before we go home. I'll need your insurance card to fill the prescription."

"Sure." He leaned back against the headrest and closed his eyes.

I parked in the lot of a local drug store and turned off the motor, hesitant to wake him.

"Stephen, do you have your card with you?"

He opened his eyes and glanced around the lot. Sighing, he leaned over and pulled his wallet from his back pocket, giving me the card without a word.

In the store, I waited in a folding chair while the pharmacist filled Stephen's prescription. I couldn't shake my nagging worry. In the past few days, Stephen's mental state had changed. It seemed as if a curtain had fallen between us, keeping me from the brother I loved. Today's news seemed to have turned the curtain into a lead shield.

My brother was slipping away.

While the pharmacy staff answered phones and rang up sales, I fretted. Perhaps I'd only imagined the change. After all, with so much going on in his body, Stephen had no extra energy to waste socializing. Could this withdrawal be a symptom of his current pneumonia?

No. Something had changed and I knew it. Stephen was sliding into a cavern of depression. While his lungs battled a fungus, his emotions battled a hopelessness more black than any I had observed before. I found myself replaying the conversation in Dr. Kurian's office. Something Stephen said bothered me, but I could not recall the words.

The memory returned, shocking and painful. Stephen saw this pneumonia as the beginning of the end.

No matter what the truth was, Stephen could not survive if he believed that he had already lost the battle with AIDS. He needed to believe in the treatment, believe in his chances of survival. Without hope, the depression would surely steal his will to live, and eventually his body would obey.

How could I pull him out of this emotional dive? As I sat there, in the midst of customers and clerks, children and product displays, I begged God for insight.

Stephen needs hope, Lord, I prayed. *And outside of you, I don't know what hope I can give him. He's right. He's going to die, eventually. But he has to live long enough to see you. Show me what I can do to reach him. Tell me what to say. Lead me as I try to break through the wall surrounding him. More than his health is at stake.*

Show me how to reach his soul.

~ ~ ~

At home, I gave Stephen his Bactrim and brought him a tall glass of juice. As I handed him the glass, I realized that neither of us had managed to remember the antiviral medication schedule during our long and hectic day. I wondered too about his blood sugar. I could not remember seeing Stephen use his glucometer.

I went back into the kitchen and brought out the schedule of medications.

"We've messed up today, Stephen," I said, laying the sheet on the table between us. "We need to figure out how to get back on track. Do you know which of these are most critical? Which ones can we just start again tomorrow?"

Stephen, sitting in the barrel chair in the living room, did not even look at the sheet. Instead, he leaned his head back over the chair. "No. I don't," he said. "It doesn't make any difference anyway."

"Of course it does."

"You heard the doctor, Colleen." Stephen leaned forward, cradling his face in his hands. "The medications are failing. I might be able to beat this pneumonia, but then what?" He looked directly into my eyes. "I'll tell you what. After the pneumonia, I'll get something else. And then, something after that. And I'll continue with one disease after another until I'm so thin that you can count my ribs. And then my muscles will go, and my body functions."

Stephen's voice remained completely flat—calm and unemotional—as if he were describing the death of a tomato plant. "Please don't talk like this, Stephen," I begged, as tears began to roll down my face. "It doesn't have to be that way."

"But it will be that way. I've seen it. Over and over and over." His voice grew more intense, as though he had to convince me of the inevitability of his demise. "I've seen it in my friends. I saw it with Glen. It'll get so bad that I'll beg God for mercy. But I won't die. I'll have bloody diarrhea seven times a day. I'll lose my ability to read and to talk. I'll lie without moving for days at a time. My skin will decay on my body. And if I am very, very lucky, I'll lose contact with reality."

He stood up, walking slowly to the stairs. "After all of that, I'll die. Just like all the rest."

"Please, Stephen," I said again, following after him. "You've got to have a little hope. You can't just give up."

He turned to face me, his left hand on the banister, his eyes boring into mine. "Look. I've lived through this hell for fifteen years. I've tried the positive self-talk. It doesn't stop anything." He put one foot on the stair and began the slow climb to his room. Without turning, he continued, "Don't talk to me about hope, Colleen. Don't ever say anything to me about hope. Not ever again."

Hearing the door close at the top of the stairs, I turned toward the kitchen. Not two steps later, spinning on my heel, I headed back for Stephen's room. To tell the truth, I wanted to pummel the guy. I know that I should've felt sympathy for his emotional state, but I didn't. I felt angry, and for long moments, as I stood panting at the bottom of the stairs, I couldn't put my finger on the source of my overwhelming anger.

I decided to bake bread.

Baking bread involves kneading. And when I wanted to knead my brother's skull, kneading dough seemed a more appropriate response.

Still steaming, I sat down at the counter and pulled out my recipe file, removing a well-worn copy of a Scandinavian rye bread that Jackie had introduced to our family. Slamming the card onto the counter, I began rummaging through the kitchen, assembling the required utensils, spices, and ingredients. I heated milk and butter in the microwave, measured molasses and yeast, and poured flour into my mixing bowl. Moments later, soft dough bounced around the inside of my mixer.

I turned the sticky, sweet-smelling concoction onto a thick layer of flour and began beating it like a mad woman, desperate to exorcize my frustration with Stephen. I must have looked like a student in an anger-management class, sweating with effort, tears spilling down my cheeks.

Eventually, exhaustion got its way, and I fell into the rhythmic push and fold of kneading. I took comfort in the repetitive movements: Push. Fold. Add flour. Push again.

In time, I felt the tension in my neck and shoulders begin to ease. My thoughts found expression in frustrated, staccato prayer. I kept at the dough until at last it began to feel smooth and elastic. The phone rang.

"Hey, Colleen," Carrie's voice came through the handset. My heart sank. Carrie was the very last person I wanted on the other end of my telephone. "I just called to find out how Stephen is doing."

"We spent the day at the doctor's office," I said, avoiding the question.

"Can I talk to him?" she asked.

"I can check. He's resting. Hold on." I put the receiver down and started up the stairs. I opened Stephen's door quietly. He was in bed, his face turned toward the window, the lights out.

By the light in the hall, I crept around the bed. "Stephen," I said. "Carrie's on the phone."

He did not answer.

"Don't you want to talk to her?"

A racking cough began at the bottom of his chest and folded him in half, his face diving back under the covers. I waited, but he did not emerge.

"I'll tell her you're not feeling well." I backed out and closed the door. Seeing him so weakened, so abused by the infection growing in his lungs, my frustration with him eased. I could not hold a grudge against someone so sick. Perhaps when he felt better, he would think clearly.

"Carrie," I said into the telephone. "Stephen has pneumonia. The doctor in Wenatchee says we caught it early, but he's really under the weather. Talking is difficult."

"So, put him on."

"You don't understand." I made a mental note to be patient with her. After all, Carrie hadn't been through the last three weeks with us. "I went upstairs, and he said he isn't up to talking right now." I sat down at the counter. "Maybe you could leave your number and he could call you tomorrow. The medicine should kick in by then."

"So you're back to it already."

"Back to what? He has a fever and a terrible cough."

"Back to protecting him. Back to having him all to yourself."

"Listen, I'm sorry you have this, this"—I struggled for a word—"this false perception. I've never tried to keep you and Stephen apart."

The bitterness in her voice came through the hundreds of miles separating us. "Yeah, right." I heard voices in the background and Carrie said something that I could not hear. "Look, Colleen. Don't bother to have Stephen call me back. If he doesn't want to talk to me, that's fine. I was only trying to be part of the family. I wouldn't want to come between the Bobbsey Twins."

"Carrie, please don't talk that way. If you were here—"

"But I'm not there, am I?" she answered. "You have him secreted away in that little Hollow of yours, all to yourself. No doubt you have designs on his soul too, don't you?"

For the life of me, I still could not get my understanding wrapped around Carrie's hostility. I had no desire to ask what had I done to deserve her wrath. I took a deep breath, letting it out slowly.

"I have designs on every soul, Carrie," I answered. "Even yours."

"Well, don't bother with me," she said, and hung up.

With the utmost care, as if her words had no effect at all, I put down the receiver. Then I poured myself a glass of milk and ate a Christmas cookie.

~ ~ ~

I did not sleep well that night, tossing and turning all alone in my big bed. All through the night, I heard Stephen coughing in his sleep, and as the noise drew me from my fitful sleep, I prayed for him.

I dreamed as well, an endless succession of nightmares pulling at my already fragile emotions. In one horrible sequence, Carrie and I fought over Stephen's body, pulling at him like contestants in a tug-of-war. When his flesh began to split in half, I woke sweating and I turned on the bedside lamp.

After a glass of cool water, I sat down on the loveseat in our bedroom with my Bible. I'm not superstitious. I don't use the Bible as some use a dream catcher. But I felt lost, like a hiker shrouded by a deep and sudden fog.

I needed to find my way.

I settled into the corner of the couch, tucking my feet under the second seat cushion. In an effort to stave off the nighttime chill, I wrapped myself in a cotton throw. I opened my Bible to my bookmark and began to read at exactly the same place I left off the night before. I had no more noble purpose than seeking solace in the Lord.

I had not read four verses in Psalms when I recognized the Lord speaking directly to me. I'd sensed this before, over the years, a time when the words jump off the page and into my soul. In those moments, almost as if by magic, I understand what the words mean—not in an academic sense—but in clear, succinct directions. In those moments, the Lord tells me exactly what to do.

With a yellow highlighter, I underlined the first lines of Psalm 107:

> Give thanks to the Lord, for he is good!
> His faithful love endures forever.
> Has the Lord redeemed you? Then speak out!
> Tell others he has saved you from your enemies.

I read the rest of the passage with eager, frightened eyes. Eager because I understand that for this human woman, such divinely inspired moments are rare occurrences. And in these priceless seconds, the Lord is so close that I can almost smell my Creator's breath.

Yet, I have learned that obedience is not always easy. And this expectation, that I should obey the One who speaks, frightens me. What if he asks more than I can do?

The verse reminded me of Dwayne's Christmas message. Was the Lord asking me again to tell my brother everything about my past? Even if it were forgiven and forgotten? Would the Lord ask that of me? Could I obey?

I read to the end of the passage, wondering if more instruction awaited me. As I got to the end, I read these words:

He changes rivers into deserts,
and springs of water into dry land…
But he also turns deserts into pools of water,
and the dry land into flowing springs.
He brings the hungry to settle there,
and build their cities.

And as I read the words, I began to cry. Stephen was living in a dry
desert. Not only was the disease a physical desert; his soul had shriveled
up as well. Stephen had given up on life. I laid my Bible aside and
stretched out over the back of the couch, praying as I cried.

*Oh Lord, Stephen is so hungry he doesn't even know it. He is so dry
that he is about to blow away. I need you to help Stephen in this desert. And
I need you to help him build his city there.* And then, in one last effort to
avoid obedience, I prayed. *Don't ask me to do it, Lord. Don't ask me to
dig up the past.*

~ ~ ~

I woke up after eight, groggy from the short night. Downstairs, I
made coffee and toasted rye bread. I moved silently about the house,
wanting Stephen to have as much sleep as he could get. Perhaps sleep
would brighten his outlook.

To stay busy, I tackled my refrigerator, this time in earnest. Moving
everything onto the counter, I disassembled the drawers and washed
all the shelves and parts in the sink. I threw away all the fuzzy foods
and disinfected their storage containers.

I filled a bowl with soapy water and washed all the condiment jars
as I put them back on the door. I made a grocery list of the fresh fruits
and vegetables we needed. Finished, I turned the refrigerator on and
closed the door, happy to complete such a mundane chore. I wiped
the kitchen counters and looked at the clock. Nine-thirty.

I wondered about Stephen, about his medicines, and about how
hungry he might be when he woke up this morning. I thought about
fixing breakfast and bringing it up to his room. Inside, a battle waged.
Part of me wanted to check on him, to get his medicines started, and

get on with the day. Another part wanted to let him sleep, hoping that rest would help him heal.

I stood at the bottom of the stairs and listened. Nothing, no movement, no coughing. Relieved, I decided to let him sleep longer, and went back in the kitchen.

No coughing. The realization nagged at me, and I tried to replay the sounds I'd heard during my long and sleepless night. Yes, Stephen had coughed all through the night. Almost endlessly.

And now, no coughing?

Concern twisted my stomach like a wet dishrag. Why had the coughing stopped? I took a sip of coffee and slipped onto the barstool. A nagging, urgent voice inside me said, *Go check. Go check on Stephen.*

Even as I got off my chair, I felt foolish, like an overprotective mother checking on a newborn every four minutes. I started upstairs anyway. I knocked quietly at Stephen's door. He did not answer. I almost turned away, but the voice spoke again, urging me inside. *Check on Stephen.*

I tiptoed around his bed, moving through the darkened room to the window, where I opened the blinds. Sunlight broke into the darkness, and for a moment I paused to enjoy a brown rabbit having breakfast in our back yard. But again the voice urged, *Check on Stephen.*

I turned to face the bed, moving forward quietly. I touched Stephen's shoulder, "Stephen, good morning."

He did not open his eyes.

"Stephen, how are you feeling this morning?"

He did not respond.

A chill of alarm ran along my spine and I shivered, struggling with the bedside lamp. I wanted to see my brother's face. But when the light came on I saw that Stephen had left his insulin kit—the black case containing all his diabetes supplies—open on the table, a used syringe cast carelessly on top.

I felt my chill turn to panic, and I shook Stephen's shoulder violently. "Stephen, wake up!" I shouted the words again, pulling on his arm.

This time, his eyes fluttered open, a blank stare escaping before the lids drifted closed. In that instant I saw the truth in his blank, incoherent look.

Stephen lay at the brink of an insulin-induced coma.

CHAPTER
Twenty-Six

Stephen's eyes fluttered open once again, a blank, lifeless stare. I felt panic rise in my chest as I shouted, "Stephen, what have you taken?"

His eyelids drifted closed again. His face shone with perspiration, a slick beading across his forehead and upper lip. I grabbed his lower jaw. Holding it tightly in the vise between my fingers and thumb, I shook his head. I'd have shaken his eyeballs loose if I thought it would help.

Over and over I shouted his name, as if by increasing my volume I could somehow break through the fog of chemical incoherence that held my brother in its grip. His features went slack. Whether from growing up with a diabetic sister, or from some other source, something inside of me shouted. *Sugar! Give him sugar!*

Under normal conditions, I would add sugar to orange juice and force Stephen to drink. But in this condition, Stephen could not, would not drink. I felt quite certain he could not even swallow. I grabbed the insulin kit and began to rifle its contents.

I needed something more than juice, something more effective, more immediate, something to save him from the coma that lurked just beyond his loss of consciousness.

On one side of the kit, I found a vial of test strips along with his glucometer. Beside these, I found sterile packages of insulin syringes. In another pocket, I found a large tube of glucose—not unlike a tube of toothpaste—still wrapped in its cardboard-and-plastic packaging.

I tore it open, throwing the waste aside, desperate to read the directions.

The instructions demanded the patient eat the gel from the tube; Stephen was in no condition to eat. I tossed the tube aside and unzipped another section of the kit.

Inside this pocket, I found another, smaller tube still wrapped in plastic and cardboard. I turned the package over and held it under the light of the bedside lamp. I read quickly, scanning the tiny print on the back of the package. This sugar, the label said, could be absorbed through the membrane inside the patient's cheek or gums.

Trembling, I tore open the package and squirted the clear gel onto my index finger. Standing beside the bed, I brought my hand to Stephen's face, opening his lips with my left hand while I tried to sneak my right index finger inside his mouth. He bit down, pulling his head away, unconsciously resisting the very substance that might save his life.

Most of the gel dripped off my finger and onto his chin. The second time, I put the gel on my left hand, using my stronger right hand to open the way. This time, while trying to avoid the unpredictable motions of his teeth, I managed to get some of the fluid inside his cheeks. Even as we wrestled, I hoped Stephen would not remember this struggle.

As soon as I let go of his face, my brother's body went limp, lost to the blackness of insulin-induced hypoglycemia. I sat down exhausted, certain somehow that I had not managed to get enough sugar into his bloodstream. In my mind, I pictured my mother in this same position, leaning over Carrie's limp body, desperately trying to raise her blood sugar. What would she have done?

What more could I do?

Feeling the tube in my hand, I twisted open the lid and jammed one end inside Stephen's cheek. I tried not to imagine the skin I tore away with this rough treatment. With my fingers, I pinched his lips closed as I squeezed the contents of the tube into his mouth. Gel began to run back out onto his chin.

Forget dosage. At this point, I'd get whatever I could inside his body even at the risk of having him choke.

For a few moments, I considered calling an ambulance. But as I recalled these episodes with Carrie, I remembered that my mother gave her twenty minutes to respond to the emergency treatment. If the low blood sugar continued longer than that, Carrie went to the hospital in an ambulance. I looked at my watch.

So far, Stephen's face showed no sign of responsiveness. I took hold of his shoulder and shook him again, though more gently this time. "Stephen, swallow," I told him. "You have gel in your mouth. Swallow it."

He did not move. I looked around the room, wondering what else I should do. The cordless telephone was downstairs. I would have to leave him to call an ambulance, and I didn't feel comfortable doing that. What if he began a seizure? *Father, help me. Show me what to do next.*

I spied the glucometer on his bedside table and wondered if I should try to measure his glucose level. I picked up the device, about the size of cell phone, and dropped it beside my brother. I remembered the test strips I'd thrown on the floor and dropped onto my hands and knees to recover them.

Grabbing the tiny clear bottle, I popped the top and removed a test strip. I stuck the strip in the monitor and waited as the power came on. Only then did I realize that I had not yet drawn a droplet of Stephen's blood for the sample.

Setting the monitor aside, I found a lancet to puncture his skin. My fingers trembled as I held the device, so unlike the one my sister used. How did it work? Could I stick Stephen with this thing?

I played with it, cocking the trigger and setting it off until I figured out how to get the automatic puncturing device to successfully stab the air. I prepared to poke Stephen's finger.

I clenched my fists, repeatedly opening and closing my fingers, hoping to overcome my own trembling. Then, holding Stephen's middle finger, I lanced the end and squeezed, forcing a tiny drop of blood from Stephen.

I caught this droplet on the test strip, already shaking again as I waited for the monitor to respond. Though I'd watched Carrie so many times, I felt unsure of myself, unsure of my ability to obtain accurate results. What would happen if I made a mistake?

I waited, my eyes fixed on the digital readout, as the machine calculated the level of sugar in Stephen's blood.

The number appeared, black and flashing. Fifteen.

I expected that he would need to be somewhere near fifty before he reached consciousness.

From Stephen's hospitalization, I knew that my brother needed a special hormone shot, and I would have to figure out how to give it to him. "Stephen, wake up!" I said, hoping that by some miracle he would respond.

"Can you hear me? I'm going to have to give you a shot," I said as much to boost my own confidence as to speak to my brother. "I'm going down to the kitchen to get the Glucagon. Don't you go anywhere. Hear me?" I stood up, squeezing my hands together. He needed the shot. I had no choice but to do it myself.

I ran downstairs to the kitchen, grabbing first the medicine from the refrigerator and then the cordless telephone. If I needed to, I could call for help from his bedside.

When I returned, Stephen had not moved, though his sweating seemed slightly less pronounced. "Stephen," I said, "I'm going to give you one of these shots."

I pulled the packaging from the syringe and set it aside. Then, taking the tiny glass container of freeze-dried Glucagon, I stuck the needle into the vial, injecting the solution inside. I shook the bottle, hoping to accelerate the mixing of the liquid and powder. In my enthusiasm, I shook too vigorously, and the syringe flew off the lid and landed somewhere across the room.

I said a word most Christians would never consider saying.

I put the bottle down on the bedside table and went off in search of the needle, which I found beside the chest of drawers, inches away from the trashcan. I picked it up and blew on the contraption as I brought it back to the bedside; it was Kevin's pacifier-sterilization technique. "Stephen," I said, only half joking, "If you've ever considered prayer, this might be the time for it."

I unwrapped an alcohol swab from its foil container and gave the syringe a thorough cleaning. Quite certain that Dr. Erickson's nurse would fire me on the spot, I reinserted the syringe into the vial and drew up the clear liquid.

I don't mind admitting that needles make me slightly dizzy. Between the close proximity of this particular needle and the serious nature of Stephen's condition, I felt like a nurse in a gyroscope. My stomach objected to my activity with a nausea I barely restrained.

As I approached Stephen's bare arm with the alcohol swab, my hand shook until the needle blurred in my vision. I wiped an area about the size of a football field over Stephen's shoulder. Then, slowly I approached the skin.

I held the needle there, waiting for something, though I didn't know what. I couldn't do it. I couldn't puncture Stephen's skin. What if I was wrong? What if I'd made a mistake?

Do it, the voice instructed me. Holding my breath, and aiming from a distance of about five inches, I threw the needle at his arm, almost like a dart at a carnival game. As the needle punctured the skin, I had to look away. I pushed in the plunger and withdrew the syringe as quickly as I could, swallowing to keep my stomach in place.

Now there was nothing to do but wait.

Ten minutes later, I checked my watch. Should I test Stephen again? Though I'd lived with Carrie's diabetes, there was so much I didn't know. I'd never attended a diabetic education class. I threw a prayer heavenward and grabbed the phone, dialing Jackie's number.

When she answered, I praised God I'd found her at home. "Jackie," I said, "Stephen is in trouble. Could you call the prayer chain?"

"What happened?"

"Too much insulin."

"Do you need me to come over?"

I smiled as I imagined Jackie rushing through the rain to our house. "I need prayer. And if you can find Raisa at home, would you ask her to call? I could use a nurse's advice." After promising to keep in touch, we hung up.

~ ~ ~

After another ten minutes, Stephen's blood sugar had risen to forty-seven, and he opened his eyes. Clearly awake, he seemed slightly out of touch with his surroundings. "Stephen," I said, "it's me, Colleen."

Though he looked directly at me, he seemed not to recognize my face. He blinked and looked around the room, apparently confused. "What?"

"You've had low blood sugar," I explained. "I've given you a shot and some glucose."

He nodded, reaching up to brush damp hair from his forehead. He coughed again, a dry, unproductive cough that sounded painful. I can't tell you how glad I was to hear it. "Can I get you anything?"

"Water?"

"Promise to stay put?" He smiled. I went downstairs and poured a glass of orange juice, adding additional sugar. Wanting to give him a long-lasting source of carbohydrates, I threw together a ham and cheese sandwich and cut up an apple. Grabbing a bottle of water, I headed back to his room. Whatever happened at this point, I felt more confident dealing with too much sugar than what I'd just been through.

As I brought the food to Stephen, I found him dozing. He woke easily as I placed the tray beside his bed, and he worked his way into a sitting position. "I feel as though I've been dragged through a sewer line."

"Start with the juice," I told him, handing him the glass.

I sat beside the window in an old dining-room chair my mother had given me, waiting quietly as Stephen ate. From the window, I watched a breeze ruffle the grass in the lot behind ours. I'd lost most of the morning to this event, and as yet, I hadn't even paid attention to the weather.

It was the first time I sensed Stephen's illness pulling me away from the outside world.

As I watched the wind in the grass, I wondered about Stephen and about the episode we'd both just survived. Why had he given himself an insulin shot without making certain that he had food? Had he measured his blood sugar before taking the insulin? Was this near-death experience an accident or, as I suspected, had Stephen done it on purpose?

I needed to know. I deserved to know. I realized that the incident with Stephen had changed me, forced me to move beyond the superficial relationship I'd recently shared with my adult brother. The little girl who used to live with an elephant in the living room no longer existed. She had died while trying to save her brother's life. In the last hour a new woman, a stronger woman, had taken her place. She was an adult—an adult who would ask the hard questions and wait for the answer.

By taking too much insulin, Stephen had crossed some invisible line, changing everything between us. If he hoped to die before I found him, then we could never go back to the kind of relationship we'd shared only the day before. He had destroyed my trust.

I wouldn't leave the room until I knew for certain how this thing had happened.

I waited as he ate his sandwich. I watched as he ate the pieces of his apple. I held my tongue as he opened the bottle of water and took a long deep drink. "I feel better," he said finally. "Thank you."

"For the food?"

"Yes," he said, avoiding my eyes.

"Stephen, I have to know what happened here. Why did you give yourself too much insulin?" I crossed my arms and waited for his answer, my heart pounding against my chest, the blood echoing in my ears. Even when change is right, it is never easy.

Stephen did not answer immediately, but I refused to rescue him.

"It's hard. I've only had to give myself shots for a few weeks."

"I know it's hard. Are you telling me it was an accident? You didn't mean to do it?" I waited patiently, looking directly into his face.

Again, he looked away.

"Stephen, you did this on purpose, didn't you? You gave yourself a shot. One, maybe even two, and you hoped that I wouldn't come up here and find you until it was too late. That was what you planned, wasn't it? That I would be too late."

Though I wanted to remain calm, I couldn't. The fear I'd felt while trying to rescue my brother exploded into anger like fire raging through a dry forest, whipping itself forward, exploding from treetop to treetop.

"You wanted to end your life, and you had the nerve to do it at my house," I said, my voice rising. "Did it ever occur to you what that would do to me? Did you ever think, even once, about what I would have to remember for the rest of my life? That I found my dead brother? That my brother killed himself in this bedroom because I was too late to save him? Did it ever occur to you to think about the guilt I would have to live with? Why didn't I see it coming? Why didn't I stop him?"

As I spoke, my imagination took over, and I saw myself finding Stephen lifeless in a darkened bedroom. I felt the pain of the discovery, the anguish and guilt I would carry forever. And the more I realized how close we had come to disaster, the more angry I became. I stood up, striding over to his bed. "Or do you just not care about anyone else? Is Stephen all that matters here?"

He turned his face away, tears streaming down his bony cheeks. "You don't understand. I can't do this. You can't expect me to do this."

"No, Stephen," I said, sitting down beside him. My voice became calm, authoritative, daring him to challenge me. "You are the one who doesn't understand. You just changed the rules. And now you're the one who's going to have to live by them."

He looked at me, his eyes questioning.

"If I told your doctor that you tried to commit suicide today, you could be sent to a mental hospital. No matter what anyone thinks about euthanasia, suicide is still grounds for hospitalization. And when you stop making reasonable decisions for yourself, you lose the privilege of making your own decisions."

I was bluffing and I knew it. Though suicide could get a depressed patient admitted to a hospital, I had no idea if anyone in authority would take this morning's event as seriously as I did. But bluffing seemed to be my only hope. I had to. I had to do something to change Stephen, and I would use any tool to get his attention. At that moment, all the anger and horrifying fear I felt collided with enough force to give me the strength I needed to confront him.

"I'm telling you, Stephen, you just gave your privileges away. You aren't going home. You aren't going back to school. You aren't going anywhere.

"You can sell your house. You can quit your job. You can work from here. But you are staying here. Right here. Right under my nose. We'll make room for you. We'll make sure that you get the care you need. But you are living here with us, where I can keep an eye on you. There won't be any of these 'accidental' overdoses ever again."

I reached out and turned Stephen's chin toward me, looking directly into his eyes. "We can get through this. I don't know how. I don't expect you to know how. But we will. We can do it. And we'll do it like we've done everything we've done up until now. We'll do it together."

He blinked and a fresh pair of tears rolled down his cheeks.

Twenty-Seven

As I look back, I think that Stephen's next words were the door through which a miracle walked into my life. He said, "Alright, Colleen. You win."

I leaned forward and wrapped my arms around his shoulders, holding him tightly as we cried together, rocking gently back and forth. It felt so good to hold him like that, almost as though, for the first time in years, he had let down the wall that separated us.

I'll never know exactly why it worked, but it did. After all, why would Stephen suddenly decide to listen to me? Why would he fall for my bluff? For some reason, my strong-willed, independent brother chose to let go.

With a final squeeze, I sat back, nose running, tears dripping onto my sweater, and laughed. Stephen looked as worn out as I did. But he looked relieved too, as if by promising to help him carry this burden, I had effectively cut it in half. His face seemed less tortured, his moist eyes less haunted.

I reached over to the nightstand and pulled several tissues from the box. Handing them to Stephen, I pulled two more for myself. I blew my nose and wiped my face. "Good. That's settled then. You take your blood sugar again, and I'll bring up your morning meds." I dropped the monitor and lancet into his lap. "And don't try to mess with me. I'll check it when I get back."

While I was downstairs, the phone rang. Raisa's voice, calm and confident, asked, "Colleen, Jackie called. She asked me to check in with you. Is Stephen alright?"

"I think so. We had a low-blood-sugar episode. I thought I'd have to call an ambulance."

"How is he now?"

"Awake. Coherent."

"Sounds like you did well. The ambulance might have been too late. What are his numbers?"

"Almost fifty the last time I checked. He's up checking them again right now."

"Have you called the doctor?"

"I'm planning on it."

"What did you give him?"

I laughed as I remembered the gel dripping off of Stephen's stubbly chin. "Well, I tried to get gel in through his cheek and gums. I don't know how much got through though. Most of it ended up on the sheets. And I gave him a shot."

"Ooh, I'm impressed," she said. I heard the laughter in her voice. "Has he eaten yet?"

"He's had a sandwich and juice. And an apple."

"Good job, my needle-phobic friend. Sounds like you've made it through this one. Be sure to let the doctor know what happened, though. The nurse will give you instructions about monitoring sugars today. The Glucagon could make him vomit, and you might have to manage sugar spikes today."

"He has pneumonia too."

"Then you have your work cut out for you. Want me to drop over?"

"Thanks, Raisa. I think we're okay for now." I felt tears again, and scolded myself for being so overly emotional. "It was so scary. I didn't know what I was doing."

"Everyone feels that way. You did fine."

"Thanks for calling. I really appreciate it."

After we hung up, I called the internist we'd seen at the hospital, reporting most of the morning's events to his call nurse; however, I left out the bit about the needle flying across the room. And, of course, I neglected to explain why Stephen's blood sugar had dropped so low in the first place. Somehow, I felt the need to protect Stephen.

As had Raisa, Dr. Erickson's nurse reassured me that I had managed the emergency correctly. After another ten minutes of instruction, she hung up, promising to check in again with me in the afternoon.

I spent that first day checking on Stephen continually, hovering around his room while trying not to look as though I were afraid to leave him alone. Working around the house, I dropped by his room every time I went upstairs. By the end of the afternoon, his blood sugar had stabilized, and he managed to get up and move to the family room, where he watched the last half of an old movie on television.

Still, his energy level was very low, and he continued to cough. I heard him panting as he climbed the stairs to the bedroom after dinner.

I tried not to think about telling Kevin that I'd asked Stephen to live with us. I tried not to imagine what Kevin would say when I told him. After all, the deal was done. Anyway, Kevin generally let me make serious decisions all by myself. I'd chosen our couch by myself. I'd even found my car in the want ads. He'd be happy for me. I'd made the offer; Stephen had accepted. My brother would live with us for as long as he needed to.

On the second day after our crisis, we took a walk outside, walking down our long driveway and circling the cul-de-sac once before returning to rest on the living-room couch. Just as we came back in the front door, we heard the telephone ring. Though I tried to catch it, the caller hung up.

Stephen spent most of the third day out of bed. His afternoon fever did not return, and he had taken over responsibility for all of his own medications. Unfortunately, a heavy rain kept us both inside. Around four, I caught him in the kitchen with his watercolors and paper spread across the breakfast table. "What are you up to?" I asked.

"I'm tired of being sick."

I smiled. "I feel that way every time I get the flu. It's happens right after you stop feeling like you're going to die and before you're really well again." Pulling out the chair beside him, I sat down. "My mother-in-law used to say, 'You know you're still sick because you see how much you'd have to do, but you don't feel well enough to do it.'"

Without looking up, Stephen nodded, frowning as he sketched light lines on a piece of tracing paper. I leaned toward him, trying to catch the scene he created with a pencil. "What are you working on?"

"I'm just getting started," he said, pushing a picture toward me, a photograph of a garden torn from the pages of a magazine. In it, a single Adirondack chair sat on a brick patio, surrounded by lush perennials all in a mass of bloom. The sun broke through the vegetation in bright patterns of light, shining on the bricks, warming the wood. Everything about the picture invited the viewer to sit down.

"It's beautiful. You're going to paint this?"

He nodded. "Hope to. Not all today, of course."

I felt a ripple of envy. "I wish I could do that."

"You can."

"Not me. I haven't a single artistic bone in my body."

"Nonsense. You knit."

"It's not the same. I pick a pattern and buy some yarn. You're the one who reminded me that I can't draw anything."

Stephen's pencil stopped moving and he looked up at me. "Of course you can. You just haven't tried. I promised to teach you, remember?"

The doorbell rang and I stood up to answer it. "Well, I won't hold you to it," I said as I went through the swinging door toward the entry hall.

I opened the front door to find two strangers, one African-American, the other Caucasian, huddled together under a black and white golf umbrella. For a moment, I suspected they were selling door-to-door religion. I stood gaping, looking back and forth between them, unable to guess why they had come.

"Hello, Colleen," the smaller one said, dropping the hood of her coat to expose beautiful graying hair. "I know we should have called. But your telephone was busy."

I stared unbelieving. "Gloria!" I glanced at the tall man beside her. "Come in," I said, opening the storm door for them. "Please. Come inside."

"Have we come at a bad time?" she asked, giving her coat a shake. "We could come back. We were out in the neighborhood and decided to see if you were home."

"No. Of course not. This is great," I said, standing back to let them inside. "Can I take your coats?"

The tall man extended his hand. "I'm Noah," he said, a smile spreading across his broad face. "Noah Armstrong." As his enormous hand swallowed mine, I noticed that Noah's smile did not diminish. Instead, he seemed to glow effortlessly, like the happy expression on a new bridegroom.

Gloria slipped out of her coat. "I'm sorry, Noah. I always forget introductions." As she adjusted her hair, she spoke conspiratorially. "I've known Noah for years. Pastors a little Baptist church over in Cashmere."

Oh, no. Could Stephen survive another pastoral visit? I shook off my fear. "I'm so glad you came," I said, with less-than-authentic gratitude. "We haven't had much company."

In truth, Stephen and I had been alone for the entire week. No visitors. Few phone calls. I'd already begun to develop the first symptoms of cabin fever.

"I brought Noah over to meet your brother," Gloria said. "I thought Stephen could use a man friend. Too many women are never good for a man."

Noah laughed. "Now, I don't know about that, Gloria. But every man needs a friend. That's true," he nodded.

I showed them into the living room, and excused myself to get Stephen. In the kitchen, I leaned over the table. "Remember the lady I met at Dr. Kurian's office?" I said. "She's here."

"Here?" He looked up, confused. "Why would she come here?"

"She came to visit you," I said, gesturing toward the living room. "Actually, she brought a man along. They're waiting to meet you."

"Oh no," Stephen ran a hand through his hair. He glanced at the door to the dining room, as if by bolting he might avoid meeting the strangers. "I don't know why she would do that. She doesn't even know me."

I shrugged, holding up both hands. "I didn't know they were coming. I've never met this guy before."

"Alright," he said, standing up. "I'll do it this once. But don't expect me to do it again."

"Don't look at me; I just answered the door."

When I offered refreshments to our unexpected guests, Gloria came to the kitchen to help me. I expected her to explain more about the mysterious man she'd dragged along to visit my brother. Instead, she filled the teapot with water and arranged the last of our Christmas cookies on a plate. "Noah loves sweets," she said, smiling innocently at me. "He'll think he's died and gone to heaven."

While we were in the kitchen, I worried about Stephen and Noah. After all, the last time a pastor had dropped by to see my brother, he'd asked me to make sure it never happened again. "Gloria," I said, "Stephen had a really bad experience with our pastor. What if Noah makes the same mistake?"

"Oh honey," she laughed. "You don't have to worry about ol' Noah. He has a special understanding with these boys. You'll see."

In the living room, I sensed an awkward discomfort in Stephen. As always, I felt it my duty to make everyone feel at home. "We've had a nasty week this week," I said, offering the tray of hot drinks to Noah. I caught a warning look from Stephen but stumbled on. "Stephen caught a little bug and hasn't been feeling well."

"I'm sorry to hear that," Noah said. "Are things going better?"

"Not really," Stephen said. "I have AIDS you know." Leave it to my brother. Obviously, Stephen meant the announcement to have shock value.

Noah did not seem the least affected by the declaration. In fact his smile broadened. "From what Gloria said, I guessed that."

"AIDS doesn't bother you?" Stephen said.

"It doesn't frighten me, if that's what you mean," Noah said, picking up his cup. "I know lots of men who live with AIDS. Some are sicker than others. But they all have the virus, just the same."

I saw Stephen's eyebrows shoot up in what I assumed to be grudging admiration. "Others in this area?"

"A few," Noah admitted. "Gloria here makes dinners for them. She runs errands, picks up medicine, goes shopping. She even drives some patients to their doctor appointments. That's what she was doing at Dr. Kurian's. Whatever they need, Gloria here takes care of it."

Stephen looked at Gloria, who wore a thigh-length sweater and baggy silk pants. Silver bracelets jangled from both wrists. Today, she had twisted her wavy hair into a thick French roll and fastened it in place with a leather-and-bamboo clip. To me, she looked more like one of the Potter's Hollow clay artists than a church lady. I wondered what my brother thought of this woman.

"Actually, I have a group of women who help me," she said, putting one hand on her chest. "I don't do it all myself. And sometimes, Noah here helps too. This morning, we took one of our clients out for breakfast. Noah helped me get him in and out of his wheelchair."

Stephen nodded.

Gloria looked at me. "Sometimes, just getting out of the house is a treat." I was beginning to understand that feeling myself.

"So, you see, AIDS isn't a scary thing to us," Noah sat back in his chair and crossed one ankle over his knee. "We know how lonely it can be to be sick all the time. Gloria here thought you could use some company." He folded the leg of his pants over his ankle as he spoke. "So here we are. Tell me, Stephen, you aren't from around here. Where do you live?"

I wondered if Stephen would tell Noah about moving across the state to live in Potter's Hollow. I half listened as Noah drew Stephen into a conversation as ordinary as any I'd heard between new acquaintances. They talked about hobbies. Stephen admitted a passion for watercolor. Noah told Stephen that he loved stream fishing.

As they spoke, I watched Noah, wondering who he was and why Gloria had brought him along. His words betrayed no past. No reason for his passion to help Gloria. My curiosity aroused, I listened to the conversation, hoping to catch the story behind the story.

Noah was a big man, broad in every dimension. I guessed that he might be in his late fifties, though his body looked youthful, sculpted by exercise. His short black hair showed tiny flecks of gray. A well-defined widow's peak left him with a broad, deeply lined forehead. These lines jumped when he laughed or smiled, and the whole effect reminded me of the animation of a marionette, eyebrows dancing as the puppeteer worked the strings.

But Noah had no strings.

As he spoke, he waved his broad hands, the pale palms flashing against the dark of his navy sweater and dark gray slacks. Noah's whole body participated in his conversation; in every way, Noah was fully present.

When Stephen spoke, Noah leaned forward in the chair, resting his elbows on his knees, keeping his full attention on Stephen's face. He nodded often and asked thoughtful questions whenever he needed clarification. Noah laughed in all the right places.

He asked about Stephen's disease, conversing easily in all the details of cell counts and viral loads. Obviously familiar with these medical terms, Noah understood their meaning in the context of the disease. Stephen volunteered the latest developments, including details of both the diabetes and the pneumonia.

Stephen did not tell Noah about the low-blood-sugar episode.

Gloria stayed out of the conversation. Instead, she seemed content to drink hot tea and focus her sparkling eyes on Stephen and Noah. Though she did not participate, I don't believe she missed a single word.

In her behavior I recognized the well-executed scheme of a loving mother and caring woman. Determined to make a difference in the world around her, no doubt Gloria had arranged to bring Noah to our home. She had a plan and I loved her for it.

They did not stay long. "We need to be going," Gloria said as she put her mug down on the table beside her chair. "I have to get back and start dinner for my husband." She stood up. "Noah, what do you think?"

He looked at his watch and shook his head. "I've talked your ear off, Stephen. I'm sorry to stay so long."

"It was good. I miss seeing people," Stephen said, and then he laughed. "Well, I miss them, and then I start a new quarter, and I can't wait to get away from them."

"I know," Noah said. "Like the old story about the pastor who loved his job but couldn't stand the people."

"It was so nice of you to come," I said, following them to the hallway.

They put on their coats as I opened the front door. "Good-bye," Gloria said, taking a step toward me. Wrapping me in her bony arms she hugged me, whispering in my ear, "Don't give up." As she stepped back, I thought I saw tears in her eyes.

Just as I leaned into the storm door, pushing it open for them, Noah caught Stephen in a giant bear hug. From where I stood, I saw Noah's back and watched Stephen's face freeze in a confused expression, his hands waving loosely in the air, unable to choose the appropriate response. But as the hug continued, Stephen closed his eyes and patted the giant man on the shoulders as if surrendering to the emotion of the moment.

This time, I had tears.

As I closed the door behind them, I felt wrapped in the warm glow of their compassion. How wonderful it felt to be understood without explaining. How good to be accepted, in the desperate condition of our physical ailment. I thanked the Lord for sending them.

I picked up the dishes in the living room and headed for the kitchen, where I found Stephen checking his medication schedule, a pencil in one hand. "We need to talk," he said, his tone serious.

I felt my heart tighten. Though I was so grateful for our visitors, I wondered if they had somehow offended Stephen. Did Noah say something?

"Okay." I pulled out a chair and sat down.

"I need to ask you something. And I need the truth."

"Sure. I always try to tell the truth."

"I need to know about Tuesday," he said. "I need to know if you really meant to invite me to stay here." He paused, his chin in his hand, his face soft. "I need to know if you want me."

His question made my heart ache. How often I've wondered the
same thing. Wondered if anyone wanted me. Wondered if I could be
loved. Wondered if those who promised to love me really meant it. Or
would they leave?

"Stephen," I said, solemnly. "I want you. I want you here with me.
With us. It's what I want more than anything else in the whole
world."

CHAPTER
Twenty-Eight

Because we expected Kevin and the kids home late on Sunday afternoon, Stephen and I spent Thursday evening making plans for a two-day trip to Seattle, intending to leave Potter's Hollow early Friday morning. Whatever Stephen needed to accomplish in order to move in with us had to be finished before my piano students resumed their regular schedule. I planned to start teaching again on the Monday after New Year's.

We put a full day of activities on the agenda, hoping that Stephen could make it through without total exhaustion. We would list his house with a real-estate agent, write and deliver a letter of resignation to the community college, and pick up whatever belongings he wanted from the house. Of course, we also had to pick up Colleen, Stephen's golden retriever, who was staying with a friend. Colleen-the-dog would also join Stephen at the Payton household.

We had no plans to close the house or to remove the furniture. We knew that furnished houses sell faster. At some point, those details would have to be covered, but we agreed to hold them off as long as possible.

On this trip my brother also wanted to request a copy of his medical records be mailed to Dr. Kurian. In order to care for Stephen, she would need a full record of his disease, including all of the lab records accumulated over the past fifteen years.

I did not envy the person who would copy Stephen's records.

We set out Friday morning before the sun rose and arrived at Stephen's home in Seattle just after ten. He went over to a neighbor's

to pick up his mail while I let myself inside. I made a quick tour of the
kitchen, wondering which things we should bring back to my house.
The freezer was full, and the pantry easily held two boxes of cans.
The refrigerator held nothing more than condiments and eggs. At
least the cans could wait for another trip.

Stephen brought in the mail and called a Realtor, who agreed to
come by the house at four-thirty. "I'm going to go type the letter,"
Stephen said, hanging up the phone. "Would you go down in the
basement and see what I have in the laundry? I think we should wash
and dry laundry before we leave tomorrow."

With a determined face, Stephen headed for the stairs.

When I flipped the light switch in Stephen's basement, I discovered an open room with posts supporting the rest of the house. The
space had never been finished. A cement floor and bare studs lined
the four walls, leaving pipes and electrical wire fully exposed.

In a single turn around the room, I found a wealth of things in that
basement, things that described an adult I had never fully known,
the man my brother had been in his healthier days. The discoveries
surprised me.

From a ceiling rack, Stephen had hung a fairly new twenty-seven-
speed road bike. Tennis rackets and shoes sat beside Rollerblades on
the shelves lining the basement walls. On another shelf, Stephen
stored a pair of snow skis and sleek modern boots.

Though we had skied as teenagers, I had never considered
Stephen an athlete. He had never shown any interest in varsity ath-
letics at school. Sometime in his adult life, Stephen had taken up
recreational sports I knew nothing about.

In the opposite corner, boxes of books, each of them labeled and
filed alphabetically by author, stood against the wall. I walked over to
the collection and opened the top box. Dust burst into the air, and I
sneezed. By the quantity of books in the corner, I guessed that
Stephen could start his own public library.

I found the washing machine in a well-organized corner of the
basement, laundry soap in a cupboard above the dryer. Three canvas
bags hung from a chrome frame standing beside the dryer. Each bag
had a label: "whites," "darks," and "other."

He had a load of jeans and sweatshirts waiting to be washed; I put them in and started the machine. Turning to go upstairs, I looked around the big room again, wondering about the active life these items represented. As I climbed the stairs, I could not help feeling a little sad. There was so much about Stephen that I would never know.

On the second floor, I found Stephen in his office. "Tell me what things you'd like to bring along today, and I'll start packing."

"We don't have to take everything," he said. "We can always come back." While Stephen wrote his letter and sorted his mail, I filled boxes with winter clothes. I included personal items from the bathroom, and the pictures and books I found scattered about. I filled a box with shoes, socks, and underwear, and was about to go into his office when Stephen met me in the hall.

"I just called the school. Dr. Dennison can meet me in a half hour."

"Do you want me to ride along?"

"We can pick up Colleen at the same time. Would you drive?"

"Sure," I agreed, shaking my head at the notion that I might ever get used to sharing my name with a dog. "I'll meet you at the car."

We parked in the staff lot at the community college. "Why don't you wait for me in the student-union building. I'll come and find you."

"Sounds fine. I'll be in the bookstore."

I stood by the car, watching as Stephen started across the courtyard. He walked slowly, his shoulders drooped, he head hanging. I wondered if his posture reflected his illness or his reluctance to finish this particularly difficult chore.

Stephen did not want to quit teaching.

"Wait," I called, running to catch up with him. "What about your office? Should we get your things today? Won't they need the space?"

His face fell, and he glanced away, putting one hand over his chin. "I hadn't even thought of that." He shrugged. "I guess we should."

He looked so lost, so dejected, that I volunteered, "How about I get some boxes from the bookstore, and I'll meet you at the entrance toward the quad." I pointed to the English building. "There. I'll be just inside the door. You come get me when you've finished with the meeting, and I'll help you with your office."

Nearly an hour later, I sat reading a new book when Stephen came out of the elevator at the end of the main hallway. I glanced up, anxious to gauge the effect of his resignation. "How did it go?" I asked. "You okay?"

"He wouldn't take it."

"Wouldn't take your resignation?"

Stephen nodded. "He asked me to write a letter requesting a medical leave. Though I won't be paid, I'll be eligible for continued coverage with the group health insurance, as long as I pay my own premiums."

"That sounds great. I didn't know that was an option."

"Neither did I." He put his hands on his hips. "I'm not even sure it was. I think he made it up." Stephen chuckled, a bemused smile on his face. "I'm not sure the comptroller will buy it. So it isn't a sure thing."

"It could be a lifesaver."

"That might be stretching things."

Together, we packed up his office. Stephen began with his desk, emptying his file drawer and then packing the books on the shelf behind the door. While he did this, I packed the office decorations. On one of his walls hung six years' worth of programs from the productions Stephen had supervised during his tenure at the college. Each had been carefully matted and framed. Most were covered with the signatures of students who had participated.

I took them down one at a time, carefully wrapping each frame in a sheet of newspaper before placing it in a box on the floor.

"Don't bother with those, Colleen."

Holding a frame in one hand, I asked, "Don't bother?"

"Where will I put them all? Just leave them. Someone here will throw them away."

I looked back at the wall, a virtual tour of Stephen's mark on the school. "You can't leave them. They're your work. Your influence."

He stood up and glanced over the frames. I read the memories as they crossed the features of his face. Reaching out to take one from the wall, he said, "This one was a nightmare. The lead broke her foot during the dress rehearsal." He handed the program to me. "Who'd want to remember that? Just dump them."

I don't think until that very moment, as I saw the anguish on his face, that I understood what quitting meant to Stephen. I could hardly hold back the tears.

We picked up Colleen-the-dog at a house about twelve blocks from school. The dog nearly knocked Stephen over, putting her front paws on his chest, licking his face, wagging her tail, and whining with pure delight. With effort, he got Colleen-the-dog to mind her manners. Stephen thanked his friend and put the dog in the car.

She rode all the way home with her chin resting over Stephen's left shoulder.

Back at the house, I made lunch for both of us. My brother looked like he'd just shoveled a snowy driveway. He pushed his plate away.

"You should eat."

"Are you going to spend the rest of my life nagging me?"

I winced. So many painful meanings. "I will if you'll let me."

He smiled. "I'm honestly not hungry."

"You're a little depressed."

He put his chin on his hand. "You wouldn't be?"

"I think I would."

"I knew this was coming. I could see it. I've been through it with Glen. But I still don't want it to happen. I want to stay here, doing my thing, living my life the way it is, forever."

"I understand."

"And it isn't like I absolutely have to leave. I'm not that sick."

"No, you aren't. Not right this moment. But we both know you can get sick at the drop of a hat. You need people around to take care of you. It isn't like you're going to live at a nursing home. We aren't that bad."

He laughed.

"It'll be alright," I said.

He nodded, but I saw in his face that he didn't believe me.

~ ~ ~

We worked in Stephen's upstairs office until the doorbell rang at four-thirty. Colleen-the-dog, who had not left Stephen's side since we came home, followed my brother down to the front door. I continued working while Stephen met with the Realtor, folding clothes in the kitchen while they talked contracts in the formal dining room. As they finished, I made a snack for my brother.

Stephen brought the paperwork into the kitchen. He sat down at his table, his shoulders sagging, his face discouraged. I put a plate of cheese and crackers and a glass of milk in front of him. "I think you need to eat. It's been too long, hasn't it?"

He played with a slice of cheese and leaned his chin on one hand. "Well, it's all settled. I shouldn't feel this bad. I can't take care of the house myself any more. I don't have the energy to mow the lawn or wash the windows or clean the gutters."

I sat down beside him, waiting.

He rubbed his forehead with his hand. "I just didn't think that it would hurt this much. It's a stupid house. Small and narrow." He gestured around the kitchen. "It's older than the Roman Empire." He looked at me. "But it was mine, you know?"

"It's still yours. You don't have to sell. You could rent," I said. "Maybe it isn't time yet."

"I have to. I need to pay off my debt. If I don't work, how else will I pay for insurance? I won't survive two weeks without insurance paying for my meds."

I nodded. "It's hard."

"I don't think you have any idea." He took a drink of milk. "This whole disease is about giving away your life. First you lose your friends. Then someone you really care about. And then, bit-by-bit, it steals away your energy, and your abilities, your body, your happiness. I still remember the day I decided that I couldn't play tennis anymore. I just didn't have the energy to run. When your hands are empty, you lose your privacy and your dignity."

"And now this," I said.

"But it isn't just this," he said, spreading his hands as though to entreat my sympathy. "I mean it's the house, yes. But it's more than that. It's the independence. I don't want to have to live with someone. I don't want to be a burden. Not to anyone. Not even you."

"I understand. I don't think I'd want to either."

"And I don't want to quit my job. It's who I am, you know. I'm a teacher. I love being with the kids, seeing them grow as people and actors. Now I'm forced to give that away too. It's too much. Way too much. Why do I have to live through all this?"

I was beginning to see how much I had asked of Stephen by having him live with us. Perhaps I shouldn't have. Perhaps I could have come up with some other solution. As I listened to him, I began to wonder how I could arrange things at the house to give him a sense of control over his own life, a sense of independence. "You're right. Until today, I hadn't really understood."

"You aren't alone. Unless you're living through it, no one can."

"You aren't alone either, Stephen. You might have been before Christmas, but that has changed. You aren't alone any more."

~ ~ ~

On Saturday, with Stephen's Subaru Outback loaded to the roof, we headed for Potter's Hollow. As I traveled, I glanced at the drivers around us. How different their New Year celebrations would be from ours. They looked forward to a new year, excited about new opportunities, new relationships, new beginnings.

But on that New Year's Eve, as we drove east across Washington, Stephen and I saw not beginnings, but endings. Not potential, but losses.

Life must have felt a little like a poker game to Stephen. He had begun the Christmas season with a full hand of cards—a hand full of potential. But somewhere in the season, life had snatched his most valuable cards right out of his hand.

He had wanted to fold early. Now, because I insisted, Stephen had to stay in the game.

He slept through most of our trip, waking only at a rest stop when I dragged Colleen-the-dog to a grassy rest area. He used the bathroom, measured his blood sugar, and went back to sleep. His cough had begun to subside, but the fatigue continued.

Colleen-the-dog continued her vigil from the back seat, her paws between us, her chin resting on Stephen's shoulder. I had to give it to her. She never moved from his side.

At home, I insisted that Stephen go inside while I emptied the car. I put box after box in the entry hall, pushing aside the anxiety I felt about leaving them there. If we hurried, we could sort and store everything before the kids came home. That way, I could explain things to Kevin before he figured it out himself.

When the car was completely empty, I changed into a pair of sweats and came back downstairs to fix some dinner. As I passed by the telephone on my way to the refrigerator, the blinking light caught my attention. Messages. I dialed the number for voice mail and punched in our security code. "You have four messages," the automated voice declared.

I listened as one of Mallory's friends invited her to an afternoon movie. I smiled as Raisa checked on Stephen. Then came the message I'd hoped for, and I warmed to the sound of Kevin's voice, low and rich over the phone line. "Hey, we miss you too much to stay and ski on Sunday. So we're heading back early in the morning. Should be there around dinnertime. The kids are fine. Mallory misses you. All Travis wants is food."

I laughed. Of course Travis wanted food. His life had become a perpetual hunt for empty calories. I erased Kevin's message, smiling as I thought about having my family home again. Sometime soon, I'd have to tell Kevin about inviting Stephen to live with us. But in that moment, in the warmth of the kitchen, I believed Kevin would understand.

The final message took the smile right off my face. According to the automated date and time stamp, the call had come late Friday. The first few words of the message passed before I recognized the distinctive clipped accent of Dr. Kurian.

"It is imperative that you call my office immediately," she said. "This afternoon if possible. I will be here until six." She paused, apparently considering how much information she wanted to leave on an answering machine.

"I have the results of your blood work, Stephen."

CHAPTER
Twenty-Nine

On Sunday morning, Stephen rested while I went to church. I could hardly focus on the service, worrying about Stephen at home alone. Part of me worried that Kevin might call. Would Stephen say something about living with us?

Afterward, I made lunch and we began the seemingly endless chore of putting away the bags and boxes we had temporarily stashed in the entry hall. I brought a portable table in from the garage and set it up in front of the window in Stephen's bedroom.

At one end of the table, I placed an old two-drawer file cabinet I'd kept from my college days. With my mother's old chair, we created a comfortable mini-office for Stephen. "I'll figure out how to get you connected to the Internet later," I said, tucking the chair under the desk.

"No hurry." Stephen lay on his back under the table, connecting the lines of his equipment. Though I tried not to be obvious about it, I kept an eye on Stephen as he worked. He rested frequently.

"You feeling okay?"

"Are you going to ask that every five minutes?"

"Yes," I said, gently kicking his leg. "Get used to it."

He shook his head. While he set up his computer and printer, I moved Mallory's clothes from the guest bedroom onto a pile on her bed. I hadn't known she'd taken over the guest bedroom closet; we'd have a little mother-daughter talk when she returned.

I hung Stephen's jackets and shirts in the closet and made a neat stack of his shoes along the floor. We moved his folded clothes into the empty dresser and put his collection of pictures and memorabilia around the room. By the time we'd finished, the place looked distinctly his own. "Look better?"

He glanced around the room. "My home away from home." I heard no trace of humor in his voice, not a single drop of happiness. Could Stephen be happy without being independent?

I looked at my watch. "It's getting late. The kids should be home soon. I think I'll start some dinner."

"Mind if I rest?"

"You should. We've worked really hard this afternoon."

I went downstairs to the kitchen, stopping in the entryway to condense the rest of Stephen's things. Though we'd managed to put most of his stuff away, we had several boxes left. As I slid the remainder closer together, I tried to ignore the tension I felt in my neck and shoulders. Kevin would be home soon.

Even after so many years together, my husband still surprises me. I knew that I should have talked to him first, wished that I could have. But the fact was, Stephen's attempt to end his own life had forced my hand. I'd made a decision—a radical, impulsive decision, granted—but it had to be done. I was the one who would pay for it, more than anyone else in the family. I would take responsibility for Stephen's care.

If Kevin loved me as much as he said he did, he would soon have a chance to prove it. And though I believed that our relationship was solid enough to handle this potential crisis, at that moment, I wished that I hadn't chosen to put our love to the test.

In the kitchen, I browned beef for stew and cut up vegetables. I threw together cornbread from a mix and brought a gallon of ice cream in from the garage freezer. I put candles on a tablecloth and set out our good water glasses.

Surveying the table afterward, I wondered if I'd gone overboard. I reconsidered the decorations. Would Kevin feel manipulated?

I was just starting a salad when I heard the Jeep come down the driveway. Moments later, the kids burst through the mudroom, their faces pink with exertion and sunshine. "Mom," Travis said, hugging me, "you missed a great trip."

"The weather was really good," Mallory added. "No wind or ice."

"Great snow," Kevin said, wrapping his arms around me. "Missed you," he whispered and kissed my cheek.

"What's for dinner?" Travis asked, lifting the lid on the stew. "Mmm, smells good." He opened the cookie jar and threw me a grieved look.

"No cookies, sorry," I said. "I've been too busy to bake. We're having stew and cornbread." I pointed to the bags that my children had dropped on the kitchen floor. "Take your bags up to your room, please, both of you. And drop your laundry down the chute."

"Do I have time for a bath?" Mallory asked.

"About fifteen minutes."

The kids disappeared, and Kevin chose a chair at the kitchen counter. "So, what have you been up to?" he said, as he sorted through the week's mail. "I noticed that Stephen's car is still here. I thought he'd have gone home today. Doesn't school start tomorrow?"

"I think it does," I said, swallowing the awful fear I'd been battling all week. It had come, the need for this confession of mine, more quickly than I'd expected.

"Shouldn't he be on the road by now? He's going to have to go over the pass in the dark." Kevin paused to open a bill from the phone company. "Where is he?"

"He's resting," I said. Crossing the kitchen, I leaned against the counter, folding my hands to keep them from shaking. "He isn't going back to school."

Kevin looked up, confused. "Why not?"

"Stephen got pneumonia, and I took him to the infectious-disease guy in Wenatchee—only the guy was a girl, a woman actually. Dr. Kurian said that the pneumonia was a very bad thing."

Kevin smirked. "I guess so."

"No, I mean more than that. It's a sign that Stephen's disease has progressed."

Kevin put the mail aside. As he listened, he leaned on the counter, his chin in both hands, fully focused on my words. "Progressed?"

"It's getting worse. The number of healthy cells in his blood is going down. The amount of virus is going up. It's a bad combination."

Kevin nodded. "Go on."

"He was so sick, Kevin. Coughing, fever, out of breath all the time. Anyway, when we got home from the doctor's office, he was also depressed. Very depressed."

"That would be pretty normal." Kevin said, dismissing my brother's emotion.

I felt something inside me rebel. How dare he? "He tried to kill himself, Kevin."

He looked up, clearly surprised. "You're kidding." He smiled, unwilling to believe my explanation. "Stephen wouldn't do that. What are you saying?"

I found my anger with Kevin growing. My voice took on an irritated tone. "I'm saying he tried it. He almost succeeded."

"How? What did he do?"

"He gave himself too much insulin, counting on the fact that I wouldn't find him until it was too late."

Kevin shook his head, clearly confused by this recent turn of events. "I'm sorry, Colleen. You shouldn't have to put up with that kind of behavior."

"Attempting to kill yourself isn't misbehaving."

"I didn't mean it like that," he said. "What I mean is that you shouldn't have to deal with that. What if he'd succeeded?" Kevin shuddered. "What would that do to you, finding him like that? What was he thinking?" I heard the change in Kevin's voice as he made the mental shift from interested listener into protective husband. "So did you call an ambulance?"

"I got through it by myself, amazingly. You know how long an ambulance can take to get here. I gave him glucose. I managed to get a shot into his arm. I called the doctor from here." I shook my head. "It was a nightmare. But the nurse at the internist's office said I did everything right."

"Did you talk to him about it? I mean confront him? Maybe it was an accident."

"It was no accident."

At that moment, Travis came into the kitchen. "When can we eat?" he asked. "I'm starved."

"You can pour water in the glasses," I offered, turning toward Kevin with one finger over my lips. I said to Travis, "And put the dressing on the table. Is your sister out of the bathroom?"

"I'll go check," Kevin said. "I have to take my bag upstairs. Is dinner ready?"

"As soon as everyone comes down," I answered. "Would you knock on Stephen's door and tell him dinner's ready?"

My son's interruption had saved me from giving Kevin the worst of the news, and though I knew it had only delayed the inevitable, I couldn't help but feel relieved. I didn't want to tell Kevin the truth anyway. How do you confess to your husband that you invited someone to live with you, but you neglected to check with him first?

I was about to figure it out, but I was in no hurry to learn.

By the time our family sat down to dinner, I suspected that Kevin already knew the truth. While the kids chatted about the trip, Kevin played with the stew in his bowl. Once, over ice cream, I caught him looking at Stephen with a peculiar expression of distaste.

Perhaps the things in the entry way had clued him in, or the changes in the guest bedroom. It didn't really matter how he figured it out.

After Stephen and the kids went to bed, I found out how accurate my guess had been. Kevin found me in the laundry room, sorting clothes. "Could you come out to the garage?" he said, his voice low and intense.

"Why? We can talk here."

"I don't think so. I think we need a little space." He turned and left the room without another word.

I put on a coat and mittens and headed for the garage. Outside, the wind rushed through the trees, howling through the spaces in the back fence. The cold air slapped my face, and I knew from the temperature that a Canadian cold front had dropped over Potter's Hollow. I zipped my coat all the way to the collar and turned my face away from the wind as I walked across the yard.

For the first time, I was glad that we hadn't attached the garage to the house. This way, no matter what Kevin had to say, Stephen would never hear the discussion. It might be miserable for me, but at least Stephen didn't have to suffer through it.

Inside the garage, I found Kevin near his workbench, two lawn chairs waiting. I sat down in one. A space heater blasted warm air at my feet. In spite of the heater, anxiety drained the blood from my hands and feet, leaving me chilled before I began. My mouth went dry.

Kevin took the other chair. "What's going on here, Colleen?" he said, leaning forward. "And this time, I want the whole story."

"Okay. The whole story," I repeated. I thought about a long preamble. I considered explaining how much I believed Stephen needed us. How I hoped that our love would help him move toward salvation. I thought about reviewing the physical struggles that Stephen faced. But as I sat there looking at Kevin, remembering how much I loved him, how much I wanted to please him, I found myself tongue-tied.

I couldn't think of a single place to begin. There was so much to say. Too much.

He waited.

"The whole story," I said, shaking my head and clenching my teeth to keep them from chattering. "Alright," I took a deep breath and plunged forward. "When I found Stephen unconscious, I was so scared. I've never been so scared in my whole life. I was sure that I'd lost him, that he would die and it would be my fault. I thought my heart was going to burst through my chest. And I was all alone trying to think of something, anything that would save his life. I was so frightened."

Though I tried to control myself, I found my words rushing out, tumbling forward. I sounded like a teenager caught driving a car without a license. All of my excuses seemed quite foolish when examined in the broad light of the detached garage.

"And then, after I gave him the gel, and then the shot, something changed. I got angry. Really angry. I couldn't believe that he would do that to me. And I wanted to kill him myself." I shook my head. No matter how I tried to explain what had happened with Stephen, my words didn't carry the impact of the experience. "It was like I became a completely different person," I said. "Kinda crazy huh?"

Kevin's face was a mask. His unwillingness to show himself, his cold, frozen features, frightened me. What had I done to my normally jovial and loving husband?

I stumbled on, "Anyway, as I sat there by the window and watched him eat, I knew what I had to do. I had to move Stephen into our house. With us. I just knew that it was the right thing to do."

Kevin's mouth became very tight, and his eyes narrowed. "You decided, without asking," he emphasized the words. "Without asking?"

"I didn't need to ask." It sounded ridiculous. What was I thinking? My stomach rolled and I felt a little nauseated.

"How can you make a decision like that without asking?"

"I don't know. I just knew it was right. I didn't have to pray about it or think about it. I just knew that we had to do it. We had to. We're Stephen's only hope."

Kevin's eyes bored through me, his voice intense. "That's a big responsibility to hang around a human neck. God is Stephen's only hope."

I glanced away, avoiding those eyes. "I know that. But he's given up. He was ready to end his own life. How can we let him do that?"

For the first time, Kevin raised his voice. "What on earth made you think this would be okay with me?"

I clenched my fists, trying to control my raging emotions. "Because I thought I knew you. I thought I knew how you felt about Stephen. I thought you loved him as much as I do."

"Of course I care, Colleen." He leaned back, throwing his hands up in frustration. "That isn't the point at all."

At that I lost my temper. No matter how Kevin felt about it, I couldn't change things now. If I took back my offer, what would Stephen think about believers? I took the offense. "Then what *is* your point, Kevin? That you didn't have the last say? That you care about Stephen as long as it doesn't interfere with your happy little life?"

My words hit home and I saw Kevin wince. "That wasn't fair. I do care about Stephen."

I shifted gears and stood up. Pacing along the back of the garage, I looked for the words that would make him understand. "Look, Kevin. I would have asked. But it looked like my only opportunity to help him. Don't you see? If he lives with us, he won't be surrounded by his old friends. They won't be pulling him away from God. We can make a real difference in his life."

Kevin did not stand. He did not even move. "I know you have this whole scenario all scripted, Colleen. Just like a good play. But what about our own kids? Travis can hardly stand being around him. What are we telling our kids by having him live with us?"

"I don't know," I said with sarcasm. "Something like, faith isn't faith unless it finds a way to work in your life?"

Kevin retaliated. "Or perhaps that the gay lifestyle is okay for those born to it?"

"Oh come on. Give your kids credit for more intelligence than that." I felt my face grow flushed as my frustration grew.

"What about you, Colleen? How long will this last? Are we his last stop on the way to death? And what about you? How long can you keep this up? How will you manage to keep the house and the kids and the students, and take care of Stephen too?"

"What you're really asking is how long will it take for Stephen to die."

"You don't have to put it so bluntly." Kevin ran his hand through his hair, pausing to scratch at the top of his head. "You're trying to make me out like some kind of jerk. I'm just trying to tell you that you didn't count the cost. And we're going to have to pay, all of us."

"Because we're family."

"Right. Because we are family, we're all going to have to participate in this. How could you commit us to something this big without talking to us first?"

I took a deep breath. "Look, I've admitted that I shouldn't have done it. I confess, alright?" I paced two or three steps. "I should have asked first. But I didn't. And now here we are. We can't throw him out. I can't take the offer back. Wouldn't you have said yes, anyway?"

In the silence that followed, I heard a broken branch slam against the roof. The wind whistled through the trees and the window rattled.

Kevin wiped his face with his hands, pausing to rub his eyes. "I don't know what I would have said. I'm tired, Colleen. I still can't believe you would do something like this."

I turned to face him, the one I loved more than any human on earth. "It's done, Kevin. I did it. I'm not going backward." I put my hands out, palms up. "Can't you see how much this means to me? Stephen is my flesh and blood. I have to help him.

"On our wedding day, we promised to take one another for better or worse. Can't you just call this the worst?"

Kevin stood, his sweatpants bagging at the knees, holes in the elbows of his flannel shirt, face unshaven, red-blond hair wildly askew. "This is the worst, alright. You've stolen something from me. You took my life and you gave it away without asking. It hurts that you didn't even care enough to ask me first. I don't know how we'll get through this. But right now, I can see that you don't even realize how much damage you've done." He shook his head. "You really have no clue."

CHAPTER
Thirty

On Monday, the second of January, I made breakfast for the kids and sat down with them while they ate. I told them about the progress of Stephen's illness and about my decision to let him live with us. I didn't quite tell the whole truth. I told them it was our decision—meaning Kevin's and mine.

The cardinal rule of parenting is to present a united front.

"It was the right thing to do," Mallory said. "We can be his family. He needs us now."

Travis said nothing, but his face betrayed his anger.

I touched his forearm. "Travis, what are you feeling?"

He shrugged my hand away. "Nothing."

"I'm not blind."

"Well, if you're so sensitive, then you figure out what I'm feeling." He took his dishes to the sink and stomped out of the room.

"Don't worry, Mom," Mallory said. "He's a guy. Guys take longer with these things."

After the kids left, Stephen called Dr. Kurian's office and made an afternoon appointment. "She said I could come in at five," he said, hanging up the kitchen telephone.

"I have piano students; I won't be able to come along." I was disappointed.

"I can drive myself."

"Driving isn't my concern. I wanted to hear what Dr. Kurian had to say." The serious tone in her telephone message had frightened me. Stephen might not tell me everything.

272

"I know. You want the whole scoop."

"All the details."

"Colleen, just because I live here now doesn't make you my mother."

I felt my cheeks turn pink. "I don't want to be your mother. But what if something happens to you while you're here, and I don't know what is going on? How will I know what to do? How will I take care of an emergency?"

"You worry too much."

"I can't help it. But you don't have to make it worse than it is."

He came across the kitchen and drew me into a hug. "I promise, I'll tell you everything I can remember."

"Write it down?"

"Don't push."

~ ~ ~

That afternoon, I taught piano with one eye on the clock. As usual, none of my students had bothered to practice over the vacation. By five I was ready to tear out my hair. By six, I wanted to tear out someone else's hair.

When Stephen hadn't returned by the end of my last lesson, I assumed that Dr. Kurian had been delayed. I fed the family and cleaned the kitchen. By seven, I'd begun to worry about what might be keeping him. I dialed his cell phone and left a message.

At dinner, Mallory asked me to listen to her newest essay for a private-college application. Travis asked for a set of reed-making tools. Apparently all the great reed players make their own reeds.

Later, while Travis practiced his saxophone and Kevin watched television, I worked on Stephen's sweater. His illness had influenced my choice of patterns and yarn. I wanted something that would knit up quickly—a simple pattern with few cables, written in a large gauge. I tried not to think about why it was so important I finish it. I told myself that I wanted him to wear it during the coldest part of winter in Potter's Hollow.

In truth, I wanted him to wear it before he died. I'd begun to pray for Stephen as I knit, trying to concentrate on a single petition through an entire row of stitches. Before that winter, I would never have guessed that knitting and intercession went well together.

Stephen came in around seven thirty, his dog padding down the stairs behind him. No matter how many times I'd seen him, I was struck again that night by the way his body had changed. His face, which used to be full and soft, had grown angular, like chipped marble. His dimples had changed to crevices, and his laugh lines had become creases. From the side, the bone around his eye stuck out through the flesh, leaving deep hollows at the temple and where his cheeks used to be.

My handsome brother now looked like a drug addict.

Even through jeans, I could see the long unpadded bone of his thigh and notice the absence of muscle to sit down on. I could trace the bones in his hands all the way from his wrists to his knuckles.

Stephen looked spent. He sat down on the couch beside me.

"So how did the appointment go?" I asked.

"Well, I'll have to give her this. She isn't in any hurry to rush you through."

I smiled. "That's good news. What did she say?"

"The CD4 has dropped, which is why she called. At least she thinks it has. She hasn't gotten the records from Seattle yet. Probably won't until the middle of next week."

"How much has it dropped?"

"I stopped paying attention awhile ago. The doctor has tracked it every three months for seven years. But I'm pretty sure it wasn't this low the last time."

"What was today's number?"

"One ninety-two."

"She said it would be under two hundred."

"She wants to test for viral replication."

"What's that?"

"A test to see if the meds are keeping the virus from reproducing." He scratched his nose. "If the meds are still holding it at bay, we continue them, even if the CD4 count is dropping."

"So, did you do it?"

"Of course. What's another trip to the hospital for blood work?"

"That explains how long you've been gone."

"Some of it. She had another idea."

I perked up. Another idea? Anything that might help Stephen live a longer, fuller life sounded promising to me. "What is it?"

"There's a new antiviral just approved by the FDA. The clinical trials are over, and it should be available to the public in the next month or two. It will be expensive, but it might bring my CD4 count back up."

I smiled, leaning over to pat his knee. "Wouldn't that be something?"

"Don't count on it, Colleen. I've been down this road before. It will cost plenty. And remember me? I don't have a job anymore. I have to pay my own health insurance. And even with insurance, I have to come up with the co-pay. I don't have any extra money to cover a new medicine."

"Stephen, can't you just wallow in the good news for a couple of minutes before you start shooting it out of the sky? This might be the break we've been waiting for."

"Maybe. But how will we pay for it? It won't help if we can't afford the medicine."

"Let's cross that bridge when we come to it."

"That's my sister, Colleen-who-lives-in-dreamland." His dog sat up and whined. "Not you, mutt."

"Come on, be kind."

"To the dog? That's the best I can do." He stood up. "Until the medicine becomes public, sometime in March, we have to monitor my CD4 more closely. Hopefully it will stay where it is for a while." Stephen paused, yawning. "Right now though, I'm going to be kind by heading straight to bed." He stood up and walked toward the stairs. Colleen-the-dog followed on his heels. "Good night."

"Wait. Did you eat anything? Have you taken your meds for the night?"

"Good night, Colleen," he said, this time with emphasis.

~ ~ ~

And so the Payton family welcomed a new member into its midst.

We spent January and February falling into a routine of sorts. While keeping my teaching schedule, I managed to get the kids off to school every morning and do most of my housework before Stephen woke up. On the days I taught piano before school, Stephen learned to sleep through the noise of lessons.

Most days, Stephen finished breakfast and dressed and then felt well enough to write for a few hours at his desk. After lunch, we went for a walk, sometimes all the way to the river, but most often we took a short trip around the neighborhood.

He read for a while every afternoon and nearly always took a nap while I taught piano. Wanting to help around the house, he asked for a job. I put him in charge of the dishwasher, asking that he empty it every afternoon before dinner. This he did with the regularity of a rooster crowing at sunrise, with the methodical precision of a neurosurgeon.

I once caught him washing the silverware tray with a Q-tip.

We made a weekly trip to the library, where Stephen checked out books on nearly every topic. Along with these, he brought home magazines, dissecting articles as he perfected his own writing skills.

He longed to see his work published in a periodical.

More than once I caught him gazing at the pages of a travel book, full of glossy pictures of far-off lands, and I recognized in his eyes an unquestionable understanding that travel would never be part of his life. And though it hurt him to look at the pictures, Stephen dreamed anyway.

Once every week, we made a trip to the post office, where Stephen mailed his queries and articles to the professional magazines and journals he hoped would publish his teaching and theatre articles. Stephen did daily reconnaissance at our mailbox, checking for some indication that his work had made it past the next publishing hurdle.

Day after day and week after week passed with no word. Though he kept up a brave front as he returned from the mailbox, I recognized

Stephen's disappointment. Editors who once seemed eager to read his work apparently disappeared as soon as we mailed the requested manuscript.

While they took their time to respond, Stephen clicked off the weeks of his life. They had forever; Stephen was living on borrowed time.

He waited too for news of his house sale. From Potter's Hollow, we hired a yard maintenance crew to clean up the lawn and garden. We paid a group to clean all of the windows inside and out, and we hired a cleaning crew to put everything in order for a showing. The Realtor sent us a picture of the house, all clean and waiting for a buyer. Still, he had no offers.

Selling the house became Stephen's only hope for overcoming his never-ending struggle with finances. He had some savings, but these would not hold him for long. Though we did not charge him for staying with us, Dr. Kurian and the lab continued to bill for services. His portion of the hospital bills, combined with his current medical expenses, amounted to an astronomical number. It was enough to send a child to Harvard.

Stephen could not refinance his house. In spite of low interest rates, no bank would consider working with someone who was currently unemployed. Every other week, Stephen portioned out his savings and sent a small check to the hospital and another to Dr. Kurian. The pressure of mounting debt weighed heavily on him.

During January and February, Noah Armstrong became a regular at our house. Most often, he arrived on Thursday afternoons, just about the time I began teaching piano lessons. While my students struggled through their major and minor scales, Noah holed up with Stephen at the dining-room table. His visits became so ordinary that he began letting himself inside, sometimes visiting with Stephen and leaving without ever speaking to the rest of us.

Once, when Thursday came and went without Noah's arrival, Stephen noticed.

When he came downstairs for dishwasher duty, I was making marinade for chicken. "Did Noah call today?" he asked, opening the dishwasher.

"I didn't take a call," I answered. "He might have left a message while we were out."

Stephen walked over to the phone. "There's a message," he said. "Can I check?"

I nodded and Stephen punched in the number for voice mail. He added the security code and listened through two long sales pitches. I didn't have to ask if Noah had called. Stephen's disappointment showed in his face. "Nothing there," he said, his eyebrow furrowing. "I hope he's okay."

"I'm sure he had something he had to do."

"It isn't like he's obligated to come."

"Maybe you should go visit Noah."

Stephen considered my advice and then shook his head. "No. I don't want him to feel obligated."

I laughed. "Stephen, if you're friends, you're friends. It's okay to care about someone, you know. You can go visit a friend."

My brother didn't answer. But in his concern, I recognized a deepening connection with Noah Armstrong. Secretly, I rejoiced over their friendship.

Once or twice a week, Stephen brought his drawing pencils down to the kitchen where we sat at the table for my drawing lessons. Stephen assured me that I could begin painting as soon as I felt comfortable with the pencils. At first, I was horrified to expose my lack of skill. Eventually though, I learned to laugh at myself, relaxing under the guidance of my brother's gentle instructions.

His methods were strange, unlike any art class I'd had in school. One day, he crumpled a piece of notebook paper and had me draw nothing more than the uppermost edge of the paper, following the edge with my eyes as I let my fingers draw along on my own sheet.

"Don't look at your hand," he said.

"How can I draw without looking?"

"Like you play the piano without looking at the keyboard," he answered. "Your fingers will find a way."

"Ah," I laughed. "Drawing by faith."

"You could call it that."

We progressed to drawing our hands, then our shoes, and eventually simple shapes from magazine ads. My skill improved, although it couldn't have been too hard to improve from where I started.

At the same time, Stephen continued to progress at the piano. Of course, he had a much stronger foundation in music than I had in art. When we were children, we learned music by rote, with no explanation of the structure behind the notation. I began by teaching him how modern music used the major scales to create three simple chords. These primary chords, I told him, the building blocks of all music, are in the same place in every scale.

As the weeks passed, we found those three chords in the keys of C, G, D, and F. I taught him to play his scales and use the chords to accompany himself. Stephen caught on quickly, learning to invert the chords and accompany the same scales in three positions.

Week after week, Stephen begged me to play "real" music. I tried to put him off. At first he wasn't ready. Eventually, he had progressed until he needed to practice with simple melodies in major keys.

I decided to let him learn folk songs and simple Christmas carols. I wrote the melodies on plain staff paper, rewriting the melody in several keys on every sheet. I made him play the tune with one hand and guess which chords supported the melody. At first, it was painful to hear. But eventually, Stephen conquered "Merrily We Roll Along" and "Good King Wenceslaus."

I have to admit that my brother was a good sport about the whole thing. Not many forty-somethings are willing to suffer through that kind of torture for such a modest payoff. Stephen was determined.

As Stephen learned from me, I learned from him. In the midst of our sharing ourselves, something marvelous happened. My brother and I found each other again. We laughed. We touched. We appreciated one another almost as freely as we had when we were children.

At the same time, something marvelous happened with Travis.

During the last week of January, I added about twenty appointments with high-school band students to my regular piano schedule. As an eligible pianist in a small town, I share the dubious privilege of accompanying these students for their solo contest.

Fortunately, the same instruments often choose the same pieces, making my work much easier. I find that contest is a great way to add a little padding to my savings account.

I played for Travis that year, and on the Saturday of the contest, we were both surprised to see Stephen sitting with Kevin in the classroom where we performed. Truthfully, I've always hated playing for my own children; I can hardly overcome my nervousness for them. Travis did well, and I was relieved when it was over.

Outside, Stephen greeted us with a large plastic shopping bag, which he handed to Trav. "You did great in there," he said, full of obvious pride. "I don't know what the judge thought, but I was really impressed. I bought this for you. You've worked really hard for this day. I know you'll always play the sax, and I thought you'd like one of these."

Travis opened the bag to find a soft leather gig bag. "I can't believe you did this, Uncle Stephen. You shouldn't have." He unzipped the bag and felt along the inside pockets. "It's just what I would have chosen." And then the miracle: Travis gave his uncle a hug.

I like to think that it was more than the gift that won over Travis. Stephen had recognized what was important to his nephew. Together they shared a common interest. Stephen's understanding broke through Travis's resistance.

I won't say that having Stephen with us was easy. It took time to get used to having another adult in our home. At first, I felt as though our family was on display, being evaluated and judged by Stephen as we interacted together.

I had a hard time learning to act naturally, to speak and touch and love my family—even correcting the kids—with my brother constantly present. But I worked at it, and eventually I decided that I could be myself in front of him, warts and all.

Kevin continued to struggle with having Stephen in the house. Though he was civil, he never quite entered in. I missed having the real Kevin at home.

Another thing, an unavoidable part of the process, gave me great pain as well. As the weeks passed, I watched Stephen continue to deteriorate. Though he tried to take care of himself, he tired more easily. There were days, several every week, when getting up was more than he could manage, and he spent the day in bed, dozing and reading. Though these occasions were rare, they seemed to take more out of Stephen's confidence than they took from his body.

The bedridden days reminded him of his own mortality; I think that explained why his mood became especially sour and demanding. On those days I felt as though I'd become nursemaid to a crotchety millionaire. I tried to be patient, but patience isn't natural to anyone. Especially me.

On the last day of February, Stephen and I celebrated the sale of his first article to a journal for elementary-school teachers. He had written about using drama to teach literature. Though the piece would not be published until early fall, the company promised to send a check as soon as Stephen signed a contract. The success gave him a huge lift, and I couldn't thank the Lord enough for his kindness toward my brother.

Early in March, during one of Noah's visits, I went into the kitchen for a glass of water. I discovered the two of them bent over the current Sport Fishing Rules for Washington State. On the table, Noah had spread an extra-large desk calendar representing the months of March, April, and May, and below this a huge map of the state.

"What are you two up to?" I asked as I filled my glass.

Noah looked up and smiled. "Fishing," he said. His voice was so full of reverence that I nearly laughed.

"On the table?" I teased. "Don't leave any fish guts."

"If you must know," Stephen explained, "we're planning the lakes where we can fish until the stream season opens. So far, we have Trapper, Clear, Fish, and Chelan on the schedule. Then, we'll hit the Yakima and move on from there."

"I didn't know you knew how to fish," I said, leaning against the counter.

"I don't," Stephen said, a sheepish expression on his face.

"Not yet," Noah added. "I figure anyone who can play the piano and do a little art can learn to fish. It's never too late to learn to fish."

I left them to their planning and returned to my next piano student. As I taught, I refused to let myself become anxious about Stephen going out in the cold spring air to fish in a lake. That night at dinner, Stephen invited Kevin to join the fishing expedition.

"That sounds like fun," I said with overzealous enthusiasm. "You love to fish, honey," I said, passing roasted vegetables to Kevin.

"I don't know if I can get away," he said. "When are you planning to go?"

"We aren't sure yet," Stephen said. "Noah has to schedule time away from the office."

I wondered how Stephen and Noah dared to make these kinds of plans. With Stephen's unpredictable health, making plans seemed an extraordinary expression of faith. "You can take some time away, can't you?" I asked Kevin. He threw me a look that said, *Enough, Colleen*, and I frowned at him.

"I'm not sure. We have some heavy meetings this spring," Kevin said. "We're planning the budget. Since I'm in charge of the meetings, I can't exactly get out of it."

And as soon as he said it, I knew that Kevin hadn't quite forgiven Stephen for accepting my invitation to join the family. Kevin loves to fish. Ordinarily, nothing would keep him from joining anyone— even a serial killer—for a fishing trip.

Kevin's rejection did not seem to bother Stephen. But I could not let go of it. How could Kevin hold my failure against a dying man? Stephen had never done anything to deserve the callous treatment he received from Kevin.

That evening, sitting around the kitchen table, I realized that Kevin and I would have to talk. Though I did not know when, I knew we'd have to hash things out.

Before I got the chance to talk with Kevin, another complication hit Stephen—though whether from the disease or the treatment of the disease, I don't think we'll ever really know. I was downstairs vacuuming the family room when I heard a tremendous crash in the entry hall. I turned off the vacuum and listened carefully. A gentle moaning floated down the stairwell.

I ran up to the entry hall, where I found Stephen lying crumpled on the floor. "Are you alright?" I asked, squatting down beside him.

"I don't think so," he groaned. "My ego is definitely bruised."

"Can you get up?"

"Sure. Give me a minute though. My knee hurts."

I sat beside him, waiting while he stretched his legs. "I missed a stair. No big deal."

"Missed a stair?" That didn't sound like Stephen.

He frowned at me. "Don't tell me you've never missed a stair."

"Of course. Everyone expects it of me. But you?"

He rolled onto his back, bringing his knees up to his chest. "Lately, I've had trouble with my feet. They feel sort of weird."

"Weird?"

"Strange. Sometimes numb. Sometimes burning. Once in a while, I just don't quite know where they are. Really it's no big deal."

"Have you told the doctor?"

He gave me a scolding look. "Yes, Mother," he exaggerated. "Okay, if you must know, I have the beginning of peripheral neuropathy."

"Neuropathy?" I stood up.

"Nothing. Just changes in the nerves. It happens." He shrugged. "Now, if you'll just help me up, I promise not to tumble down your stairs again."

I offered him my arm and leaned back as he pulled himself up. "I hope not. Nearly scared me to death."

My problem with Kevin compounded. He developed a pattern of coming home late, leaving for work early, hiding behind the newspaper, and spending much time in front of the television. One night, after the kids were in bed, I tried to talk to him about it. "Kevin, what's going on with you lately? I feel like you're avoiding me."

"I'm not avoiding you. I live here."

"You can live here without being really present."

His eyebrows rose. "I think you're overtired."

I couldn't solve a problem with Kevin until we agreed that there was one.

Two weeks later, Stephen and I were working at the piano when one of my students came to the door. Normally, I leave the house unlocked, allowing my students to enter quietly and wait for their turn at the piano. This prevents doorbells from interrupting my lessons, and Travis and Mallory don't spend the afternoon answering the front door.

Generally it works.

But on this day in mid March, one of my students came in with her mother. Eight-year-old Chelsea sat down in a barrel chair swinging her legs as Stephen played through his weekly assignment. Her mother came around our half-wall, eyes down, digging through her purse. As she stepped into the room, I happened to look up. Chelsea's mother looked at me, surprise in her face as she glanced from me to Stephen and back again.

I recognized the expression; I'd seen it before. The eyes widening in horror as she saw Stephen touching the keys of my grand piano.

I smiled at Chelsea. "You're early today," I said.

She smiled back, patting the books resting on her lap. "I'm all ready."

An expression of confusion crossed her mother's face. She looked again at Stephen, and then made up her mind. "Actually, we came early to tell you that we aren't going to be able to have a lesson today," she said, stumbling over the words as they poured out. "I'm sorry about the mix-up. I know we should have called. But I have an appointment I can't avoid."

Chelsea's mother walked across the room, reaching for her daughter as she spoke. "So, we have to be going, don't we dear?" Yanking her daughter's hand, she hauled Chelsea across the carpet to the entry hall, the child's feet literally dragging along on the carpet behind her. The last thing I saw were two little black rain boots sliding around the corner.

Stephen and I sat frozen as the front door closed. And then, catching a glimpse of my brother's face, I burst out laughing.

"I'm glad you think that's funny," he said.

"I can't help it. Did you see her face?"

"I recognized the look," he said, bitterness creeping into his tone.

"Me too," I said through giggles. "I knew it was coming as soon as she saw you. I'm sorry, Stephen, it was cruel, really it was. She was terribly unkind. But it was so funny, the absolute shock, you know? And then the way she tried to get out of here. You'd think we had Legionnaire's disease."

He smirked as I continued, "She couldn't have been more shocked to see Al Capone, or Beethoven himself." Stephen's smirk grew into a smile. "I wish I had a picture of her face." He finally broke into a grudging laugh. "I have to admit. I don't think I've ever seen anyone move away that quickly. It had to be some kind of record."

And the more I thought about her face, the more I laughed. And the more I laughed, the more Stephen joined in. Though I tried to stop myself, I could not.

"It would be horrible if it wasn't so funny," he said, holding his stomach. "I wish I had a video clip. My drama students could use it as a model."

During the rest of the afternoon, the two of us enjoyed the event over and over again, a sick humor having overwhelmed our slightly twisted brains, until we began laughing as soon as we looked at one another.

I was still chuckling long into the evening, even after Chelsea's mother called to tell me that her daughter would not be taking any more lessons. I giggled about it for three more days. But when the fourth student called to tell me that she had decided to quit piano, my laughter turned to anger all over again.

Dr. Kurian had been monitoring Stephen's blood levels every three weeks through the winter. With God's grace, Stephen's health remained fairly stable, in spite of a steady loss of CD4 cells. It seemed that the switch to new medicine was inevitable. Stephen asked Dr. Kurian's office to check with the insurance to see how much of the expense they would cover.

The insurance manager reported that the new medicine would be covered at the usual rate, as long as it was fully approved for use with his diagnosis by the Food and Drug Administration. The usual rate left Stephen with half the retail cost.

It didn't sound like a problem to me, not until I discovered how much half represented. In this case, Stephen's monthly portion would be $850.

While we waited for the new medication, Stephen worried about the sale of his home. He called the Realtor and found that no one had yet gone to view the house twice. Stephen lowered the asking price.

In the meantime, he made arrangements to liquidate the last of his retirement funds. Though he could hardly afford the financial hit for taking the funds early, Stephen had no choice. If he didn't take the funds, he would not live to pay his taxes again. He wrote one large check to the hospital, another to Dr. Kurian, and put the remainder in his savings account.

It would have to be enough to cover his new medication when the time came.

≈ ≈ ≈

In late March, Gloria and Noah asked Stephen out for dinner and an evening of amateur theatre. The Little Theatre, a group in Potter's Hollow, was putting on *The Diary of Anne Frank*. I found him in the living room with yet another magazine. "They aren't coming until six, are they?" I asked.

"I know. I didn't want to keep them waiting."

With a dress shirt and tie under the new sweater I'd just finished, Stephen looked especially handsome. The teal in the sweater made a striking accent to his blue eyes and blond hair. Still, looking at Stephen in his dress shirt, I felt a little sad. He had lost so much weight that the tie essentially gathered the neck of the shirt onto his body. Every reminder served as a new source of pain; Stephen was wasting away.

As I saw him waiting, I regretted that we hadn't done more to get Stephen out. He had spent three long, dark months at our house, and I realized how house-bound he must have felt going from a full work-week to complete disability in such a short time. I made a personal commitment to do more to get Stephen out and about.

Noah rang the bell at five minutes to six, and I walked both men out to the car. "You guys have a really great time," I said as they climbed inside the minivan.

"I'll have him home by midnight," Noah said, and laughed.

When the car door opened and the overhead light went on, I saw that the little minivan carried other passengers. It looked to me as though they had filled the car with sick men. I wondered if all of them were as desperate for friendship as my brother. I saw hope in their smiles, an earnest desire for a night off from illness.

Mallory had plans for a birthday party that night, and Travis was headed to a movie with friends. That left Kevin and I sitting home like old fogies, which I anticipated with pleasure. It was the first time we'd been alone in three months.

After dinner, I made a hot-fudge sundae big enough to share and brought it down to the family room. Kevin was immersed in The History Channel. "I brought you something," I said, sitting down beside him. I handed him a napkin and spoon. "Don't spill on the couch."

"Oh, stop my pounding heart. Dessert. What possessed you to let me have ice cream?"

"I'm celebrating. It's our first evening alone in years."

"You're exaggerating."

"Who, me?" Just as I reached for the bowl with my spoon, Kevin deftly moved it sideways, slightly out of my reach. "Don't you think you should share?" I asked.

"I wouldn't want you to be sorry in the morning."

"Get it back here, buddy," I said in my most menacing tone. I glanced at the television. "Haven't we seen this Civil War series a couple dozen times?"

"Not without listening to you complain."

"I think the war is over."

Kevin aimed the remote at the screen and turned up the sound. I put on my best pouting face. "I really did want to talk to you about something important."

"Well, that explains the ice cream." He looked at me for a long moment and then back at the screen. With a sigh, he turned off the television. "I guess I won't get to see it tonight either. So what is it? What do you want to talk about?"

"I just wanted to talk to you about Stephen."

I felt his defenses go up. "What about him?" He took a spoonful of ice cream.

"I've noticed the way you treat him. And I'm wondering if you could make a bigger effort to be kind."

"I am kind." He rolled the edge of the spoon through the fudge and brought it to his lips.

"Kevin. I'm not talking about being polite. I'm talking about loving him."

"Look, he lives here. Isn't that kind enough?"

"No. It isn't."

"I speak nicely to him. I pay for his groceries. I let my wife wear herself out taking care of him. Certainly that's enough?"

I leaned forward, placing my spoon on the coffee table. "No. I don't think so. You never initiate a conversation with him. You don't take any interest in his world. You don't go up to see him when he's had a bad day. He can tell that you're just tolerating him."

"He can tell? What, he's clairvoyant?"

"I can tell. Anyone can tell."

"Alright. So Stephen isn't my best friend. I'll give you that. Why does he have to be?" Kevin leaned over and put the half-finished bowl of ice cream down on the table. "I never planned to have him live here. It was all your idea. Isn't it okay if I keep my distance? What difference does it make to you?"

"It makes a huge difference. I want your support in this. Not only do you ignore Stephen, but you've started to ignore me. We don't talk any more. You're never home for dinner. You bury yourself in the newspaper."

"Look, Colleen, you're getting everything you asked for. Your brother is here. He's safe. You can keep an eye on him. What more do you want?"

"I want you to be kind to him. And I want a relationship with you. A real, husband-wife relationship."

"You want more than kindness. You want me to have a relationship with Stephen."

"I want you to *create* a relationship with him. It isn't there now. It won't happen by accident." I turned my palms up. "What I mean is, I want you to find a way to reach out to him, even though it takes effort."

He shook his head, crossing his arms across his chest. "I can't do that. I can't just make something out of nothing." He let those words sink in for a moment. "He's your brother."

"He isn't taking anything from you. He pays for all his own stuff. A small butterfly eats more than he does. Why is this so hard for you?" I didn't like the whining of my own voice, but I felt my emotions surging just below the surface. *Why wouldn't Kevin reach out to Stephen?*

"I could ask you the same question. Why are you pushing so hard? This is your crusade, Colleen. It isn't just kindness or compassion. I've known you too long to buy that as an excuse. Something inside you is driving this crazy need to save your brother from himself. What is it? What's pushing you?"

I'd never expected this conversation to go this way. I'd hoped that Kevin would see things my way and agree to try harder. Instead, his questions triggered something. For the first time I realized that my "crusade" for Stephen had nothing to do with my need to save him from himself or from the consequences of his choices.

I'd been driven by love.

The love Stephen and I had sought our whole lives had found me, and I desperately wanted it to find my brother too. Suddenly I realized what I had to do. My palms broke into a sweat, and my breathing came fast and shallow. "What's pushing me?" I repeated. Without another word, I stood up. "Just a minute and I'll show you."

With my heart pounding, I left the family room and headed upstairs. In all the years I'd been married, I'd been anticipating this moment, dreading it as one might dread oral exams or a speech before an audience of thousands. My knees turned to jelly and I wished with all my heart that I had not eaten a bite of ice cream.

How could I get through this? How could twenty years of antici-pation and fear suddenly give birth to the truth?

Would Kevin ever understand? Could he ever accept what I had done?

In our bedroom, I turned on the light, opened the closet door and pushed all the clothes into one corner. I opened a step stool and climbed up. Nausea rolled through my stomach and I bent over, trying to grab hold of my emotions before they took hold of me.

My knees shook so hard that I had to keep one hand on the shelf as I stood on my tiptoes and reached for the box. From this position, I couldn't grasp the little gray safe, hidden in the far corner of my top shelf. With one finger, I slid it across the shelf, dropping it over the edge, catching it with one hand.

With the little metal box safely in my arms, I climbed down and went into the bedroom. I knew this day would come. I'd anticipated it, dreaded it. But who would have thought it would come like this, in this context?

I thought of dear, sweet Kevin. This moment of truth would for-ever change everything between us. He didn't deserve what I was about to tell him. And yet, he deserved nothing less.

In the top drawer of my bedside table I retrieved a small key. I turned off the bedroom light and walked downstairs, praying for the strength to tell the truth. And I prayed for Kevin.

When he saw me standing beside the couch, the box in my arms, the key in my fingers, he stiffened a little and patted the spot beside him. "This looks serious."

"It is."

"Okay," he said.

I gave him the key. "Do you remember when you first met me?"

He nodded. "Stephen introduced us at the cast party."

"Do you remember the night that I told you I hadn't been raised in a Christian home?"

"We'd been dating a couple of months." His eyes narrowed, confusion in his features.

I thought back to the night in the library with Kevin, picturing his young face intense and full of love. "We talked for hours in the third-floor study room. I cried and you didn't quite know what to say. By then I knew that I loved you, and I had to tell you the truth about me. Do you remember what else I told you?"

He nodded, more slowly this time, his eyes searching mine. My questions baffled him. "You told me that you had gotten involved with a guy at your last school. That it went farther than you wanted."

"I told you that I had sex with him."

Kevin blanched. "I remember."

"There was more to it than that," I said, turning in my seat to face him. "Much more than that. I was too afraid to tell you everything. I thought you'd leave me."

"I wondered," he said. "I never asked, but I wondered."

"Kevin, when I was a junior in college, I left the state to attend Indiana University School of Music. Stephen didn't go. He wasn't interested. It was the first time we'd ever been apart. I'd never been alone before, and I was so miserable that I thought I was going to die. It was a mistake to go.

"But I wanted to be grown up. Wanted to feel grown up. But inside, I was frightened and horribly alone. There was a man at school. A graduate student who taught my music theory lab. His name was Rob. He asked me out and I accepted. It progressed. He was older, more experienced. He told me he loved me.

"I don't know if you can believe me—especially after all these years. But it was the first time any man had ever said that to me." My voice trembled, and before I could stop it, a tear escaped. Kevin reached over and took my hand, massaging my palm with his thumb. "I know now, looking back, that my father never once said those words. Not once in my whole life, did my father ever tell me he loved me."

Kevin winced.

"I wanted to be loved so much that I believed this guy. I went along with it. We had sex." I wiped my nose with one hand, sniffling. "I don't want to blame him. I made the choice, you know? I did it."

"You don't need to tell me all of this," Kevin said, his face tightening in pain. "We've been over this. It's past. It's done."

"But it isn't done," I said. "That's what I'm trying to tell you. It's forgiven, yes. I mean, the whole mess was part of the reason that I needed Jesus. He's forgiven me, but it isn't done." I buried my face in my hands, wanting more than anything to bury this secret one more time.

"What isn't done? What could be more important than being forgiven, Colleen?"

"Nothing is. I know that. Really I do. I've worked through it. But I've never been really honest about my past. Not with you. Not with anyone. Not until now."

I took a deep breath. "I got pregnant. That's what I've been hiding all these years." My voice shook as I choked back the sobs. "I had a baby, and in all these years, I never told you."

CHAPTER
Thirty-Two

With my face in my hands, I cried—loud, racking sobs punctuated by gasps for air; it certainly wasn't the gentle feminine tears of daytime soap operas. Kevin did not speak. Instead, making no effort to stop my tears, he used the palm of one hand to rub my back.

Through tears, I continued. "Rob didn't want me. He didn't want the baby. I didn't have anywhere to go, no one to tell. I mean—can you imagine trying to tell my father about what had happened? He would have killed me. It would have humiliated him. I couldn't go home.

"Even though I hadn't attended church, even though I had no faith of my own, I went to talk to a pastor near campus. He found a family who took me in. I moved out of the dorms before anyone could see that I was pregnant. I paid for my room and board by helping to care for the children where I stayed. I finished the semester without my classmates knowing.

"I never told my mother," I said, smiling a rueful smile. Even now, I would never consider telling Mother this juicy bit of information.

"The baby was due in August, and by early summer, the pastor located a couple who wanted the child. I stayed in Indiana long enough to give birth, and after it was over I went home. I couldn't tell anyone about what had happened. I had so much shame. I was depressed and had to see a therapist. Even though I could hardly put one foot in front of the other, I went back to school in the fall."

"That was when you started attending the church on campus," Kevin said.

That was the only part of the story I had told Kevin. "I don't know where I'd be without that church. My past was eating me alive. I'd never heard about forgiveness. And that was what I needed. More than anything in the world, I needed a fresh start."

Kevin pulled me into his embrace, encircling me in his arms, patting me as I cried. "We all do, Colleen. We all need forgiveness." He tipped his head, resting his face on my hair. "And I'm sorry, Colleen," he whispered. "Rob didn't know what he was missing. You're the most wonderful thing that ever happened to me. I don't know how he left you behind. What a fool."

I wiped my eyes with my palms, and managed a meager smile. "But don't you see?" I asked, "I gave the baby up for adoption. And he's out there somewhere right now. I haven't heard anything from his parents since he was six months old. That was the arrangement."

I handed Kevin the little steel safe. "It's all in there. All of it," I said. I took a deep shuddering breath. "Open it."

Kevin used the tiny key to unlock the lid. Gently, he lifted the contents from the box, placing them on his lap. On top of the pile, he found a plain white envelope. He opened it and looked inside, lifting out a tight blond curl.

"His mother sent that with his picture."

Below the envelope, Kevin found a photograph. A curly haired blond boy sat clapping his hands and grinning at the camera. He wore a navy blue sailor suit and white oxford shoes. His short dimpled legs stuck out in front of him. "He was beautiful," Kevin said. "A beautiful boy." He reached out to give my hand a squeeze.

By now, my sobbing had subsided. As I looked again at the picture, tears flowed freely, silently down my face and dripped onto my jeans. I could hardly see the baby's smile.

As I watched, Kevin read the note from the baby's mother. Because I had memorized the words, I did not try to read the handwritten note with him.

"Jonathan is a happy, healthy baby. He sits by himself and will crawl soon. He plays peek-a-boo and pat-a-cake and loves our pet collie. As we promised, this will be our last letter to you. No words can accurately express the gratitude we feel for Jonathan. He has forever changed our lives. Your courage in giving him a future and a family has cost you much. We will pray for you every day of our lives."

Kevin folded the note card and replaced it in the envelope. "I didn't know. All these years, you've been carrying this, and I didn't know."

"I should have told you. I know that. But the longer we were together, the more I convinced myself that it didn't matter. And the longer I let it go, the harder it was to bring it up. I finally decided that I couldn't tell you. It had been too long."

"He's old enough to come looking for you now."

"It's possible. But boys rarely go looking for their birth mothers, unless they need health information. That's why I have so much empathy for Stephen. Don't you see?" I stood up and crossed the room. I grabbed a box of tissues and carried them back to the coffee table, where I sat facing Kevin.

"I guess I don't understand," Kevin said, still holding the photograph.

"Stephen and I lived in the same house. We had the same father. Dad provided for us. He came home occasionally. But he was never home emotionally. I don't know why. He just couldn't do that. He drank too much. He was angry all the time, even though he didn't beat us. My father had a wall inside that kept him from us. I guess it was just too big for him to climb over. No matter how much we needed a father, all we got was an army officer.

"I grew up so hungry for love that I fell into a relationship that I shouldn't have. And so did Stephen. He was as vulnerable as I was— only in a different way. We both wanted a man to love and approve of us. We were desperate for it. Don't you see? We both made the same mistake, for the same reason."

Kevin thought for a moment. "That would be true—if Stephen had gotten into an immoral relationship with a woman. But he didn't."

"He got into an immoral relationship. What difference does it make who it was with? Is one kind of immorality different than another? He was vulnerable. He wanted to be loved, just like I did. We aren't excused. I'm not saying that. I'm saying we were *both* wrong.

"I have to be there for Stephen because I understand. I've done the same thing."

"I follow your reasoning," Kevin admitted. "But I don't agree. It isn't really the same."

"Today, Stephen is living with the consequence of his sin," I explained, desperately seeking the words that would help my husband understand. "I didn't experience the *same* consequence. But I had a consequence too. And someday, my consequence might show up on our doorstep—just like Stephen's disease. I don't have AIDS, Kevin. Not because I'm such a moral person. Not because I don't deserve it. I do.

"How can I sit in judgment when I'm as guilty as he is?" I said. "You asked me to tell you why taking care of Stephen is so important to me. This is the reason:

"When I was guilty and facing a pregnancy alone, the love of a church and a family saved me. I want to do the same for my brother." I reached up to caress Kevin's cheek, rubbing my thumb along his cheekbone.

"You've heard the expression 'except by the grace of God'? That's me. I'm only here because of God's grace. I want Stephen to experience grace too. I want it so much that I'm willing to do whatever it takes. I want to do it with you. I want you to want it too. But I understand that you have to decide. That much is up to you."

Taking both my hands, Kevin pulled me toward him. He put one arm around my shoulder and sat quietly for a while. "I'll think about it, Colleen. I promise. But you know, I've got to say, you missed your calling."

From inside the protective circle of his arms, I looked up at his chin. "What?"

"If you'd gone to law school, we'd be rich by now."

The next morning, Stephen bubbled over with enthusiasm. I think it was the happiest I'd seen him all winter. "It was really fun,

Colleen. We went to dinner at that underground soup kitchen over in the tourist district. It was funky, but the food was great." He opened his pill minder and began downing tablets with milk. "The play wasn't bad either. For community theatre, I thought they did exceptionally well."

"Maybe you should volunteer. They could probably use some experienced help."

"Actually, I've thought about it." He threw another handful of tablets into his mouth. "But I have something more important to do today."

"Oh?" I took oatmeal off the stove and poured a bowl for myself.

"Last night one of the guys talked to me about my insurance problems. He told me that I should apply for a disability. I might qualify for Medicaid. I won't have to make any more of those crazy payments to the insurance company."

"Will they cover your care?"

"As soon as the paperwork goes through. Of course, I won't drop my insurance until the disability is approved."

"How do you do it?"

"I'm going to drive into Wenatchee and get the paperwork today. I have to drop it by Dr. Kurian's office for her signatures. I have to get a CD4 today anyway; I can do both in one trip."

"Are you starting to feel like a pincushion?" I poured myself a cup of coffee and sat down at the kitchen table. The lab had drawn Stephen's blood once a week all winter long.

"Have for a long time," Stephen said. "Dr. Kurian has been watching me like a hawk."

"When will the new medicine come out?"

"I think it's available now," Stephen said. "But she doesn't want to use it until she has to. Who knows how it will affect me? We're assuming it will help. But maybe it will mess something else up."

He sat down beside me. "Speaking of available. Is the rest of the oatmeal spoken for?"

"It's all yours."

≈ ≈ ≈

Stephen spent the next few days working on his disability application. His house still hadn't sold, and though I didn't know any of the details of his financial situation, I knew he felt pressure. I saw it every time he opened his bank statement.

I saw it too when we went shopping and Stephen bought only the least expensive store-brand items. Standing at the checkout counter, he'd lay out his coins with the miserly care of a street urchin. He picked up pennies in the parking lot.

Without a paycheck, he made his house payment out of his savings account. That combined with his insurance payments ate away at his little stash like spring caterpillars nibbling down an apple tree. We talked about renting the house, but he decided to hold out a little longer.

On the Sunday after his excursion to the theatre, Stephen woke early. I found him in the kitchen with Colleen-the-dog. "What are you doing up so early?"

He looked a little sheepish. "Actually, I'm going to church."

"You are?" My voice held equal measures of disbelief and delight.

"With Gloria. She's driving me over to Noah's church. Her support group is making brunch for everyone after the morning service."

I tried not to let my disappointment show. After all, why should I care which church my brother attended? "That sounds good. I wish someone would make my lunch after church," I teased, gently elbowing him in the side.

Stephen winced and moaned.

"I'm sorry," I said. "What's hurting?"

"I don't know. My skin, I think." He pinched his sweatshirt and held it away from his chest, as if the feel of the fabric was painful. "Probably just the neuropathy."

"Have you checked your temperature?"

"Please, Colleen. I've felt great for a few weeks here. Let's not go looking for trouble."

If Stephen felt great, I had to be missing something. But I chose not to mention his list of current aggravations. "Sorry. You're an adult. I know it. I just need to spend the rest of the week repeating it to myself. Stephen is an adult. Stephen is an adult…"

He laughed, and I reveled in the sound of it. "I love you, sis," he said.

After Stephen left with Gloria, we did church as usual, stopping for groceries at the warehouse on the way home. The kids talked us into lunch at a burger joint, and we made it home before three.

Stephen's car was in the driveway, but he was not downstairs. I assumed he was taking a nap and chose to let him sleep. Because it was a relatively mild day in early spring, Kevin and I worked outside, picking up branches from the yard and sweeping needles off the deck. My husband even mowed the back lawn for the first time that season. When the time came to make dinner, I felt happily exhausted, looking forward to full-blown spring in Potter's Hollow.

With seafood chowder bubbling away in a pot and fresh garlic bread browning in the oven, I went upstairs and knocked on Stephen's door. "Dinner is ready."

He didn't answer. I opened the door and found the room completely dark, heavy snoring coming from his bed. "Stephen," I said, touching him on his shoulder. "Do you want to come down for dinner?" Spending the day with so many people had exhausted him.

"Hmm?" He rubbed his eyes and rolled over. "Ah," he cried out, putting his hand to his side. "Ah. Shoot."

I turned on the light beside his bed in time to recognize the agony on his face. "What is it?" I asked. "What hurts?"

Stephen's face was flushed; perspiration covered his skin. He spoke through gritted teeth. "My side. It burns. Like it's on fire."

"Can I see?" He pulled up his T-shirt, exposing the left side of his rib cage. I bent over, trying to see what might be causing his pain. "Turn toward the light." Obediently he rolled, at the same time twisting his neck around in an attempt to examine his own skin.

On the side of his chest, just below the nipple, a faint rash appeared in a wide stripe. There were no localized spots, no sign of infection. "It's red," I confirmed. "Looks just like a plain old rash. Did you scratch yourself?"

"Not that I know of. What do you think it is?"

"I don't know. I'm guessing here," I said. "Maybe we should we call the doctor?"

"Not on a Sunday night. I'll be all right. As long as I don't touch it."

"Do you want to come down for dinner?"

He shook his head. "I'm not hungry. I ate a lot at the brunch."

I imagined the tiny portions of food my brother might have managed to force down. "I'll bring something upstairs." I called the dog as I left the room. After so many hours, she needed a trip outside. She refused to leave Stephen's side.

On Monday morning, after the kids left for school, I went up to check on Stephen. I found him lying on the bed with his shirt off, unable to bear the touch of fabric on skin. The redness on his side had intensified and spread. Several small lesions had appeared in the midst of the rash.

"I'm thinking it looks like shingles."

"Oh great. Shingles." He threw his arm in the air. "What next?"

"I think we should call the doctor," I said, handing him the cordless phone.

"You planned this."

"Not the shingles, silly. I assumed we'd have to call Dr. Kurian. Now dial the number."

Abandoning my plans for the day, I drove Stephen to the doctor's office. Dr. Kurian had us enter through a rear door and wait in a secluded exam room. Apparently, according to his nurse, patients could contract chicken pox from his lesions—if in fact they were shingles.

"I'm waiting for the results of your latest CD4," Dr. Kurian said, sitting on the stool in the corner of the exam room. "But there isn't any question. You have shingles. We'll do our best to treat that right away. Your lab results should be back tomorrow, Thursday at the latest. I'll give you a call. I'm thinking it's time to start the new medicine. We've waited long enough."

I needed clarification. "Are you saying that the shingles are another sign of weakness in the immune system?"

"It would be for anyone," she answered. "No one comes down with shingles unless they are weakened in some way—could be stress or age or fatigue. I just want to know where Stephen is before I start the new medication."

"Will we stop all of the others?" Stephen asked.

"No. I'm going to switch the new med for one in your combination. I think we'll see a rebound in your CD4 count, and that should lower the number of viruses in your bloodstream."

"Well, let's hope so," Stephen said.

"I'll give you something for the pain," she said. "These lesions can be as painful as kidney stones." Twelve minutes later, we left with prescriptions for antiviral cream and tablets and a strong pain reliever. Stephen dragged down the hall to the elevator and punched the down button. "Well, I guess it could be worse," I said.

"I should expect it by now," he said, standing perfectly still, holding his arms away from the painful skin under his T-shirt. "This is the way AIDS goes. I know it. You know it. Why do I even hope for anything else?"

"Because we're going to keep swinging away until we get a hit," I said, punching the elevator button impatiently. "Big hitters don't worry about strikes. They just get up to the plate and swing away. That's what we're going to do. We're gonna keep coming to the plate."

"Who made you color commentator for the Mariners?"

"Preseason baseball is the only hope I have for summer."

The elevator doors opened, and we stepped inside. "I'd recommend you lay off the television," Stephen said. "You're starting to scare me."

CHAPTER
Thirty-Three

By the next day, Stephen's shingles had spread over his lower chest. When he woke in the morning, hundreds of pustules covered the rash. The pain so debilitated him that he stayed in bed, lying for hours on one side, infected skin exposed to the air.

I moved a space heater into his bedroom, hoping to keep him warm.

I learned to apply the antiviral cream with sterile gloves, but no matter how I tried, Stephen found my touch excruciatingly painful. Though he hated narcotics, he was grateful for the drug-induced stupor they produced, grateful for the few hours of relief. Only then, immediately after his dose of pain medication, did Stephen sleep.

My job—between piano lessons, cooking dinner for the family, driving Travis to his saxophone lessons and school soccer practice, and helping Mallory to address her graduation announcements—was to keep an eye on Stephen's AIDS medications, his antiviral medications, his pain pills, his blood sugar, his insulin dosage, and his food intake. Other than that, I had it pretty easy.

Oh yes, I had to drag Colleen-the-dog outside occasionally.

Dr. Kurian called just after lunch on Thursday. Unfortunately, Stephen had already fallen asleep. "He just took his pain medication, and I think he'll sleep for quite a while. He's been waiting for the test results," I said. "Can you give me the numbers?"

"I suppose I can do that. The viral load hasn't changed much," she said. "But the CD4 count has dropped again. Stephen is at 98."

"That's quite a drop."

"You're right. It isn't good." I heard a telephone ringing in the background. "I've already called your pharmacy. They've ordered the new medication. It should be in tomorrow by noon. I want you to start Stephen on it right away. It's critically important."

"What about his other meds?"

Dr. Kurian went over the collection with me, detailing how often and when Stephen should take each medicine. I took notes on a yellow legal pad I kept by the phone. "Now, do you have any questions?"

"None that I can think of."

"I want you to call me at any time," she said. "I'll do a blood test every two weeks to see how he is doing. If the meds are working, we should be able to see the changes fairly soon. He'll feel better, look better, and the shingles should start to heal."

"That's the way I'm praying."

I heard a long pause. "Well, let's hope it works," she said. "There's one other detail I should mention. This drug is the very latest thing. It may save Stephen's life. But it is very expensive. A one-year course should run around twenty thousand dollars."

I swallowed hard.

"Are you there?" she asked.

"I was just gasping for breath."

" Have you gotten an appointment for Stephen's disability interview?"

"Not yet."

"Well, don't count on hearing anything soon. In my experience, even when you qualify it takes about six months to get approval."

"That makes quite a crack to fall through."

"It does indeed. At least when things go through, you won't have to worry about medication costs any more."

When I hung up, I couldn't help but wonder. Where would Stephen get that kind of money? What would he do until the house sold? Would he even qualify for Medicaid?

I wandered into the living room and sat down at the piano. For a moment, I sat still, staring at the photo of Stephen had brought me on that first visit last summer. In spite of my love for him, I felt completely helpless, unable to rescue him from the battle he now faced.

Opening the lid, I stretched out my arms and began a gentle worship chorus. With nothing more than a simple melody line and block chords, I began "His Grace Still Amazes Me." Then, warming up, I elaborated the chorus, adding fills and counter melodies. Eventually I used the entire piano, letting the sound rise up and swirl through the house.

I'm quite certain that the Lord does not inhabit my piano skills. If he did, I think I would play better. But, he certainly fills me with peace as I play. Refreshed, I brought the music back to earth, ending with a lilting repeat several octaves above the melody. And as I lifted my hands from the keyboard, it occurred to me.

How much is a six-foot Kawai grand worth?

Friday morning I called Jackie to stay with Stephen. "I need to go to the pharmacy for his new medicine. I hate to leave him alone. He can hardly move. Mallory and Trav have a band rehearsal. If you could come by after school, I could run to Wenatchee and be back in an hour, tops."

"I can't," she said. "I have a hair appointment. I'd cancel but I'm getting a color, and canceling would leave a huge hole in my hairdresser's schedule."

I took a deep breath. Jackie has been my friend longer than anyone in Potter's Hollow. But clearly, she had distanced herself from me. Had I focused so intently on Stephen that I'd isolated myself from those I loved most?

I called Gloria. "I hate to bother you. But the only place I can get this medicine is in Wenatchee, and I hate to leave him alone that long."

"Sure," she said. "I'm supposed to work in the yard today, but I'd rather come visit Stephen any time."

"There won't be much visiting," I said. "He sleeps all day. Could you come around two?"

Early that evening, I gave Stephen his first dose of fusion inhibitor. I couldn't help the excitement I felt as I gave him the pill. It was possible, I told myself, that this new medicine could completely turn things around. With it, he might achieve undetectable viral loads again. He might even recover a fully functioning immune system. Did I dare hope for this much?

I had to laugh at myself as I handed him a glass of juice. I'd never even held a $55 pill before. It felt a little like asking him to swallow a diamond. Stephen missed the significance of the event. He barely woke up to swallow.

I went down to the family room, where Mallory and a girlfriend were watching a video, and Kevin was reading the evening paper. I sat down beside him and picked up my knitting. "I gave it to him."

He moved the paper slightly, nodding.

"I meant to tell you, I wrote a check for the drugs."

"You did?" He folded the paper. "How much?"

"I wrote it down in the register. For one month, $850." I watched his mouth drop open. "I already transferred some from our savings account to cover it."

He whistled. "Quite a sum. It'd better be a miracle drug."

"That's what I'm praying."

"Have you heard anything from his Medicaid application?"

"Just that the doctor thinks it will take about six months to process."

Kevin set the paper aside. "What about his house?"

"Nothing yet."

"What's he planning to do? Pharmacies don't sell drugs on the easy payment plan."

"He plans to use his Visa card."

"And pay it back with what?"

"I don't know, Kevin. It doesn't matter if he can pay it back or not. This stuff is our only hope. We'll just have to beg or borrow or steal." I put my knitting aside. "Or something."

"We?"

"I'm not going to let him go without the medicine."

"We don't have that kind of money."

"I know." I crossed my arms. "I've been thinking about it." I hated to say it out loud, hated to even let Kevin know what I'd been thinking.

Somehow, he sensed it.

"What are you thinking?"

"I'm thinking that I don't need my piano."

"What?" The volume of Kevin's voice drew the attention of the girls, who glanced up, curiosity on their faces. He smiled at them. "Sorry."

"Shh. I don't need the piano. I can practice at church. I'm almost through with my teaching schedule. I could sell it now, and use the money for Stephen's medicine until his disability comes through."

"You'd do that? Sell your piano?"

"Honestly? I don't know." I shook my head, still thinking about it. "But I might. If it came right down to it, I would."

Kevin sighed. "You might as well cut off your hands," he said. "I never thought I'd hear you say that."

The new medication gave Stephen an immediate boost. Between his $3,500 shingles medicine and the new AIDS drug, he looked more alive than he had in months. He got back to his usual routine, working for a few hours every afternoon, sending out articles and queries. His rash cleared slowly, changing from vesicles into a hard brown scab. Eventually, pale pink skin began to reappear, though this time it was covered with patches of scar tissue.

The pain from the shingles eased, though it never went away completely. Dr. Kurian told us that it might last forever, depending on the damage done to the nerve endings during the acute phase of the disease. Stephen took this bad news with some resignation and stopped using the pain medication.

For some reason, Noah began to come by more often. And frequently, in the late afternoon, he and Stephen walked down to the river to sit on the same little bench where Stephen first told me of his disease. After these visits, Stephen came home laughing and refreshed. The change in Stephen was so profound that I could not help but thank the Lord for sending Noah Armstrong to the Payton household. I considered him an angel in disguise.

We greatly welcomed the continued improvement in Stephen's health, no matter how slowly it appeared to come. He had fewer bad days, fewer days in bed, shorter naps, and more energy.

Two weeks after Stephen quit his pain medication, he and Noah took their first trip lake fishing. To my surprise, Kevin took the day off and joined them. When they left, I gave my husband a very warm kiss.

That night, we shared trout with Noah and his wife, Jan. The table conversation was lively and even though I saw how tired Stephen was, I saw his happiness too. His eyes had a sparkle I had not seen in months. Stephen had spent a whole day doing something other than being sick. He'd been outdoors, enjoying the cold air and spring sunshine in the company of healthy men.

Sitting at the table with my children and guests, I didn't think things could get much better. We said goodnight to Noah and Jan and went into the kitchen to clean up. Stephen and I carried dirty dishes to the sink while Travis rinsed and put them in the dishwasher. Mallory put away food and wiped the counters. On our second trip from the dining room, I saw Stephen wince and bend forward, putting a hand over one eye. "Something the matter?" I asked.

"I have a little headache," he said. "Probably too much sunshine today. I forgot to wear sunglasses."

"That would give me a headache," I agreed, trying to push aside the strange quiver of fear that tightened my stomach. "Why don't you go on up to bed? We'll finish up."

"I do have a lab appointment tomorrow," he said. "If you don't mind, I think I'll turn in. I'm feeling pretty bushed."

I put down the water glasses I carried and went around the table to give Stephen a hug. "Good night, little brother. I'm glad you had such a good day today."

"Who'd have thought?" he said, and smiled.

After two lab reports, Stephen's CD4 counts had risen steadily. We still faced the pressure of coming up with the medication costs once each month. Stephen had run out of money and his house in Seattle had not yet sold. I was feeling desperate. I didn't want to encourage him to use a credit card.

One night, as Kevin and I lay in bed, we talked about the problem. "The lab results are great so far. The new stuff is working."

"Have you had to renew the prescription yet?"

"We've ordered it. I have to pick it up at the end of the week."

"That doesn't leave us much time." I had not missed Kevin's choice of words. *Us.* I smiled into the dark.

"Do we have any savings that we could liquidate?" I asked.

"We keep a little savings, but it wouldn't go far. Not with those kinds of costs."

"What about a certificate of deposit? Do we have one coming due?"

"Not for another couple of months. The interest rates are so low I've tied up most of our finances for longer terms."

I sighed and rolled over.

"Don't worry about it, Colleen," Kevin said into my hair. "We'll think of something."

We had two more reports of improving CD4 counts before things started to go wrong.

On the last Friday in May, Stephen ate lunch with me. In an effort to help him gain weight, I'd made a Mexican lasagna, a chicken-and-tortilla dish slathered in cheese and sour cream. Though I encouraged him to eat high calorie foods, I seemed to be the only one gaining weight.

After we finished, I brought him his noontime pills and a glass of water. "Here you go. You wouldn't want to miss the opportunity to take a $55 pill."

I watched as he took the pills, several at a time, and followed them with water.

After lunch, I went down to the family room, where I'd laid out some things to air dry. I checked the clothes and pulled them off the couch, dropping them into a basket as I worked. When I finished, I turned around and nearly ran into Stephen.

"I need my noon pills," he said.

I laughed. "You just took them."

Stephen's brows wrinkled in confusion. "I don't think so."

For a moment, I wondered if he were teasing me. "You don't remember?"

With a straight face, he shook his head. "Why would I forget?"

"You must be tired," I said, excusing his confusion. With gentle persuasion, I convinced him to head upstairs for a nap. By the time I closed the door to his room, I believed that his forgetfulness was simply a reflection of his fatigue. Nothing a nap wouldn't cure.

That afternoon, Kevin came home from work early. "I have something for you," he said, pulling a small piece of paper from his coat pocket. "But you have to kiss me first."

"Oh, please. We've been married too long to play."

"You're going to feel really bad if you miss out on this one."

"Okay. You're up to something." I stood on my toes and gave him a kiss on the cheek.

He shook his head. "Not good enough."

"Shouldn't I be the judge of that?"

He handed me the paper, unfolding it as he did. "Be my guest."

I took the paper, recognizing it as a personal check. "What's this?" I held it out in the light, trying to read the handwriting. It was made out to Kevin, from an engineer he worked with. "Why would Mark Toloffson write you a check?"

Even as I asked the question, the number written on the check sank into my consciousness. "Ninety-five hundred dollars? Kevin, what is this?"

"I sold the boat," he said, shrugging. "We need the cash, and the boat seemed to be the way to get it quickly. Mark has wanted our boat for a couple of years. I figured he might as well get it now as later."

CHAPTER
Thirty-Four

For his gift, I gave Kevin more than a kiss.

Three days later, with the children at school, I sat in the living room working on a rough draft of the program for our spring piano recital.

Stephen was upstairs, taking his morning shower. Like a new mother, I'd begun listening to him, constantly aware of his moving about in the house. I heard the bathroom shower go off and the shower door slide open, and then closed. I heard him turn on the exhaust fan, and then the hair dryer. And then I heard a crash, which included the rattling of the shower door and something hitting the upstairs floor. I knew without thinking that Stephen had fallen.

I threw my music on the floor and flew upstairs, pulling myself up by the railing. At the bathroom door, I paused to knock. "Stephen," I called, "are you alright?"

At that moment it hit me that I'd been here before, and I wondered why so many of our crises seemed to revolve around the bathroom.

I turned the knob and found it unlocked. Inside, Stephen lay wrapped in a towel, slumped against the bathtub, his legs sprawled across the cold linoleum floor, in the midst of what appeared to be a seizure.

His mouth worked, though he did not speak. His right arm and hand made movements, though these seemed without purpose. I called his name, but he did not respond. Though his eyes focused on me, my brother was clearly out of touch.

I felt fear rise up inside my chest like a tidal wave. Shaking his shoulder, I screamed his name. The seizure, if that's what it was, continued for what seemed like hours. When it was over, he blinked and looked at me, confused about what had happened. "What are you doing here?"

"You fell, Stephen. I came in to see if you were alright."

He sat up, feeling the back of his head. "My head hurts."

I ran my hand over the part of his skull that had hit the tub doors. "Looks like you really hit hard," I said. "You're going to have a nice goose egg for that one. Can you get up?"

"I don't feel quite right." Stephen seemed groggy, thick.

"So, why don't we check your blood sugar while you're down?" I went into his room and got the diabetes kit, snatching a cotton throw from the foot of his bed. In the bathroom, I wrapped his shoulders with the throw and checked his blood sugar like an old pro. The monitor read 115. Though high blood pressure might cause a seizure, it had not caused his most recent problem. "I think we should call the doctor."

He shook his head. "No doctor."

"What about your head?"

"It's fine. No problem, really."

How I wished he would give up this stubborn streak. "What if this is serious?"

Though Stephen got up, he returned to bed and slept the rest of the morning. Before lunch, I caught him in the kitchen, taking acetaminophen. "What's that for?"

"A headache. Must be from the fall. I'll be fine."

When Noah came to visit that afternoon, Stephen begged out of his usual walk. The two of them sat in the kitchen, drinking cola and visiting. As soon as Noah left, Stephen went back to bed for a nap.

At four in the afternoon, I took a break between piano students and called Dr. Kurian's office. She returned the call within fifteen minutes. After questioning me carefully about Stephen's fall and his activity over the rest of the day, she instructed me to take Stephen to the emergency room in Wenatchee.

"He won't want to go," I told her. "He doesn't even know I'm calling you."

"Colleen, seizures are serious business. I wouldn't advise taking him to the emergency room without a reason." She paused. "It's four-thirty. I'll meet you there as soon as I've finished with my patients. Maybe I can admit Stephen and order the tests myself. We'll see."

"I'll get him there as soon as I can." I canceled the rest of my piano lessons and called Kevin's office, leaving a message that I'd taken Stephen to the hospital. I explained things to Mallory, who was reading in her room, and asked her to find a ride home for Travis after soccer. "I won't be home in time to pick him up," I told her.

It took all the coercion techniques at my command to get Stephen to the emergency room. I wondered as I argued with him if he suspected something frightening. He didn't want to know what had happened in the bathroom. Finally, his unrelenting headache provided the winning argument. "At least you can get something to kill that headache," I said. "It could be a migraine you know. You might just need the right meds."

As I drove Stephen to the hospital, I tried to fit the whole scenario under the category of migraine. I'd known friends who got dizzy when they had headaches. Perhaps a headache had made Stephen lose his balance and fall.

By the time I pulled into the emergency-room parking lot, I'd almost convinced myself. After all, a migraine would be treatable and have nothing at all to do with his AIDS diagnosis. Another medication certainly couldn't interfere with our routine. We checked in with the clerk at the outpatient desk. "Ah yes, Dr. Kurian is waiting for you. I'll page her."

As we took a seat in the waiting area, it occurred to me that neither of us had eaten since lunch. "Are you hungry?" I asked Stephen.

"Not at all."

Starving, I went to the snack machine and put in a crisp dollar bill, choosing a bottle of pink grapefruit juice. I offered Stephen a sip.

"No thanks," he said, waving me off.

Dr. Kurian came in through the double doors of the emergency clinic. "Ah, Stephen. I've arranged to use an exam room in the clinic. It's pretty unusual to meet my own patients here, but once in a while, when things are quiet, they let me get away with it."

Stephen followed her through the doors. This time no one invited me to come along. I waited with growing alarm as the minutes passed. Whatever Dr. Kurian had discovered was not a simple thing. Since I was the only one waiting at that hour, I asked the clerk to change the television channel to FOX news.

Watching the struggles of other humans reminds me of how grateful I really should be. I began to thank God for his work in Stephen and me. We were changing, the two of us. And though I would have liked to see more definite changes in Stephen's life, I decided to be grateful for those I could see. The old Stephen would never have attended anyone's church. He would never have become such good friends with a pastor. He would never have welcomed visits by one so clearly sold out to Jesus. Though I couldn't tell where he was on the inside of his soul, he had begun to take steps that undeniably moved him in the right direction.

I'd changed too. I'd learned to speak up over the past five months, to say what I felt. To tell the truth when it needed to be told. I'd learned to risk relationships by being a real human being—one with feelings and opinions and passions, one with faults—instead of a chameleon, blending in with the expectations of others.

God had certainly done a good thing. And even as I thanked him, I asked for continued guidance in this present predicament.

About forty-five minutes after he went into the clinic with Dr. Kurian, Stephen came out, pulling his sweatshirt down around his waist as he walked. His doctor approached. "I've decided to admit Stephen for the night," she said. "I want to order some tests right away, and I want your brother under close supervision until we get the results." She sat down across from me.

"What kind of tests?"

"He needs a lumbar puncture and a CAT scan. I'll have the lab do a complete workup on his blood. Then, if we see anything, we may order a PET scan. I'm also going to call in a neurologist."

"What are you thinking?"

"I'm not prepared to make a diagnosis," she said, though her solemn face betrayed her concern. "I don't have all the information I need. At this point, guessing won't help anyone." She folded her hands on her lap. "We'll begin by eliminating the possibilities. We should know more in the next twenty-four hours."

I stayed with Stephen until he had checked into a second-floor room. Then, when he'd settled into his new bed, I kissed him good-bye. "I'll be back tomorrow morning."

"You don't have to. I'm just here for tests."

"I want to."

He squeezed my hand. "Okay, you can come."

"It's going to be alright," I said, returning the squeeze. "I'll pray for you."

"Thanks. I guess I need it."

As I stepped out of his room, I looked back at my brother. His face had the most forlorn look of hopelessness I had ever seen on a human. It was everything I could do to force myself down the hall to the elevator.

The next day, after I got my family off to their respective obliga-tions, I cancelled piano lessons. I had no idea how long it would take to identify the source of Stephen's problems, but I knew that I wanted to be present when his doctors made their rounds. If I missed them, I might spend days trying to catch up on the latest news. I'd rather miss lessons than miss information about Stephen's illness.

At the hospital, nurses told me that Stephen had gone downstairs for tests. I opened my knitting bag and began working again on Mal-lory's graduation sweater. I'd nearly finished the sleeves and was close to putting the whole thing together. As I knitted, I prayed for the doctors, for the tests, for the diagnosis, and for my brother.

Before Stephen returned, Noah Armstrong stepped into the room. "Where's our boy?" he asked after we greeted one another.

"A scan of some kind," I told him.

"What happened yesterday?"

I told Noah about the struggles that had dogged Stephen over the past few weeks. "I don't think it's an infection," I said. "His blood sugar is fine. He doesn't have a temperature or any other sign of infection. I just don't get it."

"Confusing," he agreed. "Usually, opportunistic infections are the culprit. I've seen it time and time again."

"We've had our share of those," I explained. "But he's on a prophylactic for almost everything that could come along. His CD4 counts are going up. He should be getting better. And now this. What are we supposed to do?" I shook my head. "It seems like we can't win."

Noah laughed. "We win alright," he said. "I've read the end of the book. And we win. Absolutely."

"I don't know, Noah. Stephen won't talk to me about spiritual things. I know he needs forgiveness. His eternal life is so important. But I can't work on the eternal; he shuts me down all the time."

"You don't need to worry about the eternal things," Noah told me. "He's listening. I promise you. He's listening."

At the same moment, we both heard a wheelchair rolling down the hall toward Stephen's room. The door swung open and my brother, clad in hospital pajamas and a robe, entered, smiling, followed by a nurse in green scrubs.

"Ah, my favorite people," he said.

Noah bent over Stephen, giving him a man-sized hug. "I'm glad to see you so well. When I heard you were in the hospital, I thought maybe you were sick. They don't usually put big healthy guys like you in here."

"Enough with that," Stephen said, climbing into his hospital bed. "I'm not sick. But I saw the neurologist this morning. Since then I've been poked and prodded and stared at and photographed until all I want to do is go home. If they take one more picture—"

"You'll what?" His nurse, a cute young twenty-something, folded up the wheelchair and backed out of the room. "I don't give in to empty threats," she said. "We get orders, we obey them, whether you like it or not."

"See what I mean?" Stephen asked.

Thinking of Noah's words, I decided to give the two men time alone. "I'm going downstairs for some coffee. Can I bring you anything?" I asked.

"Nothing for me," Stephen said. "Unless you can find something to kill this headache."

"I'm fine," Noah said.

"I'll just leave you to visit then," I said. As I ducked out the door, I hoped more than anything that Stephen would really hear all that Noah had to say.

Later, around the change of shift, we heard from the nursing staff that Stephen would be discharged as soon as the neurologist came by to check on him. Taking that as a positive sign, Stephen got dressed and sat on top of his bed, waiting to go home.

Kevin came into the hospital after he finished work, and it was so good to see him that I think I may have clung a little when I hugged him. No matter how much I tried to calm myself, I had the distinct feeling that something horrible was about to happen. The two of us sat with Stephen while he waited for the neurologist.

Around six a man with dark hair and dark eyes entered the room wearing the typical white doctor's jacket over a striped shirt and dark tie. He introduced himself as Dr. Frank Barelli. "I'm the neurologist Dr. Kurian asked to look at Stephen," he said, offering his hand to each of us in turn.

After we introduced ourselves, Dr. Barelli asked Stephen, "Would it be alright if the three of us talked about what I've found on your tests today?"

Stephen shrugged. "Colleen and Kevin are family," he said. "I want them to know everything." I couldn't help the tears that filled my eyes when I realized what Stephen had said.

"Let me bring in another chair," Dr. Barelli said.

As he left the room, I reached up to touch Stephen's shoulder. "It's going to be fine," I whispered.

He nodded, his fists clenched on the sheets beside him.

Dr. Barelli returned, dragging an oak chair behind him. I held my breath while he placed the chair. It had come, the answers I'd worried about for days. The constant fear I'd fought since the episode with Stephen's noon medicines was about to come home to roost. I prayed for strength.

With Kevin on one side of the hospital bed and I on the other, Dr. Barelli sat down, crossing his legs before he spoke. "Stephen, how are you feeling this evening?" he asked.

"The headache again," Stephen answered. "Other than that, about the same."

"I'm going to prescribe something for the pain," he said.

"I'd like to know what's causing it," Stephen answered.

"We're getting to that," the doctor said. "Today's tests revealed some difficult news. The CAT scan showed small lesions in your brain. They're probably the cause of the headache you've been struggling with, and I suspect they caused the episode you experienced in the bathroom the other morning."

"What kind of lesions?" Kevin asked.

"I can't be absolutely certain without a biopsy. These kinds of lesions aren't easy to identify. They could be tumors, or they could be inflammation caused by bacterial or viral infection. Normally, with AIDS, I might suspect CMV—a virus.

"However, the ones I saw in Stephen's scans do have suspicious characteristics. Your lesions are periventricular, with ring enhancement. They show less edema than similar tumors."

Oh great. Medi-speak again. "Is that good?" I asked. "I'm still confused. Are you saying that he has an infection in his brain?"

The doctor smiled. "These lesions can be confusing. Right now, I'm saying that I'm going to have Stephen's spinal fluid evaluated by a molecular cytologist, and then I'm going to go ahead with a PET scan tomorrow. It will probably be a couple of days before I can be absolutely certain what kind of lesions we are seeing in his CAT scan.

Even then, the only way to be one hundred percent accurate is to have a biopsy."

"A biopsy? You mean surgery?" Stephen asked.

Dr. Barelli nodded. "It would give us the most accurate diagnosis. But, remember, you're on Bactrim for the PCP. That should provide prophylaxis for other infections. That raises our concern about these lesions."

Stephen sounded incredulous. "Are you asking for permission to do surgery?"

"Not right now. I honestly don't think it will be necessary." He uncrossed his legs and stood up. "What I want you to know is that we can see something very wrong going on in your brain. We have to get to the bottom of it quickly."

"If you were a betting man," Kevin asked, "what would you bet this is?"

The doctor's face betrayed no emotion. "Doctors don't bet. Besides, without the proper information, there's no need to worry you unnecessarily."

Two days after his discharge, tests confirmed that Stephen had developed primary central nervous system lymphoma. The news came as a blow to the whole family. Noah took it especially hard. After he left the house, I watched from the dining room window as he leaned against his car and cried. Even from a distance, I saw his shoulders heave with sobs.

Stephen seemed to take the diagnosis better than anyone. "At least I know why I'm forgetting things," he told me. "I'll bet you wish you could say as much."

We met with an oncologist, Dr. Woo, who encouraged us. "Your CD4 count is high for this diagnosis," he told Stephen. "Generally, PCNS lymphoma happens with counts below fifty cells per milliliter. Higher numbers improve the odds. And, since the new medicine seems to be helping your cell counts rise, I think we have a chance for a good result."

Whatever the chances were, he was not willing to verbalize the odds on Stephen's survival. I began to prepare myself for the worst.

Dr. Woo planned to have Stephen continue his current antiviral protocol and start a three-course chemotherapy trial at the oncology clinic in Wenatchee. These treatments would be followed in six weeks by a second scan to evaluate Stephen's response. If all went well the lesions would shrink, or perhaps disappear entirely.

In a normal patient, steroids would reduce the pain caused by the pressure of the tumors. But because steroids impair the immune system, a patient with AIDS cannot afford that luxury. Stephen was forced to cope with a constant headache, using nothing more than ordinary pain medications.

I made some drastic changes in my personal life. I apologized to my students and cancelled the spring recital. Then I refunded tuitions for the month of May and closed my piano studio for the year. Stephen would need all my energy.

Though the spring schedule included receptions and teas for the graduating class of Potter's Hollow High School, Mallory made every effort to help where she could. She cooked on the afternoons that Stephen and I went to doctors' offices. She did laundry; she cleaned the kitchen.

At the same time, I watched her cope with events by herself. Instead of asking for help, Mallory made do. For instance, she found and purchased her own dress for senior prom, leaving me out of the process. I felt both sad and relieved that she went shopping with friends.

Even Travis helped. He took complete responsibility for the lawn and all the weekly vacuuming. He even washed the cars without being asked.

Kevin kept going to work. It was all he could do. And when I cried, he held me.

The first chemotherapy was an all-day ordeal for Stephen. I waited with him in Dr. Woo's Infusion Center. Though the room was beautifully decorated, the lights low, the furniture soft and luxurious, I couldn't escape the strange atmosphere of death as I considered the deadly poison dripping through the IV line into my brother's body.

For Stephen, the combination of AIDS and chemo compounded his already-severe risk of secondary infection. The oncologist put him on prophylaxis for everything and gave us special instructions for boosting his immune system with food supplements and vitamins. Stephen's drug regimen doubled and then tripled in complexity.

We cooked organic. We ate health food.

Even so, Stephen barely swallowed anything. Food, he said, had a metallic taste that made it nearly impossible to eat. Though he had gained some weight with the new medicine, he quickly lost this while on chemo and reverted to his haunted, skeletal appearance.

Chemotherapy robbed Stephen of his energy, and he spent most of every day resting. Just days after the first chemo, Stephen stopped me as I passed by his bedroom door.

"Can I get you something?" I asked.

"Could you come and sit for a while?"

"Of course. I'd love to." I sat down on the end of his bed and we talked for a few minutes.

"I wanted to show you something," he said. "Could you open the bottom-right dresser drawer?"

"What am I looking for?"

"Below the sweater," he said. "It's a large black box. Flat."

I found the box and brought it around to him. He patted the bed beside his knee and I sat down. "Open it," he said, handing me the box.

I lifted the top and discovered the same photograph album I'd first stumbled across in Stephen's Seattle house. "It's beautiful. What do you want me to see?"

"I just wanted you to see what I've been working on. It's a record of my life—of our lives actually." He reached out and ran his finger along one black page. "I started it just before I came to Mother's birthday party last fall. Last summer, I asked Mom for all my childhood pictures. She hadn't put them in an album herself, and she sent them to me in one big box. I think that working on the photo album made me want to come home again. I wanted to start over, to make things right."

I smiled at him. "I'm so glad you came that day."

He laughed. "Me too. Even though it didn't turn out quite the way I wanted." He pointed to the book. "Turn the pages."

I opened the book and began looking through the pictures. Stephen had not cropped the pictures or added any extra trims or artwork. Rather, he had mounted them simply, with black corner mounts. Under most, he added simple captions in white ink.

I stopped at one that said, *Stephen and Colleen, Second Birthday.* "I'd forgotten this picture," I said, fingering the black paper. "I've forgotten so much of our early days." I pointed to another picture. "I remember that. I hated that dress—so scratchy."

I turned the page, and discovered that he had stopped with the picture of our first day of school. He smiled. "It isn't finished, Colleen. I want to finish it."

"You can do it. You have lots of time to finish."

"I don't know how much time I have. Can you help me? I don't want to leave it undone."

"Of course I will."

We started that very day, spending the early afternoon choosing pictures for the next several pages. Stephen directed me as I mounted them on the pages. Then he wrote the captions. This simple activity exhausted him, and an hour later, I left him napping.

His cell count took a hit with the chemotherapy, and Dr. Woo decided to reduce the dosage on his second round. Still, Stephen continued to lose weight. He became so weak that we rented a bedside commode to conserve what little energy he had. He could no longer shower by himself; we hired a home health aide to help him bathe twice a week.

Stephen's hair came out in clumps, on the pillow, in his brush, on the shoulders of his clothes. Eventually he asked me to shave his head. I did it with trembling hands, using a clipper I borrowed from a neighbor.

When the time came for his next scan, Stephen felt fairly certain of the results. He told me, "It won't be good, Colleen. You need to prepare yourself."

The size of the lesions had not changed.

Every day we saw Stephen's strength ebb. One morning, three days before Mallory graduated from high school, he woke with numbness on the right side of his body. Though he could move his arm and leg, he could not feel them.

"It's like walking on a tree stump," he told me. The fingers of his right hand refused to cooperate when it came to fine motor skills, and I was forced to take complete responsibility for his diabetes management. I became Stephen's hands.

We made another trip to the doctor. This time, in the quiet, softly lit office at the rear of the Infusion Center, Dr. Woo explained what he believed to be the case. "One of the lesions is pressing on the nerves that tell you where your arms and legs are in space. I think we need to try radiation."

"Will it cure the lymphoma?" Stephen asked.

"Not usually," he said quietly. "It may slow the deterioration. That would be our only expectation. I think that you should know that you qualify for hospice services; you should consider contacting them. They provide excellent care. In the meantime, I want you to know that I will continue to care for you, no matter what happens."

"You're saying we can't fight the lymphoma," Stephen said.

"I'm saying that you have an illness no human can cure." He took off his glasses and rubbed the bridge of his nose. "That doesn't eliminate the possibility of making you more comfortable, even more functional. It certainly doesn't eliminate the possibility of a miracle. Miracles happen. I've seen them."

I couldn't speak. No matter how Stephen had tried to prepare me for this moment, I couldn't believe it was actually happening. I began to tremble, though I could not think, or reason, or cry. Stephen wrapped one arm around me, reassuring me as I continued to shake. Dr. Woo set up appointments for radiation therapy, and we went down to the lobby and called Kevin. Somehow I drove home, where Kevin was waiting for us.

Dr. Woo had asked that we consider an end-of-life plan. He'd given us brochures and handouts. Though I couldn't look at them, Kevin and Stephen read them together while I lay on the living room couch, crying. Stephen chose the hospice program provided by the hospital. Together, they filled out the questionnaire, and Kevin agreed to make health care decisions for Stephen, should he become unable to decide for himself.

Neither of them thought I would be able to think clearly when it came to Stephen's death. They were completely correct.

The next day, Kevin stayed home from work. Quietly, with authority and kindness, he arranged to have a hospital bed delivered to the house. "Stephen shouldn't be held captive in his room," he told me over morning coffee. "We don't want him to waste energy on the stairs."

He contacted hospice and arranged a primary consultation.

He ordered a wheelchair and drove to the medical-supply store to pick it up. We needed to be able to transport Stephen to and from the doctor, should that become necessary, without having to call for help.

Part of our agreement with hospice involved a commitment to avoid further emergency-room care and hospitalization.

While Kevin did these things, I spent the morning with Stephen. Sometimes, while he slept, I sat beside him, waiting quietly, watching him breathe. When he woke, he insisted we continue our work on the album. His weakness grew worse, until he could no longer hold a pen. Then he told me what to write and, obediently, I printed the captions below his pictures.

On the third day after the diagnosis, we moved Stephen into the living room. Kevin and Noah carried him down the stairs. His headaches became more difficult to manage, and we were forced to use stronger medications. These he resisted, because they made him drowsy, and he hated to waste what little time he had on sleep.

On that day, Stephen found a picture of the three of us—Carrie and Stephen and me. He and I sat on opposite seats of a chair-swing. Carrie stood balanced on the bar between us. "When was this taken?" I asked.

"Maybe you should call her," he whispered.

On the fourth day, Noah came to help me take Stephen to his radiation appointment. Together we helped Stephen into his new wheelchair and out to the car. The first treatment lasted nearly four hours, and Stephen came into the lobby with his bare scalp covered in black markings.

As we headed for the parking lot, Noah pulled a navy blue, hand-knit cap from his jacket pocket and handed it to Stephen. "My Jan knit this for you," he said. "She was worried your head would be cold."

Stephen took the cap and put it on. "Thank her for me."

"I will," Noah answered. "I don't understand it though. I been goin' bald for the last fifteen years, and she never knit me a hat."

"That's a woman for ya," Stephen said.

"I resent that," I said. "Besides, Noah, I'll knit you a hat. Anytime."

"I'd be obliged, Colleen," Noah said, smiling. "I'd be much obliged."

~ ~ ~

Thankfully, the radiation relieved some of the pressure in Stephen's head. His headaches eased, and his strength returned, though not in full. We continued to work on his album because he insisted, attaching photos, writing captions, and reminiscing about the fun times we'd shared together growing up. We sorted pictures, adding them to the black pages in chronological order. Year by year, the pictures told the story of our lives.

When the pictures my mother gave him ran out, Stephen's own skill with the camera took over. The number of Stephen's photos surprised me. Though I knew he'd taken pictures during our high-school years, I had no idea how many. There was no way they could all fit in the book. Most of the pictures were of the two of us at high-school dances, music events, and school programs.

Some were of me that Stephen had taken himself. Others were taken by friends with Stephen's camera. He became quite selective as we worked, directing my every move before fatigue rendered him completely unable to continue. Then he slept.

I called Carrie and told her about the album and about the photo we did not recognize. "We need you here," I told her. "Not just for the pictures. I can't do this without you."

Carrie and Tim came for a weekend, and as angry as I'd been with her, I couldn't help but forgive when I saw how much Stephen's illness hurt her. She stayed in a chair beside his bed for the entire weekend, never moving, never letting anyone else do anything for him.

I let her hover. It was healing for her, I think, and healing for me as well. I needed to be reminded of her love for her baby brother. We never spoke of religious things. When she left, she hugged me. "I know how much this hurts you," she said, crying. "I was wrong to be jealous."

As the days passed and Mallory's graduation weekend approached, I began to worry about how I would be able to leave Stephen. I knew that I had to attend graduation, to see my oldest child make this milestone in her life. Stephen knew it too. "You have to go, Colleen. You have to be there for me."

Because the graduation was scheduled for a Sunday I could not ask Noah or Gloria to stay with Stephen. Instead, I called Jackie. "Could you spend Sunday with Stephen?"

She hesitated. After a long pause she said, "Of course I can. I'm happy to help."

When Jackie arrived on Sunday morning, we were still scuttling around trying to get ready. I let her in and poured her a cup of coffee. "We've moved him into the living room. He's strong enough to feed himself again. And he can use the bedside commode by himself. So you don't have to worry about any of that. He just needs someone to fetch things for him and to make sure he doesn't fall."

Jackie looked terrified, her shoulders tense, her face pale. Instinctively, I knew it had taken all her courage to come and care for my brother. Recognizing her fear, I suddenly realized why she hadn't called or come by in the six months that Stephen had been with us. I took her in my arms, and gave her a warm hug. "I can't tell you how much I appreciate your doing this. I consider it a gift."

"You need to be with Mallory." She smiled.

"I know this is outside your comfort zone."

She nodded. "A little. But it's good to stretch."

"Shall I introduce you?"

We went into the living room, where Stephen was finishing his breakfast. I took his tray and introduced him to Jackie. "She sang that song you loved so much," I said. "Remember the tape I played for you?"

"Ah," he said. "The voice of an angel."

That was all it took. Jackie loved Stephen immediately.

During Mallory's graduation day, I felt traitorous. Every time I let myself be fully present, I felt guilty about enjoying myself. And when I thought about Stephen, home without me, I felt guilty for not being emotionally present with Mallory on this special day. We took our daughter out to dinner at an expensive restaurant. She was radiant with happiness, proud of her awards and accomplishments.

I was miserably torn between two loves.

I think she knew how I was feeling, though I never said a word. When the waiter came to offer us dessert, Mallory looked at Kevin and said, "We can have dessert at home, Dad. Mom needs to get home to Stephen."

≈ ≈ ≈

During all this time, these weeks of progressive illness, I remembered the times that the Lord had spoken to me. I remembered the verse he'd given me in the middle of the night. And though I knew he expected me to obey, to tell Stephen all that I had gone through, still I hesitated. Though I begged the Lord to show me what to say, I never found the courage to speak.

When it finally happened, it was as if Stephen knew my struggle and wanted to ease my discomfort.

His weakness grew with every passing day, until in the end he spoke very little. Still the album drove him on, and somehow I knew he would not die until it was finished. Even in this condition, he pointed at pictures and I mounted them on the page. Then, I leaned down and he whispered a word or two, and I would try to come up with a caption that fit. If I did well, his eyes smiled.

When we came to my junior year in college, there were no more pictures of the two of us together. Suddenly our progress came to a halt. "Tell me," he whispered, pointing at the blank page.

"Tell you?"

"What happened?" he said.

I knew what he meant. And with his invitation, I found the courage I needed. Beginning with our father, I explained how desperately I felt unloved. I told him about the loneliness of being away from my twin brother for the very first time.

And I told him about Rob and the baby.

"Those things," I explained, "the shame of being pregnant, the foolishness of loving a man who never meant to love me back. They made me realize what a mess I had made of my own life. When someone told me about Jesus, I was primed and ready.

"I needed a father who loved me. I needed forgiveness for my own failures. I needed strength to make up for my weakness. Jesus was what I needed. He was all of those things wrapped into one person." I began to cry. "The time was right for me. I needed a fresh start and a new purpose. That was what happened in this year," I said, pointing to the blank page.

I took the white pen and steadied the book in my lap. Drawing carefully, I made the simple outline of a white cross on the black page. "I spent that year here," I pointed. "At the foot of the cross." And Stephen smiled.

We took a reclining chair from the family room and put it beside Stephen's bed. During the day, if he felt well enough, we transferred him into the chair, letting him feel as though he were up during the day.

At night, one of us slept in the chair beside him.

My mother asked one of her friends to drive her across the state and deliver her to our doorstep. When I answered the doorbell that day, I nearly fell over in surprise. "I've come to take care of my boy," she said, standing on my front porch. "I'll sleep on the couch if I have to, but I want to be here. This is where I belong."

During the last two weeks of Stephen's life, the five of us, Noah and Gloria, Mother and Kevin and I took turns staying with him around the clock. Mallory and Travis sat with him during some of the day shifts. Each of us slept when we could.

Other than going outside when she absolutely couldn't hold it any more, Colleen-the-dog never left Stephen's side.

Gloria often stayed with me, even when it wasn't her turn to sit with Stephen. Her arms held me when I cried, prayed for me as I grieved, and handed me tissue when it became absolutely necessary that I blow my overflowing nose.

One day, while Noah was sitting with Stephen, she and I sat down at the kitchen table. I asked her, "Why do you do this? Why do you keep coming back? I know it isn't because you want to see my puffy red eyes and stopped-up nose. Why do you put yourself through this much pain?"

She smiled, a soft knowing smile. I noticed that her eyes filled with tears, and for a moment, as she held her lips together, I sensed that she could not speak. "Once, I heard a terrible story on the radio," she said, controlling her voice with obvious effort. "It was about an airplane crash that killed everyone on board. The news reports said that the passengers knew for three minutes that they were going to die. They knew that nothing the pilot could do would save them. It took three minutes for that plane to fall out of the sky. When I heard that story, I was so angry with God that I had to talk to him about it.

"I said, 'God, how could you be so cruel? How could you put those people through that kind of terror, knowing for three minutes that they were about to suffer a gruesome, indescribable death? How could you?' I poured out my anger. And I waited. For a while I didn't hear anything at all. And then, it was if I heard him say, 'Gloria, it wasn't cruelty that made them face their death like that. It was grace.

" 'It was grace that gave them three extra minutes in the face of irrevocably certain death. They had three full minutes to remember the truth about me. Three minutes to change their mind. Three minutes to make the right decision. Three minutes to decide what it was that they truly believed about me.

" 'Gloria, it was three minutes of grace,' he said.

"And I've never forgotten that experience. When my son was dying, the church told me that AIDS was a punishment—that he deserved to die. But I knew that none of these boys deserves death any more than any of the rest of us deserve it. Because we all do, you know." Gloria reached out and patted my hand. "We all deserve death.

"Anyway, as my son lay dying, I saw him turn from a bitter, angry boy into a grown man who came to faith in God. He was changed. Just as surely as an egg is changed when you boil it, my son was changed on the inside. And the change made him strong enough to go through the process. He died with Jesus."

Gloria leaned one elbow on the table and, tucking her chin into her palm, continued. "In my mind, AIDS wasn't judgment, it was grace. Plain and simple. There isn't a day goes by that I don't thank God for what happened to my boy." As Gloria paused, two slick trails made their way down the soft skin of my friend's cheeks. She blinked, but did not wipe away the tears.

"I keep thinking," she said, tipping her head to one side, a mischievous look in her eyes, "that this disease is a season of grace for everyone involved. If I'm here while these men face their last days, I get to see it over and over and over again. And sometimes, I get to help in the process." She stopped and gave a little laugh as she toyed with her wedding ring. "You might as well ask why a woman becomes a midwife. Sure, the process is full of pain. But when the baby is born," Gloria winked, "all the pain is worth it."

Though I understood what Gloria meant, I was not yet ready to join her position. So far, I'd only seen the pain. As far as I knew, death would mean the ultimate separation of the MacLaughlin twins. I'd barely survived the years Stephen had been away. How could I survive eternity?

≈ ≈ ≈

In the days that followed, I continued to wonder about Stephen's spiritual state. Had anything really changed inside his soul? If so, he hadn't talked to me about it. He wasn't talking to anyone anymore.

Stephen spent most of his days lying or sitting perfectly still, his eyes open, staring into the distance. He rarely responded to us. We developed a blink code. One blink meant no. Two blinks meant yes. We used it for water and food, for blankets and pain medication.

Seven days before Stephen died, Noah sat with him. Though I have no idea why, Noah began reading the Psalms out loud. When Noah had to leave, he closed his Bible and set it aside. Stephen became agitated, as if he were frightened. I called Mallory in to sit with Stephen while I walked Noah to the car.

The sun was shining through bright green leaves as we paused in the driveway. "Noah, I need to know. Have you talked to Stephen about making a faith decision?"

"Of course I have, Colleen. There hasn't been a day go by that I haven't talked to him."

"Can you tell me what happened?"

"What you want to know, Colleen, is whether or not Stephen is saved."

Leave it to Noah to cut right to the point. "Okay. Yes. I do. It's important, Noah. I need to know. I can't let him go without knowing for certain that he is safe."

"Well then, honey, you can let him go."

"You mean...?"

"I mean that we talked after the service the very first time he visited my church."

"Why didn't he tell me?"

"I can't explain everything," Noah laughed. "I don't know why he didn't tell you. Maybe, in his own way, he thinks he has."

I put both arms around Noah's broad shoulders and hugged him, crying and laughing at the same time. "Noah. How on earth did you get through to him? I've done everything. He wouldn't listen to me. He told me not to ever mention it again. He had so many pent-up issues. I couldn't talk to him at all."

Noah smiled. "It wasn't hard," he said, as he leaned one hand up against the roof of his car. "You see Colleen, I used to be just like him. I lived the same lifestyle."

My face must have registered complete shock, because Noah nearly broke in two laughing. I stammered as I tried to back out of my surprise.

"You don't need to apologize," he said, still chuckling. "I don't tell many people. Most folks are as surprised as you. I still get a kick out of the astonishment it creates."

"So that's why Gloria told me not to worry about you."

"I suppose so." He took me in his arms and hugged me again. "It isn't easy, this dyin' stuff. But we all have to go through it. It should be better knowing he's going home."

"We won't be separated for long," I said into the shoulder of Noah's jacket.

"Not for long," he said, patting my back. "Not for long, honey."

When I went back inside, Stephen's agitation continued. I tried without success to settle him. Finally, as a last resort, I asked if he wanted me to read the Bible. Stephen blinked twice, and thus was born the continuing habit of reading the Bible whenever he was awake. The Word of God literally gave Stephen peace.

≈ ≈ ≈

Stephen slipped away in the early morning hours of June 30.

I published his obituary in the Seattle paper, and in the community-college paper, as well as the local papers on the east side. Though I didn't expect his friends to come to his service, I felt they needed to know what had happened.

We celebrated Stephen's life at Noah's church in a memorial two weeks later. Jackie sang her song again, though she used the accompaniment tape we'd made for practice. Noah gave the sermon, and Dwayne gave the opening and closing prayer.

Even though I knew that Stephen was safe, the letting go nearly killed me. I don't think it's possible for anyone to understand the life of a twin. We had begun life completely intertwined, not as two people but as one. We had the rare privilege of ending life in the same way. But when Stephen ended, I had to go on. It felt as if part of my body had been severed and buried.

I was surprised by the number of people who came to his service, considering Stephen had lived in Potter's Hollow for such a short time. Many of his friends and professional acquaintances from Seattle made the trip across the state. Several of his students came to give a last tribute as well. His nurses and caretakers attended.

When we opened the microphone, a number of people came forward to share bits and pieces of Stephen's life with the rest of us. Some spoke of how often they had prayed for him. Many talked of his devotion to his students.

Travis spoke of how much he loved his uncle, and how glad he was that Stephen had spent his last months in our home. When Travis sat down, Kevin wiped a tear from his cheek and squeezed my hand. Of all the people in the audience, we knew more than anyone the true value of that two-sentence tribute.

Four weeks later, early on Saturday, July 26, the Payton family, along with Noah and Jan, Gloria and her husband, all met together at the little bench beside the river. We'd been working at our project separately for several weeks, and on this morning, this gloriously hot summer morning, we planned to add the finishing touch.

We'd replaced the old wooden bench with a wrought-iron model we'd bought from a commercial garden company. Noah and Kevin had spent two weekends laying a concrete pad and installing the bench. The kids and I planted a dwarf apple tree beside the pad and surrounded it with a small stone wall.

Inside the wall, Gloria planted rockroses.

On that day, we planned to place the plaque we'd commissioned for the tiny park we'd created in Stephen's name. Kevin carried wet concrete, and Noah the granite marker.

"Alright, Kevin," Noah said, sitting down on the bench. "Go ahead and fill in the frame."

Kevin used a trowel to smooth the cement into the metal frame. Then, with deft strokes, he wiped the excess off onto his pallet. "Your turn, Noah," he said.

Noah knelt beside the frame and lowered the granite stone. With a gentle push, he settled the plaque into its new home. From his back pocket, he produced a shop rag and wiped away the last trace of concrete. "I think we should pray," he said. Together we joined hands around the little green frame.

"Father, we thank you for this place. For the beauty of these mountains, and this river, and this town. We thank you that in your divine plan you brought the bunch of us together, and that you used us to reach just one for your glory. We thank you for that one. What a wonderful thing you did in Stephen's life, and in ours through Stephen.

"And now, Lord, we dedicate this place to you. Use it to remind us always of your grace. May we never sit here without remembering your sacrifice on our behalf.

"And we ask that you would continue to use us, Father. And all God's people said, 'Amen.'"

We chorused a collective amen as we wiped away fresh tears.

From where I stood, I could not read the gray-pink granite marker. I stepped around the monument, letting my shade fall over the letters. And then, through tears, I read it one more time:

In this river, some cast for fish.
On this bench, another fisherman
Cast for a single soul.

In Loving Memory,
Stephen William Payton
1960-2003

About the Author

Bette Nordberg graduated from the University of Washington as a physical therapist in 1977. In 1990 she turned from rehabilitation medicine to writing and is now the author of *Serenity Bay*, *Pacific Hope*, *Thin Air*, and numerous dramas, articles, and devotions. She and her husband, Kim, helped plant Lighthouse Christian Center, a church in the South Hill area of Puyallup, Washington. Today, she writes for the drama team and teaches Christian growth classes. Along with teaching writing workshops, Bette speaks for audiences around the Northwest. Married twenty-eight years, Bette and Kim have four children, three living at home.

Bette may be contacted through her Web site:
www.bettenordberg.com